THIEF OF LIVES

Barb & J. C. Hendee

www.orbitbooks.co.uk

An *Orbit* Book

Published by arrangement with Signet, a member of
the Penguin Group (USA) Inc.
First published in Great Britain by Orbit 2005

A CIP catalogue record for this book is available from
the British Library.

ISBN 1 84149 365 1

Typeset in Bembo by Palimpsest Book Production Ltd,
Polmont, Stirlingshire
Printed and bound in Great Britain by
Mackays of Chatham plc, Chatham, Kent

Orbit
An imprint of
Time Warner Book Group UK
Brettenham House
Lancaster Place
London WC2E 7EN

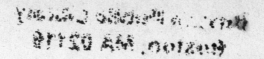

Barb and J. C. Hendee live just outside of Boulder, Colorado, close to the Rocky Mountains. He teaches English for the Metropolitan State College of Denver, and she teaches for the University of Colorado at Denver. Barb's short fiction has appeared in numerous genre magazines and anthologies. She is the author of the novel *Blood Memories*. J. C.'s poetry, non-fiction and short fiction have also appeared in many genre magazines.

Find out more about Barb and J. C. Hendee and other Orbit authors by registering for the free monthly newsletter at www.orbitbooks.co.uk

By Barb and J. C. Hendee

DHAMPIR
THIEF OF LIVES

Look out for . . .

SISTER OF THE DEAD

The follow-up novel to *Thief of Lives*

by

Barb and J. C. Hendee

orbit

www.orbitbooks.co.uk

For brother Al, our biggest fan

Prologue

He neither relished nor anticipated the task at hand. It was simply one more step upon the path, and he had always been capable of doing whatever was necessary.

Street lanterns, lit by the night watch, hung from high posts and building-side iron mounts at more regular intervals along this street than other places in the king's city. Dim light shimmered on wet cobblestone rather than packed earth, on stone dwellings instead of wattle and daub or timber buildings. This was an elite district, where gentry, dignitaries, and city officials lived just outside the walls of the castle grounds. Light, warmth, and an aura of comfort flowed out between half-drawn curtains hanging in windows with actual glass panes. Here, at night, all was serene.

He watched the street from a side corner, making certain no guard or watchman would pass by anytime soon, then stepped along the cobblestones at a quiet pace.

Night air was seasoned with the wet scent of the bay on the city's west side. The cool breeze carried some chill, but he did not notice the cold. Still, he shifted the long black wool cloak closer about him. Its dark color, melting into the night, protected him from errant gazes by any occupant peering out a window before settling to bed. He tugged his black lambskin gloves, flexing his fingers until the material was smoothed comfortably in place.

Arriving at the house he sought, he entered the iron yard-gate and walked up the path. His hand rested gently on a side railing as he climbed the three stone steps to the large front door. Ornate ash wood was stained in multiple tones to accent detailed doves and vines a patient artisan had carved in its panels. Two lanterns glowed to either side of the door. He reached up and twisted their knobs, first the right then the left, until the wicks retreated and their light dimmed just short of going out altogether. Grasping the large brass knocker ring, he announced his arrival with two raps and no more.

Moments passed. The door cracked open.

A young feminine face peered out. She was small for sixteen, with dark brown ringlets hanging to her shoulders and a dress of muted lavender with light saffron trim. Her expression was hesitant at first, but then she smiled with warm recognition.

He knew she would answer. Her father was away this same midweek evening, playing faro with other gentlemen and nobility. This young one always took pity on their overworked servants, giving them a secret night off without her father's knowledge. She was alone in her house, in the quietest, most respectable of neighborhoods.

'Oh, Father isn't home tonight,' she said. 'He's gone to the Knight's House for cards again.'

He did not answer her. His left hand shot out, gripped the back of her neck, and jerked her toward his open mouth.

She heaved in a breath but never released it.

He bit her exposed throat before her hands could push at him, elongated canines sinking through her skin. His jaws snapped closed as he ripped away flesh to expose open veins. Pain and trauma paralyzed her body, and there was no way she could scream. Her hands, almost to his chest, dropped limp in spasms.

Her weight was nothing, and he supported it by the hand clamped about her neck. Her heartbeat slowed, its rhythm shallow and irregular, so he shook her until the blood flowed freely. It soaked her collar, spreading from the wound, and he watched the red seep into her bodice and across her chest, and downward over her shoulder until it ran along her left arm to drip from her slender finger. The heartbeat weakened until even he could not hear it anymore. He watched as her eyes grew cold and vacant. A ringlet of brown hair adhered to the wet flesh on her throat as her head rolled in his grip.

With his free hand, he ripped her dress open, exposing the bloodstained white shift she wore underneath. He shredded that as well and dropped her body upon the porch like a soiled, broken doll. Turning, he walked back out the front gate to the street, stopping briefly to check both ways. Once certain the path was clear, he returned the way he had come.

Fishing a handkerchief from his pocket, he wiped his mouth.

The coming days had been successfully set in motion.

1

It was the place he'd nearly died, and here he returned every day before dawn.

Leesil stood sweating in the forest clearing's cold air, surrounded by sparse-limbed, shaggy firs. The sun had crested the high eastern tree line, and winking sparks of sunlight skipped between ocean wave tops below to the west. Along the shallow bay's coastal edge sat the small port town of Miiska, its rooftops brightened by the dawn.

White-blond hair matted flat to Leesil's neck, shoulders, and his narrow face, letting the blunt tips of his oblong ears peek out. Faded but still visible scars lined his tan-colored throat and the lower right side of his jaw. The thin beige cotton shirt clung to his back, and his feet felt wet with perspiration in the soft leather boots. Breathing hard, he scowled in irritation, wiping away sweat running into his eyes. He shivered briefly. The chill of a late-autumn morning encouraged him to keep moving for warmth.

'*Valhachkasej'â!*' he muttered, though not completely certain of its meaning.

His mother – Nein'a, Father had called her – would whisper it under her breath when angered or frustrated, or when she cut herself accidentally while sharpening a blade. Her narrow, triangular face of smooth caramel skin would wrinkle slightly, and high, thin wisps of white-blond eyebrows would cinch together in a scowl as she shifted unconsciously into her native Elvish.

She refused to teach Leesil her language, and her large, slanted eyes would narrow whenever he asked. At her occasional slips, he'd listened carefully to the way she spoke and silently mouthed the words in turn, trying to unravel their meaning. Leesil had heard enough foul exclamations in varied tongues to guess at the meaning of this exclamation. Childhood obsession became unconscious habit. A few times, she had spoken his name with strange inflection − Léshil − and more than once referred to him or herself as '*anmaglâhk*,' but he never unraveled its meaning.

Shaking off the memory, Leesil returned to training, collapsing low in a buckled crouch. His right leg shot out to the side.

Momentum pulled him into a backward spin toward his outstretched leg, body pivoting quickly on his left foot. When his right heel had traced one-third of a circle, it bit into the clearing's earth.

His torso spun around, and both arms swung over to his right side. Hands slapped flat against the ground to brace his weight, and his left leg whipped upward.

Today he trained later than ever before. There was so much to remember, to relearn, and it was the last morning he could slip out alone before anyone, including his companion, Magiere, arose for the day. Their routine would soon shift to nightlife again, as they fell back into their roles as the owners and proprietors of the Sea Lion tavern. She would handle the bar, while he ran the card games at their faro table.

He looked down the slope to the town again, his gaze settling upon the nearest building with its new roof, new everything, rebuilt from the ground up. The fresh cedar shakes looked too vibrant amidst the other weathered rooftops. The new Sea Lion tavern was finally finished.

Farther up the shoreline before the small docks was a large empty plot of burned earth between surrounding buildings. The vacancy was easily three times the size of any other building in the town. Although the structure's charred remains had been cleared away, months of fall weather hadn't washed the blackened stain from the ground where once stood Miiska's largest warehouse. It had burned to ash and cinders . . . burned down by Leesil.

He looked back to the Sea Lion once more. It, too, had been a charred patch, but was now reborn from the ashes, a little bigger and certainly brighter than its bleached and wind-worn predecessor. It would be home once again for him and Magiere, and for their dog, Chap, as well.

And somewhere beneath it lay the powdered bones of monsters.

But not the one who'd been here in the forest clearing and nearly crushed the life out of him. Not the one he'd let slip away.

He pictured in his mind the three undeads he and Magiere had faced. Two were destroyed, but the last, Ratboy, had escaped.

Leesil turned to the clearing's east side, where a large, scarred fir tree stood. Each morning he brought a small box wrapped in canvas sailcloth and set it at the tree's base. The fir was old and solid, and wind and rain had carried away soil, exposing lumps of deep roots. One bare patch revealed where bark had been torn away and a lower limb was raggedly broken off. These injuries were not so old.

The undead of Miiska were gone. All three of them, but this brought Leesil no relief.

It wasn't over. He couldn't tell this to Magiere, who wasn't ready to hear it. Not just yet.

Crossing to the scarred fir, Leesil unrolled the sail scrap to reveal the long box of dark wood, its length equal to his forearm. It was flat enough to slip inside a baggy shirt without leaving much of a bulge. A flick of fingertips opened the lid, and his shoulders knotted in apprehension at its contents, gifts from his mother on his seventeenth birthday so many years ago.

Inside lay weapons and tools the like of which could never be bought openly from a weaponer or metalworker. Their origin unknown to him, Leesil could only guess they'd come from his mother's people, though why the elves would make such things he couldn't imagine.

He studied the distasteful items. A garrote, its handles and wire of the same metal as his good stiletto, both a tone brighter than silver. A small curved blade that could be palmed but would easily cut through flesh and bone. And inside the lid behind a foldout cover, a row of a dozen thin struts, wires, and hooks, again of the same metal, and suitable for picking any lock. The final item was a hilt that matched the better of his two sheathed stilettos. Its blade was missing, snapped off a finger's breadth from the guard.

Leesil picked up the bladeless hilt, and a rush of unwanted memories hit him.

Ratboy, the filthy undead street youth, brown eyes shining with hate and triumph. In Leesil's pain-fogged vision that night, the little monster had looked so human.

'Perhaps we could call this a draw?' Leesil had joked, trying to sound confident. 'I promise not to hurt you.'

Ratboy's sharp features made his smile seem out of place and pasted on.

'Oh, but I want to hurt you.'

The dusty undead hopped like a rat leaping at a larger opponent, and kicked Leesil in the chest. Leesil's ribs cracked audibly as he was thrown halfway across the clearing. Before his vision cleared, Ratboy crossed the distance to snatch him by the shirt.

As Leesil was pulled to his feet, he curled his hands

up and flicked open the holding straps of the sheaths on his forearms. Stilettos dropped into each hand. He thrust both hilt-deep into Ratboy's sides.

'One good . . . turn for another,' he gasped out, and then wrenched the hilts downward.

Beneath the sound of Ratboy's cracking ribs came a muffled metal clink. The right blade snapped, sending a jar through Leesil's arm and into his battered body. Ratboy's mouth gaped, soundless beneath wide eyes, and he flung Leesil at the trunk of the old fir.

The lowest branch shattered as Leesil fell across it on his way down to the forest floor. Impact with the ground sent so much pain through his body that it became distant and unreal, and he dropped his one whole blade and the hilt of the other. Clutching at the ground, he gripped the severed half of the branch. When Ratboy came again, Leesil let the vampire's own momentum and weight do the work.

Ratboy pulled himself up and stumbled back, face filled with anguish and fear as he clutched at the branch protruding right of center from his chest.

'Leesil! Where are you?'

A voice called out Leesil's name, but Ratboy's gaping mouth had not moved. Half-impaled, the dusty undead bolted into the forest before Magiere broke into the clearing. Leesil lay on the ground trying to stay conscious.

The wiry, filthy little vampire had escaped.

And now, months later, Leesil looked over the instruments in his box. He dropped the bladeless hilt and picked up the garrote, looping it as he gripped the handles. With a quick jerk, he pulled it tight. The wire snapped straight, and a thrumming tone filled the air with a vibration that made Leesil's stomach lurch.

Time to relearn lessons from his mother and father,

to reclaim part of a sickening heritage. There had been so many nights when he drank himself to sleep so dreams of a nightmare childhood couldn't wake him. But he would never again be caught so ill prepared.

Because it wasn't over.

Rumors would slip quietly along in one direction or another. He and Magiere had wanted a quiet life in Miiska, but word of her deeds would reach the desperate. They'd freed Miiska, a whole small port town on the main coastal shipping route of the Belaski kingdom. And they'd done it right out in the open.

Magiere, hunter of the undead, would never be allowed any lasting peace.

Leesil dropped the garrote into the box, shut it, and wrapped it in the sail scrap. He gathered his bundle and turned toward town, and the new Sea Lion tavern, where Magiere might now be preparing for their opening night. He wished he could speak to her, tell of his fears for her and how much he wanted to protect her from what he knew was coming. But that was just one more thing she wasn't ready to hear.

'Oh, Magiere . . .' he whispered sadly, heading down the forest slope toward their new home. 'It's never going to be over – not now. And you can't even see, can you?'

After months in this small port town, Magiere never tired of hearing waves lap upon the shore. It puzzled her that she'd lived nearly all of her twenty-five years so far inland, only recently discovering her love of existing on the edge of an ocean. Not given to romantic notions, she now found the sea a mystical wellspring of life. The salt-laden air was cleansing. She walked with long strides along the docks toward a small warehouse.

Black tresses pulled back with a leather thong, she felt

the tail swing like a pendulum between her shoulders. She cared little if people stared at the sun-sparked scarlet glints in her hair. Like a birthmark, they were simply part of her now. She rarely wore her leather hauberk anymore, preferring the soft comfort of dark breeches, a loose white shirt, and an oversize leather vest. Her two small amulets hung in plain sight around her neck — one a simple topaz set in pewter, and the other a half oval of bone set against a tin backing.

At her side trotted Chap, tall and wolfish of build with silver fur and translucent blue eyes. Occasionally, the dog's ears perked and his gaze darted quickly about the crowd of dockworkers, bargemen, and local merchants. But nothing seemed important enough for him to bolt off on his own, so she didn't worry about him. She couldn't say the same for Leesil.

Her half-elven partner had taken to disappearing before dawn into the wooded hills above the south end of town. Magiere had no idea why or what he did there alone, but she somehow felt reluctant to ask. She'd taken careful note of his return each morning and, by that measure, he was late. Today of all days, his presence would be useful. At least that was the reason she held on to when she peered between buildings to the tree-coated slope south of town.

Their tavern had been burned little more than two moons past. With the townsfolk's help, the Sea Lion had been rebuilt. She'd ordered two casks of wine, three barrels of ale, and stocks for the kitchen in anticipation of heavy patronage. Tonight would be the grand reopening.

When she'd stopped by the tavern to check on the stores, nothing had been delivered. Not a tankard's worth. Leesil was better — more tactful, he would say — at dealing with such matters, but she'd waited until nearly noon for his return, and then decided to take matters into her own hands.

Chap bounded away to sniff at a stack of crates. An old man nearby, sewing up a net, looked down. The dog lifted his muzzle in reply, and the man reached in his pocket to pull out a tuft of jerky and toss it into the air. Chap caught it, barely chewing before the morsel was down his throat. He barked once, tail switching expectantly across the dock planks.

'Chap,' Magiere called out. 'Come on.'

The old man laughed, holding up empty hands as a sign he had nothing more to offer. Chap's tail stopped, and he let out a groaning whine, hanging his head in pitiful disappointment.

Magiere had the strange notion the hound might well have learned this ploy from watching Leesil wheedle extra cream cakes at their friend Karlin's bakery. She closed her eyes briefly.

'Chap, enough begging!'

At Magiere's insistent tone, the hound loped after her, and she headed down the waterfront. Sometimes Chap displayed startling intelligence.

And sometimes he just acted like a dog.

As she approached the run-down warehouse, the number of dockworkers seemed fewer than normal. Too few. People were everywhere along the docks, more than she'd seen in the past, but it was different. So many new faces made up the surplus, and that made her strangely anxious.

Amidst common waterfront faces were now others. Merchants were present, but not all of them were making arrangements with warehouses, as was standard practice. Instead, they haggled directly with outgoing barge masters and mates of small ships that bothered to stop in this lesser port. Peddlers actually worked the dockside, and farmers tried to engage merchants and traders directly with wagons full of bundles and bales.

Magiere watched men and a few women haul and stack crates and barrels and bundles. They seemed shabby, thin, and more tired than she'd seen before, or perhaps she'd just never paid attention until today. For some reason she couldn't pin down, she felt responsible.

Before she'd come to Miiska, her life consisted of cheating peasants out of anything valuable they possessed and then moving on. She and Leesil had earned their living by traveling from village to village in the inlands of the northeastern country of Stravina – or anyplace where peasants died of illness or other unexplained cause. She convinced the inhabitants that they were plagued by an undead and that she, the hunter, the dhampir, could save them for a price. At night, Leesil would masquerade as a ghost-white monster, 'the vampire,' appearing in the village pathway to dart in and out of the darkness between their homes. In a violent battle, Magiere would 'stake' him, and the village was saved.

But constant travel and uncertainty became too much. She'd secretly saved enough profit to purchase a tavern sight unseen in this little coastal town. She wanted peace and quiet and to spend the rest of her days simply running a tavern with Leesil. How ironic that turned out to be. A fake and cheat, playing hunter of the dead, she'd bought a tavern in likely the only town in Belaski with a trio of undeads nestled in its midst.

And worse, her rumored reputation followed her to spread slowly through Miiska. Everyone expected her to have the skill and knowledge to fight such creatures, and the vampires themselves believed she'd come to hunt them. Unable to avoid this conflict, she destroyed two of the undeads, including their leader, Rashed.

Now, Magiere looked back down the waterfront. She'd actually walked right past the charred earth today and not even noticed the vacancy. Leesil had burned Miiska's largest warehouse, covering their retreat from the undeads' hiding place in order to save her life. But Leesil's action had other consequences.

Rashed may have been a monster masquerading among the townsfolk, but it seemed he'd also had a head for business. His warehouse had employed many dockworkers as well as being the mainstay of export for the local area.

Magiere finally recognized the source of her seemingly pointless guilt.

'Move it, you lazy grunts!' shouted a foreman in a sleeveless shirt. 'There are plenty around to take your place if you can't keep up.'

She and Leesil had saved the town from its undead plague, but without Rashed's establishment for competition, the two other smaller warehouse owners could now pay workers substandard wages for longer hours, as well as choke off the prices for abundant goods with less opportunity for storage and export. Anyone who protested was dismissed. There were simply more workers than jobs, and worse, more business than these small warehouses could handle. People watched their livelihood go to waste or be bought out for low return.

Magiere tried to take no further notice. She had a business of her own to manage. She grabbed a ragged worker by the shirtsleeve.

'Where's Master Poyesk?'

The man stared at her in exhaustion, and his eyes narrowed slightly as his back straightened. She realized that he recognized her and met his gaze without flinching. A long moment passed, until the silence was too much.

He pointed toward the warehouse's doors. 'Inside.'

Magiere nodded, and Chap followed as she entered the dimly lit building. She choked on the dust while her eyes adjusted to the decreased light. Crates of wool, casks of ale, and other packaged goods lined the walls. She spotted a short, weasel-faced man writing on a torn bit of parchment.

'Master Poyesk!' Magiere called out with an edge of anger.

Poyesk turned, slightly surprised by her presence. 'Mistress Magiere,' he said in an oily tone. 'I was expecting your partner.'

Although he was dressed like a merchant in a burgundy velvet tunic, Poyesk's teeth were yellowed, his hair greasy, and his nose pockmarked. Magiere was too irritated to be revolted.

'If you're expecting my partner, then you know why I'm here,' she stated. 'My tavern opens tonight, but my stocks haven't been delivered. I paid in advance, so what is the delay?'

He set the parchment on a nearby crate and rubbed his hands together, smiling apologetically.

'Yes, but as you see, business has been slow in Miiska of late. Fewer ships come to trade and there are so many workers to employ. My overhead is climbing by the day.'

Confused, Magiere wondered where this was leading.

'I paid the delivery fee as well,' she added.

He paused as if weighing his words, and tapped one finger lightly against his lips.

'Of course, but there are other considerations. With so few handling all of Miiska's trade these days, I have to consider who to serve first based on which customers are most . . . profitable.' He shrugged, as if there were nothing he could do. 'Otherwise, I won't have the coin to pay workers to serve the next customer.'

Poyesk's meaning settled upon Magiere.

Leesil would handle this differently, but he wasn't here.

She reached to her hip for the falchion's hilt, but that wasn't here either. She'd stopped wearing it around town in broad daylight.

'Are you asking for a bribe?' she said. 'You want a bribe to deliver goods I've already purchased . . . with a delivery fee paid in advance?'

She heard Chap growl softly at Poyesk, the low sound rolling up his throat to vibrate through half-exposed teeth. Master Poyesk didn't react, picking up his parchment again to return to business as usual.

'Setting your dog on me won't get you your ale.'

Magiere was about to explain what she could do with a bailing hook and his various body cavities, when a familiar voice called out from behind her.

'Ah, there you are, Magiere. Caleb said you'd come down here.'

Magiere turned to see two familiar men entering the warehouse, Karlin Boigiesque, the town's baker, and Darien Tomik, constable and head of the guard.

Karlin's presence usually put her at ease. Portly, smooth headed, and always smelling of clove-spiced soap, he was more than just a baker. He now served on the town council and had been her main advocate in getting the town to rebuild her tavern. He was a good man to the core and her friend. She didn't have many friends.

Darien, on the other hand, she didn't know well. He struck her as competent and quiet, though he hadn't held his position long. Tall to the point of being lanky, he stood almost a head above Karlin and gazed seriously at her. She realized her face must be flushed with anger.

'This little weasel just asked me for a bribe to deliver an order I've already paid for,' she snapped.

Darien looked at Poyesk and asked softly, 'Is this true?'

'Uh, no . . . I think Mistress Magiere misunderstood.'

Poyesk became slightly nervous. 'I was explaining that her delivery had to be moved into the afternoon schedule. We're running behind today.'

'Behind . . . *something*, certainly,' Magiere snapped, her hand still on her hip.

Karlin settled one thick palm on Magiere's shoulder in a friendly manner. Darien stepped in on her other side. The quiet, dour constable was appropriately outfitted in leather hauberk, sheathed short sword, and a small cudgel tucked in his belt.

'But all is well now?' Karlin asked, polite and jovial. 'You'll send her order this afternoon?'

Poyesk smiled with yellowed teeth and backed farther away. 'Yes, of course. She'll have everything well before dusk.'

Magiere realized Darien's presence made Master Poyesk extremely nervous, more so than seemed appropriate for one attempt at gouging a customer. Darien's attitude stepped beyond mere disapproval from a town constable. She wondered who else Poyesk was attempting to extort and felt less inclined to let the situation drop so easily. Karlin, however, gave a slight tug on her shoulder, and began rushing her toward the doors. Darien hesitated before following. Magiere glanced back at Poyesk.

'I hope there won't be any further misunderstandings to straighten out. And you'd better hope my partner, Leesil, doesn't come in my place.'

Master Poyesk only smiled again.

Magiere shielded her eyes from the bright sunlight as they emerged from the warehouse.

'It's fortunate you two happened along,' she said, blinking as she lowered her hand.

Karlin didn't answer and walked slowly down the water-front. She and Darien fell into step beside the baker.

'All right, you going to tell me what's going on?' she asked.

Darien remained silent, and Karlin rolled his shoulders as if shifting an irritating shirt seam to a more comfortable position.

'We went to speak with you at the Sea Lion,' Karlin began slowly. 'When Caleb said you'd gone to the docks, we thought we'd take a walk and see if we could find you.'

'And you did,' Magiere added. 'Is anything wrong?'

'Yes and no,' he answered. 'You must be aware that things have changed in Miiska of late. When you and Leesil . . . when Rashed's warehouse was burned, the town's economy was altered.'

She took a slow breath. Again, everything came back to Rashed's warehouse.

'Where we once had a surplus of money,' Darien cut in, his voice even but hard, 'is now a nearly empty purse. The small warehouse like Poyesk's are claiming they earn no profit, and months ago, town funds were drained in helping those who lost livelihoods after the fire. We have almost no community surplus left from taxes.'

Magiere kept stride, but she was uncertain why they wanted to chat with her about problems with the town's treasury.

'What is it you think I can do about this?' she asked.

'Pay your back taxes,' Karlin said plainly.

Magiere came to a sudden stop, looking in confusion between the corpulent baker and the lanky town constable. 'Back taxes?'

'There's a tax for trade and business, which in turn is split between community funds and what's owed to the kingdom. Fortunately, we're a free township and don't pay a percentage to a local fief. Of course, you would know that. It's just that you've been so helpful to Miiska that the council never thought it right to insist. But we're in a crisis, and everyone must do their share. Now that you're reopening, we can expect a payment from the Sea Lion as well.'

Among all the reasons Karlin would need to speak with her, this was the last thing Magiere expected. Why had no one ever mentioned this before?

For ridding Miiska of undeads, she and Leesil had been gifted some payment, but nearly all of that had gone into rebuilding the Sea Lion. She'd used up the remainder restocking to open for business. She couldn't tell this to Karlin and Darien, though.

'Leesil handles our account sheets,' she lied, clearing her throat. 'I'll need to speak with him.'

'Of course.' Karlin nodded. 'We know you're just reopening and things might be a bit scattered. I must be off now, at any rate. A town council meeting was called this afternoon over a letter from Bela. Apparently, the news it contains warrants an immediate discussion, but I'll stop by the tavern tonight.'

Darien gave a nod of acknowledgment and farewell and headed into town. Karlin patted her on the shoulder before following him.

Magiere watched her own feet step along the water-front planks. Where was Leesil, indeed, now that she needed him?

She passed beyond the commotion of the docks and turned inward to the closest street paralleling the shore. Shops around her grew dense and more closely connected, side streets occasionally reaching inward to the heart of town. Her stomach was in knots. She had until evening to come up with taxes on the Sea Lion. Miiska was in trouble, and she and Leesil were partially responsible. The least they could do was pay their fair share. But how?

She passed the stable down the road from the tavern and saw Lila, the cobbler's wife, walking toward her. A large woman with a mass of burnished auburn hair, she carried a basket of bread loaves and fruit. It was a cheerful sight, as if some part of the world were calm enough to simply worry about pies and apple butter. Lila smiled when she spotted Magiere. Not everyone blamed her and Leesil for Miiska's troubles.

As Lila passed an open alleyway, two teenage boys burst out, as if they'd been lying in wait for a passerby. For a heartbeat Magiere froze in disbelief.

The first swung his fist and caught Lila across the jaw. She dropped instantly in a heap on the dry, dusty street. The second grabbed the basket and turned to flee. All the day's frustrations found welcome release in Magiere's anger.

'Chap, get him!' she shouted as she took off after the first boy.

He was fast but didn't notice Magiere until too late. She snatched him by the shirt collar, spun him around, and flung him up against the cobbler shop's wall.

The boy turned as if ready to fight, but he looked terrified, breath coming in ragged gasps and eyes wild with panic. His collarbone poked sharply out of a ripped shirt. His raised fists were bony at the ends of thin arms. At most, he was fifteen years old.

Magiere's anger drained instantly, and she heard Lila calling out her name.

Hesitant to take her eyes off the first boy, Magiere glanced quickly toward the stout woman, who was pulling at Chap.

'Magiere, help me. Call him off,' Lila shouted.

Magiere stepped back, watching the first boy until she was at a safe distance. She had little choice but to let her quarry go and run back to Lila.

Chap snarled and barked at the other thief pinned against a pile of empty crates blocking an alley. Magiere saw that the dog wasn't trying to harm the boy but merely make enough of a show that the young thief would cower down and be still. Lila, on the other hand, didn't know Chap well enough to understand what was happening.

'Call him off,' Lila repeated. 'They're just hungry boys.'

'Chap, that's enough,' Magiere said. 'Leave him be.'

The dog snarled once more and pulled back next to Magiere. The boy whimpered softly, rolled to his feet, and started running.

'Wait, take this,' Lila called out. She held out a loaf of bread from the fallen basket.

The boy never looked back and disappeared down a side street.

Magiere stared at Lila's swollen jaw. It would be black and purple tomorrow. 'You're trying to feed the thief who attacked you?'

Lila's expression grew sad, so sad that Magiere fell silent.

'They're just children, and they're hungry,' Lila said softly. 'There's not even enough work for their parents, if they have any, so how can they feed themselves?'

Magiere had no response. The knot in her stomach tightened as she escorted Lila safely home. Turning away, she headed back toward the south end of town, Chap beside her.

The Sea Lion was nestled at the base of a small, forested peninsula forming the southern side of the bay. Stout and cleanly cut plank walls, freshly whitewashed shutters, and an ornate sign depicting a sea lion riding an ocean wave greeted her as she stood outside her reborn establishment. The front door was shaped from solid oak this time, with iron bars and locks that Leesil had requested. Enough fair-grade glass panes had been found for the upper-floor windows, and shutters were in place on the ground floor. The whole of the place was at least half again as long as its previous incarnation and shone like a new copper coin in the sunlight. Even in hard times, people spent what little they could afford for the comfort of ale in good company by a warm hearth. The Sea Lion fairly burst with promise of laughter and profit. But at the moment, Magiere did not feel like laughing.

Chap scurried to the front door and sat waiting, but Magiere held back.

Somewhere inside, old Caleb, the caretaker they'd inherited, was likely putting things in order. Little Rose, his granddaughter, would be playing in her new bedroom, probably waiting for Chap, her favorite 'pull-toy.'

This day already weighed too heavily upon Magiere. She could imagine the activity that would grow through the afternoon, until the place opened for business.

The last time she'd taken on the role of bartender, both Miiska's desperate townsfolk and the vampires they feared had found her too easily. The memory, as well as the revelations about herself that had emerged, still haunted her. In facing the truth behind her life of deception and lies, Magiere had also faced more of herself than she'd ever wanted to know. In the presence of vampires, rage and strength filled her until she began to change, manifesting attributes only vampires themselves possessed . . . canines elongating to fangs amid sharpening teeth . . . healing herself by drinking mortal blood. It terrified her, even though it became necessary both to her own survival and to protect Leesil. And they had grown closer during the crisis.

Magiere felt suddenly cold and exposed.

In the aftermath, Leesil was so badly injured that all she could do was care for him until he could walk again.

During that time, they didn't speak much of their experience together, because she decided it was best to put it all behind them.

He began slipping away by himself each morning. Perhaps that was best. Her cool manner was obviously troubling him, but his life had been endangered because of his connection to her, and a certain distance was for his own good. A lonely thought, but true.

Magiere looked southward across the coastal road out of town and up to the forested hills that lay inland. Leesil was late.

'Advance,' Chane instructed, trying not to yawn from tedium, 'and again. No, master, keep your blade level and then settle your weight back. Do not lean into your front leg.' He lazily parried but did not take advantage of the blatant opening his opponent had left again – and again.

Toret, his pupil in swordplay and his master in all else, halted in frustration.

'My sword is straight!' he snapped. His voice echoed off the walls of the enlarged cellar cleared for their use in training and other clandestine pursuits. 'Why do you keep repeating that?'

Their three-story stone house resided in the upper-class quarters of Bela, the kingdom capital of Belaski and its major port of call. Acceptable and perhaps extravagant by middle-class standards, it was not what Chane had been used to in life. The city's population was so diverse almost anyone could fit in. However, since he'd risen from death, Chane felt nothing but out of place in his master's company.

A recent Noble Dead, or vampire specifically, Chane still understood the walls between classes. In mortal life, he had been a minor noble of an outlying barony, familiar with the politics and social strategies customary among the gentry. And now – as in most of his conscious moments – he assisted his creator, his master, in elevating himself. That contradiction, as well as the contrast between them, was so beyond comic it struck Chane as absurd rather than amusing.

Chane was tall, with thick auburn hair cut just below his ears. Dark ginger breeches and a midnight-blue tunic were tailor-cut for him, framing broad shoulders over a long torso. Fluent in four languages, with a noble's education and self-schooled in less acknowledged arts, he handled a long sword as if born to it.

Herein lay the contemptible irony of this new existence with his *master*.

Toret was thin-armed, seeming a youth no more than seventeen years, and small for the age. Even scrubbed clean, his skin was tinted as though covered in a constant layer of filth. His dirt-brown hair stuck out in tufts and cowlicks. He bore scars on one wrist and his cheek. He conversed well enough in Belaskian, the common language throughout most of the region, and seemed to speak the vulgar tongue of the Suman Empire across the ocean and far to the south. But despite this, so far, he could barely read or write any language, regardless of tutelage. His expensive burgundy brocade tunic made him look like a houseboy playing dress-up while the manor lord was away.

But Toret had trapped and turned Chane, pulled him from death into servitude. Now Chane could not refuse the smaller undead's most menial whim. Once created, a vampire could not refuse its master. Chane was a slave.

'No, master,' he said with forced politeness. 'Your blade is not straight, and you throw your weight too far. Observe me.'

Chane stepped precisely through three connected advances but did not believe for a moment that Toret would catch the finer details.

'Well, I think you're doing . . . splendidly!' came a high-pitched voice from across the cellar.

Both Toret's and Chane's attention shifted toward the voice. Chane suppressed a sneer of disgust as their household's third member forced her presence into his awareness. Toret smiled, exposing straight but lightly stained teeth.

'My sweet,' Toret said with relish. 'Have you been shopping?'

Flouncing toward them was another painful reality of Chane's new existence: Sapphire.

Some would find her alluring or desirable, in a vulgar way, but to Chane she was the most repulsive creature to invade his existence, before or after his death.

Sapphire wore a low-cut satin gown so starlingly pink it might be called magenta, and dark blond curls sculpted into sausage ringlets framed her round and often pouting face. Red-stained lips stood out between her smooth, pale cheeks, while gaudy ruby earrings that could feed a large village dangled from her earlobes. No matter how much money Toret heaped upon her for clothing and jewelry, she retained the appearance of a well-paid but tasteless prostitute. Her only untainted feature was a set of bright sapphire eyes, and hence the name Toret had given her.

To think of this creature as a Noble Dead was a constant source of disquieting irony. But when Toret looked at her, Chane saw in his master's hungry eyes that she might as well have been the queen of the Fay. It was nauseating, and reminded Chane of a childhood time when his family's cook served a salmon left unprepared too long in the summer heat. Chane had spent three days kneeling over a bucket.

'Splendidly?' Chane said, masking the sarcasm in his voice. 'Did you learn a new word today?'

Both Toret and Sapphire blinked once, and she pretended he hadn't spoken. Chane knew his companions often had difficulty distinguishing whether he was being polite or insulting.

'Not shopping,' she said to Toret, smiling coyly with a tilt of her head as she fingered the front of his tunic. 'To my dressmaker. Charlotte got in some lovely mustard-yellow silk, and I've had a new gown made. Of course, her ideas for the cut were dull, so I've insisted on alterations.'

No doubt, Chane thought, trying not to imagine what overtly provocative choices passed for style in such a creature's thoughts.

Chane had managed to find bankers, merchants, and dressmakers who remained open for business far into the evening. Appropriately handled, such requests weren't suspicious in a city the size of Bela. Half the gentry he'd known slept all day and spent all night in social politics or discreet debauchery. Toret and his companions were simply 'eccentric' for their late business hours. They paid well, and no one complained.

'Have you fed yet, my dear?' Toret asked Sapphire. Clasping her hand, he pressed its palm firmly against his mouth, closing his eyes halfway.

'No, I was waiting for you.' She smiled at Chane and added, 'For both of you.'

Chane nodded as coldly as possible without appearing rude. No matter how badly he treated her, she played the coquette with him, though never openly enough to annoy Toret. She believed all men found her charms irresistible and constantly played up to this self-image.

'I want to go to the Rowanwood,' she announced quite happily.

Toret shook his head. 'It's too soon.'

Sapphire had a penchant for elite prey, a dangerous indulgence, from Chane's perspective. She fed on the rich as often as Toret allowed. The Rowanwood hosted wealthy patrons, if not the most sophisticated. Chane did appreciate its lush atmosphere, suitable for upper classes looking for a less stuffy night's entertainment. But frequent hunting near a prestigious establishment gained unwanted attention.

Sapphire's smile faded, replaced by a pout, and Chane steeled himself. It was time to repeat the ritual of manipulation.

'Well, where do you want to go?' she asked Toret, her voice pitched so high it hurt Chane's ears. 'Some dockside tavern to feed on stinky fishermen? Do you want to smell ale and sweat all night? I don't. I don't! I want to go someplace nice!'

Toret sighed, walking to the cellar's far wall to place his sword back in the rack.

'Did you hear me?' Sapphire called, astonished at being ignored. 'Ratboy! Did you hear me?'

Toret froze in midstep. When he turned, his face was a tight mask of rage, and his dust-colored skin appeared to turn hoarfrost white.

Ratboy? Chane had no idea why she called him that. Perhaps some peasant's insult? Indeed, it had an unimaginative sound. During frequent fits of temper, Sapphire called Toret all sorts of names and threw herself into sorrowful pouts until he relented to her whims.

Toret snatched a parrying dagger from the rack and closed the distance to Sapphire. Before she could dart away, he gripped her by the throat and pressed the blade's point under her chin.

Chane felt something near to astonishment. It was quite pleasing. He'd never once seen Toret lay a hand on Sapphire in anything besides affection or desire.

'We discussed this,' Toret hissed. 'I made you, and I can unmake you. You will never call me that again. Understand?'

Sapphire's eyes widened as one tiny drop of dark fluid ran down the blade from under her chin.

Chane felt a moment of pure pleasure at the open terror on Sapphire's face. The evening was not a complete waste after all. The little bitch had given up something new to consider.

Ratboy.

Whatever the meaning, it displeased Toret more than anything Chane could recall, and this was worth remembering.

'I'm sorry . . . Toret,' Sapphire stammered. 'We can go anywhere . . . anyplace you like . . . I'm sorry . . . anywhere.'

Toret lowered the blade and slowly released his grip on her throat. He then looked troubled, of course, perhaps realizing he would later pay for his actions. And pay he would.

Chane kept his sigh of boredom silent. So tediously predictable.

'It's all right, my dear,' Toret said, his abrupt calm a counterpoint to his rage from a moment ago. 'We can't go to the Rowanwood again so soon . . . but we haven't been to the Damask Throne in a while.'

Daggers and threats forgotten, Sapphire's face lit up. 'Oh, yes, the Damask Throne? That would be . . . splendid.'

Chane inwardly groaned. She *had* learned a new word. After changing into suitable attire, complete with evening cloak and gloves, he went to fetch a covered carriage for hire.

In the far-past time of the first king, Bela had consisted of a castle stronghold. Over time, villages close by spread into towns and then into a surrounding city. The castle itself grew. As the city spread outward, new fortification walls were erected for its defense. The king's city of Bela now consisted of three walls that ringed the city at nearly equal distances from its center castle grounds. Most banks, municipal buildings, wealthy homes, and upscale establishments existed within the inner ring wall, where they were best protected. Though there were main avenues of commerce and city life running from the center of Bela to the waterfront docks, such as Harbor Street, as one moved outward from the city's center, one moved downward in society.

The night air was crisp with a rare seaward breeze that pushed back the odors of wood, rope, fish, salt mill, and other harbor smells. It was a short ride from their home until the carriage stopped near the Damask Throne. Toret assisted Sapphire from the carriage while Chane paid the driver.

Even with large, burning street lamps positioned every thirty paces, the night felt comfortingly dark. Chane looked his part of protector in a long wool cloak with the point of his sheathed sword just visible at the bottom. Toret and Sapphire appeared a wealthy couple.

The carriage moved off down the street, and Sapphire walked toward the luxurious inn while Toret and Chane waited outside – a typical game played many times over. Chane crossed his arms and stood in the shadows. He rarely spoke to Toret unless spoken to first. Toret sighed, watching Sapphire disappear inside the Damask Throne.

'She is lovely, isn't she?' he asked.

'Yes, master,' Chane answered flatly.

In a short time, Sapphire emerged from the inn with

a young couple. A female victim in the mix surprised Chane, as Sapphire usually brought out only drunken men, all ne'er-do-wells and blueblood want-to-bes. But aside from the woman, the couple was no different from a typical set of well-off merchants.

'Oh,' Sapphire exclaimed to her new companions as they crossed the street. 'Here are my friends now. I told you they'd be along soon.'

She introduced the couple as Simask and Luiza. Toret shook the man's hand and politely greeted the woman.

'Simask is the son of a Stravinan winemaker, and he's in Bela on business,' Sapphire continued. 'They don't know anyone in town, so I offered to show them a few of our evening attractions. But now that you're here, you can help me entertain them.'

Chane focused upon the woman: in her early twenties, with pale skin and dark hair swept up under a little red velvet hat. He was suddenly struck by the growing tingle of hunger. His normal disdainful thoughts were replaced by images of Luiza's soft, warm throat drawn close to his mouth as paralyzing fear stained her face. Even now, he could feel the slight and slow shift of his teeth, canines elongating as saliva built up until he quietly swallowed it down.

One of the few times Chane forgot his unfortunate state of servitude was while he hunted.

Toret smiled at Simask. 'Come, come. There's a much better inn down the street called the Rowanwood. The food is excellent, and they have the best wine cellar in this part of the country.' He paused a moment, then feigned a surprised epiphany. 'Perhaps you can do business with the proprietor.'

Toret's relaxed and friendly manner put the young couple at ease. They strolled down the street, occasionally passing another late evening citizen enjoying a walk, and once, a city guard who returned them a polite nod.

Chane remained silent while Sapphire and Toret chatted away with Simask and Luiza. They turned onto a sloping road toward a merchant district outside the inner wall. The area had grown unfashionable over the years, and after hours was all but deserted. Chane was almost bored by the time Simask suddenly stopped and looked around, realizing the street lamps had grown scarce, the buildings were dark, and there were no other people about.

'Did we miss the Rowanwood?' he asked. 'Perhaps we went too far.'

Without warning, Toret grabbed him. He slammed Simask hard against the clay-plaster wall of a closed shop.

Chane had long since ceased being surprised by his small master's speed and strength. Toret's lips curled back to reveal elongated canines. He exhaled into Simask's face once before releasing him.

'Run,' he whispered.

Toret rarely toyed with his food. Chane preferred such pretense and foreplay himself, but understood Toret's concern for secrecy. Most Noble Dead could muddle or smother their victim's memories, so normally they left their prey alive but disoriented. Some developed more pronounced abilities, but neither Chane nor Sapphire could do more than simply blur a victim's recollection.

There was a difference in Toret's attitude tonight. Chane silently rejoiced, anticipating a brief respite, and the release of all the frustration of his slavery spread through him like warmth.

Simask tried to dodge around Toret and reach Luiza, but Sapphire stepped in his way, laughing.

'Not that way,' she said, and pointed down an alley. 'That way.' Another low-voiced laugh exposed her fangs.

Simask ran. Luiza screamed in shock as her husband's form receded into the dark. She backed into the middle of the street.

Sapphire started after the husband. Toret hesitated long enough to look to Chane.

'No one knows them here. Do what you want, but leave no trace when you're finished.'

Then he was gone down the alley after Sapphire.

Chane saw Luiza staring at him in a mix of terror and . . . pleading hope? He knew his appearance suggested a vassal lord or liegeman who protected women like Luiza, the fair and fragile.

'Sir,' she said. 'Please . . .'

He walked quietly toward her, backing her up until they reached the alley's other half across the street. He tilted his head toward the opening.

'Go,' Chane said.

Luiza sobbed once and tripped over her skirt as she turned to flee. She managed to catch herself and keep moving.

Chane let her run. He waited just a little longer and then followed.

Her head turned once as he trotted steadily after her, not caring for silence any longer. She sobbed loudly again and screamed for help at the footfalls closing quickly behind her in the alley's darkness. No one would hear her. Or if they did, they wouldn't care.

He caught Luiza effortlessly, and as he grasped the little red hat and a handful of her hair, he felt a slight disappointment.

There were appropriate times for a quick and poignant kill. But not now. This was too easy.

To his surprise, she twisted away and with both hands grabbed an empty vegetable crate on the ground. With all her strength, she struck him across the side of the head. The crate shattered around him.

The impact almost hurt, and elation returned.

Chane snatched her wrists and bound them in one grip. He grabbed the front of her clothes with his other hand. He slammed her body up against the alley wall, pinning her arms above her head.

He forgot Toret. He forgot Sapphire. He forgot his lost mortal family and his mother and all the trappings of life that he still missed. This mattered. This moment.

Luiza struggled, and for a short while Chane allowed her to. It was fascinating how easily he could push his dead form to accomplish anything he demanded of it, and what little the living could do to oppose him. He felt her useless squirming in his grip begin to weaken. Looking down, he took in the horror on her face and watched as her cheek brushed against him and her tears disappeared, soaking into his black cloak.

Chane let himself feel the shiver and heat of her skin against his fingertips, and then he concentrated until his fingernails hardened under his will and ever so slightly elongated. He pulled his hand back, slashing away her coat, blouse, and all fabric from around her throat. His mouth closed down on flesh.

He rarely tasted blood until a short while after feeding, and then there was only a salt-laden, coppery residue. During the act, he only felt warmth and strength filling him, as if blood were only a medium carrying the power of life into his possession. Nothing in his memory compared to this. It was the only aspect of his undead existence that brought him joy. Chane knew it was time to stop only when he could no longer sense any life pouring into him, and the mix of oblivion and euphoria faded.

He returned to his current existence – a slave.

Toret expected him to drop the woman's empty husk down a sewer grate, where it would not be found immediately. Such a grate was only twenty paces away. He remained still in contemplation.

After a moment he dragged Luiza's body with one hand down the alley closer to the main street and dropped her. He then ripped her dress further open, shredding it and the undergarments. She must look savaged and mutilated by something unnatural.

The night Toret turned Chane, he'd ordered, 'You will stay in Bela and serve me.'

Chane could not disobey, but there were loopholes to consider. If the bodies of lovely young women were found with throats ripped and clothing shredded, would the constabularies or city guards begin an active hunt? Chane could take care of himself, but if fate were kind, Toret could lose his head.

He crouched down for one last look at Luiza's still open eyes. His body coursed with life's energies now, but he felt sad as he wiped the blood from his mouth. The hunt had been so short and staged. Straightening his cloak and pulling his gloves on, he walked back toward the Damask Throne.

2

Leesil shifted cards about the faro table that evening, stealing brief glances at Magiere, who stood behind the bar pouring drinks and talking sparingly with patrons. Everything should have felt like it had before the events of months past. The Sea Lion was fully restored – better than restored. He should have been happy.

After the fire, only the common room and kitchen hearths remained. A local carpenter who remembered the old bar quite well had created a nearly identical version. It glistened with dark, fresh stain. The building had been lengthened and slightly widened, and the common room hearth now stood near the room's center, its backside open like the front. Patrons circled around it or nestled close to either open side for a little extra warmth.

Hanging above the hearth facing toward the bar was a sword. Regardless of how much Caleb had scrubbed it, the blade remained partially blackened and marred. Leesil considered having it polished and restored but then thought better of it. This was Rashed's sword, the warrior undead that Magiere had tricked into the flames as the old Sea Lion burned. She'd fished the blade from the ashes as a reminder of what she and Leesil had accomplished for Miiska. Displayed not in pride or triumph, it was a tribute of respect for those who died and shouldn't be forgotten – Brenden the smith and his sister, and Bethrae, Caleb's wife, among others. That blade symbolized what had been finally faced and overcome at a severe cost.

The upstairs bedrooms were larger. Before the fire, he and Magiere each had their own room, but Caleb and his five-year-old granddaughter, Rose, had shared one. Now Rose possessed a bedroom to herself, and Leesil had whitewashed the interior for her. Every child should grow up with a place that was all his or her own.

Leesil took in the room with its new wood walls and secondhand tables and chairs donated, bought, or scavenged from around town. It struck Leesil as bizarre that, had Rashed not burned down the original Sea Lion, their establishment wouldn't have become what it was now. His gaze swung back to the warrior undead's sword above the hearth.

'Perhaps we should thank you,' he muttered, but there was more sarcasm than irony in his voice. He turned again to watch Magiere.

The long battle with Rashed and his 'family' had altered her. Before, she'd started to become more open to him. Close comradeship seeded the possibility of more, but in the past month, that warmer Magiere seemed to fade. She smiled occasionally, treated him well as partner and favored companion, and yet drifted back out of reach. Once in while during the evening, he caught her standing quietly behind the bar, watching him intently with her dark brown eyes. He was careful not to let her notice his awareness and thereby scare her away even more. There seemed no clue as to how to close this new distance between them, let alone fathom its cause.

Tonight, in celebration of the grand reopening, Magiere's long hair was loose from its braid and hung in gentle waves across the shoulders of her blue dress, bodice laced in tightly but not uncomfortably. It was only the third time Leesil had ever seen in her anything but breeches and boots, and either a shirt and vest or her leather hauberk. To his knowledge, she owned only the one dress. Seeing her in it was painfully pleasant. He was careful not to stare, or, out of irritation and spite, she might store it away, never to be seen again. Usually she was the warrior, falchion at her hip and black hair bound with a leather thong, and that look as well had its appeal. He'd become fond of both her aspects, wanted them both, but seldom had the opportunity to see her as she was tonight.

No patrons were interested in a game, so Leesil stacked up the cards and worked his way through the crowded room to the bar, smiling innocently at Magiere. She was hesitant and then smiled back.

'Like old times?' she asked.

'Not too old,' he answered. 'We didn't have the place long before someone turned it into a pile of charcoal.'

Her answering scowl made him smile again, honestly this time. An irritated Magiere, at least for a moment, was the true Magiere, who always had at least one thing in every day to smolder about.

'I know,' she said, pouring an ale and setting it on a tray for Caleb to serve. 'But we're finally home again.'

Melancholy struck Leesil. If only the world could stop, and, like some mage who'd ferreted out the secrets to cage eternity in the wink of an eye, he could keep her in this one night forever. Oblivious to his wistfulness, Magiere knitted her brows.

'We need to talk . . . later. We have to raise quick money . . . more than I'd thought, and I'm not sure how.'

Leesil was immediately on edge. It wouldn't be the first time she'd kept something to herself until she had no choice but to spit it out. The last time, she'd confessed to hoarding away money when he wasn't paying attention, just to buy this tavern.

'It's for the back taxes,' she added.

'Back what?' Leesil raised one eyebrow.

'I've been a dolt on the business end of things,' Magiere said. 'Karlin came looking for me today, and you haven't . . . there hasn't been time to talk to you about it.' She folded her arms and took a long, slow breath. 'We've back taxes to pay. I don't suppose you have any coin hidden away?'

He blinked, about to laugh, and then realized she wasn't joking. With a grunt, he gave her his wide-eyed look of sincere naiveté.

'Are you actually aware of who you're talking to? Me?'

Her jaw tightened as she glared at him. An angry Magiere was sometimes even more real than a smoldering Magiere.

The tavern's front door swung open and a handful of sailors entered.

'That's my call,' Leesil said. 'They'll start gambling soon. Pour me some tea?'

D'areeling red wine had been his preferred evening drink but not in the last two months. He needed to be sharp and clearheaded every moment if he were to be truly useful to Magiere. She took a teapot from under the bar, where it rested in an iron basin filled with hot coals from the hearth, and poured spiced tea into a chipped pottery mug.

'We're not done talking,' she insisted, and handed over his tea. 'This is serious, and we have to deal with it, or all of this' – she swiped a hand through the air, indicating their new home – 'could end up lost.'

'Duty calls,' Leesil replied. He took the mug from her and headed back across the room before she could say anything more.

Early patrons were usually townsfolk coming for fish

chowder, ale, and a bit of company. The later crowd consisted more of sailors and off-duty guards looking to drink and gamble. At the moment, they were between the two crowds, and the place felt a bit full. Young Geoffry, Karlin's son, had volunteered to serve tonight, since they expected an unusually large crowd, and Magiere had employed a girl named Aria on a permanent basis. With old Caleb serving as well, Magiere pouring drinks, and Leesil running the games, they were well staffed in a room that was well stuffed. Everyone enjoyed the new surroundings as if trying on a set of clothes fresh from the tailor.

Everyone except Chap.

The silver-blue hound circled the hearth for the hundredth time, wolfish ears pricked in agitation. Sitting near the old Sea Lion's fireplace, he easily surveyed the whole room, from hearth to bar, front door to kitchen doorway. But the new enlarged common room changed all of that. Now, to check on any unusual ruckus or raised voice, he was obliged to plod around and around the fireplace all night, unable to take in the whole room at once.

With the noise in the room, Leesil wasn't certain, but he imagined a never-quite-ending low rumble issuing from the hound. He steered a wider course toward his faro table rather than pass too close to Chap at the moment.

The tavern door opened again, and Leesil saw Karlin enter – a welcome sight, as Leesil had wondered why the portly baker hadn't been at the door the moment they'd opened. Karlin was a true friend, and his money was no good in the Sea Lion. When someone else entered behind the baker, Leesil's attention fixed on the new arrival.

Karlin's companion was slender and tall, with a gliding step that immediately reminded Leesil of his mother even before he took full notice of the man's features. Silky, wheat-brown hair was pulled back behind his pointed ears. Large, almond-shaped eyes of amber were sharply slanted in a narrow and long triangular face. The man's skin was a darker tan than Leesil's, but with a perfect complexion akin to his mother's. Standing with Karlin was a full-blooded elf.

Magiere had mentioned Loni, so Leesil knew one of his mother's people lived in Miiska, but he'd never felt the need to seek out this person. His own mother never saw fit to teach him anything of her people, even their language. The elves were reclusive, not generally mixing with the other races, which itself made Leesil's own heritage an oddity.

Since Loni ran the Velvet Rose, Miiska's most expensive inn, he had little call to visit a common folk's tavern like the Sea Lion. So why was he here, and with Karlin of all people? Leesil held his place, halfway to his faro table, where sailors nearby eyed the cards. He watched Karlin lean over the bar's end to catch Magiere's attention.

Magiere hurried down the bar's backside with a slight smile. The baker spoke briefly, perhaps discussing the tedious tax issue, and Leesil felt suddenly annoyed. Why did so many people dwell on such things? It would be handled soon enough.

Loni, the elf, tapped Karlin on the shoulder and, with a serious look, tilted his head toward Magiere. Karlin reached into his vest, withdrew a piece of rolled parchment, and handed it to her. She frowned in confusion, then unrolled it and began reading.

Magiere's mild moment of happiness melted from her pale features.

Brows knitted in puzzlement, and then her eyes widened. When she lifted her gaze to Karlin, the clench of her jaw was plain to Leesil from across the room. The elf spoke, and Magiere threw the parchment at his chest as she began shouting. Several patrons at the bar shifted away toward the kitchen side as Leesil quickly pushed his way back across the crowded room.

He couldn't make out what she said, but he did catch 'bastard,' and some Stravinan term that sounded worse. Chap had somehow wormed through the room and beaten Leesil to the bar. The dog growled at Karlin and Loni – mostly at the elf, for Chap was as fond of the baker as anyone else living at the Sea Lion. Background noise began to fade as more and more people turned their heads toward Magiere's raised voice. Leesil planted one hand on the bar, vaulted to the backside, and caught her arm.

'Quiet, you dragon,' he whispered playfully. 'You're frightening the peasants.'

Her pale skin was flushed, and the glare she returned made him think better of any further jest. She moved back from Karlin and Loni, and closer to him.

'Leesil, get them out of here . . . or I'll do it my way!'

Leesil abandoned any further thought of disarming the situation through humor, and slipped around Magiere between her and the end of the bar.

'Into the kitchen,' he said softly, and then looked over his shoulder. 'Karlin, you come now.'

Leesil steered Magiere down the bar toward the kitchen's curtained doorway. He was thankful she didn't resist. She did, however, pull away from him and nearly rip the curtains off their rod as she swatted them aside on her way through. Leesil hurried after her.

'What's wrong?' he asked. He pulled a stool to the kitchen table and literally pushed her down to sit on it. When he did, he felt her shoulders shaking with tension. 'This can't be about back taxes?'

The curtain pulled aside and Karlin entered, followed

by Loni. The baker looked stricken and shamed, a troubling contrast to his cheerful nature. The elf stared at all of them, attentive and watchful but otherwise expressionless.

'You could just say no, Magiere,' Loni said. 'This drama is unnecessary.'

'Get out,' she answered with enough hatred that Leesil balked at her tone.

'And then what, send the offer back?' Loni tossed the parchment on the table in front of her. 'You know this money could rebuild the old warehouse, this time to be operated as community property. More merchants working the coastal route would once again stop here. Commerce would flourish instead of wither. Dockworkers could earn a decent wage, forcing Master Poyesk and his like to pay well or close up. Outlying farmers and local crafters could collectively wholesale their goods once again.'

'What is going on?' Leesil demanded, lost amid the argument.

Karlin stood in helpless silence.

'I can't believe you'd ask this of me,' Magiere whispered.

Her gaze locked on Loni. She wrapped one hand on the table's edge, as if bracing for a lunge, her whole body tensed.

Leesil quickly stepped into her way, not the best place to be if Magiere succumbed to a fit of dhampir rage. Almost as tall as him, in such a state she could take down a trained undead warrior one-on-one.

'Show it to him,' Loni ordered her, nodding at Leesil. 'He burned the warehouse – correct? Perhaps he'll comprehend the potential of what you choose to ignore.'

Leesil twitched reflexively at Loni's dispassionate barb, and then he felt Magiere's fingers pulling on his own.

The touch drew his attention, and he looked down to find her pushing the parchment into his hand.

'Read it,' she said quietly.

The rolled parchment was partially flattened from handling, but enough of the wax seal remained to see its imprint. In the center was the Belaskian royal crest under the tasseled banner of the king's city of Bela. Leesil's melancholy reared again. He unrolled the parchment.

To the council and governing members of the free town of Miiska in his majesty's kingdom of Belaski:

Through Sir Vidor Chàsnitz, ship owner and member of our city council, we have learned of your recent economic difficulties related to the loss of your largest warehouse. We send our and his majesty's hope that your situation will improve. It is partially in this interest that we address you with a request which might be fulfilled best by one of your own citizens and in turn serve the recovery of your community.

From other sources, we have learned that in your respectable town resides one known as Magiere, a reported individual of special talents with whom we seek contact. We have heard with great interest of her skills put to the service of your town, and it is such skills and service that we in turn wish to engage from her. Our concern is that our great city of Bela may be plagued in the same manner as Miiska was until recently. The pattern of crimes pertinent has only of late come to the council's attention and by the worst possible means. The daughter of our prominent council chairman was killed upon the front steps of his home. The circumstances leave little doubt as to an unnatural perpetrator which continues to elude our city guard and constabularies.

*We ask your council or its agents to bring this to
the attention of Mistress Magiere, and that if she is
willing, she should travel to the capital with all possible
haste. To that end, we include documents to secure her,
as well as the companion with which she is reputed to
work, immediate free passage without question on any
kingdom ship bound for Bela.*

*In exchange for her services, the council has been
authorized to offer the sum of fifty gold sovereigns of
the realm, notwithstanding any bounty offered by
private parties. We anxiously await your reply and hope
that our offer meets with acceptance, compassion, and
duty.*

With sincerity,
Crias Doviak, Secretary
Acting for the Council of Bela

Leesil set the parchment down and leaned back against
the table, blankly staring at the floor. Loni allowed little
more than two breaths to pass before breaking the silence.

'You do not seem surprised by this,' he said.

'No,' Leesil answered.

'But . . . how?' Karlin started, attention hopping
between the others in confusion. 'Darien just brought the
letter to us this afternoon. And you already knew about
it?'

'No,' Leesil repeated. 'I didn't know about the letter
or what was in it. I knew something like this was coming
. . . eventually, though it's sooner than I'd hoped.'

'What are you saying?' Magiere's voice was harsh but
quiet.

Leesil lifted his head just enough to find her looking
up at him. Confusion filled her eyes, but her nearly white
cheeks were still flushed.

'What did you expect?' he snapped more bitterly than intended. 'If you think you had a reputation in the backwoods of Stravina, think again. We waged open battle with three undeads right before the eyes of an entire town . . . a port town sitting on the coastal sea lane of the whole nation, with sailors, merchants, and others passing through for two moons – even with the dropoff in trade. Worst of all, we won. This isn't peasant superstitions and rural rumors anymore.'

Anger drained from Magiere's face as her large brown eyes filled up with barely suppressed panic.

The letter was only the beginning, and it was never going to be over.

Magiere sank in her chair with eyes closed. Leesil looked back at Karlin.

'They know,' he said. 'They know Magiere and I are responsible for the warehouse, and they're coming at her through guilt. Otherwise they would have offered the money directly to her. They knew she'd refuse, didn't they?'

After a moment's contemplation, Karlin nodded, his round face too sad for speech.

'You *are* responsible,' Loni said with a hard glance at Leesil before focusing once again upon Magiere. 'Would it be so terrible to go destroy their undead, to help others as you have helped the people here? No one denies the good you have done, but the repercussions cannot be ignored. You have a chance to make amends. Do you not owe this to Miiska? Hunting the undead is what you do.'

The last statement made Leesil cringe. How could he or Magiere ever tell anyone that until they'd come to Miiska, their entire reputation was built on a charlatan's game for cheating peasants? Magiere put her head in her hands.

'Go home, Loni,' she said. 'Nothing you say can make me go to Bela . . . nothing.'

The dreamer shifted in his slumber. All around him, below and above, was boundless dark, the dreamer suspended at its center. He hung there in silence, waiting.

Until the dark began to undulate.

It rolled like desert dunes under a starless sky. But when the stars did come out, they blinked not from sky but from the crests of those black dunes all around. The movement sharpened slowly into clarity, and stars became the glitter of an unseen light reflected upon black reptilian scales. Dunes covered in those scales became a mammoth serpent's coils, each larger than the height of man. They circled on all sides of him, and above and below. They writhed with no beginning, no end, no space between, as if ancient and eternal and all-encompassing, perhaps stretching back into the time of the Forgotten, and the lost history of the world.

'Where?' he asked again. 'Where is it? It has been so many years . . . decades. Am I closer?'

The same questions as always, and little by little, small, cryptic images and words floated through.

High . . . in the cold . . . and ice. The weight of those whispering words slipped into the dreamer's mind and suffocated his own thoughts. *Guarded by old ones . . . oldest of predecessors.*

'How can I find it?'

The dreamer tried to peer beyond the black coils and envision what he sought, but he as yet did not even know what it looked like – only what the coils, his patron of dreams, promised the object could provide. Once acquired, it would forever alter the nature of his existence. Nothing would be needed from the outside, and all would be met from within himself.

The coils began to close in upon him with fear and exhaustion. These dreams with his nameless benefactor filled his mind with knowledge one grain at a time, but drained him quickly. He wanted to remain and ask more but could not.

Welstiel Massing opened his eyes, alone, lying upon a large, canopied bed in his rented room as the black coils faded from his thoughts.

It was like any dream one might have, sharp in its experience and dull in its aftermath. He remembered coils in the dark, but neither their look nor the feel of his patron's voice. And with each dream, the voice provided fewer new answers. In the end, if he acquired the promised object, it would free him. This much he did believe – and remember.

Rising, he settled at his desk with quill in hand and opened the top thin volume of a stack of journals. He'd procured private rooms in one of Bela's more respectable inns, affording him the privacy he required. Without contemplation, he wrote down what little he remembered from the dream. His hand shook slightly and his normal clarity was fogged, but he had a few more pieces to add, even if they did not all fit together well.

The object was hidden at an elevation cold enough for ice and snow to remain all year. And 'predecessors,' old ones, guarded it. That in itself wasn't new information, but still left Welstiel uneasy, as this detail recurred time and again. How old? As far back as the creation of this object he sought? From the time of the forgotten history perhaps, and so old it might predate the Great War.

He could not fight these predecessors alone; that he'd surmised by the patron's implications over the years, but he'd long been preparing to address this obstacle. Plans laid with patience were now ready for further momentum.

Welstiel made the bed and dressed with meticulous attention to each fold of shirt, breeches, and vest. He combed dark hair back to reveal two small, equally white patches at his temples. He used his right hand, as his left was missing the first digit of its little finger. He donned an expensive black cloak and pulled up the cowl.

Finally he opened a small jade box and removed a thin ring made of brass with minute, fine symbols etched around its inside. He slipped this onto the first finger of his right hand, bracing himself.

As always, everything around looked the same but felt as if the world suddenly separated from him, almost unaware of his presence. It had been many years since he'd made the ring, and he seldom succumbed to a self-appraisal when donning it. He looked into the small mirror on his desk.

His own familiar image was there in the glass, but it felt as if he stared at the reflection of a finely crafted painting. Though outside his appearance remained unchanged, what he held within — thought, feeling, and presence — would be imperceptible.

Before leaving, he took one more look about to be sure nothing was out of place. His journals were of no concern, written in the tongue of his homeland far across sea and land in the northern Numan territories. As to the other books stowed under the bed, their locked straps might intrigue anyone foolish enough to search his room but were far beyond the capability of any thief to open. If they were forced, the result would be most unpleasant.

On the bedside floor rested a frosted glass globe on a plain iron pedestal. Within the glass moved three dancing sparks that glowed enough to dimly illuminate the small room. It was the oldest thing he possessed, having been the first thing he'd ever created in his long studies. He opened the door to leave, speaking sharply without looking back.

'Darkness.' The sparks in the globe winked out.

After Karlin and Loni's departure, Magiere managed a polite front for her patrons until the last of them left past midnight. She thanked them and invited them to return again. Across the room, Leesil followed this same ritual as the final would-be gamblers gathered winnings and bemoaned losses. Caleb collected dishes and mugs from tables onto trays, and Aria took the trays into the kitchen to begin washing up. Magiere mindlessly continued closing down for the night. When Leesil nearly pushed the last gambler out of the tavern, he went to the curtained kitchen doorway.

'Aria, leave all that,' he said. 'I'll take care of it in the morning.'

'Sir?' her questioning voice floated out. 'Come morning, it'll stink like a broken ale keg in here.'

'It doesn't matter. Just leave it.' He looked back to Caleb, who was straightening up chairs. 'Could you walk Aria and Geoffry home?'

Normally, Leesil would have played escort for their young helpers, who'd as well been assisting with preparations before the grand opening. With Caleb on such a duty and little Rose in bed, it was obvious to Magiere her partner was getting everyone out of the way.

'I don't need Caleb to take me home,' Geoffry said indignantly. He dumped a load of firewood by the hearth and glared at the half-elf. Under a mop of auburn hair, his plain face expressed righteous indignation. 'For the love of mutton, Leesil, I helped you fight wolves and vampires. I can walk Aria home myself.'

'Come, come,' Caleb said, gathering his cloak from the hooks by the front door. 'Your parents may well be waiting up, even to this hour. We should walk in numbers.'

'Well, you'll still be walking back here all by yourself,' Geoffry answered, not quite ready to give in.

Caleb was over sixty, slightly stopped, with thick silver hair. He seldom spoke but had a presence that made people to stop and listen when he did. He looked at Geoffry in mild displeasure.

Geoffry sighed, walked to the door, and jerked his cloak off the hook. He grabbed Aria's as well as she emerged from the kitchen. Leesil ushered all three out into the night.

Magiere went to sit on the hearth's edge. Her knees up in front of her, she reached out to where Chap lay nearby and stroked between the hound's tall ears. Chap rolled his head to lick her hand. His silver-blue fur was soft, and his clear eyes seemed to express sympathy, as if he understood her suffering. A foolish thought, and Magiere shook it off.

'Are you all right?' Leesil asked, walking toward her. He pulled the tied scarf from his head, shook his long white-blond hair loose, and scratched at his scalp for a moment.

Stupid question. She didn't answer.

'It had to happen eventually,' he said. 'I've been waiting for it, though you hadn't really thought it through until today. And it won't be the last time. Word is spreading. Maybe some of them are going to want help . . . and some of them . . .' He paused, seeming hesitant to finish. 'Well, some might offer a great deal of money.'

'We don't need their money!' she responded.

It was a lie. She knew it and so did he.

'Yes, right, of course we don't,' he said, mockingly

agreeable. 'But for the moment, I'm not talking about us, and you know it.'

Leesil crouched on the floor in front of her, bringing them face-to-face.

Amber eyes just slightly almond shaped, and not as slanted and large as Loni's, stared back at her from under thin white-blond eyebrows. Magiere wanted to look away but wouldn't. It was so hard to look him in the eyes without memories surging into her thoughts – frightening and bloody memories. She wanted to see no more pain on his face and no more scars on his body. Her gaze drifted down to his wrist and then back up.

Even with his thin-lipped mouth always on the verge of a wry smile, he seemed almost sad – or perhaps bitter.

'Loni may be rude,' Leesil continued. 'But some of what he said is true. I burned that warehouse down and . . . I'd do it again without a second thought – given the same need.'

Magiere remembered nothing of their flight from the warehouse, when Leesil had set the building on fire to cover their escape. But from what she'd later learned, he'd been rather thorough and zealous in executing that chosen task. They'd tried to take the family of undeads in their underground tunnels beneath the building. The heated memory of fighting Rashed flashed unwanted into her head. She'd been in bloodlust, her dhampir nature consuming her with hate and hunger as she fought with the warrior vampire. Then his longsword sliced through the side of her throat, and she collapsed into darkness.

There was no memory of how Leesil had gotten her out of there. The only thing she did remember was awaking to Leesil *healing* her by feeding her blood from his own wrist – and wanting him to go on and never stop.

The start of a cold sweat broke out across Magiere's skin, and nausea rose in her stomach. She swallowed hard, not wanting Leesil to notice.

'Miiska now suffers for what I did,' he continued with a shrug. 'There is a chance to make amends. Plus maybe something for ourselves. The payment will be made to you, not the town, regardless of what that letter implies. And a rebuilt warehouse run by the town doesn't mean we can't get a piece of it for having funded the whole thing.'

His schemes aside, Magiere couldn't believe what she heard, and then realization struck her.

'You want to go. You *want* to do this.'

He dropped his head until his long hair hung forward around his face and across his ear tips.

'No. It's not about what I want. I don't see how we can refuse.'

'Easy, I just did. Or weren't you listening in the kitchen?'

Leesil rubbed his temple with one hand, pushing his hair back and letting it fall again like a curtain.

'You want to stay here and have us run this business forever? Fine. What if things continue the way they're going in Miiska? Where's our business going to come from with no spare coin in anyone's pocket? What happens to Karlin and Geoffry? To Aria and her family? How are we even going to pay Caleb enough to properly care for little Rose?'

Magiere couldn't see Leesil's expression hidden behind his hair, and a numb feeling crept through her. There was more behind his words than Miiska's welfare. He'd never wanted the Sea Lion in the first place. She'd purchased it on her own, and he'd fought her, conceding in the end only when she wouldn't change her mind. Now it seemed his mind was changing. She leaned against the stones of the hearth.

'If you want to do this,' she returned, 'then be honest about it and stop hiding behind concern for the town.'

Leesil's head jerked up, anger plain on his face.

'It's not that way, and you know it!' He dropped onto one knee, bringing him close enough to lean his hands against the hearth's ledge to both sides of her legs. 'You're just trying to make it simple enough to ignore, and it's not.'

Magiere was forced to look him in the eyes again.

Leesil leaned farther toward her, and Magiere's whole body tensed.

He turned, pushing his side between her knees as he settled to the floor between her feet and leaned slowly backward. It took several breaths as he settled there with his back toward her, coming closer to contact with her, until Magiere realized she wasn't breathing at all. She took a slow breath, forcing her limbs to stop shaking.

His weight against her was no more than a feather quilt at first; then it settled warm and firm as the back of his head came to rest against her breastbone.

'Nothing is that simple for us,' he said quietly.

His body felt slender, warm, and solid. She'd spent so much time watching over him every moment after the final battle, tending his needs to be sure he survived. Though she'd stripped, bathed, and bandaged him, and did whatever else was necessary to keep him recovering, they'd not touched like this, both of them fully aware of the other.

She could smell his hair, filled with forest scent, lavender soap from an afternoon bath, and remnants of ale, pipe smoke, and other lingering scents of a night in the tavern. He was still and quiet, pressed against her. Her gaze traced down his flaxen hair running across the front of her dress and his own shoulders. Instinctively, she lifted her hands to rest on his shoulders, and then her gaze fell on his left arm against her thigh.

Shirtsleeve loose, it exposed the wrist sheath holding his remaining slivery stiletto strapped to his forearm. Just below the downward-pointed hilt were the scars on his wrist.

Memory boiled into Magiere's mind, calling back her first waking awareness after flight from the burning warehouse. Blood filled her mouth, running across her tongue, and bringing life into her body as she swallowed.

Leesil's blood.

She remembered her teeth set into the wrist he'd slashed open in order to feed her. He'd straddled her on the bed and pressed that wrist against her mouth until running blood awakened her. In those early days in Miiska, she'd already begun to think more on him each day, and that fixation mingled in her hunger. He was right above her, and her teeth sank deeper into his flesh as she pulled him close.

He was so warm, so near that everything she felt might have been poured from him right into her. And she was killing him. Had Brenden not been there to pull him away . . .

From that moment, part of her became linked to the world of the undeads she'd destroyed. She was a danger to those she cared for, and deadly to the one closest to her. Leesil never saw this, would never accept it. Magiere didn't know which horrified her more – what she was, or what she could do to him if she ever became a dhampir fully again.

The scars on his wrist from her own teeth would never fade.

Magiere pulled out from behind Leesil and was at the kitchen doorway before he could get to his feet. She gripped the curtain's edge so tightly that her forearm ached, and she calmed herself before looking back at him across the room. Leesil watched her in confusion. Even Chap lifted his head.

Leesil was at least right about Miiska. At some point, if the town continued to wane, it meant the Sea Lion would have few patrons left. Any hope for building a new life here would be hollow. If the town died, so would the life she'd wanted.

If saving their life here were truly Leesil's only reason for accepting the letter's offer, she might have felt some peace in agreeing. But he wanted to be on the move again, always onto something new, and would never settle for what they had here.

'Go to Karlin in the morning and tell him we'll take the offer,' she said. 'We'll sail for Bela on the next northbound ship and destroy their undead. When we . . . when the payment is delivered, the town can rebuild the warehouse.'

Uncertainty filled Leesil's voice. 'Magiere—'

'It's all right,' she said. This wasn't his fault, not really. 'We should start packing.'

She left him and headed through the kitchen to the back stairs. She was thankful he didn't follow.

Magiere paused upon reaching the upper floor. Leesil's door was the first on the left. He'd chosen it, wanting to be the first line of defense should they ever have another assailant enter their home. He swore that if anyone who didn't belong there tried to walk up those stairs or crawl through the hallway window, he would know. When he said it, she believed him. Leesil had very good hearing.

The next room down the hall was hers. Since the downstairs hearth was now near the center of the common room, its chimney rose through the upstairs floor between her room and Leesil's, and its warmth permeated her private space. Caleb's room was at the hall's end, and inside it to the left was a door leading to the fourth and final room, belonging to Rose, his granddaughter.

Inside Magiere's room was a narrow bed with a goose-down comforter – a gift from Aria's mother – and a small table and a chest. Opening the chest, she planned to pull out her old pack, a leftover from the days she and Leesil had spent in the backlands of Stravina. But of course the pack had burned with everything else.

So much lost. The blue dress she wore had been spared only because she'd changed at the Velvet Rose and left it with Loni the night that the tavern burned. Leesil had few things left besides his weapons, but he seemed to need little else. He'd always liked traveling light.

She fingered the amulets hanging around her neck. Tools of the trade. The topaz stone glowed brightly when-ever a Noble Dead was near, though it gave off no heat. She had to see it for its property to assist her. The other amulet was more ambiguous: a small piece of bone set against an oval tin backing. She'd used it only once. Well, Leesil had used it.

He'd learned its property from the stranger named Welstiel Massing, who'd advised them concerning the Noble Dead. A dhampir, injured to the point of needing to feed on someone's blood, must place the bone side against his or her bare skin in order for the life force to be properly absorbed. Leesil had pressed it against her flesh before feeding her. There were times since when she'd wanted to smash it but could not. Amulets and fal-chion were all that had been left to her by her father.

Born in the inland country of Droevinka, she'd never

known her father, but throughout childhood learned bits and pieces about him. A transient noble vassal, he belonged to the class that ruled the peasants for the lords and collected rents due on land plots. Staying in one place for months or sometimes years, eventually they always moved onward to wherever the higher lord sent them. Few had seen him except on late-evening collections, after daylight faded and everyone could be found in their hovels and cottages, retired from labor. Her mother was just a young woman from a village near the barony house. The nobleman took her for his mistress, and she remained mostly out of sight for nearly a year.

Her name was Magelia, and she died giving birth to Magiere. Her father was assigned to another fief and left his infant daughter with her mother's sister, Bieja. Magelia had been lovely, with a mass of black hair but no glints of crimson, as shown in Magiere's. She was also said to have been quiet, composed, and gentle. Although Magiere looked like her mother, she'd been born fierce, with a temper. Rumors that her father had been an unnatural beast who feared daylight dominated her childhood. She was hated and shunned by all in her village except her aunt. On her sixteenth birthday, Aunt Bieja gave her an inheritance left by her father: two amulets, leather armor, and a falchion with a strange glyph on the hilt. Magiere took them, and eventually fled from the village to fend for herself in the world until she met Leesil.

She now knew her father had been one of the Noble Dead. For some reason, her father had left her the tools to fight his own kind, but she didn't know why.

So much time had passed since the days with Aunt Bieja. Sitting in her new room, Magiere leaned her head against the edge of the open chest. There was little she needed to pack. Tonight's profits would be left with Caleb to keep the Sea Lion running until she returned. With or without Leesil.

Outside in the hall she thought she heard soft footsteps and the sound of Leesil's door quietly opening and closing.

Toret lounged on a mauve velvet divan in his lavish sitting room, feeling quite satisfied with the state of his domain. He fixed his eyes on his glorious beloved. His beautiful Sapphire paraded before a large oval mirror in her new mustard yellow satin gown. Dark blond ringlets framed her round and sensuous face.

Chane, his servant and bodyguard, stood near the dead hearth, leaning against the solid stonework and looking as bored as always. Although useful, Chane had little imagination, rarely spoke, and spent most waking hours sporting a flat, dour expression. He was quite . . .

What was the word? Tedious? Yes, he was quite tedious, really.

But Toret didn't care. He'd come so far in the span of two moons. Was it only two since he had abandoned Rashed and Teesha in Miiska? It seemed much longer, and puzzling that he'd lived under Rashed's oppression for so many years, never realizing how capable he was of creating his own perfect world.

Traveling up the coast to Bela, he discovered the joy of a large city. He killed and fed at will, stole money from his prey, and remade himself anew, dressing as Rashed had dressed, like a nobleman – only better. Then one night, while hunting near a brothel, he saw the most perfect woman in the world, with brilliant eyes that made him think of the bright daylight sky he hadn't seen in many decades. He could never destroy her, never simply consume her. She must belong to him. His Sapphire.

She was a goddess.

She stirred his desire to remake himself anew. He changed his name from Ratboy – an insulting label thrust upon him by his own undead maker – back to Toret, his given mortal name left behind long ago.

But Sapphire had needs and desires beyond what he could afford. When Toret found and turned Chane, a spoiled and arrogant young noble, their situation was safeguarded. Chane had come into his inheritance, and the amount was substantial enough to keep them all in comfort. Toret used part of the wealth to purchase their three-story stone house on the edge of an elite district of Bela inside the second ring wall. Why hadn't he struck out on his own sooner? Why had he endured all those years under Rashed's command? Well, now Rashed was dead, or so Toret had heard, and so much the better.

'Isn't it perfect?' Sapphire asked, looking blissfully at the folds of her new gown. It was cinched so tight a mortal woman wouldn't be able to breathe, but the effect raised the tops of her smooth breasts high into view through the plunging lace bodice.

'Yes,' he answered. 'But you would look perfect in anything . . . or nothing.'

Chane made a strange sound as if choking.

Toret looked over in mild concern as the taller undead appeared to clear his throat. He made that sound so often that Toret wondered if he'd carried some physical defect from life into afterlife. But since the problem didn't interfere with Chane's ability to serve, Toret never bothered to ask.

This room pleased Toret more than any other except for the bedroom he shared with Sapphire. She, of course, had her own room for her jewelry, clothing, and accoutrements, but he insisted she rest with him by day.

Chane had ordered the furnishings for the sitting room, and Toret approved of his choices. When they bought the house, this room already boasted fine craftsmanship in its gray hearth and hardwood overlaid floors. Chane had thick Suman carpets of amber and soft russet delivered, and Droevinkan pastoral paintings graced the stairway walls leading to the upper floors. He contrasted light oak tables with dark mauve velvet furnishings.

If Toret hadn't known better, he would've sworn Chane took a modicum of pride in the finished effect. But there'd been that one tense moment when Toret hung a life-size portrait of Sapphire in an ornate bronze frame on the sitting room's west wall. What could be more beautiful, more the finishing touch to anything, than Sapphire?

The house had belonged to a wealthy but solitary merchant who died of consumption. Ownership reverted to the city, and it had been for sale nearly a year when Toret bought it. One attraction was a hidden passageway in the wall adjacent to the staircase, making him wonder just what the old merchant had been involved in. But one thing Toret had learned from Rashed was the absolute need for alternative escape routes. Each floor possessed a hidden entryway to the passage at the landings of the main stairway, and all three members of the house knew where each entry existed.

Since he and Sapphire both kept rooms on the top floor, the second floor was empty. The main floor consisted of the lavish sitting room and the dining chamber and the kitchens. The main area of the cellar was where they practiced swordplay, and Chane kept his own things squirreled away in a smaller room behind this.

Turning away from the mirror's reflection, Sapphire beamed at Toret.

'Are we going out tonight? I want to show it off.'

'We hunted last night. None of us need to feed yet.'

Her smile faded. 'I didn't say anything about feeding, did I? I said I want to go out in my new gown.'

Toret found just 'going out' to be quite dull. If he refused, she was going to pout all night – and possibly throw things – but he felt like staying in.

'Chane, could you?'

His servant appeared lost in thought, but the last of the conversation caught suddenly in his awareness. For a second, a flicker of fright crossed his lean features.

Toret stared at him. Chane probably didn't care to take Sapphire out to frolic any more than he did. But Chane seldom displayed any expression besides boredom – except when he was hunting, and then there were moments when his nature surprised even Toret. Chane stood at full height and crossed his tightly muscled arms.

'I was to finish some studies tonight, master.' Chane fingered what appeared to be a small brass urn or vial on a chain about his neck.

Sapphire's pout shifted dangerously toward impending temper.

'Yes, yes,' Toret acknowledged quickly, 'but that can wait. Your lady wishes to be entertained, and you don't want her to be unhappy?'

All he really need do was give an outright order, but Toret had always hated being ordered around, so he tried to avoid doing it whenever possible.

Chane blinked, his gaze shifting between Toret and Sapphire. He was about to speak when a knock sounded from the front door.

Toret frowned. In their charade as landless gentry, there were social contacts they'd made in order to keep up a good front – some even as high up as the city council – but it wasn't likely any would come calling here. This was probably another delivery for Sapphire. He'd tried to stop this, but the more money she got her hands on, the more baubles and garments she ordered.

'Chane, could you get that?' Toret said.

'I was going to my rooms to study,' his tall servant answered.

All of Chane's dour nature had returned, and Toret's irritation got the better of him.

'*Get the door,*' he said more slowly.

Chane's muscles jerked once. Toret saw him shake off the compulsive sensation and, once composed, walk instantly into the foyer. When Chane returned, he handed Toret a small folded paper sealed at the center with wax.

'This was delivered for you, master.'

A message? Toret was tempted to have Chane read it to him but was worried that might make him look weak. He broke the seal, unfolded the paper, and read one short line.

I will visit you near the mid of night with information regarding your past in Miiska. Be alone.

There was no signature.

'What is it?' Sapphire asked. 'An invitation? Is there a party?'

Toret's reading skills were limited, and he read the note twice before fully comprehending every word. Anxiety overran him.

Rumors had spread through bayside taverns and inns that a 'hunter' in Miiska had destroyed all of its undead, which wasn't exactly true. Toret had survived. He heard enough variations on the tale that his amusement had waned and he'd tired of it. It was seldom repeated these days. But as he stared at the note, his imagination worked feverishly. No one knew of his time spent in Miiska.

What if he hadn't been the only one to escape?

What if Rashed, the desert warrior, had actually survived and come to Bela, tracking his old companion – the one who'd run out on him?

That pompous, arrogant, sand-born, bastard of a . . . Images of the tall, perfect Suman undead smothered all other thoughts, wiping away Toret's contentment. Rashed with his crystal-blue eyes, so unnatural for his mortal race, and his ridiculous code of honor, and his ability to command. The idea of Sapphire coming under such influence made Toret squirm in agitation.

How long before the apex of the moon?

'Chane,' he said quickly, 'get your lady's cloak and take her wherever she wants to go.'

Sapphire frowned briefly, then brightened. Toret knew she didn't relish Chane's company, but at least she could take her new dress out on the town. Chane hesitated.

'Now!' Toret barked.

Chane twitched again, glowering openly as he headed for the foyer.

'I don't want a cloak,' Sapphire whined. 'It'll wrinkle my dress.'

'You'll look odd without one,' Chane said. '*Ladies* wear cloaks.'

'When I want your fashion advice, I'll ask you,' she snapped.

'He's right,' Toret said. 'Put it on.'

Sapphire obeyed, taking her cloak from Chane's long, outstretched arm.

'Hurry,' Toret said. 'The night is half-over. It's not long before the inns close.'

Chane glanced suspiciously at him and at the folded paper. Toret stuffed it inside his tunic and grasped Sapphire's pale hand to kiss it.

'Bring me back some entertaining stories, my love.'

Sapphire returned Toret only a slight smile, apparently uncertain whether to be angry because he was sending her off with Chane or content to have her way.

'I'll have to go someplace expensive to be appreciated. Some extra coin would be helpful.'

Anxiety was turning to fear. Toret jerked the purse from his belt and pushed it into her hand. 'Here, this should be more than enough.'

With a gasp of delight, Sapphire flounced out the door with Chane following.

'Take care of her,' Toret called after him. And they were gone, and he was alone.

He had a little time to think. Perhaps he jumped to ridiculous conclusions. Rumors regarding Miiska's undead had usually been consistent. Everything pointed to the fact that Rashed's charred bones were buried in the remains of that accursed hunter's tavern. But if Rashed were dead, who else could have sent the note? No one in this city knew he came from Miiska.

A knock came at the front door. Toret hesitated.

Despite his rationalizations, he half expected to open the door and see Rashed towering over him. Ratboy would run for the back door, but Toret wouldn't be driven from his own territory, and Rashed be twice damned! He walked to the door, gripping the latch firmly, and opened it.

A stranger stood before him. Taller than Toret, the man was not nearly Rashed's height. Middle-aged, with clean features and dark brown hair, he had stark white patches at each of his temples. An expensive black cloak was wrapped around his frame.

'Good evening,' he said in a cultured voice. 'Thank you for sending your companions away. I have news of your past you may not wish them to hear.' He paused and took in Toret's appearance. 'You've changed a great deal. May I come in?'

Caught off guard by this stranger's familiar manner, Toret stood uncertainly in the doorway, but curiosity nagged him. How did this man know him? If nothing came of it, Toret could, of course, just kill him and be done with it. He stepped back.

'Of course, come in.'

The stranger entered and walked to the parlor to look around.

Toret sniffed the air deeply to sense the man's blood, his presence. He forced in air, letting it fill his head as his irises opened wide to expand his range of vision. He focused on the stranger with all his senses keyed to their fullest extent.

And he felt nothing.

There was no scent, no tingle to the air. There was no thrum of heartbeat or blood rush inside the man's body. That in itself made Toret suspicious, but he sensed nothing else as well, not even tepid temperature. Even Noble Dead generated a presence, but except for his physical appearance, footfalls, and the rustle of his clothing, it was as if this strange visitor weren't here at all.

'Who are you?' Toret asked bluntly.

The man stepped to the hearth, examining the stonework, then turned to take in the life-size portrait of Sapphire with one raised eyebrow.

'A friend,' he said. 'I followed you from Miiska. I watched what happened there, what the hunter and her half-blood companion did to your home and comrades.' He almost smiled. 'I came to warn you – the hunter is coming here, and you must prepare.'

Toret's throat closed, an old mortal reaction that had

stayed with him, though he no longer needed to breathe. The only person in the world he feared more than Rashed was the hunter.

'How . . . how do you know this?'

'I've made it my business to know.'

The man's features were serious, earnest, and yet so distant. He had the same practiced stance as Chane, straight-backed, head high enough that the back of his neck touched his collar. This visitor was noble or had lived among nobles at one time. But Toret was not so easily dominated.

'How do you *know* . . . and why are you telling me?'

The man paused, weighing his words.

'Bela's council made an offer she could not refuse. She is coming here to destroy the night creatures the council believes plague the city. You must be ready to fight. Your servant, the petulant one, deals in certain forms of the arcane arts, yes?'

Toret nodded slowly.

'Use him. The dhampir hasn't faced magic, real magic. And this time will be much harder than the last. She will not make the same mistakes twice, and neither will her companion. Do not try to repeat previous tactics, or you will pay for it.'

With that, the man swept past Toret toward the front door.

'Wait,' Toret nearly cried out, losing any control he might have gained over the exchange. 'Why are you telling me this? What's in it for you?'

The man stopped briefly.

'Prepare yourself,' was the only answer Toret received as the stranger slipped through the front door and closed it behind him.

Toret rushed after him, flinging the door open and

stepping out into the night. Standing upon the front steps, he peered up and down the street, his vision stretched to its full range once again until he could distinguish the varied shades of black in the thickest night shadows.

The street was empty.

3

The sun rose on a crisp, clear morning as Magiere stood with Leesil and Chap on Miiska's docks preparing to board a schooner for departure. They'd waited several days to find a ship heading north that could carry them, and a handsome, two-masted vessel floated gracefully on the waves near the harbor's mouth. It was too large and deep-keeled to dock in Miiska's shallow waters, so a skiff would take them out to begin the voyage up the coast.

Magiere's hair was pulled back in a tail with a leather thong, and she wore black breeches and a russet shirt, along with thick leather boots. Her falchion was once again on her hip, and the two amulets hung in plain view. Her few extra clothes and a new pack, as well as hauberk, supplies, and Leesil's toolbox, were stored in the small chest from her bedroom, which now sat on the dock beside her.

Leesil, as always, gave little thought to his attire and wore an old pair of loose, faded breeches, soft boots worn thin, and an oversize banded-collar shirt that been hand-mended one too many times. He carried no visible weapons, but that was the deception he carefully maintained. Magiere knew there would be stilettos sheathed upon his forearms, and perhaps other small blades hidden in places from his bulky shirt to his boots. He was, however, wearing his green scarf about his head to hold back his hair and cover the tips of his ears. They'd passed through Bela a number of past times but had never seen any of his mother's people. Leesil preferred to mute his appearance and not draw too much attention.

'You don't need that yet,' she said, gesturing to his scarf. 'We haven't even boarded the ship.'

'I'm practicing my disguise,' he responded. 'It gives me something to do.'

At another time she would have smiled or scowled, or referred to his highly visible and oddly colored eyes, but his humor wasn't welcome this morning. They'd barely spoken since the night by the hearth. Now they were off to Bela, where she might become the dhampir once more. If she lost control again, and Leesil was close by . . .

Magiere shook off the thought. For once she wished he would be serious and say what he was truly thinking. He was almost as wryly playful as he'd been all those years in the backwoods of Stravina. Perhaps that was what gnawed at her the most. He looked forward to the journey, to an adventure – to anything besides life at the Sea Lion.

The long dock stretched back to the shore as they awaited a large square-bowed skiff coming toward them to collect passengers. All around them flat-bottomed barges and smaller ships were docked for cargo transfer.

'Hullo!' a voice called, and Magiere turned to see Karlin trotting toward them.

She was glad of it, although she'd never admit it under the circumstances. He was a symbol of what she held dear regarding life in Miiska. His generosity of spirit and calm ability to see an answer to any problem gave her faith in the world, in people.

At the sound of Karlin's voice, Chap dashed off to meet him. When the two of them jogged up together, Magiere noticed Chap fidgeting, nearly beside himself looking out at the approaching skiff.

'Not you too,' she muttered at him.

Leesil blinked. 'Too? What about him?'

Chap stopped and looked up at her, ears stiffly attentive.

'Nothing,' Magiere answered.

'We came to see you off,' Karlin puffed, out of breath. His apron was covered in stains of melted butter and dusted with streaks of flour.

'We?' Magiere asked.

Down the dock behind the portly baker came Loni, walking toward them at a more sedate pace. The wind blew back his long hair, exposing his ears and making him appear strange and otherworldly with his narrow frame, long, triangular face, and large amber eyes. Loni walked up and took her hand.

'Thank you,' he said seriously, his manner completely altered from their last meeting. 'What you are doing will be greatly appreciated by all.'

Only slightly moved by his words, Magiere pulled her hand away.

'I'm not doing it for you.'

Undaunted, he nodded. 'I thank you anyway.'

'Yes, yes,' Karlin said. He turned pointedly toward Leesil and made a half bow, as Leesil often used when dramatically charming his way into someone's graces. 'We thank you both. There is no way to express how much. Once more, you have come to Miiska's aid.'

He clapped Leesil on the back and stepped up to embrace Magiere. She noticed her partner was glowering at Loni, who seemed oblivious, but before she could consider the matter further, Karlin wrapped her in a bear hug.

His large, ale cask body was comforting. She had no wish leave him or Miiska. He held her for a moment and then pulled back to face her.

'We'll return as soon as we can,' she said, trying to

smile with encouragement. 'Bank draft in hand and ready to start rebuilding.'

He patted her shoulder, and a tear gathered in his right eye.

'Oh, you'll need this,' he said, and held out a small pouch. 'Traveling money. It's the last of our community funds, but your trip is an investment. No, no,' he added when she backed up. 'You'll need food and lodging and who knows what else. Take it . . . or I'll just give it to Leesil.'

Magiere glanced at her partner. The community purse in Leesil's care?

'I'd best keep it,' she said.

'Pardon me?' Leesil asked with a frown.

In truth, they needed the money, and she took it with a nod of thanks as the skiff pulled up to the ladder hanging down from the dock. Chap whined once, pushed his head into the back of Karlin's knee, and before anyone moved to collect luggage, he jumped off the dock and down into the skiff. The small vessel rocked sharply, and its two rowers began cursing. Chap merely sat down between the benches and stared up at everyone, his tail thumping a hollow rhythm against the skiff's bottom.

Leesil looked down at Chap and back to Magiere. 'Well, at least we don't have to talk him into going,' he joked.

Or you, Magiere thought. As she helped him gather the chest, she noticed Karlin's attention focused down the dock.

'What is it?' she asked.

'Oh, Poyesk is leaning on his warehouse door, watching us,' he answered.

Indeed, following Karlin's gaze, Magiere saw the spindly man on the shore.

'He does own a warehouse. He might be here on business,' she said.

'Perhaps,' Karlin answered slowly. 'But he was against our even showing you that offer from Bela. The last thing he wants is competition from a community-owned warehouse.'

The two sailors helped passengers load their belongings. The schooner, filled with cargo for return to Bela, had simply stopped at Miiska out of habit to pick up possible fares. Besides Magiere and Leesil, three other men waited with little baggage. From their dress, she took them for unemployed dockworkers.

Magiere suddenly wished Karlin hadn't come to see them off. It only made things harder.

'Well . . .' she said, uncertain how to finish.

'Good-bye, Karlin,' Leesil said. 'We'll see you again, soon enough.'

'Yes.' Karlin smiled. 'Soon. Off with you both. Chap's waiting with his tail in the air.'

Lighthearted banter made things easier. Magiere nodded to Loni as well and climbed down into the boat. Leesil followed.

The sailors untied the docking lines and shoved off. Magiere knelt down near the side of the skiff and ran her fingers through the blue-gray water. It was bitingly cold and refreshing, drifting past in the autumn morning air. As the gently rocking boat moved out to the waiting schooner, the harbor appeared to open wide to the ocean. The cloud-pillowed sky looked larger than it did from the streets of Miiska, and a twinge of guilt needled Magiere for being so hard on Leesil in her thoughts. There was something to be said for the journey, and some small part of her – a very small part – might find pleasure in at least these first few days at sea. She watched Leesil sitting next to her, enjoying the sea air as well, strands of yellow-white hair fluttering out from beneath his scarf's edges. He appeared lost in thought, watching the dock grow smaller behind them. Ahead, furled sails, masts, and rigging covered the sky as they approached the schooner.

'What are you thinking?' she asked.

'I'm thinking how much I hate that elf,' he answered. 'Who exactly does he think he is to us, grabbing your hand like that?'

She shook her head. 'Well, we may never have to see him again. We may never see Miiska again.'

'Don't be ridiculous,' he scoffed. 'Of course we will.'

'You know what we're facing.'

He paused. 'How much money did Karlin give you?'

'I haven't counted it. Why?'

'As soon as we reach Bela, I need to visit a decent smith's shop and have some new blades made.'

Magiere glared at him.

'Yes, I'm listening, and I know what we're facing,' he answered.

A change came over his face as he stared toward the docks. His eyes lost focus and his thin brows lowered as if he contemplated something inside himself with weighted awareness. There was no hint of a wry smile on his lips. His jaw muscles clenched slightly, and he appeared stern, without his warmth and innate humor.

'I have a few ideas . . . to make sure we come back alive,' he said.

Magiere found herself both apprehensive at his expression and surprised at his words.

'So you want to come back?' she asked.

His slanted brows wrinkled in puzzlement, and the moment of cold withdrawal washed from his features. 'Of course. Why would you even ask me that?'

She shook her head, feeling a little better but determined not to let her guard down. Let them stay in their current state and be nothing more, no matter what he, or she, might think to the contrary. It was better to have one close companion than . . . something more . . . bloodless and buried in a grave.

The long, two-masted schooner bobbed on the waves beside them as deckhands dropped a rope ladder. One of the skiff sailors grabbed her trunk, placed it on his shoulder, and climbed up effortlessly.

'You'd better have that letter from Bela ready for the captain,' Leesil said. 'He may not be overjoyed at the prospect of stopping for five passengers only to find out two of them, and their dog, are traveling for free.'

She hadn't considered that. 'Can you carry Chap and still scale that ladder?'

He grinned. 'You'd be amazed what I can scale.'

'No, I wouldn't,' she said frowning. They never talked about his past before they'd met, but during their battle with Rashed and his band, she'd realized Leesil was much more than a vagabond thief. How much more, she was still uncertain.

'Chap, up!' Leesil barked, and he bent over with his back to the dog.

Chap vaulted up, and his forelegs hooked over Leesil's shoulders. Leesil quickly climbed the rope ladder with one hand behind his back to support Chap's haunches.

Once up, he peered over the deck rail and said quite seriously, 'Are you ready?'

'No,' Magiere answered, but she grasped the rope ladder and followed.

Leesil's poorly hidden enthusiasm drained rapidly over the following four nights.

As much as he relished the idea of fresh sea air and
the rushing wedge of white water slipping past the prow
of the wind-bound schooner, sea travel was new to him.
By the second midday, the queasiness in his stomach grew
to full nausea. Saliva continuously filled his mouth
between intermittent dry spells, and food was about as
appealing as the slop bucket the cook had just poured
over the side. Perhaps there was a reason his mother's
people didn't travel.

He stayed on deck in the open air as much as possible. Eventually the wind would pick up, the ship's rock
and lunge would increase, and he would stumble below
deck to curl again upon his bunk. All he could do, between
heaves, was mope and sulk for the rest of the day. His
vision of this journey was a far cry from the reality.

He'd hoped traveling the open waters with Magiere
and altering their routine might present another opportunity to close their distance. Instead of daily matters at
hand, there would be the plans, strategies, and tactics that
had brought them so close once before. It should've been
an opportunity to be off with Magiere, living in inns,
eating when and what they could, and sharing days
without scheduled responsibilities or mundane tasks of
any sort. The old days once again.

So far, none of this had happened.

Besides being sick, he was almost reluctant to open his
mouth, not knowing what might uncontrollably come
out – or up. In addition, their cabin was the size of a
closet with two bunks and barely enough floor space for
their chest and Chap. It was probably the largest private
space for purchase on a small but swift cargo vessel where
passengers were an afterthought.

Leesil looked around the cabin illuminated by one lone
lantern hung from a hook in the corner. It swung slowly

back and forth, making the shadows undulate in a manner his stomach didn't appreciate.

When they first saw the cabin, Magiere nearly backed over him trying to leave the room. They'd slept for years out on the road with nothing between them but a campfire. Once, after a fight with an undead and the first emergence of her dhampir nature, he'd sat up all night with her sleeping in his lap to make sure she was warm and recovered by morning. Now she balked at sharing a cabin with him?

Leesil lay curled on his lower bunk, eyes shut, almost wishing they'd never left Miiska. He felt snuffling near his face, and then something warm and wet dragged across his nose. He opened his eyes. Chap licked his face once more with a soft whine that sounded almost sympathetic. Leesil barely patted the dog's silky head and felt his stomach lurch at the smell of Chap's breath.

'Oh, hell's abyss!' he groaned. 'What've you been eating now?'

The cabin door slowly creaked open, and Magiere leaned in as if snooping to see if he were asleep. With mild annoyance, he noticed that she appeared to feel fine. Her smooth, pale cheeks showed not the slightest tint of sickly yellow and green undertones.

'Any better?' she asked.

He grunted in answer. 'How much farther to Bela?'

'Captain says we could reach port tomorrow if the wind holds. If the wind calms, it might be longer ... but he also said you'll probably stay sick either way.'

Oh, merciless saints, how wonderful, Leesil thought.

Magiere's brows knitted. 'I guess some people get seasick and some don't, but once it sets in, apparently it takes a week or more to develop what he calls "sea legs" and grow accustomed to the motion.' She hesitated in the doorway. 'Are you going to sleep? Do you need some time alone?'

Time alone? What did that mean?

When he was in the cabin, she'd find a reason to be elsewhere. Really, where else was there to go? The schooner wasn't that big. Then it struck him that she was the one who wanted the cabin to herself, and that filled him with enough anger to quell his nausea. Here he was, sick at the mere thought of food, and all she could think about was her privacy. Leesil rolled off the bunk before his stomach tried to stop him.

'Where's that coin purse Karlin gave you?' he asked.

'The coin purse?'

'Yes, I'm going to buy some wine to settle my stomach – up on deck,' he said, then added with barely disguised bitterness, 'and you can have the cabin to yourself.'

She frowned, started to respond, and then went to their chest and removed the purse.

'How much do you need?'

Anger became incensed outrage, which made his stomach feel worse. So now she wouldn't trust him with their coin?

'I don't know!' he snapped. 'How much do sailors charge at sea for their stash of wine?'

From her stunned expression, Magiere was plainly confused by his outburst, but if she had the sensitivity of a tree stump, she'd have an inkling that she deserved it. He couldn't believe she was this thickheaded. He snatched the pouch from her, poured a few coins into his hand, and handed it back.

'For safekeeping,' he said, 'before I gamble it all away . . . or worse, drop it over the side while puking up the dinner I haven't even eaten yet.'

'Leesil . . .' Magiere's own anger began to show. 'You're

ill, you half-wit, and wine isn't going to help. Just lie back down and rest.'

'Oh, I think wine is an excellent idea.' Even with the possibility of retching as a real threat, he swept his arm out as dramatically as space allowed and gave her a shallow bow. 'I leave you in peace.'

He pushed past through the narrow door into the small hallway and up the steps to the deck. She didn't follow, but he didn't expect she would.

Leesil leaned against the rail, one hand clasped tightly around the braid of a rope ladder leading up into the rigging. Nightfall sometimes brought a calmer sea and smoothed the ship's rolling. He breathed in mouthfuls of fresh night air and felt his stomach settle to a low grumble.

Embarrassment filled his slightly cleared head. Behaving like a peevish child wasn't going to make Magiere wish to spend time with him. Hearing voices, he turned toward the stern.

Just below the ship's elevated rear squatted four sailors playing cards by lantern light. Now and again, they passed a large gourd, stained dark around the neck from years of wear by rough, sweaty hands. Leesil forgot the lingering seasickness, his mind now better occupied.

In addition to the lean, weathered captain, the schooner boasted a first mate, eleven hands, and a cabin boy. These four were apparently off duty, and a round or two of cards might be distracting. Leesil walked over but didn't sit down uninvited.

'I don't suppose there's D'areeling wine in that gourd?' he asked with an overinnocent smile.

One sailor with a missing ear and only three fingers on his right hand paused and looked up.

'Of course, and we'll make you a roast pheasant with almond gravy for a late supper.'

The others laughed, but no one asked him to join the game. They sat on small casks or piles of canvas and rope and used an old empty crate for a playing table. One large, off-white sail flexed above them in the breeze.

This was a rough life, and Leesil had already surmised that most sailors found passengers to be little more than a necessary annoyance, if not an outright inconvenience. However, he knew the most common way to find acceptance at any gaming table, and he gently clinked the coins in his hand.

'Well, wine or no,' he said, 'this damned seasickness won't let me rest. Could an honest and sleepless fellow join your game for a while?'

The sailors exchanged glances, probably thinking him a witless ne'er-do-well riding on some recent rise in fortune. The earless man handed him the gourd.

'Don't ask what's in it. We make it out of whatever's handy.'

Leesil smiled broadly, playing the fool, and took a long pull on the gourd. He regretted it immediately.

The liquid burned down his throat and tasted like rancid potatoes. His empty stomach lurched, threatening to expel what he'd just swallowed. The sailors laughed again, and the youngest with salt-crusted blond hair grabbed an empty box and pushed it toward Leesil.

'You'll get used to it,' he said good-naturedly, while shuffling the cards. 'You play Jack o' Knives?'

Leesil had been playing Jack o' Knives when Chap was a pup still peeing on the floor.

'Hmmm, I may have,' he said. 'Tell me the rules again?'

While the rules were explained, he took another long pull on the gourd.

He lost the first game on purpose with a small bet, and his third pull on the gourd actually made him feel better. The burning lessened, and there was no desire to retch. His head felt lighter, and he suddenly didn't care that Magiere wanted him out of the cabin. Why should he care?

And he took another gulp.

He won the second hand, making it look like a spot of luck. No one seemed suspicious, and the one-eared sailor handed him the gourd again. Leesil knew better than to drink while gambling, but whatever was in the gourd drowned some of the nausea. He'd been thrown out of his cabin and deserved a little indulgence.

His head began to swim, and his fifth hand of cards held nothing of note.

Leesil decided to bluff, and built the pot up with a few extra coins to scare off those with too little to lose. The youngest sailor called him and took half the money Magiere had given him.

No matter. He'd just win it back.

He took another drink from the gourd.

Alone in the cabin, lying in the lower bunk while Chap dozed on the floor, Magiere puzzled over Leesil's outburst. Though he was seasick, he wasn't given to childish fits of temper. He'd snapped at her and stormed out. That wasn't like him.

He was the type to keep arguing until she wanted to strangle him or stuff a wad of wet wool in his mouth to shut him up. She'd briefly considered following him and then changed her mind. Was he worried about the coming days and too proud to admit it? She quickly rejected that thought. Leesil didn't fear anything he could fight.

Magiere unbelted her falchion and laid it on the floor next to Chap, who watched her with miserable crystalline eyes.

'Oh, don't be so tragic,' she said. 'He's just seasick. He'll be fine once we reach Bela.'

She rolled over and ignored the little voice in the back of her mind.

Leesil knows you're avoiding him . . . feels you pushing him away.

No. He didn't like being fussed over. Her mother-hen ministration annoyed him while he finished healing in the last month. Why else would he have disappeared all those mornings? Perhaps he needed a bit of time by himself.

The cabin was so small that all she saw in the low lantern light was faded and bleached wood. She'd meant to turn out the lantern but thought better of it, in case Leesil should return. Shifting about on the old, flattened bunk pad, she tried to get comfortable and half closed her eyes.

Why exactly did he want wine? She hadn't seen him touch a drop while he was healing, not even on the tavern's opening night.

Magiere scrunched her eyelids closed and tried to push her petulant partner from her thoughts. Sleep would make everything fade, and things always looked better in the morning. That was what her Aunt Bieja always said, and from time to time, it was true. The bunk felt hard beneath her back, so she rolled to her side again, willing slumber to take her.

Chap growled softly from the floor.

'Shut up,' she muttered. 'It's hard enough to sleep without your noises.'

She considered getting up and going after Leesil and then heard the door creak open. He was back, and unexpected relief washed over Magiere. Hopefully he'd crawl into the upper bunk and rest, so she sat up, prepared to suggest just that.

Magiere tensed and froze.

One of the tattered dockworkers who'd boarded the schooner with them in Miiska stared in at her with equal surprise. There was a knife in his hand.

He'd probably expected to find her asleep or out of the room so he could rob the traveling chest. So many people in town were struggling, and sometimes failing, in the months since Rashed's warehouse burned.

But in that breath of moment, he never once looked toward the chest or anything else in the room except her.

Chap growled, already on his feet, with soft jowls curled back over sharp canine fangs. Magiere grabbed the falchion from the floor.

Any would-be thief with half a set of wits would have turned and run at the sight of a wide-awake, armed occupant and a large, angry hound. Even the desperate wouldn't risk serious injury for unknown profit. Instead, this one rushed her.

Caught off guard, Magiere had no time to unsheathe her weapon. The other two dockworkers from the boarding party were right behind him, pushing their way through the narrow door. Her eyes widened as the leader raised his dagger up, ready to strike, and he kicked out at her sword.

Magiere pulled the falchion out of the way. Bungling dockworkers they might be, but this was no robbery. She raised the sheathed blade with both hands as a bar to block his strike and kicked out into the man's gut.

The dockworker fell back against the pair behind him. There was a moment's jostling as the other two struggled to push him aside, but he tripped over the chest and toppled into the room's corner.

Chap launched at the men in the doorway, colliding with the second one, who was quite portly. Forepaws striking the dockworker's chest, he toppled against the third, who backpedaled into the hall. Both dog and man collapsed in a tangle at the foot of the bunks.

Chap began barking full-throated. Not the eerie wail for hunting or the vicious utterance used to keep someone cornered, but deep, long woofing sounds as if calling for attention.

Magiere assessed the leader toppled in the corner. Medium height, medium build, with plain brown hair and eyes, and clothes that were faded and worn. There was nothing distinctive about him. He was the type whom everyone forgot immediately. For some reason, this disturbed her.

It had been a long while since she'd fought a living opponent, and chasing down would-be thieves in the streets wasn't the same. When she fought the undead, strength, speed, and rage poured into her. That was her advantage even if it unbalanced her self-awareness. She was at a loss without the rise of her dhampir side, and uncertainty made her hesitate too long.

The leader drew himself up, eyes narrowed, and rushed her again. She jerked the sheathed falchion up to guard herself, and he half spun in the small space, kicking the blade from her hand.

When he charged for real, Magiere rolled from the bunk, hoping he'd land in her place and she could come up behind him. He did land on the bunk, but she hit the floor hard and, before she could spring back up, he rolled off the bunk on top of her.

Chap's snarl came from somewhere near the door, followed by the frightened outcry of the man he'd pinned.

Magiere's attacker struck down with his knife. She snatched his wrist and pulled it to the side in midswing, adding her own strength to its downward momentum.

He looked shocked when his blade stuck into the floor next to her left shoulder. She slammed her forehead into his face.

Blood spurted from his nose across Magiere's chest as his head snapped back. She followed with her right fist against his mouth, and he tumbled backward, shoulders striking the edge of the lower bunk.

Magiere twisted left on the swing's momentum and jerked the knife free from the floor. By the time the man rebounded, she had the blade in motion as she swung back. It slid fast and deep through his throat.

His hand instinctively flew to his neck. Blood running from his nose across his jaw mingled with dark red seeping between his clenched fingers, and then it began leaking from between his lips.

Magiere shoved him aside and scrambled to her feet, holding the knife out. The dockworker crumpled to the floor, gagging, and she turned quickly toward the cabin doorway.

Chap clenched the portly man's upper arm between his teeth, and raked at him with front paws. The man screamed hysterically for help, but no one came to his aid. His shirt was already shredded and stained with his own blood. Magiere kicked the hound's opponent in the head, and the man fell silent and limp. Chap instantly shifted on top of the dazed attacker, snarling and watching intently.

Magiere breathed hard for a moment. Where was the third attacker?

Had he panicked and run, seeing how quickly his partners went down? She stepped around Chap and his prisoner, and looked out the door toward the steep stairs to the right. Dim yellow light seeped down from the hatch leading to the deck. There was a flicker of shadow from her left.

Something heavy and hard collided with the back of Magiere's skull. Everything flashed white and then snapped to darkness, as if the lantern had flared and snuffed out. Her legs folded uncontrollably as she fell against the hallway's far wall. She knew she'd hit the floor only when the sensation of motion ceased, and her whole body went limp.

She tried hard to lift her face but managed only to roll over onto her back. Her right hand closed but was empty – the knife had fallen from her grip. Above her was a soft, dim oval materializing from shadow. The blurred shape slowly sharpened. An illuminated face appeared above her.

A young and slightly built man with dirty-blond hair and angry, determined eyes stood over her with an iron cudgel gripped in both hands. He'd let Chap maul his companion while he waited outside the door for her to emerge.

Magiere tried to gather strength, to think, to act, as he raised the cudgel again. The most she could manage was to lift one arm that wavered.

A shadow passed across the young man's face. Something had blocked the light filtering down through the hatch. He paused and looked up.

Slender legs in faded canvas breeches shot through the air above Magiere, and their feet covered in low leather boots struck her attacker in the face. His cudgel flipped out of his hands as he tumbled backward down the dark hallway out of Magiere's sight.

The booted feet swung up to the planked ceiling, followed by the legs, and behind them came a torso clad in a loose, worn-out shirt slightly too big for the wearer.

Leesil let go of the hatch's top edge and quickly tucked in midair above Magiere. She caught only a glimpse of his face surrounded by whirling white hair broken loose from his falling scarf as he flipped past her out of sight. She felt the impact through the floor as he landed in the hallway at her feet.

Magiere clawed at the passage-side wall to pull herself up on one elbow. Her head felt thick and too heavy to hold up.

Leesil half crouched, his back to her, with a stiletto in each hand. Magiere heard Chap's muffled snarls and barks from behind the cabin's closed door, likely pulled shut by her attacker to keep the dog out of his way.

Around Leesil's legs, Magiere made out the young dock-worker's shadowed figure getting up. The man slipped a hand behind his back, and when it came into view again, he held something long and dark. He rushed forward. Before the slender man closed, Leesil spun on his right foot in the narrow hallway.

His left leg folded up next to his body as he pivoted. As it cleared the close walls, his leg shot out and connected with the dockworker's jaw and cheekbone. Before the man's head had fully recoiled, Leesil followed instantly with the pommel of the left stiletto, striking precisely the same spot. The man spun and tumbled down the hallway wall. Leesil settled to both feet again, and staggered forward.

Staggered? Magiere pushed herself further up. Was Leesil injured?

'Be careful!' she managed to shout. 'They're not thieves.'

Leesil righted himself as the dockworker threw whatever he wielded, and the object clattered along the floor. The man turned and ran the other way down the hall into the dark. Leesil started after the fleeing figure but didn't get far, and Magiere's breath caught in her throat.

His feet tangled in the skittering object, and instead

of stumbling, he toppled straight over and slammed into the floor.

'Leesil!' Magiere got out.

From somewhere up on deck she heard running feet, shouting, and a splash.

She climbed up the wall to her feet. The back of her skull ached, and her ears rang ceaselessly, but she was more concerned for Leesil. As she took two unsteady steps, he came toward her. His stilettos already tucked away, he carried the object that had undone him – another iron cudgel. He dropped it, grabbed a rung of the steps up to the deck, and stood swaying slightly.

Magiere reached out to him and stumbled closer, leaning against the ladder's steps. She ran her hands over his arms, shoulders, and chest, pushing the folds of the loose shirt around to check for rips or signs of blood.

'Hurt?' she managed to ask. 'Did he hit you?'

Leesil's narrow, tanned face lifted, and he looked at her in some confusion.

'I'm all right . . . I'm . . . fine . . . that skinny toad ain't never gonna get near you . . . promise.' He put his hand on her cheek a little too roughly, making her vision spin, and then leaned his face close to hers. 'All right . . . you're all right now.'

Magiere jerked her head away, which made the whole world jump before her eyes. His breath reeked, and she stared at Leesil's face in the dim light.

His eyes were bloodshot.

Assassins had attacked her, and he was drunk.

4

Two nights after Chane escorted Sapphire around town to show off her new gown, he walked the dark streets outside of Bela's middle ring wall in a rare mood of contentment. Once per week, Toret gave him leave to do whatever he liked. He always chose the same destination: the new Belaskian branch of the Guild of Sagecraft. On such nights, he wore a casual white shirt, brown breeches, and a simple brown wool cloak – without his sword. This was his usual attire for such visits, as he preferred to be viewed as nothing more than an avid pastime scholar of minor noble birth. His only accoutrement, tucked beneath his shirt, was the small brass vial on a chain around his neck.

He strolled along the cobbled street toward the southern side of the city. A coach for hire would have expedited his journey, but he preferred to walk. His body did not tire, and he liked the older districts with their motley architecture marking the history and growth of the city. They held an aging charm that as yet had not slipped into decay.

It had taken half a decade for the city council to negotiate arrangements for these foreign scholars, these sages, to come to Bela from a great distance. As rumor had it, the council was pleased, for it meant a partial library of historical scrolls and documents would exist within the city, along with highly learned men and women who gathered and preserved such archives. Eventually, a full library would grow from this small start. This was the first such branch of the guild on this entire continent. In his regular visits with the sages, Chane had learned much about their origins.

Started nearly two centuries ago, the sages' founding branch was in a country called Malourné, west across the ocean and to the far coast of that distant continent. Their homeland guild grounds were actually that kingdom's old keep and castle, given to the guild in bygone days when newer structures were built for their monarchs. Malourné was the oldest of kingdoms in what they called the Numan lands.

There was also a guild branch on the continent's southern half in the imperial city of Samau'a Gaulb – 'Heart of the Heavens' – capital of both the country of il'Dha' ab Najuum and the Suman Empire as a whole. A third established branch was said to be in elven lands somewhere in the middle of the continent.

After the Great War, thought to have occurred half a millennium ago, civilization on the far continent had been thrown into ruin and nearly obliterated. So much was lost that the Guild of Sagecraft was founded in the early days of Malourne's monarchs as a safeguard against another such holocaust.

Chane had read the few histories that reached back before the kingdoms of Belaski, Stravina, and Droevinka were established here. It was likely that this same war that the sages spoke of had touched this continent as well, though the thought of such a wide-reaching conflict seemed too fabricated at times. There were tales of monstrosities and unnatural horders, and of years' worth of battles and skirmishes with invaders from across the ocean. Those speculative histories suggested that the first peoples of this continent faded as well, to be later replaced by migrating tribes and clans from elsewhere.

And now the auspices of the guild had come to Chane's own homeland.

Those distant libraries and archives the size of castles overwhelmed his imagination. Someday he would see them with his own eyes, feel their parchments beneath his fingertips, read strange tongues that spoke of forgotten days and lost mysteries, and quench his mind on centuries of knowledge gathered by the learned. How many new insights into his conjury might he find in such vast repositories? And what might be known of the Noble Dead, with some detail of knowledge that might finally free him from Toret's domination? There was now a guild here, and perhaps that would be enough to uncover a key to his freedom.

The piecemeal vision still lingered as he absently rounded a street corner onto an intersecting cobble road. A short distance ahead was an open archway in the city's middle wall. Two ring-mailed Sträzhy-shlyahketné, the city's official guards, stood relaxed but attentive to either side of the massive granite portal. They gave him little more than a passing glance.

Chane's destination was only a short distance inside the ring wall. When he reached it, he paused to take in the sight illuminated by the street lanterns' dim yellow light. His vision of grand, scholarly enclaves faded like smoke in the night breeze.

City space was scarce and, from all whispered suspicions, the city council had decided it best not to house these highly valued but 'foreign' emissaries too close to the royal grounds. What stood in front of Chane as the new Belaskian branch of the Guild of Sagecraft was an old, decommissioned barracks.

In years past, the guard outgrew these accommodations, and two new barracks were constructed – one near the outer ring wall and one near the inner. The old building stood empty for over a year, until the sages arrived. Weathered and aged, it was reasonably well kept and rose to two stories of sound timbers attached directly to the city wall's inner side. But as much as it had been adequate for a barracks, it was not what the sages had hoped for. There simply wasn't enough space inside to house their necessary wares, let alone build a library.

Chane lifted the front door's latch and entered, his welcome established months ago. He turned left down the narrow central passage toward where the Strãzhy sergeant's quarters were once located. Apprentices and hired scribes trundled up and down the stairs with careful armfuls of scrolls, sheaves, tablets, books, and the occasional oddity he could not immediately identify. A few nodded a greeting as they passed.

The old sergeant's front chamber, once used as an impromptu courtroom for petty crimes and civil disputes, was transformed into a study area with tables, chairs, scribe desks, and shelves. Around the room were a few curious glass lamps filled with glowing light that never flickered.

Two sages in clean gray robes – one of medium size, the other slight and small – sat together at the rear table carefully considering a leather-bound box. But they were also waiting for him, and both looked up when he entered. The taller of the two was the old domin, or grandmaster sage, Tilswith.

'Right . . . right time,' he said in broken speech with a warm smile.

Though he was well into his sixties, Tilswith's vivid green eyes were keen of sight, though occasionally he used a reading glass to magnify small script. His gray hair possessed a hint of its once coal-colored shade, and he wore it cropped short with a close-trimmed beard to match. Though lined, his narrow face and long hands were not harshly wrinkled.

'Come . . . sit,' Tilswith said with a welcoming wave of his hand. 'We may have . . . new clue to . . .'

The domin faltered and, with great frustration, hastily motioned to his colleague, who leaned close to whisper in his ear. Though he was engaging and wise, the elder man's command of local languages was not all it should be for the head of such an establishment. Tilswith tapped fingertips to forehead, letting out a grunt of frustration as if the term that escaped him were now obvious.

'Yes, yes – Great War . . . the Forgotten.' He sighed deeply. 'Pardon . . . days I think I never learn speak your language.'

Tilswith's smaller companion shifted out of her stool to offer it up. Slightly built and barely reaching Chane's collarbone, Wynn Hygeoht was twenty years old at best, yet already Tilswith's primary apprentice. Light brown hair hung in a neat braid down her back. Her olive-toned face was round and unpainted, adorned only by small features and a pair of rich brown eyes. As assistant to Tilswith, and an initiate in the Order of Cathologers, Wynn specialized in the knowledge of knowledge itself: the preservation, organization, and coordination of libraries great and small, and always knowing where to find the last forgotten corner note that only one person in a decade might care to retrieve. She could read, write, and speak a half dozen languages, including Belaskian. Though she seldom spoke without something specific to say, it was always engaging to converse with her. After nights of Sapphire's inane chatter, the fewest words spoken by Wynn were soothing to Chane's ears.

He found true contentment during only three types of moments in his existence – on the hunt, delving some new depth of conjury, or engaged with Tilswith and Wynn. Any other moment was little more than the lingering of servitude.

He looked down at the table and this new object of interest.

'Would you care for tea?' Wynn asked in her soft tone.

'No, I am fine. How old is this parchment?'

Tonight he was especially anxious to push the world aside. He sat on the stool, Wynn just behind him, and watched as Tilswith opened the elongated leather-bound box.

From within, the sage removed a scroll. The sheath, as well as the spindles' yellow wood, looked new, and Chane wondered what could possibly be contained in this recent acquisition. From Tilswith's solemn state of excitement, it was obviously nothing he had brought with him on the initial journey to Bela.

The domin slipped the sheath off and unrolled the scroll on the table, leaning forward to inspect the contents.

'Is copy – or . . . original found after we leave and is stored safe in home guild in Calm Seatt. No date on original. After copy, one copy sent us, me to judge . . . judge . . .'

'Authenticity,' Wynn supplied.

'Authenticity?' Tilswith glanced over his shoulder, uncertain of his pronunciation until Wynn nodded. 'Great War my field. Think this part' – he pointed to the current section displayed – 'write by soldier before or after battle.'

Chane blinked. 'Highly unlikely. Even the highest-quality parchment would not survive well for half a millennium, and I doubt such was given to soldiers in the field. If that is the true nature of the original document.'

Tilswith listened carefully. It took a moment for him

to comprehend Chane's speech, and then he nodded agreement.

'From notes, and marks here' – he pointed to a strange row of dots spaced between the foreign characters – 'original not whole but better . . . better than other old texts. Look.'

Tilswith slowly rolled the scroll, pointing again and again at repeated, irregularly placed rows of dots between and within passages of texts.

'Dots where scribe find no text can read. Copy match mark place, size, and more from original. Some text lost, but much survive . . . more than hope for this old. Puzzle how could be.'

'Can you read this tongue?' Wynn asked over Chane's shoulder.

'No,' he answered. The marks appeared to be tiny pictures instead of letters, all arranged in rows as writing. He'd seen few such pictographic texts during his studies, and they had all been attributed to the same source. 'It looks like some form of ancient Suman?'

'Good!' Tilswith nodded and pointed to a brief one-line passage of two characters. 'This name of woman. Rest may be life in soldier camp . . . and what eat for dinner.' His finger moved down to the first full section, but he read it from right to left. 'Interest . . . writer common soldier write letter to home.'

'But why would he write it on a scroll instead of a single parchment sheet?' Wynn asked, 'A single page would be dispatched more easily to its destination.' As she leaned in for a closer look, her braid slipped over to the side, across Chane's shoulder. She did not seem to notice.

The same question had occurred to Chane, but none of them could think of an answer to share. The two sages' enthusiastic curiosity was infectious. He briefly wondered if Toret or Sapphire would give a whit about the possibility of a five-hundred-year-old epistolary journal written by a nameless soldier in a mythical war. Though indeed much more than a myth, it seemed.

'So what makes you think this man was writing in the time of the war?' Chane asked.

'This' – Wynn pointed further down the parchment – 'is a reference to the forces of the "night voice," the unseen leader or messiah of the enemy. Here he mentions being in K'mal, a region near the southeast edge mountains that rim the vast desert north of the Suman Empire. Over many years, some evidence has been found of possible large encampments and battles fought in this area near the beginning of what we think of as the Forgotten, the lost time. We know almost nothing of the history surrounding this war or what came before it.'

'Symbols most important,' Tilswith added, 'but tell little we not know. Good for theory. World was more . . .' – he faltered until Wynn whispered to him again – 'advanced, not less, before war – or advanced like now. Much . . . all . . . lost in before. This why our guild made . . . protect knowledge, never more lost.'

Domin Tilswith was passionate for history, and most particularly for the Great War said to have touched the world as a whole. Once he mentioned that in his own land there was still debate as to whether or not the war had truly occurred as thought. And Tilswith had always shown a keen interest in any mention of the 'night voice.'

Few specifics had been recovered concerning this supposed leader of the hordes that washed across the sage's continent and other parts of the world. Known by varied names depending on the cultural origin of the source, it was always coupled with mention of a voice in the dark. Rare physical descriptions were vague and varied, making it impossible to tell fact from fear-filled fancy. Tilswith suspected very few individuals of the time, if any, ever saw the being with their own eyes. Only three references recurred irregularly: It was likely male, of immense proportions, and always of midnight-black hue. Some accounts presented it as chimeric, others as reptilian, and few as humanoid, but never with detail. It was impossible to determine its true nature, or why it had led a campaign over many years, decades perhaps, apparently bent upon little more than continued spread of carnage against all sentient life not under its control. Those under its sway had no other purpose than slaughtering everything in their path.

There was some certainty that the war began in the vast desert north of the Suman Empire and far south of where Malourné now existed. Somehow the 'voice' had been defeated – some accounts said 'killed' – overnight, and it vanished from all awareness. From traceable accounts of the times that followed, civilization had been devastated into nonexistence. All corners of the continent reverted to loose clan structures battling over what little food and unspoiled land remained.

Before becoming a member of the Noble Dead, Chane had little interest in history. In fact, he learned swordplay and languages only because such was expected of a nobleman's son. Conjury had been his keenest passion, much to his father's ire, but he'd not advanced more than to calling up minor air elementals, dust devils, to cause mischief about the manor. Looking back, he saw himself as a shallow creature, some useless snob who would decay and die in scant years of time. But now . . .

Now he was ageless. Clearly, the past held much to offer for an endless future. He wanted to understand everything.

Wynn watched his intense gaze upon the scroll, and he caught her soft smile from the corner of his vision. Her face was lovely, with a balanced proportion of features set around her intelligent eyes. She would have made a fine noblewoman.

He could hear her blood, a pulse surging beneath her skin.

Unconsciously, his senses expanded until he felt her body heat spilling lightly across the side of his face.

Chane quickly focused, driving down the hunger rising in his throat. Intellectual companionship fulfilled as vital a need for him as blood. Blood could be found anywhere for the taking. The company of one such as Wynn was precious.

He turned his attention back to the puzzling parchment.

Creeping down the short ladder into the schooner's cargo hold, Leesil tried not to think. It was a pointless effort, even with his head still clouded from sailor's grog. Around his neck hung a small flask of oil and a small flask of water. He carried a lantern, and his box of tools was stuffed inside his ragged shirt.

Magiere had killed the first assailant, cut his throat. Chap had pinned the second, now locked in a storage room below deck. Leesil had let the third escape due to his own drunken incompetence.

Useful, dependable Leesil had botched things up again.

Magiere called them assassins, but Leesil knew better. Skilled assassins were shadows passing unseen and unheard even by their victims. They didn't work in groups. They didn't bungle through a cabin door, rousing their victims, nor use iron cudgels and baling knives. Someone had hired common thugs to murder Magiere – someone who wanted either a cheap kill or who had no knowledge where to hire a trained assassin. Leesil was going to find out who that person was, one way or another.

Standing in the dark and narrow passage, he succumbed to shame. After all the weeks he'd spent preparing himself for what he knew was coming her way, the first time she truly needed him, he'd been in his cups again. Wasn't that what he always did when troubled? To wash away nightmares of the betrayals and assassinations for which his parents had raised him, he'd drowned himself in wine until sleep became a dreamless escape.

No more. Not a drop.

He wouldn't give in again. For two months since their last battle, he'd consumed only water and tea, and he'd still managed to sleep through the worst of his dreams. He would be what Magiere needed, even if he never slept again.

A knife's throw down the passage was a door to a small hold for the sailors' supplies. Pulling his box out, Leesil noted he wouldn't need to pick any lock. The door's latch was sealed with a cargo hook.

He lifted the hook, quietly entered the room, and closed the door behind himself.

Raising the lantern, he saw an exhausted, overweight man shackled to the floor. The chains were old and worn but still functional. The captain had questioned this prisoner earlier, but the man refused even to speak his name. Magiere learned nothing regarding who her attackers were or who'd hired them. She didn't express fear, but Leesil knew she was troubled by this mystery. So was he.

And he knew ways of asking a question that perhaps the captain did not.

The man looked at him and blinked in surprise, his round face glistening with sweat.

Leesil removed the faded green scarf from his head,

letting his nearly white, shoulder-length hair fall around his face. He pushed it back behind his ears, so their slightly pointed tips were in plain view, and set the lantern down at the man's feet. With his amber eyes and dark skin, he knew he looked bizarre and unnatural to this common lowlife sitting before him.

He knelt down, his gaze never leaving the man's face, no expression passing across his own.

The stout man instinctively pulled back against the room's rear wall. Close to the prisoner, Leesil smelled old ale, stale sweat, and a hint of urine. The man's unkempt hair was dusty rather than greasy. Brown stubble covered his chin and jowls. His flesh hung slightly loose, as if he'd once eaten too well and then come on hard times. Perhaps he'd been a dockworker in Miiska before the warehouse burned down. Leesil didn't care. This man had tried to kill Magiere.

Leesil flashed a sudden smile. The man flinched.

'So you know who I am,' Leesil said, 'but you don't know me. I've come to give you a test.'

He opened his box of tools, displaying the white metal of the one good stiletto, the garrote, and the curved, shorter blade. Pressing the catch inside the box, he flipped open the lid's interior panel, exposing the array of hooks, wires, and probes in their fabric holding straps. He took out a thin strut of gleaming metal.

'Since you tried to murder Magiere,' Leesil continued, 'and you were obviously hired, that makes you an assassin.' He held up the wire. 'Tell me, using this, what's the quickest way to kill a man from behind?'

The portly captive breathed hard. The stench of sweat thickened around him, but no answer came.

'No guess at all?' Leesil asked. 'How disappointing.' He carefully set the wire down on the box's lid. 'But we shouldn't proceed quickly. Anything worth learning takes time.'

This time, the man blinked. His stubble-covered maw opened, then closed again. Leesil reached into his box, hesitated with his hand poised above the stiletto, and then he picked up the thicker but smaller curved blade.

'But first, I should cut you free,' Leesil said, 'My mother gave me this blade . . . you should feel privileged. I never talk about my mother.' He turned the blade slowly in the air until the reflection of the lantern's light from the metal lanced directly into the man's eyes. 'Bone is one of the lighter elements this will cut through. You won't have any hands, but you'll certainly be free of those shackles.'

The man's breath lost its even rhythm of deep heaves and grew ragged.

'What do you want?' he gasped.

Leesil let out a sigh of resignation, ignoring the question.

'I'd intended to start with your eyes. This isn't an appropriate tool for such work, but it will do in a pinch. Then again, you won't be able to watch me cut off your hands. No, we'll start at the hands and move upward.'

'Stop your blather!' the man nearly spit. 'What do you want?'

Leesil's expression remained unchanged, giving no acknowledgment that the conversation had somehow shifted directions. His voice remained casual.

'Who hired you?'

The man snorted, and the fear on his face vanished.

'That's what you're after? I shoulda known, you drunken sot. Feeling bad 'cause you was sipping grog on deck?' He sneered, and almost chuckled. 'Well, go ahead and cut me. I saw you try to bluff those sailors at Jack o' Knives. You ain't doing nothing.'

For a long moment, Leesil didn't speak, just stared into the man's eyes without blinking. Then he snapped the blade out in a sudden flash at the man's face.

The portly prisoner lurched back, his head banging against the wall. His breathing stopped altogether as he stared wide-eyed. Leesil sat with the blade again turning between his fingers. There was no blood on the metal.

The man settled again with a snicker. 'I knew it.'

'As I said, you don't know me,' Leesil replied.

A thin, dark line appeared on the man's face. It ran in a vertical line down his forehead, through his left eyebrow, skipped over the eye, and continued through his cheek to the corner of his mouth. His smile faded as the first trickle of blood spread into the creases of his eyelid. He blinked and tilted his head, trying to keep the blood out of his eye and not lose sight of Leesil, and then began to shake.

The silence grew lengthy and uncomfortable.

Leesil set the blade down in the box and pulled both flasks from around his neck. He took a candle from his pocket and lit it from the lantern with one hand, while popping the stopper of the oil flask with the other and spattering drops of oil across on the man's dirty trousers.

'Hey!' his captive shouted. 'What are you doing?'

'No one saw me come down. No one knows I'm here,' Leesil explained, as if to a child. 'Those sailors were quite embarrassed that you attacked a passenger and your companion managed to jump overboard before they could catch him. When you're found, the captain won't know who did it – or won't care. And I have a very believable face.'

He held the candle near the man's oil-spattered pants.

'You won't burn me,' the man said. 'You'll set the ship on fire and kill yourself, kill your partner.'

'Water,' Leesil answered, shaking the second flask. He popped its stopper and set it close by on the floor. 'I know how to control fire on flesh. Small flames make only thumb-sized blisters, but they often become infected after a few days. I once saw a man's legs turn green and black. Took him nearly a week to die.' He picked up the curved blade, once again flashing its gleam into the man's eyes. 'You won't see the blisters, though. I wouldn't do that to you.'

This time, open fear washed across the man's features, and he tried to back into the hull wall.

'Who hired you?' Leesil asked.

'I ain't telling you, sot!'

Leesil dipped the candle flame and ignited a spot of oil.

The captive cried out and swung his chained hand to swat out the flame. Leesil jabbed him rapidly in the throat with two fingers. The man fell back, gasping for air while his leg began to burn.

In a flash, Leesil splashed water from the second flask on the flame. It winked out in a hiss, leaving the acrid smell of charred cloth. He knelt on the man's hand, pinned it down, and held the candle close to his captive's face. His expression remained calm, friendly, even as anger and hatred crept into his soft voice.

'This could take all night. No one will check on you until morning . . . late morning, and the poor soul who finds you will most likely lose his breakfast.'

He turned, prepared to set ignite another patch of oil, and beneath him, the man writhed.

'Master Poyesk!' he shouted.

Leesil stopped the candle.

'He owns a warehouse in Miiksa,' he replied. 'Why would he want to harm Magiere?'

'To stop her,' the man rushed on. 'He don't want a warehouse run by townsfolk. He'll lose what he's got now. Don't you see? I ain't lying.'

Leesil rocked back on his heels.

Of course, Poyesk wouldn't want Magiere to return with a bank note large enough to build a town-owned warehouse. But he couldn't pass this information on to Magiere. Not yet. The only thing keeping her on their current path was the desire to help Miiska. If she knew one of its citizens had hired thugs to kill her, she'd lose what little resolve she had. Then what? Would she quit and go home? Miiska would deteriorate, and he and Magiere would go back to the tense holding pattern they'd suffered for months. No, he couldn't tell her. They had a service to render and payment to receive, or there would be no future for them. He could protect her without telling her anything about the source of these thugs.

Leesil stood and turned the oil flask over the man's head.

'No! What are you doing?' the man coughed out.

'Did he hire anyone else?' Leesil asked.

'No! No one but us. I swear.'

Leesil stared down until he was satisfied the truth had been spoken, then leaned over. The man recoiled, but the half-elf simply ripped the man's pants leg open to examine the burn. The skin was merely singed.

'If you tell the captain I was here, he won't care. All that will matter to him is what information you told me, not that I was here. And I can find you again.' Finished, he carefully repacked his tools, grabbed the lantern, and headed for the door.

'Would you have cut my hands off . . .' the man whispered, 'taken my eyes?'

Leesil left without pause, fastening the door securely behind him.

5

Magiere stood near the schooner's prow in black breeches and worn leather hauberk, with her falchion on her hip, and watched sunlit shimmers flit across the water. This morning, they would reach Bela. Strands of her hair had loosened in the autumn wind, so she retied the tail of black hair. The thong's tension aggravated the ache in her head, but the pain had decreased overnight, her body recovering quickly.

The assault in her cabin was common knowledge, and she noticed the crew pausing in their duties to stare at her, at her hair and skin. Glancing back along the deck, she spotted the captain standing beside the helm watching her as well.

Magiere faked as much indifference as she could and looked out beyond the prow. Despite Leesil's distinct features, she was now as much an oddity as him. In their backwoods travels through Stravina, her appearance hadn't been so noticeable. Thickly treed, spotted with bogs and marshes, the damp forest filtered the sunlight through its canopy on clear days. But under a cloudless morning sky at sea, she could imagine the bloodred shimmers visible in her black hair. And more.

She tugged back her left shirtsleeve to expose her forearm. Recently she'd noticed a strange sensation, neither pleasant nor distasteful, and only when she was exposed to the open sun for prolonged periods. A subtle tingle ran across her white skin. She'd always assumed it held its severe pallor because of night travels and the dim

Stravinan forests. When she and Leesil had first hit the open coastline on their way to Miiska, she hadn't noticed anything. But after months in town and days at sea under the autumn sun, it became obvious that her skin didn't tan at all. Standing next to Leesil's darker elven tint, she must look as pallid as the dead. Another reminder of her tainted heritage.

Blood-marked, raven-haired, corpse-colored, and now with night assassins with slit throats in her cabin. Who wouldn't stare at such a creature from a safe distance? Magiere wanted to order the ship about, as if that were possible, and return to Miiska, where she wouldn't have to become some half-*thing* again, no matter the compensation.

Light footsteps approached her from behind. No one else might have noticed such a soft sound, but she'd grown accustomed to it. She sent a cold glare over her shoulder.

Leesil stood rubbing his arms and hands in the crisp wind's chill. A once-green paisley scarf was wrapped around his head and held his hair tucked back. His clothes were wrinkled and creased, as were hers, from being slept in all night. Once the fight was over, he'd settled her in bed with a cold rag on the back of her head. She'd turned away from him as he sat silently on the floor, refreshing the rag now and then from a pan of water. Neither of them spoke. When she'd awoken the next morning, Leesil was in the upper bunk, snoring like a drunk.

The ship took a sudden swell, rolled slightly, and Leesil grabbed the rail, eyes scrunched shut until the ship leveled out. He was still discolored from seasickness and hadn't eaten in more than a day. Added to this, his eyes were now bloodshot and, even in the open air, Magiere still caught the thin, lingering odor of stale grog or whatever he'd been drinking the night before.

'How much longer . . . farther?' Leesil asked. It would have sounded exasperated, except it was clear he lacked the strength for his usual dramatics.

'Not far,' she answered. 'Soon.' And she turned her attention to the coastline.

'Magiere . . .' Leesil began. 'Listen, I'm—'

'I don't want to hear it. If Chap hadn't been there . . .'

'I know—'

'No, you don't!' Magiere turned long enough for her gaze to pass once over his disheveled appearance. 'Not now, or last night.'

There was nothing he could say that would justify his behavior. Three assassins had entered her room, and he was out drinking again. If it hadn't been for Chap . . .

She suddenly wondered where the hound was, now that both she and Leesil were out of the cabin. She spotted him midship, perched upon a stack of crates lashed in cargo netting. Fur rustled by the wind, he watched the sailors, who in turn gave him a wide berth. Word had spread as well about how the hound had mauled a large, armed man into submission.

'There, look!' Leesil said, a bit more strength in his voice. He pushed in close to Magiere and pointed ahead of the ship.

The coastline curved inland out of sight. In the far distance, Magiere could see where it turned outward again to continue north. The southern point of the Outward Bay was finally in view, and her ire with Leesil subsided for the moment to be replaced by a rising edge of anxiety.

Although they'd passed through large cities in their travels, they'd rarely stayed long. It'd been many months since their last and final visit to Bela, when Magiere collected the tavern's deed on their way to Miiska. Over the years, they'd briefly stopped in the capital, where she'd stored away funds, little by little, at one of the less notable moneylending and changing establishments near the southern land-side gate. Venturing farther into the city's business district for an upper-class bank would have attracted too much attention for an armed woman on the move.

The king's city of Bela rested at the base of an immense peninsula reaching over thirty leagues into the ocean from the northwest corner of Belaski. On each side of the peninsula's base were two large bays with mouths some eight to ten leagues wide. They were known respectively as Vonkayshäé u Vnútornä Zäliva, the Outward and Inward Bays, the former on the peninsula's ocean side while the latter faced northeast into the Gulf of Belaski. Bela was situated at the innermost point of the Outward Bay.

'Oh, grateful praise!' Leesil muttered. 'Dry land again. Maybe tonight I get to keep the food I eat.'

Returning ire quickly snuffed Magiere's pang of sympathy. The schooner aimed for port.

She knew nothing of sea vessels, but all sizes and makes were anchored throughout the bay's expanse. Some were as small as the schooner, but many were twice its bulk or more. Several were of unimaginable size. Passing near one hulking monstrosity, she watched its crew scurry over it like ants on the branches of a leafless bush, its six masts a maze of cables and ropes crisscrossing through the sky.

Vessels dotted the water all the way to the port ahead. Then a shimmer from the corner of Magiere's vision drew her attention. It came from the north.

At first, she couldn't be certain it was more than a glint on the water. It sparked like polished metal, but the light wavered, as if what reflected the sun fluttered in the wind or rolled on the ocean. It was a vessel, riding smoothly, perhaps even a bit high, as it skimmed across the top of the water. The shimmer came from its sails, iridescent as white satin. Magiere squinted and shaded her eyes.

Long and sleek, the bow reached out to a point like a spear. The hull gleamed sun-tinted green one moment and rich golden tan the next, and its lip appeared delicately curved like a holly leaf's edge.

Leesil pointed to it and called to a nearby sailor on deck. 'What's that over there?'

A young, sandy-haired man paused from coiling his rope to glance across the bay. 'Elven,' he answered shortly, 'from the far north, on the east side of the cape.'

'Never heard of them having ships.'

'Never heard . . . ?' The sailor looked at the half-elf as if he were a half-wit.

'Too bad we can't get a closer look,' Leesil added.

At that, the sailor took one step toward Leesil and Magiere.

'I'd sooner sail a dingy into a winter squall!' He tossed the rope aside and walked quickly away.

Magiere didn't understand the sailor's caution, but she wouldn't forget it either. The elven people were so reclusive that she'd seen only a handful in her lifetime. If Loni back in Miiska was unusual for his kind, having settled away from his homeland, she wondered what these all-but-hidden people were truly like.

'How is it you know so little about your own people?' Magiere asked, still reluctant to exchange words with him.

'They're not *my* people,' Leesil corrected. 'They're my mother's, and I know nothing more of them than what I'd seen in her . . . and that was long ago.'

He finished more quietly than he began. Magiere left the subject alone, at least for now.

'Oh, please, please let us dock directly.' Leesil looked

longingly toward the shore, his words nearly a prayer. 'I don't even want to ride a skiff in from anchor after all this.'

'Enough whining,' Magiere retorted.

The land at the bay's back was a massive, rising slope that extended all along the shore. At its center was Bela, the king's capital city. More than three centuries past, before Belaski was so named or known as a country, Bela had been a small walled keep settled at the slope's crest. Over time it grew, until now it was a visible behemoth of white granite.

Villages closest to the castle spread into a town, and a defense wall had been erected around all. But the town, eager to become a city, wouldn't be contained. The population grew, new structures sprang up, the castle expanding as well, and the capital sprawled ever farther along and down the slope. A second fortification was erected around Bela, as it came to be called. Mixed buildings hid this wall's base from sight like unkempt, wild foliage against a stone cottage. Given more years, the city still wouldn't be confined.

Now, a third ring wall with regularly spaced towers existed, which reached almost down to the shore and the expansive docks that supported moorage for scores of ships.

'I don't remember it being this big,' Leesil muttered.

'Because we always came from the flat, land side,' Magiere added, 'and never ventured far into it.'

Magiere felt even more uneasy. Foolishly, she'd not considered Bela's size, a further argument against accepting the city council's manipulative offer. In Miiska, out of necessity rather than choice, they'd hunted three Noble Dead who'd already exposed their presence. Bela was at least twenty times the size of the little coastal town. Within its three ring walls, they must now find one undead – if an undead it was — with no clue but a girl's corpse.

As the schooner drew near the docks, the slope filled Magiere's view and the outer ring wall obscured the inner city from sight. Buildings of mixed size, make, and color were mashed together so closely she made out only a few vertical roads running outward like wheel spokes from the city's center. Each such passed through the third wall via a towering, fortified gatehouse with raised iron portcullis. Trails of smoke like a thinned gray forest in the air curled upward from chimneys all about the city. Warehouses lined the shore, and the air was suddenly tainted with a myriad of scents from fish to oiled wood, salt water to people and livestock.

A noxious breeze blew across the deck, and Magiere wrinkled her nose. Down the right coast at the city's edge was a building the size of two or three warehouses. On its bayside, massive wooden sluices dribbled water into the bay, while on the structure's side towering wheels turned, carrying seawater up and into wide troughs running into the building.

'Salt mill,' Leesil choked out. 'They're harvesting salt from the sea.'

The smell clearly affected him the most, and his face turned pale and sallow before Magiere's eyes.

There were people everywhere. Uncomfortable numbers of them. Dockworkers and sailors clambered over the piers' upper and lower levels, moving cargo to and from vessels, handling mooring and rigging, and shouting to each other over the general din.

'This is impossible,' Magiere said under her breath. Her gaze panned across the sprawling city. 'How are we to find anything in all of this?'

'One step at a time,' Leesil replied.

As they drew near a lower dock, the schooner's crew

was in the rigging, taking in the last of the sails. Several sailors tossed out lines to men waiting to moor the ship, and the schooner settled to a stop.

Chap barked repeatedly, until Magiere's and Leesil's attention turned his way. He leaped from his perch of lashed crates and trotted toward the ship's dockside, where a boarding plank was being lowered.

'Come on. Time to get started,' Leesil said.

He was off at a trot toward their cabin to gather their belongings. Magiere followed in silence, sharing little of her companion's desperate hurry. As they reached the hatched stairway, the captain was waiting for them.

'No need to go below,' he said, dour and stiff, as if he disliked having to speak with them at all. He shoved a folded parchment into Leesil's hand. 'Your baggage is gathered and being offloaded. You can turn over the billing to the council's secretary.'

'Well, that's very kind,' Leesil responded with an elevated politeness his expression didn't match. 'And our thanks for the passage.'

The captain looked briefly at Magiere and then turned a hard stare toward Leesil.

'Get off my ship, before I have anything more to explain to the port officials.' He turned and walked away.

Magiere was puzzled by the last remark. The one dead assailant had been tossed overboard at sea, and another had managed to jump of his own accord. There was the third locked in the cargo hold, but the captain had questioned him and learned no useful information.

'What was that about?' she asked Leesil.

'Likely nothing,' Leesil offered, and rubbed his head before walking around to the ship's dockside. 'I think it's definitely time to disembark.'

When they walked down the lowered boarding ramp,

Chap already stood waiting on the floating dock. Beside the hound sat their packs and chest, and Magiere looked to the main pier overhead, uncertain as to how they were to get both dog and luggage up to the city level.

'This way,' Leesil said. Grabbing his pack and one end of the chest, he waited as Magiere did the same.

Following him toward the docks' shore end, Magiere saw another floating walkway along the shoreline's rock wall beneath the overhead piers. At intervals spaced between every other pier were switchback ramps and stairs leading to the city level. Along the stone wall of the shoreline, she spotted archways to the sewers beneath the city that drained brackish water into the bay.

They headed upward, hauling their belongings. Chap ran ahead, stopping now and then at turns in the walkway to look back and be sure they were following. When they reached the city level, Magiere's anxiety peaked.

Every five or six steps, they were forced to maneuver around hurrying dockworkers, milling passengers, and wandering vendors and porters hawking their goods and services. At one point, a rolling cook's cart with dangling racks of smoke-cured beef came out of nowhere, almost running them over. Magiere stopped, dropping her end of the chest and causing Leesil to stumble.

'*Valhachkasej' â*,' he muttered. 'Give me some warning next time!'

'This is insane.' Magiere looked about, but all she could see were crowds and warehouses everywhere. 'We haven't got the slightest idea where we're going.'

'Well, perhaps we should find someplace to put this stuff,' Leesil added sarcastically. 'Nearer the castle grounds, where we're supposed to go in the first place?'

'I know where we need to go,' Magiere answered in a threatening tone. 'Near the castle is too costly. We need an inn that's close enough but isn't going to eat up all of our coin. I have no idea where that is! Do you?'

Leesil crossed his arms. 'All right, then we find someone who does.'

Magiere looked through the crowd. Even the hawkers seemed unable to pause long enough for a short conversation.

'Hey, sir, help with the luggage?' a high-pitched voice wailed out.

Standing nearby, head craning to see around passersby, was a boy no taller than Leesil's stomach. His frayed hair was plastered down on top and in need of a wash, and his secondhand muslin shirt and pants were too large for his frame. He pointed at Leesil.

'Yea, you, sir,' he said, ducking between the taller bodies in his way. 'Help with the luggage? Best porters on the piers, right here.' The boy's tapered, dirty face was as serious as that of any journeyman hawking his services.

Magiere let out a deep sigh as Leesil cast her a side-long glance, something between a frown and a snicker. She scowled at him with a slight shake of her head.

Leesil rolled his eyes and looked down at the lad. 'And what do you charge, *sir*, for your services?'

'We'll take you anywhere in the city,' the boy answered, folding his arms firmly across his narrow chest, 'for two copper pennies.'

'What?' Magiere took a threatening step toward the boy, but he didn't budge. 'That's a day's wage for the strongest dockworkers, not some runt. Leesil, no!'

Chap shoved his head between Magiere and Leesil to peer at the young newcomer. The boy remained standing firm, chin up. His attention passed briefly to the hound in casual appraisal before returning to his prospective customers.

'Nice mutt,' he said.

A low growl rumbled from Chap. Leesil raised one eyebrow at the dog, shook his head, and turned back to the boy.

'Who's this *we* you keep mentioning?' he asked.

The dour little pier boy put two fingers to his pursed lips, and Leesil visibly cringed at the shrill whistle that followed.

Weaving varied paths from out of the crowd came four more boys in equal disarray. Two carried wooden poles and worn straps over their shoulders. They ganged themselves up around the first, and a fifth appeared directly from behind their leader.

This last member was barely half the spokesman's size, with cropped blond hair and a fat-cheeked face of freckles above his spindly little body. He gave Magiere a smile that scrunched his eyes almost closed. His two front teeth were missing.

'Leesil, I said no,' Magiere repeated.

In answer, Leesil simply dropped his pack on the chest. 'Give me the purse.'

'I already gave you coins back on the ship.'

'I . . . I don't have any copper. Just give me the purse.'

Magiere hesitated. After everything she'd put up with in the last day and night, she had an insatiable urge to clout him upside the head, hangover or not. She pulled the coin pouch out and handed it over.

'What's your name?' Leesil asked of the leader as he fished in the purse.

'Vàtz,' the boy answered, and he hooked a thumb toward the freckled companion peering around his side. 'This is Pìnt. And that'll be payment in advance.'

Leesil pulled his fingers from the pouch and reached out to the boy. One copper penny fell into Vàtz's open palm.

'That'll be a down payment,' Leesil said, and with thumb and forefinger, he fanned out three more copper pennies like tiny cards. 'The rest when services are complete. And I need guidance to a weaponsmith of a particular kind.'

Vàtz eyed Leesil, but his attention kept slipping to the three coins.

'Done,' he said, tucking away his one penny, and he waved his crew forward.

They descended upon the luggage with many an 'Excuse me' and 'Step aside, ma'am,' and Magiere found herself caught between backing out of their way and swatting them aside like pestering flies. Before she could decide, two boys lowered their poles to either trunk side while their counterparts slipped leather straps through the trunk's end handles, synching the trunk between the poles. All four boys positioned themselves at the poles' ends, ready to lift and haul the moment the word was given.

'So where to?' asked Vàtz.

'Wait – Leesil . . .' Magiere grabbed her companion by the arm, pulling him aside. 'What are you doing? Why do you need a smith?'

Leesil licked his lips and looked her straight in the eyes.

'I can't help you with a couple of stilettos, or . . .' – he took a breath and lowered his voice – 'any of the other gear I'm accustomed to.'

'Yes . . . your other gear,' Magiere repeated quietly, but it wasn't the time or place for what she imagined would be a long tale best told in private. 'Then we'll get you a sword, a short saber, or anything manageable.'

Leesil shook his head. 'I don't have time to learn a sword, and it doesn't fit my ways. I've something planned I think will work, but I need a weapon maker who's skilled and fast. Hopefully one with apprentices or journeymen to work on it all at once.'

'We don't have that kind of money,' Magiere insisted.

'I don't need money.' He handed her back the pouch, minus the copper to pay their porters.

'Leesil—' Magiere began.

'I've some things I can barter with,' he rebuked. 'It'll all be perfectly aboveboard.'

Magiere already imagined ways he might procure funding for the purchase, but she was too eager to get away from the throngs of people.

'Get it done and catch up to me before . . . Where are we going?'

Leesil turned about. 'Vàtz, we need an inn that's clean, cheap, out of the way, but fairly close to the castle grounds.'

The boy didn't hesitate. 'Easy enough. The Burdock. My boys know the way.'

'And you're coming with me,' Leesil added, then looked to Magiere. 'I'll meet you in time, before we go to the council – promise.' With that, he waved Vàtz to follow and hurried off.

Alone amid the milling dock crowds, Magiere felt exposed. Whatever Leesil needed to arm himself for the coming days wasn't anything she could try to deny him. Hopefully it wouldn't end with some outraged smith pounding on their door with the city guard in tow. There was little left to do but get to the inn and wait for him.

The pier boys were ready but stood suppressing snickering laughter for some reason. She looked about for her own pack.

Out ahead was Pìnt, or what she could see of him, her pack hoisted up like a bearer. As he teetered blindly back and forth under its bulk, his head had disappeared in the sagging mass that dropped down to his shoulders.

'Give me that!' She snatched the pack off of him. 'And get moving.'

Pìnt wobbled as his burden suddenly vanished, and spun completely around before his short legs righted themselves. He grinned, all fat cheeks and scrunching eyes, and scurried off to lead the way.

'Four copper pennies,' Magiere muttered, as she followed, 'to be a nursemaid.'

Leesil harbored doubts whether what he had planned could be accomplished in an absurdly short time. As he stood in the smith's outer timber stall, with Vàtz leaning impatiently against the entry, he peered through the archways to the work area of the smithy. What he saw gave him hope.

Rear doors at the room's back were opened for light, but most illumination came from the glowing forges, casting the interior and its occupants in a sweltering glow. The place was big enough to house Miiska's own smithy in the forge room alone. A half dozen men and women worked forges and fire pits. Benches and tools and materials were spread everywhere, and the air was baked with the smell of metal and coal.

Leesil turned toward the back stalls. Through a door, he saw several more people at a table polishing, sharpening, and finishing spear- and arrowheads, swords, and other armaments. Vàtz had more than adequately filled his request for a particular kind of weapon maker. Leesil fished in his shirt and withdrew a folded parchment and an old scarf wrapped around an object the length of his forearm.

Out of the workroom came a man who barely fit through the archway, a solid column of flesh with legs and arms like ship beams. Between smears of soot, sweat glistened across his skin. Even his long leather apron seemed to perspire.

'Master Balgaví at your service,' the man pronounced with a heavy, rolling voice as he wiped his hands on an over-smudged rag. 'What can I do you for today?'

'I have a job for you, something unique, and I need it fast,' Leesil said. 'Can you handle it?'

The smith shrugged. 'If you make it worth putting aside other work, as I don't lose business just to do new business. If I put enough of my people on it, we can make most any steel weapon. In as little as a few weeks, you'll—'

'No, not weeks,' Leesil cut in. 'Days.'

Balgaví's mouth slackened as his singed brows wrinkled, and for a moment Leesil wondered if he was about to be tossed into the street.

'You haven't got that much coin,' the smith growled.

'I've got something worth that, and more,' Leesil replied. 'Can you do it?'

'What's it you want?' Balgaví asked suspiciously. 'It had best not be any nonsense.'

Leesil tucked the scarf bundle under his arm, and carefully unfolded the crinkled parchment sheet.

In the woods outside of Miiska, he spent his time scribbling, rubbing out, and redrawing, until the image fit his vision. If it could actually be made, he had faith he could stand with Magiere against whatever they fought.

Its forward end was shaped like a flattened spade, tapering smoothly from the point in arcs to both sides. At the base between those arcs was a crosswise handle to be gripped in the fist so the tip could be thrust with a punch. However, one side arc of blade did not stop at the handle. It continued in an extended, more gradual curve that would run along on the outside of the forearm, ending just beyond the elbow.

'Hmm . . . intriguing, sure enough,' the smith said, taking the parchment from Leesil to inspect it more closely. 'And fortunately for you, not as complicated as I'd expected. The grip can be made by cutting an oval in the base of the head, making a handle to be wrapped like a hilt. Better than forging on a crosspiece, and it'll give some strength. And we've some similar curves of metal that could be adapted for this outside wing. That'll save some time.'

'I need two of them,' Leesil corrected. 'Mirrored. One for each hand.'

Balgaví sighed deeply. 'You'd better have something well worth this.'

'And I'll need custom sheaths to fit that will hang from a belt, with lashings to strap above the knee and hold them to the thighs.'

At that, the smith grunted. 'Go to the scabbarder. Down the road, two blocks.'

'I don't have time,' Leesil retorted. 'And for what I'm paying, you can send one of your apprentices with the drawing, easy enough.'

The smith folded the parchment in his fist.

'Let's see this oh-so-grand compensation you've been clucking about.'

As he unrolled the scarf, Leesil was careful to watch the smith's eyes. This was the moment he'd feared the most. The bulky giant was clearly intrigued, and both his irritation over the rushed work and his mild curiosity concerning the drawing meant he was likely able and willing to fulfill the request. If Leesil gambled correctly on the value of his barter, he'd know the moment the smith saw what was in the scarf.

The scarf's folds parted, dropping around his hand, and in his palm lay the elven stiletto and the extra hilt.

Balgaví's eyes blinked twice. Leesil tried not to smile.

'Where'd you get this?' the smith asked quietly, as he reached out to touch the white metal.

'An inheritance, of sorts,' Leesil answered. 'But now I need something more suitable.'

The smith hadn't taken his eyes or fingers off the stiletto. For that matter, Vàtz now craned his neck to see, and for the first time, he lost his affected stony expression in awe.

As Balgaví lifted the stiletto, it caught light from the forge room. Rose highlights shivered along its silver-white metal and sparked along its clean and perfect edge.

'Done,' the smith said simply. 'But be warned ahead. This kind of hurried work . . . I won't stand behind it. You'll get the best that can be done in the time, and that's all.'

'Fair enough,' Leesil agreed. 'Either I or someone I send will check back to see how the work goes.'

With that, Balgaví nodded, took the spare handle as well, and walked back into the forge room, shouting to his people.

Leesil headed out into the street, Vàtz trotting by his side. The boy looked at him with irritation.

'Forget it. You get paid when your work is done,' Leesil said.

'That's not what I'm thinking about,' Vàtz said with grumbling dissatisfaction.

'Then what?'

'I'm thinking I should have charged you more.'

★ ★ ★

Wynn disliked visiting the Bela council hall on the castle grounds, and she often wished Master Tilswith spoke the local language well enough to handle these meetings by himself. Now, the old domin sat beside her as she patiently waited to translate or supply any words he could not remember.

Directly in front of her, seated behind a large, cherry-wood desk in his office chamber, Count Alexi Lanjov closed his eyes and rubbed his left temple in mild frustration. He wore a perfectly pressed white shirt, black tunic, and black breeches. Wynn and her master were dressed as always in their simple gray robes.

'I understand point, Alexi,' Domin Tilswith said, 'but you admit old barracks not . . . suitable . . . our needs.'

Wynn noticed that the twinge pulsing in Lanjov's left temple became more acute as the domin went on in his broken speech, describing inadequate facilities for ancient scrolls, new volumes and books, and materials and instruments necessary for their work.

Lanjov opened his eyes to look again at the two sages seated across from him.

At the moment, it seemed the councilman had little time for the complaints of scholars, and Wynn had more understanding of his position than her master did. Lanjov spent half of his time handling the city's treasury funds at Bela's largest bank and the other half making decisions as chairman of the city council.

He was a tall man, and though he was nearing fifty years of age, his square face was unlined and adorned by a straight, slightly large nose. His hair was steel gray, short, and neatly combed.

'Your council invite us here,' Domin Tilswith said, 'start new branch our guild, serve city, kingdom, people. First on your continent, but you not . . .' He paused and, once again, Wynn leaned to whisper in his ear. 'Value?' he said aloud with puzzlement, and Wynn nodded. 'You not *value* us.'

Lanjov placed his elbows on the desk, laced his fingers, and rested his chin on them.

'Domin,' Lanjov said in audible frustration. 'Tilswith – you know we do value your presence here. I understand the barracks are inadequate, but there is simply no place to move the guild at this time. The city is growing at an unfathomable rate, and there is no building or grounds currently not in use that is large enough for what you plan. We must wait until suitable open ground is allocated to build an entirely new structure.'

Wynn had to translate parts of the councilman's response, but when she had finished, Tilswith's green eyes glittered. Wynn almost smiled in relief, hoping this would be enough for her superior. Perhaps Lanjov truly would assist them.

'Yes, yes,' Tilswith said, 'best solution! When?'

Lanjov sighed. 'I will see that the council takes the opportunity to address your concerns. But at the moment there are simply no funds available for a project of this size.'

Wynn glanced about the office, as did Tilswith, and she couldn't help a suspicious frown. Lanjov shifted uncomfortably.

Deep blue tapestries trimmed in soft cream covered the walls. On one wall hung a portrait of Chesna, his daughter, and on the opposite a portrait of the king. The imported Suman rug was thick enough to sleep on, and a porcelain tea service, with matching pitcher and wash-basin, rested on a cherrywood stand by the chamber's side door. Lanjov's inkwell and the tip of his crystal-handled quill were crafted in matching silver.

'Yes,' Tilswith said. 'We see problem . . . with money.'

Wynn felt her previous hope fade as Lanjov's expression turned from polite frustration to one of dismissal.

'I respect your presence here, and am personally glad of it,' he said seriously, 'but truly, Tilswith, we have more pressing matters. No – don't look at me as if I'm deaf. There are other matters . . . criminal matters which require the council's attention.'

These words the domin understood, and he paused in silence.

'I sorry your daughter,' Tilswith said. 'She kind girl . . . in . . . innocent.'

Wynn, too, felt sympathy. Lanjov was a private man, and the recent murder of his daughter – on the front porch of their home, no less – weighed heavily upon him. She had heard little in detail, but the brief descriptions of the body were more than she cared to know.

'I help if can,' Tilswith added.

Lanjov nodded stiffly. 'Yes, I know you would. We are doing what we can to find her killer. The council has sent to Miiska for a dhampir.' He then paused. 'Do you know of such?'

Both sages stared at him for a moment. Tilswith frowned in confusion and then leaned closer to Wynn, seeking an explanation.

Wynn looked back to Lanjov. 'What is a dhampir?'

'A hunter of the dead – or the undead,' he answered. 'Yes, yes, I know it's distasteful and superstitious-sounding, but . . .' He stopped, clear discomfort rising in his eyes. 'An unnatural creature murdered my daughter. I have no doubt of this, and the city needs an equally unusual agent to hunt it down.'

'But what is a dhampir?' Wynn repeated.

Lanjov sighed again. 'From what I've been told, legend

has it that such a person is the offspring of a vampire and a mortal and, by nature, capable of exterminating these creatures.'

Wynn paused, uncertain of what she heard, and then translated. Domin Tilswith scoffed.

'Child tales,' he said. 'We have like in stories call *àrdadesbàrn*.'

'You would say "dead's child,"' Wynn explained, 'though it is the offspring of a revenant, not your vampires. How much did you pay this . . . dhampir?'

'Tales of this person drifted along the coast,' Lanjov said, ignoring the issue of payment. 'It seems those stories are true to a point, as much as any rumor holds some grain of truth. She and her companion hunted down at least three undeads in Miiska. That she has killed at least three is verified by Miiska's town council.' Lanjov shook his head slowly. 'Undeads . . . the mere thought that such things are more than peasant superstitions . . .'

Tilswith shook his head sympathetically and scoffed again, but Wynn was curiously intrigued. A half-undead?

Domin Tilswith appeared on the verge of returning to the issue of new guild quarters, when a knock sounded at the side door.

'Come in,' Lanjov called out, sounding rather eager.

Crias Doviak, council secretary, put his head around the door.

'She's arrived, sir,' Doviak said. 'The council is gathering in the main chamber now.'

Lanjov quickly rose. 'Thank you. I will be in directly.'

Doviak nodded respectfully and left.

'I apologize,' Lanjov said to Tilswith, stepping briskly around the desk. 'Duty calls me away.'

Tilswith sputtered, but Lanjov nearly lifted him out of the chair while shaking his hand in farewell. He placed a hand on Wynn's shoulder as well, propelling them toward the main chamber door.

'We will continue addressing your concerns as soon as possible.'

Surprised by this sudden rush out of Lanjov's office, Wynn instinctively tried to plant her heels in the floor, but the councilman's large hand slipped down the center of her back with a quick shove. Before she could offer a polite good-bye, the door closed in their faces.

'*H'neaw hornunznu!*' Tilswith spit back at the closed door.

Wynn was relieved she did not have to translate such an utterance.

Leesil slowed his step as they approached the council hall, overwhelmed by its sheer size. The lengthy, three-story building also served as the city's central courthouse and hall of justice. It was bound to be more than the back room of the Velvet Rose used by Miiska's own council – but this he hadn't expected. The entrance doors were wide enough to pass through with arms outstretched. When he stepped inside, Leesil felt an anxious spasm for every questionable act he'd ever committed in his entire life.

Once inside the cathedral-like entryway, he, Magiere, and Chap waited as an interior guard sent a youthful attendant to fetch their escort, Crias Doviak, secretary of the council. The paned window arch above the doors spilled light across stone walls stained in soft green to complement a marble floor with veins the color of jade. Above them, raised into the domed ceiling, hung an iron chandelier with polished brass fittings that held at least two dozen oil-lamp receptacles in glass globes.

Leesil adjusted the faded scarf on his head and surveyed his attire in somber dismay. He felt like a dolt who'd walked home through the town market not realizing he'd sat in cattle droppings. Normally, he didn't care what anyone thought of his appearance, but this was a whole other world. They were here to play hunters of the dead – for real this time.

Magiere was oblivious, pacing in short steps back and forth around the polished floor. After Leesil left her to find a weaponsmith, she'd gone with the pier boys to a moderate inn called the Burdock in the lower-class merchant district. The inn turned out to be owned and run by Vàtz's uncle but was suitable in all other respects. When Leesil caught up with Magiere, they'd barely had time for soup before leaving to meet with Bela's council.

'Don't worry,' he said to her. 'All we do is find out about the death of this councilman's daughter, get an idea where to start looking, and Chap can take us from there. Just like in Miiska.'

'I'm not worried,' she answered.

Chap whined and pushed his nose into her palm as she passed him in her pacing.

'Stop it,' she said, pushing the dog's muzzle aside. She gave Leesil a disdainful look. 'I've dealt with enough village elders back when we were on the game. I know how this is played.'

Yes, Leesil thought, *but we're not in a Stravinan village.*

These weren't superstitious peasants awed by floating powders, clanging urns, and a half-elf dusted in flour. They were in the king's city, and this wasn't a game anymore.

He simply nodded and said nothing.

Magiere's attire was less disheveled than his own. She wore her black breeches, a loose shirt that needed a wash, and a leather vest. Her hair was pulled back in its usual tail, and her falchion rested comfortably on her hip. She appeared relaxed – except for the constant pacing.

Down a side hall came a short, well-tailored man at a brisk trot, his heels clicking on the floor. Leesil assumed this to be Crias Doviak, the council secretary. Two armed guards accompanied him, and their longer legs made their steps seem slower and more deliberate.

'The council has gathered and awaits you in the main hall,' Doviak said with a slightly affected lisp. His light brown hair was purposefully curled into small, uniform ringlets.

'We're ready,' Leesil answered.

'As a formality, you must turn over all weapons to our guards.' The diminutive secretary paused with an apologetic expression on his face. 'Who will, of course, take proper care and return them upon your departure.'

Magiere stared at him. 'Why?'

Clearly not accustomed to confrontation, Doviak stamered for a moment.

'I assure you, it is standard policy for security.' He proffered a short bow of his head. 'Though in your case, dhampir, it would simply be a courtesy on your part.'

'Oh, give them your sword,' Leesil blurted out. 'I doubt you'll have need of it here.'

Magiere scowled but began unbelting her scabbard.

'And where,' Doviak began in a cautious tone, 'will the mistress be leaving her dog?'

'He stays with us,' Leesil said flatly.

Doviak opened his mouth to argue and then closed it.

Magiere surrendered her falchion to one guard, who in turn asked, 'Anything else?'

'That's all,' she answered sharply.

The guard nodded. Leesil still wore his two 'everyday'

stilettos inside of his shirtsleeves, but he saw no need to mention them.

They were ushered down a wide corridor, Doviak leading the way, and the guards following behind. They turned into another wide hallway headed for huge double doors of carved dark wood. Along the passage were smaller side doors, and standing before one were an elderly man and a young woman, both wearing simple gray robes. Even in their plain attire, Leesil found them mildly curious and then outright unsettling as they stared back, looking him over as if he were some strange animal that had managed to get into the building unnoticed.

The young woman paused from chatting with her elder companion and absorbed the sight of Leesil, then Magiere, and finally Chap. Her face was smooth and oval, and she didn't blink once as she looked over the trio, particularly Chap. She offered a mild smile in greeting and spoke directly to Leesil.

'Majaye túâg bithva annaseach ésh äillé! Sheórsäe a'bithva?'

He didn't understand it, but felt an uncomfortable tickle of familiarity with the sounds. The woman was speaking Elvish to him, though something was different compared to the few words he had heard in the past from his mother.

'I'm sorry,' Leesil replied. 'I don't speak . . .'

'Oh.' She appeared embarrassed and confused at the same time. 'I apologize . . . I did not realize.'

Leesil looked away, avoiding the situation altogether, then noticed Chap's attention fixed upon the woman. His tail was wagging. At that, Leesil couldn't help looking back as well.

The woman gazed at the hound with eyes narrowed in puzzlement. Then, as if the moment never happened, Chap turned and loped to catch up. The huge doors opened, and Doviak ushered all three of them into the adjoining chamber.

Leesil found himself standing between Magiere and Chap in a cavernous room buzzing with hushed activity. Guards stood at all four corners, and attendants unobtrusively poured tea, took cloaks, and refilled inkwells on the immense table. Life-size portraits of unsmiling, conservatively dressed, middle-aged men hung at intervals on all four walls between cobalt curtains trimmed in white. And the table . . .

He couldn't imagine a mahogany tree large enough to provide that solid, singular piece of wood. Its oblong surface stretched over half the room's length, from door to the far wall, in all its refined glory. At least thirty men of various ages sat around it in high-backed mahogany chairs and stared at the new arrivals.

Magiere didn't appear impressed by the scene before them. She stepped up to the table's rear end, following Doviak, and the little man stopped to announce them.

'Mistress Magiere and . . .' Doviak paused, looking uncomfortably at Chap and Leesil. 'And party.'

At the table's far end, in the position of central authority, one man stood up. He was unusually tall, with broad shoulders and steel-gray hair, and everything he wore from collar to cuffs was impeccable. Again, Leesil wished he'd at least taken time to wash his shirt.

'I am Alexi Lanjov, chairman of the council for Bela,' the man said. He hesitated, looking her over with uncertainty. 'You are Magiere? The hunter from Miiska?'

Leesil sensed that Lanjov was usually skilled at guarding his thoughts, but there was no hiding the shock in his eyes. Magiere was clearly not what he expected.

Magiere looked straight at Lanjov without notice of anyone or anything else in the room.

'Yes, I'm the hunter you requested.'

Several council members whispered to each other in low tones. An old man dressed entirely in black pointed at Chap.

'Animals are not allowed in the council chamber. They are not even allowed in the building.'

Leesil put his hand on Chap's back and felt the dog tense, as if Chap knew he'd become the object of attention. Magiere's gaze shifted to the old man, resting upon him for the span of a breath. Without comment, she returned her attention to Lanjov.

'Your offer has been accepted,' she said. 'All we need now are the details. Your letter said a girl was killed on her own doorstep. We need the location and a piece of her clothing, and we will start from there.'

Lanjov's face grew pale, and he breathed in audibly. The whispers grew into muttering until a strong voice with a vaguely familiar accent rose above them.

'And what, exactly, are you planning to start?'

Leesil followed the voice to an unusual man with shoulder-length black-brown hair, a close-trimmed beard, and pockmarked ginger-colored skin. He wore a silk robe of dark amber and exuded visible arrogance.

Lanjov raised one hand in the air. 'Lord Au'shiyn . . . we addressed your concerns before, and the matter was settled.'

Au'shiyn. Leesil repeated the name in his mind. It wasn't Stravinan or Belaskian. He wondered if the man was from the deep parts of Droevinka, but the accent didn't match and his name didn't sound of that country or language. Then Leesil recognized where he'd heard such an accent before.

Au'shiyn spoke like Rashed, the warrior undead Magiere had fought in Miiska. And Rashed had been

Suman in his living days. What was a man from the Suman Empire doing on the Bela city council?

'It was not adequately settled,' Au'shiyn answered coldly, and he turned on Magiere again. 'What exactly do you believe you are to hunt?'

For the first time since entering the council chambers, Magiere's expression grew uncertain.

'Your council sent for me,' she said directly to Lanjov. 'The letter was very clear.'

'Yes, yes,' answered a young man with reddish-blond hair sitting at Lanjov's side. He appeared earnest but distressed at the dissension. 'Please understand, our offer is genuine. It is Councilman's Lanjov's daughter who was murdered at his own home. This is difficult for him to discuss.'

Lanjov nodded but looked no less troubled.

One word the younger man at Lanjov's side had used now stuck in Leesil's thoughts: murdered.

He'd read the letter sent to Miiska's council mentioning a girl killed, but he'd never heard the term 'murder' in connection to vampires. 'Killed' or 'slaughtered,' or a number of more disturbing terms. This young man's tone was different.

Lord Au'shiyn picked up on the word as well. 'Indeed, the poor girl was murdered, so I would like to know why our own city guard has not tracked down her killer.'

'Because the killer isn't natural!' the young man burst out. 'It is an undead that feeds on blood. For that, we need a dhampir. The city guard has tried and failed.'

Au'shiyn burst out laughing. 'Yes, a dhampir.' With amusement, he appraised Magiere. 'One of your parents is of these predatory corpses – a vampire? Which one? Mother or father?'

Magiere's expression turned cold. Leesil eyed the four

guards around the room and was particularly glad she'd been disarmed before entering. Even the doubtful men around Au'shiyn had the good taste to look embarrassed.

'Really,' the man next to him murmured. 'Is that necessary?'

'Enough!' Councilman Lanjov ordered. 'The dhampir has come to help us. She deserves our thanks and coop-eration' – he nodded to Magiere, briefly lowering his eyes – 'and common courtesy as well. Suitable rooms have been reserved for you at one of Bela's finest inns. I'll have guards escort you immediately. Come to my office in the morning, and I can give you the few details that I have.'

Magiere stepped back, taking in the entire scene. Leesil knew her well enough to realize this moment was crucial. She'd either tell them to burn the offer and where they could stuff the ashes, or she'd put forth the effort to gain control of the situation.

Chap whined and put his nose in her palm. She looked down at him, and Leesil watched them lock into a long gaze. Magiere gave Chap a rueful smile and stroked his head. She turned her dark, determined eyes back upon the council and walked slowly around the long, oval table.

'One of your members lost a child in a way that fright-ened the lot of you enough to send for me. If she died with her throat torn open, then you either have an inhuman predator or a sick madman on your hands. I'll assume your guards can handle a madman, so it's obvious why I'm here.' At that, her gaze passed over Au'shiyn but didn't pause. 'If it's an undead, then you need me – and them.' She pointed at Leesil and Chap. 'The only reason we're here is because you offered us enough money to save Miiska from ruin. The offer has been made and accepted. Now, all you need to do is answer our requests and stay out of our way.'

When Magiere finally stopped at Lanjov's side, even Au'shiyn remained silent. Leesil suppressed a grin. None of these men were accustomed to such blunt words.

'We've our own rooms,' she informed Lanjov. 'It won't do to have guards parade us into some upscale inn. We don't need that kind of attention.'

Lanjov's shock at having lost control increased. 'The arrangements are already made.'

'Then get your money back,' she said. 'And tomorrow morning is too late. The trail is already cold as is. We'll visit your home tonight.'

'My home?'

Lanjov faltered. Clearly, he never considered the idea, but then he nodded as he realized the oversight. Mystery still surrounded Magiere, and he probably thought she had some supernatural method for tracking.

'This evening,' Magiere said firmly. 'We'll need the location. We don't want an escort.'

The chairman sat down and resumed his calm but dominating demeanor.

'Of course,' he said. 'My aide will provide directions.'

At that, Magiere turned on her heel and headed for the doors, past the openmouthed Doviak, with Leesil and Chap stepping in beside her. She stopped briefly before the guard at the door.

'My sword,' she said.

The man handed it to her, and she continued, not even pausing until they were outside on the council hall's terrace. Only then did she close her eyes, lean on the stone rail, and let out a deep breath.

'Just like village leaders.' She didn't sound confident in the comparison. 'No matter how angry, on the inside, they're frightened. They want someone else to fight their battle.'

'Do you think it really is an undead?' Leesil asked.

'I don't know. You know as much as I do about that. But for Miiska's sake, we'd better hope so.'

'Sad thought,' he added, and then straightened in dramatic determination. 'Well, you dealt with the wolves once today, so wait here. I'll get directions to Lanjov's house.'

'Yes,' she said. 'Then we're on the hunt.'

He looked over her pale features, her hair, mouth, and her eyes staring blankly out into the courtyard, lost in thoughts he couldn't touch. At least she'd finally committed herself. He would see to it she reached the end and made it home again, no matter what else might pass between them.

'On the hunt,' Leesil agreed.

Welstiel Massing waited in the side corner of Councilman Lanjov's office. He knew the meeting taking place would soon end, and Lanjov always returned directly to his private chamber. Finally, the door opened.

Lanjov appeared drained and tense. Moving to his desk, he sank into the chair and pulled a velvet cord hanging against the wall.

Doviak poked his head in the door. 'Yes, sir?'

'I wish to dismiss the hunter and have a note immediately delivered wherever she is staying.'

Doviak nodded in approval with a quick breath of relief. 'I'll get a parchment and be in directly.'

Lanjov buried his face in his hands as the door closed.

'You would be wrong to dismiss the dhampir,' Welstiel said as he stepped out.

Lanjov started slightly and turned in his chair.

'Welstiel?' he said, regaining his composure. 'How did you . . . ? What are you doing in here?'

'Your aide showed me in a short while ago. I've been

in the cellar archives all day doing research. I heard the dhampir had arrived and came up to wait for you.'

'I did not notice you,' Lanjov answered. He leaned back in the chair, rubbing his eyes. 'You should have announced your presence.'

'The audience did not go well?'

Welstiel stepped to the front of the desk, fingers laced with his hands hanging down to rest on his belt. Lanjov's attention fell briefly on the partially missing little finger. Welstiel often wore gloves to hide the slight disfigurement, but now his hands were bare.

'A disaster,' Lanjov answered. 'You told me she was a professional.'

'She is,' Welstiel answered. 'Do not allow her appearance and manner to fool you. Only moons ago, she destroyed a trained undead warrior nearly twice her weight. She is a dhampir.'

Lanjov shook his head with uncertainty.

Welstiel had met him for the first time a month ago at the Knight's House, an establishment for the elite of Bela. Their polite acquaintance quickly grew to casual companionship, and with the exception of Domin Tilswith, Welstiel was the only friend of Lanjov's to express open sympathy at Chesna's death. Lanjov wanted justice, so he called it. Welstiel offered to help him reason through what had happened and suggested a possible solution.

'If there is a vampire in Bela, she will find it,' Welstiel continued. 'I've seen firsthand how undead beasts kill. Your daughter was taken by such.'

A brisk knock on the door sounded, and Doviak walked in.

Lanjov hesitated, and Welstiel understood his concerns. If the dhampir failed, he would be disgraced. If he sent her away now, he would look like a fool after all the pressure he had put on the council – and there would be no justice for Chesna.

'Never mind, Doviak,' Lanjov whispered. 'We will stay on our current course for now.'

Doviak glanced briefly at Welstiel and frowned, his small mouth pursed. 'Are you certain?' he asked Lanjov.

'Stay strong in this,' Welstiel encouraged. 'And let the hunt begin.'

Lanjov took a deep long breath. 'Let the hunt begin.'

6

The Burdock was a modest but clean inn, nestled in a merchant district on the south side of Bela. After council hall of elites, this suited Leesil. Magiere had paid for two small rooms next to each other, the arrangement similar to the Sea Lion's upstairs. Each room held a narrow bed, a window, a tiny side table, plus a candle for an extra copper penny. Chap wandered about Magiere's room and poked his nose through the open chest. As Leesil stood in the doorway, watching Magiere unload her belongings, a strange isolation crept over him.

Indeed, they had their own rooms at the tavern, which was pure pleasure after years of sleeping on the ground. A warm, dry bed was a luxury that never wore off, but in this little inn a new change entered Leesil's awareness.

For years on the road, they'd kept together – Magiere, Chap, and himself. On rare occasions they'd rented a room or a farmer's barn loft. They huddled in the same space to save money and maintain a sense of sanctuary in a world into which neither of them had been welcomed. At the time, he hadn't given thought to Magiere as more than a close companion and partner.

There'd been so much fear, hers perhaps greater than his, as they slowly discovered what little they now knew of her dhampir nature. Perhaps more apprehension came from what she didn't know of her past. In the face of that, he'd found himself wanting more from her. And now, in spite of her penny-pinching . . .

Magiere had acquired separate rooms.

Pulling on her hauberk, she buckled her sword belt across it, checking that the blade slipped smoothly from its sheath. She removed a brush and an extra leather hair thong from her pack and placed them on the table. It was her way now to make any space hers. He'd never realized this out on the open road, nor how important a sense of home was to her. Perhaps she wasn't aware of it herself. For Leesil, home was wherever she and Chap happened to be.

'What are you thinking?' she asked.

'That we're in over our heads, and we can't back out,' he replied. 'That pack of wolves on the council might share traits with village elders you've dazzled, but there are differences. They're landed gentry and wealthy merchants. Did you see their faces when we walked in?'

'Yes.' She stopped to pull the chest's lid closed. 'But if I think like that, I won't be able to go on.'

'Then we avoid the council.' He nodded, white-blond hair waving as he leaned against the doorway, reluctant to enter the room. 'We go to Lanjov's, and maybe Chap picks up a scent from the dead girl's clothes. Then we start hunting. We're in the largest city in the country, and this won't be simple. We aren't trackers, but we'll have to play the part and hope for luck.' He lifted his head with a narrow-lipped smile. 'Maybe if we blunder along, the bloodthirsty little monster will panic and try to kill one of us. That would get things out in the open.'

'You're not funny,' Magiere replied. 'We've done this once. We can do it again.'

Leesil wanted to believe her.

In spite of her attempted confidence, Magiere was overwhelmed as they stepped through the iron front gate at Lanjov's home. Constructed of finely masoned stone, the house was easily large enough for three families back in Miiska. When they climbed the three steps to the door, she grasped the large brass knocker, then paused and glanced at Leesil.

'You need that shirt fixed. Or better, buy a new one. You look like a beggar.'

'I could pretend I'm in disguise.'

She glared at him and rapped the knocker against the door.

Chap sniffed the front porch in some agitation. When Magiere looked to see what had captured his interest, she noticed that, unlike the clean stone in the walkway, the mortar between the left side porch stones was dark, as if stained.

A young maid opened the door and peered out, wearing a simple muslin dress covered by a clean apron, her hair tucked completely under a white linen cap. She looked at Magiere and then Leesil, and her eyes widened with fright.

'We have an appointment with Councilman Lanjov,' Magiere said quickly. 'He is expecting us.'

The maid nodded, half hiding behind the door as she stepped aside to let them enter.

'H-he . . .' she stuttered, looking at Leesil, then quickly averting her nervous eyes, 'he told me to have you wait in the lower study.'

She seemed even more flustered when Chap entered behind them. Leesil flashed her a smile, which only caused her skin to pale as she turned to lead them down a hall and through an open archway.

'Please sit,' she managed to say, motioning to a green velvet divan, and then she fled.

'Don't smile at the help,' Magiere said, settling on the divan. 'They aren't used to it.'

Leesil rolled his eyes. Instead of taking a seat next to her, he peered about at luxurious knickknacks and bric-a-brac carefully placed about the room. A crystal vase and a silver inkwell held his attention for a short while, and then he stopped at an antique gold candleholder on the end table next to the divan.

'Do you suppose this is genuine?' Leesil asked.

'Stop it!' she warned.

Leesil returned an innocent stare. 'What?'

'I know what you're doing.'

'What am I doing? I'm admiring the man's taste.'

'If anything comes up missing' – she grabbed for his arm, but he stepped out of reach – 'I'll stuff you in our trunk and save them the trouble of arresting you.'

Before Magiere could force him to sit, a deep voice interrupted.

'How kind. I see you can appreciate some of the finer things.'

Lanjov stood in the study's archway. Though he was still as freshly dressed as this afternoon, his expression was tired and worn. He'd obviously had a long day.

'I'm sorry about the evening visit,' Magiere replied. 'But we need to know more of what happened. Your daughter was killed on the front porch? Who found the body?'

'I did,' he answered with difficulty, staring at Leesil's torn shirt. He studied Magiere's partner for a moment, and a narrow-eyed expression passed over his face that she couldn't fathom. It was most certainly time to change Leesil's look, if they were to continue dealing with the councilman and his kind. Lanjov's gaze lifted to Leesil's face, or perhaps his hair, and Magiere grew more puzzled. The councilman's observation moved back downward to where Chap sniffed at the divan's legs.

'Then you weren't home?' Magiere asked. 'Where were you?'

'At the Knight's House playing cards. I came home quite late and she . . .' His gaze grew unfocused, until he finally closed his eyes.

Magiere waited, allowing Lanjov to compose himself. 'Was anyone else at home?'

He paused in thought. 'Only my cook, who also serves as housekeeper. My coachman was with me. I was unaware that my maid and my houseboy were missing. When I questioned them later, I learned that Chesna had been giving them the same midweek night off for nearly a year. I always go to the Knight's House on the same evenings.'

Leesil stepped away from the candlesticks and spoke to Lanjov for the first time.

'You leave the house on the same nights, and your daughter had a habit of letting the servants off for those evenings?'

Lanjov seemed disturbed at being addressed directly by Leesil, but he tightened his jaw and nodded. 'Yes, but I did not find this out until after Chesna's death.'

Leesil glanced at Magiere, and she knew his mind was now busy. That was what she needed. This one connection was easy to spot, but he often picked up on things she didn't.

'We'll need to speak with the servants,' Magiere said quietly.

'Why?' Lanjov was back on his guard. 'I've told you everything they told me. They feel guilty enough about their betrayal. What possible reason is there for upsetting them further?'

Betrayal? This man thought a few servants indulging in a night off was betrayal?

'You said the cook was at home,' Magiere pressed. 'I at least need to speak with her.'

With his jaw still tight, Lanjov backed through the archway to speak low and harshly to the young maid. Soon after, a portly woman in her mid-fifties appeared.

Unlike the maid, she didn't appear frightened. Her red-and-gray hair was bound in a bun, and her apron, although clean, bore a few faded stains. She sized up Magiere.

'So you're the hunter. You're not what anyone expected.'

Magiere almost smiled. 'Apparently not.' She turned to Lanjov. 'Could we speak with her alone?'

'No,' he said flatly. 'Any questioning will take place in my presence.'

It became clear to Magiere that for all his words to the council concerning cooperation, he had little intention of doing so himself. He probably expected her to stay far from him and his home, and use some mystical power to track down Chesna's killer. Then he would expect proof for the council, so they could pat her on the head, give her a bank draft, and send her out of sight.

'What's your name?' Magiere asked the cook.

'Dyta.'

'Tell us what happened the night Chesna was killed.'

'I already told the master everything. I didn't know the poor mistress had even opened the front door. I never heard the knock.'

Magiere nodded. 'No one is blaming you, but I need you to tell us exactly what you did that night. It might help us find her killer.'

Dyta pursed her lips. 'Chesna was a sweet girl. Always sent Hedi and young Andrey out for a little amusement whenever the master was off to the cards. She stayed home and read or visited with me. That night, I was busy in the kitchen, storing up dried plums for winter. I didn't hear no knocking. I didn't hear no voices, because the kitchen is out back of the house. But I did catch a sharp draft when I opened the back door for a bit of air. I thought maybe a window out front might have been left open. So I went to see and found the front door ajar.'

She stopped. Before tears could get the better of her, Dyta scowled hard, anger replacing anguish.

'I closed it. The poor lamb was lying out on the steps, and I never saw her or thought for a moment she'd be anywhere but in her room. I just closed the door.'

Lanjov listened attentively, but at those words his head dropped slightly.

'Wasn't until later,' Dyta continued, 'past midnight, I heard the master shouting. I was already settled in bed in my room out back, so I found my robe and ran out. I heard him outside and opened the door as Lord Kushev came running up the front walk.'

'Who's Kushev?' Leesil asked.

'A neighbor,' Lanjov answered. 'He was playing cards at the Knight's House with me.'

'The saddest sight,' Dyta whispered, 'with her dress all torn, and throat so—'

'Enough,' Lanjov ordered in a ragged voice. 'I don't see how any of this will help.'

Leesil raised his eyebrows, but Magiere couldn't tell what he was thinking.

'I assume you saved the dress?' she asked.

'Yes,' Lanjov answered. 'Captain Chetnik of the city guard told me that I must keep it, even after she was buried.'

Magiere committed the name to memory. So far, few people in this had shown much sense, but this captain apparently had, and it might be worth the time to speak with him.

'I'll need to see it.' She paused and felt some embarrassment. 'Actually' – she pointed to Chap – 'our tracker needs to smell it.'

Lanjov's face paled again. The thought of a dog sniffing over his dead daughter's clothing was pushing this evening past his tolerance. To his credit, he simply said, 'It's in her room. Follow me.'

As Dyta left, Magiere, Leesil, and Chap followed Lanjov back into the hallway and to the right. The hall opened up in a wider area with a curved staircase. Lanjov led them up to the third floor and into a bedroom.

Cream draperies hung from a four-poster bed with a matching comforter. Small whitewashed shelves were attached to the walls at heights low enough for a young girl to reach, and the number of dolls that filled them surprised Magiere. Leesil looked at them too. At least a score of dolls, intermingled with occasional toy animals or a foppish marionette, were displayed along one wall alone. Some were blond, some had dark ringlets, and one had hair of auburn red. All of their heads were porcelain and most wore pink, lavender, or yellow lace dresses.

'How old was your daughter?' Magiere asked.

'Sixteen,' Lanjov answered.

At that, Leesil's eyebrows rose, and he rolled his eyes as well.

'Where is her mother?' Leesil asked.

Again, Lanjov paused as if the question were not only irrelevant but impertinent.

'She died the night Chesna was born,' he answered.

Magiere couldn't help pitying this arrogant man. He'd lost his wife in childbirth, and now lost his only child. Perhaps he'd been in no hurry to see his daughter grow into a life of her own.

Lanjov opened the doors of a tall wardrobe and

removed a cloth-wrapped bundle. He carried it to bed as if it were both precious and horrifying to the touch. Inside was what had once been an elegant day dress of lavender with saffron trim. The neckline and left shoulder were stained with dried blood.

Chap trotted to the bed and looked up at Lanjov expectantly, but the councilman merely stepped back. Leesil reached out and took the dress, letting it unfold until the skirt hem touched the floor.

From its size, the girl would have stood no taller than Magiere's shoulder, but what caught her attention most was its condition. The front was shredded and torn open from bodice to hem. Magiere's stomach began to burn, accompanied by a familiar ache in her jaw that she quickly suppressed. But anger still crawled up her throat and into her head.

Those lower slashes hadn't been done to feed or kill. An ugly question needed to be asked, but when she looked at Lanjov's face, she couldn't voice it.

Lanjov stood silent and never blinked as he stared at the dress. His hands were tightly closed at his sides, and Magiere saw his throat clench as he swallowed.

Chap started at the hem of the torn skirt, pushing at it with his nose. As he worked upward, Leesil dropped down until the hound could reach the collar. Chap looked up at Leesil and back to Magiere and whined. Magiere knelt down next to the hound.

'Nothing?' Grabbing the shredded fabric in her fist, she shoved it at Chap, nearly jerking the dress out of Leesil's hands. 'Again . . . pay attention!'

It wasn't that Chap understood her words, but Magiere had come to recognize that he knew exactly what his role was in their trio.

Chap looked into her eyes for a moment, and Magiere

felt as if he returned her own dissatisfaction with a faint rumble in his throat. He again breathed in the dress, working along the folds and up to the bodice and shoulders. He finished and then whined.

'That's enough,' Leesil said. 'He's not getting anything. Perhaps it's been too long.'

'Well?' Lanjov demanded, as if expecting them to have some new dram of insight after this painful indignity.

'We need to take it with us,' Leesil said. He stood to face the councilman, leaving the dress in Magiere's hands. 'Chap might not know what he's scenting yet.'

Magiere knew well enough that her partner was now telling tales. She bunched the lavender dress in both hands. Part of her didn't want to know what had been done to this girl as she bled to death. She suddenly envisioned the mother she'd never seen being taken away in the dark to a fief keep. Rumors passed among the villagers of a woman glimpsed on rare nights, wandering, full with a child sired by what Magiere now had accepted was a walking abomination masquerading as a man. Just before her mother died, Magiere was born, unnatural and half-tied to the world of the undead. She squeezed Chesna's dress between her fingers and closed her eyes.

Teeth clamped down on her wrist, and Magiere's eyes snapped open.

Chap had her wrist wrapped in his jaws, and he tugged at her as he backed toward the door. She pulled out of his grip and looked at Leesil.

'I don't know.' He shook his head. 'Just follow him.'

At that, Chap whirled about, trotting out of the bedroom door. With dress still in hand, Magiere went after him, Leesil following, and from behind, she heard the breathy irritation of Lanjov. Chap stayed well ahead and, upon reaching the main floor, bolted toward the front of the house. Magiere chased him, coming to a stop in the main entryway. Chap stood grunting and growling as he pawed at the front door.

'It appears your dog needs to go outside,' Lanjov said coldly. 'Perhaps you gave him too much water before coming.'

Leesil turned on the councilman and was about to spit something out, when Magiere interceded. 'He wants to see the front porch again.'

Lanjov blinked. With a deep sigh of resignation, he opened the door.

Chap lunged out and did exactly as Magiere had expected. He stopped with nose down, sniffing the dark-stained grout between the porch stones.

Stepping out, Magiere studied the spot that Chap inspected. In the low light of the porch lanterns, it was hard to see it clearly. Her gaze still on the porch stones, she reached for the left-side lantern to turn up its knob and extend the wick for more light. Instead of growing brighter, the light dimmed.

Magiere looked to see if she'd mistakenly turned the wick down and snuffed it out. The wick was fully extended, and the flame burned wildly, licking the top of the lantern. The light was so bright that she pulled her gloved hand back to shield her eyes.

Her gloved hand. She didn't wear gloves.

Chap yipped, leaping aside as Magiere stumbled down the porch steps. She stood in the walkway, hand held before her, and stared at her fingers.

There was no glove on her hand.

'Magiere?' Leesil asked hesitantly. 'What's wrong?'

'It's nothing,' Magiere muttered.

When she pulled her awareness back to the moment, Leesil stood before her, studying her face with wide-eyed puzzlement.

'I'm . . .' she began. 'It's nothing.'

She glanced once more at her hand, the right empty and the left still clutching the bloodstained dress, and shook her head. Stepping around Leesil, she headed purposefully up the right side of the steps, watching the left-side lantern suspiciously. A trick of the light was all it had been, and she grabbed the railing to steady herself.

The porch was empty and silent.

Magiere stared at the closed front door with its outer carved panels of detailed doves and vines. She tried to look about and find where Leesil or Chap or even Lanjov had disappeared to, but her head wouldn't turn.

Her hand reached for the door's side lanterns, first the right and then the left, turning down the wicks until their light dimmed just short of going out. Her hand wore a well-tailored, tight-fitting, black leather glove. The hand itself was wrong, wider than it should be. It grasped the brass knocker, clacked it twice against the door, but there was no sound. Magiere tried to back away but couldn't move.

Moments passed. The door cracked open. A fresh young face peered out.

She was a pretty girl with dark ringlets of hair that hung to her shoulders. The girl released a smile, as if knowing Magiere as a familiar acquaintance. Magiere had no recollection of ever seeing or meeting her before, but something about her appearance was familiar. When the girl spoke, Magiere couldn't hear the words, but dark ringlets swayed across the shoulders of her lavender gown with its saffron trim.

'Chesna?' Magiere whispered, or thought she had. The sound never reached her ears. The only thing she heard was her heart hammering.

Jaw now aching, Magiere felt her canines elongate,

pushing against the clench of her teeth. Her gloved hand snatched the girl's neck and wrenched the young woman closer. When her mouth clamped around the girl's throat, lips sealing across smooth, warm skin, there came the scent of lilac from perfume or soap. Chesna's throat collapsed between Magiere's teeth as blood seeped into her mouth.

Magiere wanted to let go and scrape the taste from her tongue with her fingernails. Its thick warmth trickled to the back of her throat. Her head abruptly ripped back, and Magiere saw the side of the girl's throat open, exposing sinew and bleeding veins. Her hand still clenched around the girl's neck, she shook Chesna until blood soaked the lavender bodice. Her free hand came up, fingers snarling in the front of the lavender dress . . .

Chesna's empty eyes rolled.

'Stop it! Wake up!'

Magiere jerked away, both hands to her face as she clawed at her own mouth.

Her foot slipped off the edge of the porch. A hand snatched her upper arm, and she snarled in fear and pulled free, tumbling down the stairs to land facedown on the walkway.

Magiere lay still, unable to do anything but hold her bare hands across her face. She could still taste blood. Her heart raced so fast that she couldn't separate the pounding beats in her ears.

Hands grabbed her shoulders from behind, trying to pull her over onto her back. She blindly swung a backhand fist at her attacker. Her wrist was snatched in a grip that pulled her up and around to her knees.

'*Valhachkasej' â!* Open your eyes!'

Magiere obeyed.

Everything in the pitch dark around her appeared thinly luminous.

Leesil knelt before her, one hand on her shoulder, the other still gripping her wrist. The door lanterns behind him burned so brightly she couldn't look at them, and yet his face wasn't night-shadowed. She saw his features clearly, from the fine hairs of his slanted eyebrows to the faint scars on his jawline where the small undead, Ratboy, had tried to claw his throat open months ago.

'What is this?' Lanjov shouted. 'What is wrong with her?'

The councilman stood in the house's entryway back from the door and stared in horrified astonishment at the two of them kneeling on his front walk.

'Quiet, please,' Leesil snapped in annoyance.

'No!' Lanjov shouted. 'Enough of this ridiculous—'

'I said quiet!' Leesil repeated, and leaned around to face the councilman.

Magiere couldn't see her companion's face, but Lanjov's reaction was plain. The councilman lost all semblance of anger and took a further step back into his home.

Leesil turned back to her, and Magiere saw a change pass across his features. His narrow jaw tightened, and large amber eyes flinched and widened, and she felt his sudden twitch through his tightening grip on her wrist. He looked afraid. She shrank back from him, but he held her in place.

The ache in her jaw began to fade. Leesil slowly released her wrist and tried gently to pull her other hand from covering her mouth. She jerked her head away.

'Let me see,' he whispered.

This time, she let him push her hand aside. She felt his fingertips gently spread her lips. He frowned and gave a shallow nod.

'It's all right now,' he assured her. 'Nothing to hide anymore.'

'She knew him,' Magiere choked out, and ran her own

fingers over her teeth. There was nothing strange to her touch.

Leesil took hold of her upper arms and pulled her to her feet.

'What are you talking about?' Leesil asked.

'I saw . . . felt him,' Magiere tried to answer. 'Chesna. She knew him.'

'How could you see . . .' Leesil started. 'What do you mean, *him*?'

She didn't know how to explain that she'd seen through the eyes of the murderer, followed his steps, and lived inside his moment. Tasted his kill.

'My hands.' Magiere shook her head. 'They were too wide for a woman. And the gloves I . . . he was wearing were fine leather. Custom-fitted.'

'All right.' Leesil hesitated as he looked her over. He took a deep breath and let it out slowly. 'This "seeing" we'll get to later, but the gloves . . . means maybe he's masquerading as an elite or noble perhaps.'

'He didn't feed,' she continued. 'This wasn't for blood.'

'No more!' Lanjov shouted harshly through the doorway. 'I have answered your questions and let you paw over her dress. You should be out in the streets hunting this creature, not putting on a spectacle for my neighbors.'

Magiere slipped around Leesil and up the steps. 'Chesna knew him. Who else comes here? Does anyone else come regularly to the house?'

Ashen with anger, Lanjov spit his words. 'Are you suggesting the murderer is not a vampire?'

'No – he's an undead.' Magiere shook her head, the vision now crystallized in her thoughts. And that one word hung in her mind – murderer. 'But he didn't feed on her blood. I think he wanted it all over her. He wanted someone to find her that way.'

'Leave my home at once,' Lanjov said. 'My daughter did not know this creature. It . . . he is a fiend, like those of your own town. The guard captain has taken accounts from those who were either attacked or viewed attacks by this thing, and I assure you, it was not a nobleman.'

'There have been other attacks?' Leesil's voiced betrayed an annoyance Magiere could hear growing into open outrage. 'With survivors? Why didn't anyone tell us this?'

Lanjov stared blankly at him, searching for a response to a question that apparently made no sense to him.

'There was no need. The city guard took the reports, and the victims were—'

'Common folk,' Magiere finished in disgust. 'You didn't see a need to call for me until one of your own died. So some survived these attacks to report them, but what about bodies? Besides Chesna, where are the other bodies?'

'I do not know,' Lanjov answered tiredly. 'Now, please, leave my home. This is a prowling creature that kills at random. If you wish to be paid, take that dog into the sewers or any other place where such things hide, and do not mention this ridiculous theory of a nobleman again.'

He closed the door, and Magiere heard the bolts inside slide sharply into place.

'Are you all right?' Leesil asked.

Magiere ran her hand across her mouth, wiping at the lingering taste and touch.

'I saw her die,' she said. 'I saw it through his eyes. I felt it.'

'I know, and I believe you, though . . .' He paused, and then hesitantly asked. 'What did you see when you opened your eyes?'

'Just your face, the lanterns, the walkway, but . . . as if

everything were touched by a hidden, soft light that let me see it more clearly. Why?'

Leesil stepped off the porch and looked away from her as he spoke.

'Your eyes. They were completely black, like their centers opened up and swallowed all the color out of them.'

A thickness settled in Magiere's limbs. She was tired enough to crawl away into a small place, not to emerge for as long as she could remain undiscovered.

'I thought this was all done with,' she said. 'How many more twisted parts of me do I have to face?'

Leesil took her by the arm and pulled her into motion, headed for the front gate.

'We know the Noble Dead can see in the dark. It makes sense that you'd have some of that as well. It's night sight, Magiere. My mother's people have something akin to it, and I do partly as well. As to what you saw through the killer—'

'Why now?' she insisted. 'Why haven't I had visions before?'

Leesil shook his head. 'Perhaps the dress?'

'Then why didn't it happen in the bedroom when I first touched it?' Magiere held up the bunched ball of the dress.

'I don't know. It could be . . . I just don't know,' was all he could say.

'I want no more of this.'

Magiere looked about the street, its cobblestones illuminated by spaced oil lanterns atop posts or hanging from brackets fixed to the inner ring wall across the way. There was no movement and nothing to see in the empty night. Except for Chap, who had somehow passed them by and sat waiting patiently outside the gate.

'No more,' she added. 'I feel tainted all the time as it is.'

'Give me that.' Leesil took the dress from her hand. 'We won't risk setting it off again, however it happened. We'll walk until we spot a coach to take us to the inn.'

Magiere gripped her falchion's hilt, squeezing it tight like a single handhold over a chasm. Who were they fooling? She was an ex-mountebank and a tavern owner. Leesil was an ex-thief and a gambler who loved his wine too much. Yes, they could fight, even against the undead. They'd proven that much in Miiska, but this was different.

'They were right about murder,' she said, shamed at what she'd seen, her hand – *his* hand – around Chesna's torn throat. 'He slaughtered that girl with barely a swallow and left her there on purpose. What is happening here?'

'I'll find us a coach,' Leesil muttered. 'And we'll get you away from here.'

After a light breakfast of porridge and grainy apples the next morning, a hired coach took them back to the inner ring wall and the recently built barracks of the Sträzhy-shlyahketné, the royal guard division assigned to the king's city. Magiere noticed that Leesil had mended his shirt sometime in the night. Over breakfast, he'd questioned her about the vision. It was disturbing to remember, let alone ponder why it happened at all.

They knew the Noble Dead varied some in powers and abilities. Now, Magiere found her dhampir state continuing to mimic them.

She was changing. She could sense the sun. She'd awoken that morning at almost the moment it arose, though the curtains on her window were closed.

Even in the upper-class districts, people went about on daily business, though fewer street hawkers and peddlers wandered about. Most shops here served the whims and fancies of the privileged. Next to a clothier selling cloaks and voluminous capes trimmed in satins and rare furs stood a wine house built of dark timbers and white plastered walls.

They passed by other shops along the way, from a bakery with full tables of glazed goods to a large cartwright station for the sale and repair of carriages and coaches. At first, Magiere was puzzled when they entered this district rather than Lanjov's, but it made sense that even a king's guard division deployed for the city's protection wouldn't be housed among the homes of the elite. No, even the Strächy-shlyahketné were still common folk, regardless of their standing. After dealing with Lanjov, Magiere hoped this Captain Chetnik might be less deluded and caste-conscious.

Lost in thought, Magiere was jarred back to awareness as the coach rocked to a halt.

Stepping into bright daylight, Magiere shielded her eyes and looked inside the purse Karlin had given to her. Their coin was holding, but they would spend quite a bit getting around in a place as large as Bela, and she paid the coachman with reluctance. It was either coaches or buy horses, and that meant stable fees as well. On the Stravinan back roads, they'd walked or paid fare on a barge or ferry traveling the main rivers, but time meant little back then, and horses were an unnecessary extravagance. Now, they couldn't spend half the days getting from one place to another.

'Can you ride?' she asked Leesil as the coach pulled away.

'You mean a horse? Only if I have to. I don't care to be at the mercy of a bag of lunacy lunging around on four sticks.'

'Well, you may have to. The price of coaches will drain us soon enough.'

He stopped his apprehensive examination of the barracks' outer stockade and looked at her.

'You're worried about the price of coaches? Forgetful gods, Magiere, I have never met another spirit as mean with money as you.'

'Well, one of us has to be!'

Magiere pushed past him, heading for the gate to the barracks' grounds. She wasn't mean with money. She simply planned ahead. That was more than anyone could say of him.

The barracks' crafted stockade around its grounds was twice a man's height, with a double-wide gate that stood open. Four guards manned the portal, while others inside went about in the cool morning air, drilling at arms. All were similarly outfitted in ring mail beneath white surcoats and armed with sabers. Some, on their way out to posts around the city, carried long, pronged pikes and white shields emblazoned with twin sea hawks. The center ridges of their helms were trimmed in the feathers of these same birds.

Magiere paused before one gate guard. 'Pardon, I'm looking for Captain Chetnik.'

The man appraised her briefly, but spoke politely in turn and gestured toward the building directly ahead. 'In the main hall. Ask at the front entry.'

Magiere nodded her thanks and headed across the grounds, with Chap at pace beside her and Leesil following behind.

The main hall was two stories of masoned stone, the front doors propped open to let in the morning air. The entryway led into a small room, plain and sparse. From down one of the side halls came an angry voice, though

Magiere couldn't quite make out what was being said. Behind the front desk was a balding little clerk, clean-shaven and plain-clothed, who raised his head and gave them a brief and polite nod.

'How may I help you?' he asked.

'We're here to speak with Captain Chetnik,' Magiere replied. 'At the request of Councilman Lanjov.'

'And this pertains to?' the clerk asked.

'The councilman's deceased daughter,' she answered. 'We were called upon by the city council to look into her death. The captain has reports from citizens that might be of help.'

The clerk seemed momentarily agitated but, with a short sigh, nodded in understanding. 'Please wait. I'll see if the captain can meet with you.'

At that, he disappeared down the left hallway toward the voice Magiere had heard, only to return moments later.

'The captain is currently with someone, but he said you are to come in anyway.' He motioned Magiere around the desk and gestured toward the hallway. 'Just go down to the end door.'

Chap trotted ahead to the corridor's end. His whole attention focused through the open door at whoever waited inside. Magiere caught up to the hound, wondering what had his interest, when voices inside the room became clear.

'Are you suggesting my son would just leave the city without a word?'

The question came from a stout, middle-aged man sitting on the near side of the room in front of a large, dark-wood table. Dressed modestly in a short burgundy cloak with cap to match, he had an ample and sculpted beard dropping to a point from his chin.

'Captain, my son and his wife have been missing for days,' he continued shouting. 'Will you do nothing?'

Behind the table sat a hefty man in ring mail armor with a broad nose. A mass of dark brown curls hung from his head, trimmed off around his face as if his helmet had been used as a shearing guide. Among the table's clutter of scrolls and parchment was a helmet similar to those of the Sträzhy but with more ridges and one plume of feathers arcing back over the crests from the nose-guard. This, Magiere assumed, would be Captain Chetnik.

'What else would you have me do?' the captain asked, too quietly for his stature.

Magiere expected him to be bored by merchant's outburst, or at best, in a hurry to take the man's statement and shove him out the door. That had been her previous experience with constables and guards, but this captain appeared patiently sad.

'According to your statement,' he went on with equal softness, 'your son, Simask, and his wife, Luiza, were here with you on business. They went out to seek patronage for your vineyard from local innkeepers but didn't return. Guards have made inquiries, and I've notified the district constables in the area and the two local districts where they'd likely have gone. But there are no witnesses and no evidence of foul play. What more would you have me do?'

'Look for them!' the merchant answered in frustration.

'Where? In which part of the city should I search? Where were they last seen? We've had to guess at best.'

The merchant collapsed in his chair under a sudden weight of fatigue.

'We separated to work different sides of the city,' he continued more quietly. 'I didn't even realize they were missing for a full day. I don't know where they might have gone, but my son is dependable. He wouldn't have missed our meeting day.'

It was then that the captain noticed Magiere and Leesil standing in the doorway, and he stood up. The girth of his belly was wide, but appeared more muscle than the bulk of a sedentary man.

'Go back to your inn and rest,' he told the merchant. 'We'll do what we can. If there is any news, I'll send word without hesitation. Now you must excuse me, as there is another matter that needs my attention.'

The merchant's face was drawn and hopeless as he stood. Magiere pitied him, but she didn't know what to say. When he turned to leave, he spotted her in the doorway and looked back at the captain.

'Luiza is fair, almost like that,' he said, pointing at Magiere. 'And black hair, but she is shorter, smaller.'

The captain nodded. 'I will make a note of it.'

With nothing else to say, the merchant shuffled out past Magiere and down the corridor.

'Can I help you?' the captain asked, looking her up and down. He picked up a leather-bound sheaf of parchment and flipped the loose cover open. 'I don't have any other appointments this morning, but I'm due to meet with the local constabulary in a short while.'

'This won't take long,' she said. 'I'm Magiere. The council hired me to investigate the death of Councilman Lanjov's daughter.'

At her words, Chetnik scowled and shook his head as he dropped the sheaf on the table. He studied her a moment, with only a brief appraisal of Leesil and Chap. A slightly amused smile bent his mouth up as he folded his arms.

'You're the hunter. Who's he?'

'My partner, Leesil.'

Chap was sniffing the air about the room, but he looked over at Chetnik intently.

'That's our tracker,' Magiere added. 'But the trail is cold, and we need to limit our search. Lanjov said there are reports of attacks by a night assailant. We'd like to talk with some of these people. Can you give us a list of names and where to find them?'

Chetnik stood there, still smiling faintly. 'You aren't what I expected.'

If there was one phrase Magiere was most tired of hearing, this was certainly it.

'Indeed,' she responded.

Chetnik laughed aloud, and the last of the sad strain vanished from his eyes.

'No, no,' he added. 'I expected some pompous mystic or aspiring alchemist throwing potions and powders about. I was none too pleased when the council took this case out of our hands. But our hands are full, and the district constabularies are hired locals not always suited to the task. You at least look like you can handle a fight.'

His goading good humor proved mildly settling, and Magiere relaxed a little. Although Chetnik's continually eyeing her was more than a little puzzling. In fact, it made her rather uncomfortable.

'Can you give us a list?' she asked more politely.

'Hmmm . . . perhaps you've time for an exchange.' His thick eyebrows arched. 'I don't care who catches this murderer, but I want it done with.'

Leesil stepped closer. Magiere noticed that he appeared to be strangely put out by this conversation.

'What do you mean, "exchange"?' he asked.

Chetnik acknowledged him briefly and turned his full attention back to Magiere.

'No matter how good you are, you may need help

sooner or later. I've spoken with all of Count Lanjov's neighbors. I'd be willing to share their statements, if you'll tell me what you've come up with so far or what you discover along the way.'

Magiere suppressed the urge to immediately agree. Chetnik was more than a soldier. As captain, he might know the city as well as any of the local constables assigned to its separate districts. Anything the constabularies heard would likely be passed to Chetnik. She and Leesil were working blind. On the other hand, she didn't want to appear too eager. If Miiska was to be saved, she and Leesil – not the Sträzhy-shlyahketné – had to produce the remains of an undead.

Chetnik's warm eyes watched her expectantly. She returned him a shallow nod of agreement, though she wouldn't necessarily share everything.

'Have you found any bodies?' she asked.

The blunt question surprised him. Likely he thought he would be the first to get some answers.

'No,' he answered. 'We mostly hear about disappearances. One way or another such things often get resolved, for better or worse. In the last month, there've been more reports and fewer resolved. There are now more missing people than we can possibly search for at once.'

None of this made sense to Magiere. So many missing, yet Chesna had been left to die on her own front porch in plain view.

'Chesna's killer wanted her body found,' she said aloud. 'I think he mutilated her and left her there intentionally.'

'I'd considered that, but why?' Chetnik asked thoughtfully. 'It doesn't fit with any of the disappearances.'

He stepped around the table and closer to Magiere, his brows knitted. As he settled on the table's edge, he leaned toward her just a bit.

'And what makes you certain it's a man?' he asked, and his gaze wandered a bit.

Leesil let out a sharp breath. 'I think we've taken up enough of the captain's time. If you could give us the list, we'll be on our way.'

Leesil's voice was icy, and Magiere could tell he wanted out of here for some reason. The tone wasn't lost on Chetnik, who grunted and walked to a short chest of drawers against the wall.

'There isn't any list,' he said. 'I can get you started with a few statements, but I expect them back.' He dug through parchments in the top drawer and pulled out a stack as thick as his thumb. 'Names and addresses are all written out. Can you read?'

'He can,' she answered without embarrassment, giving a nod in Leesil's direction. 'But that's quite a few statements.'

'They aren't all going to help you,' he said, again rather friendly and chatty. 'A drunk or two have been known to see monsters in the dark, and there are always those who latch on to rumors and tavern tales to blame for misfortune.'

Leesil snatched the stack from his hand. 'Thank you. Let's go.'

He headed straight for the door. With little choice, Magiere hurried after him, urging Chap ahead.

'Keep me informed, and if you need anything else,' Chetnik called after, 'stop by and let me know.'

Magiere merely waved in thanks and hurried out. By the time she reached the courtyard, Leesil was already in the street hailing a coach.

Although Leesil considered himself adept at talking to almost anyone, by the time the sun dipped low at dusk, he didn't care if he ever spoke a word again. They'd been over half the city. All right, so it was probably a tenth or twentieth, but it felt like half, and they'd managed to find only eight people noted in the reports Chetnik had given them. Chap became more restless throughout their search, and twice Leesil had to go scouting about neighborhoods and markets to track him down.

Magiere had been severely shaken by her experience at Lanjov's, as had he. He'd wanted to both comfort her and fathom what was happening to her before it happened again. But in typical fashion, she grudgingly put up with a few questions over breakfast and then refused all further efforts to discuss these newly manifesting abilities. The 'sight' was not so surprising, but the vision, and what had triggered it, was another matter.

It couldn't have been the dress, for she'd handled items – even bloodied ones – from victims before in Miiska. The same reasoning stood for walking in the footsteps of an undead at the site of a killing. In spite of this unsettling awareness she'd developed, a part of him felt they shouldn't be thrown by any kind of unexpected help. They had no trail, not many clues, nothing to hunt, and on top of that, the guard captain had spent the better part of their brief meeting appraising Magiere as if he wished to make her part of his breakfast, or perhaps a late evening repast. Leesil didn't like this Chetnik one bit.

He was tired, hungry, and sick of listening to sad, despondent folk relive unsettling experiences. They'd talked to cobblers' daughters, tanners and sons, barkeeps, and even low-ranking gentry. So far, only one tanner's son and one young noble – who hadn't even wanted them in his home – had managed to produce coherent and unified stories. Both men had encountered a female with bright blue eyes in garish clothes. Of those tales, neither teller remembered what had happened, only that they'd found themselves wandering later in a befuddled and weak state, torn wounds in their throats.

'The sun is going down,' he said. 'Let's just go back to the inn. We can start again tomorrow.'

'One more,' Magiere said absently, staring at a parchment.

She could make out a few words at a time, and Leesil sat watching her read the same line of ink scrawl three times. It was getting even darker outside. Most shops they passed were closed. Chap lay on the seat across the coach, and Leesil had the oddest impression the dog looked sullen.

'Bright blue . . . blue . . . blue eyes,' Magiere mumbled as she worked word by word through the scribed report.

Leesil groaned. 'Let's at least have some supper first.'

'Isn't this another name for a brothel?'

He reached out. 'Let me see that.'

'Oh, yes,' she said in mild disgust. 'That would get your attention.'

'Not funny,' Leesil chided, and scanned the parchment.

Just over a moon ago, a woman with bright blue eyes – like 'crystals,' the witness had said – attacked a hired guard named Koh'in ib'Sune serving at one of Bela's loftier 'domvolyné,' a house of leisure. In other words, a brothel for those who preferred not to frequent an establishment that might actually be called a brothel.

'It's the same description,' Magiere said. 'Like the tanner's son and that haughty little noble.'

Leesil nodded.

'That makes three matching accounts,' she said.

'All right, all right. One more and then back to the inn. But there's no exact address.' He leaned through the coach door window and called to the driver. 'Do you know the Blue Dove?'

The driver looked at him cautiously. 'I know where it is, if that's what you mean.'

'Take us there.' Leesil ducked back inside the coach.

Chap let out a whine without lifting his head. They rode for a while in silence until finally the driver called out their destination: 'The Blue Dove.'

Leesil hadn't paid attention to their progress and was surprised to find they'd passed back into the inner wall ring. What they knew from the reports didn't add up in a way that would lead to this place.

The young noble who'd seen the blue-eyed woman lived inside the second ring wall in a respectable but not overly wealthy area. The tanner's son lived in the outer ring. The three encounters had occurred in different parts of the city, but still, it wasn't unimaginable that an undead would range so widely.

Magiere paid the coachman, asked him to wait, and then stood next to Leesil, shifting her weight from one foot to the other. The brothel was a lavish stone dwelling with two large braziers on each side of a door painted sky blue. The building's unusually small windows were shuttered tight, so no one could see inside. As they stood there with Chap looking about, a few people, particularly one elder couple, passed them with disapproving glances.

'I've never been inside a brothel before,' she said finally.

Leesil grinned at her. 'Neither have I. How tragic is that?'

'For who?' she muttered under her breath. 'You or the women?'

'The women, of course,' Leesil answered. 'And from what I've heard, these places serve a wide variety of entertainment. Some even employ young boys, and I know of a place in the Warlands with a large mastiff that—'

'Not another word.' She gripped his arm, pulled him up the steps and knocked on the door.

A gargantuan man opened it and looked down at them in surprise. His head was as clean-shaven as his wide, cleft chin, and his eyes were a brown so dark they were nearly black. But his most noticeable feature was his deep brown skin. He wore dark green breeches and an open vest with no shirt, and the handle of a flanged mace was slipped through the side of a wine-red silk belt wrapped more than a dozen times around his waist.

'You are too early,' he said.

'Uh, no . . .' Magiere stammered. 'You don't understand. We're looking for a man named Koh'in ib'Sune. Is he here?'

The man's body blocked the entire doorway.

'I am Koh'in, but I do not know you.'

Leesil noted that his accent was smooth and fluid, like Lord Au'shiyn's from the city council.

'We're working with the city guard,' he lied. 'We wanted to speak with you about a report describing a woman with crystal-blue eyes who attacked you. There've been other reports, and we're trying to find any link between them.'

Koh'in's stern expression didn't change. 'You do not look like the city guard.'

'We're not,' Leesil replied, exhaustion getting the better of him. Bluntness seemed to be the only option. 'We're vampire hunters working for the city guard. Can we come in?'

Koh'in blinked twice with a flare of his wide nostrils as his expression changed to mild concern.

'Come to the kitchen,' he said, shifting slowly aside.

'My mistress was displeased that I reported the event at all. She correctly believes such a stain on our reputation may hurt business.'

With a quick glance behind himself, he ushered them toward the back of the house.

Leesil was curious to see the parlor, but he barely got a peek from the foyer before being hurried away to the kitchens. Pillows of shimmering fabrics rested upon divans and couches, and rich, thick draperies were pulled across the windows. Following Koh'in, he looked at the man's bulging shoulders straining the back of his vest. It was likely the patrons of this domvolyné conducted themselves with every bit of good manners.

The kitchen was well kept with pottery stacked about, and a warm, low fire in the cooking hearth. The room already contained two occupants. A beautiful woman with a generous figure and a mass of chocolate-brown hair sat at the kitchen table drinking tea, while a lovely blond nymph curled the woman's already impressively spiraled tresses. They wore matching silk dressing gowns of amber with embroidered white roses.

'This is Brita,' Koh'in said, respectfully gesturing to the seated woman, and then lifted his hand toward the other. 'And young Natasha. They must prepare each other while we talk.'

'Koh'in, what is this?' Brita asked disdainfully, taking in Magiere's breeches and falchion. 'You know the mistress doesn't allow visitors at this hour. And a dog?'

'They are from the city guard,' Koh'in whispered, 'and need to ask me questions about . . . the woman.'

'Oh.' Brita immediately stood up, and at full height she was taller than Leesil. She stepped directly in front of Koh'in as if to block passage. 'Well, you can pose any questions in front of us. The guard helps us little enough, and troubles us plenty when some fop starts complaining. Ask your questions – and then leave him in peace.'

Natasha set her curling rod on the stove and stepped close to Koh'in's side, crossing her arms in agreement. Next to the tall Suman guard, she looked like a tiny porcelain figurine.

'Yes,' she said with some bitterness. 'Poor Koh'in was attacked in the alley nearly a moon ago. The slashes on his throat are already healed, yet this is the first time you decide to look into this?'

'We don't actually work for the guard,' Magiere replied, both empty hands in front of her, seemingly on the defensive. 'We're working for the city council on another matter, but it might be connected to what happened. We may be tracking whoever attacked your friend here.'

'Vampire hunters,' Koh'in whispered to Brita.

Brita snorted and crossed her arms, crinkling her amber silk sleeves.

'That's what the council is spending taxes on? What happened, some pasty-skinned noble get his throat cut? But when it happens elsewhere, it's no concern of theirs.'

Leesil shifted uncomfortably at how closely she assessed the situation.

'Can you just tell us what happened?' he asked tiredly.

Koh'in nodded. 'I always make sure all the ladies are safe, alone in their rooms, before I lock up the downstairs.'

Natasha wrapped her dainty hands around the large man's forearm. It took both hands to encompass the bulk of his limb.

'But before locking up,' he went on, 'I walk the outside, all around the house, to be sure no one remains, someone looking up at one of the windows, if you understand.'

Leesil nodded.

'That night,' Koh'in said, 'I saw a red dress and blond curls in the alley behind the house. I thought one of the ladies had been called to a party and was coming home late. I hurried to take her inside. She was not one of ours.'

'What exactly did she look like?' Magiere asked.

'Pretty. Small. Dark-blond rings of hair and bright blue eyes. So bright they made me think of gems, like they could reflect the light from the street lamps. But the mistress would not hire her to work here.'

'Why not?' Leesil asked, and Koh'in frowned.

'Her dress was rich satin, but she looked . . .' – he searched for the right word – 'cheap – not like Brita or Natasha. Perhaps it was her face, the way she looked. I cannot explain. I thought to help her, as she should not be alone in the alley. She smiled and asked me where we might go to be alone. Then I thought she was a poor street whore in a stolen dress trying to make coins from our patrons passing by. So I went to chase her off, and . . .'

The large man's eyes wandered, and he wrung his hands as Natasha leaned her head against his upper arm. He appeared shamed.

'She pushed me against the alley wall. Her mouth opened, and I saw her teeth come for my throat. They were like those of a *numår*.'

'A what?' Leesil asked.

'A large wild black cat in my homeland,' Koh'in explained. 'Fanged above and below. I threw her off, but she was strong – so strong – and I ran. I did not know I was bleeding until back inside with the door bolted. This was not a real woman.'

Natasha patted his arm softly. 'It's all right. There was nothing more you could do.'

'Did you managed to rip part of her dress or anything she was wearing?' Magiere asked.

'What kind of a question is that?' Brita snapped.

Magiere pointed at Chap. 'He tracks. If you have anything that belonged to this woman, it would help us.'

'Oh.' Brita's demeanor softened. 'Koh'in?'

The Suman shook his head. 'No. I did not think of anything but to get inside.'

Leesil hadn't expected much, but the man's description of the woman closely matched that of the tanner's son and the noble.

'So now you'll catch this thing?' Natasha asked.

'We'll try,' Leesil said, for lack of a better answer.

Brita looked at them both and said, grudgingly but politely, 'Thank you for coming. At least finally someone has.'

With a few promises and good-byes, Leesil found himself once again climbing into the coach, but this time heading back to the inn and a hot supper. Only now, he found no joy or comfort in the thought of rest and warm food. One fact hung in the silent air between himself and Magiere.

'There are two,' she said finally. 'We're hunting two of them.'

'If your vision was correct,' he added.

'My vision is correct. And we've hunted more than one before.'

'Do you think they're connected?' Leesil suggested. 'Are we dealing with another pack?'

Magiere shook her head in uncertainty.

'The council can quake in their houses for all I care,' Leesil added. 'But I liked Koh'in – and Brita and Natasha. Besides the other common folk, the pier boys and such, these are the first people I've met worth protecting.'

'And Chesna, who's now beyond our help.' Magiere glanced sidelong at him. 'We'll protect them. That's what we're here to do – so it seems.'

Leesil leaned back. A fight was coming their way, and he smiled with a mordant sense of contentment for the first time since they'd left home.

7

Past dusk the following evening, Leesil and Magiere finished another grueling day of wandering the length and breadth of Bela, speaking to as many people from Chetnik's reports as they could find. For all their efforts, they learned nothing new nor came any closer to beginning the hunt. Leesil's dark contentment faded shortly before lunch.

Magiere's concern over the price of coaches, mixed with his reluctance to ride on horseback, had resulted in a great deal of walking. Chap limped slightly, his paws obviously aching from the city's cobblestone streets. But even more frustrating to Leesil was their lack of progress.

Back at the Burdock, they sat in the common room in their dusty clothes, mildly relieved that the hard wooden stools let them get off their feet. Leesil took off his scarf and scratched his head freely, shaking out his white-blond hair.

'Are you having supper tonight?' asked Milous, the innkeeper. 'We've a nice mutton stew and fresh bread. A few barrels of Droevinkan ale just arrived yesterday. It's the best.'

'You are my hero,' Leesil replied with a weak smile. 'Stew and bread all around. Any spiced tea?'

'I'll see. And for you, mistress, the same?'

'Yes, spiced tea,' Magiere answered tiredly.

'I'll bring it directly,' Milous assured, and glanced down at Chap lying exhausted on the floor. 'Hmmm, when you say "all" . . .'

'Just find a large bowl and pour some in for him,' Leesil answere. 'A bowl of water as well.'

The stocky innkeeper sighed, shaking his head, and went off to fetch their meal.

A small hearth lit the room with a soft glow. The place was comfortable and clean, but like the innkeeper's face, merely pleasant and not truly noteworthy. There were only two other patrons. Old men sat near the front door, smoking their clay pipes as they talked in low voices, while young Vàtz brought them tin tankards on an old wooden tray.

Leesil found himself thinking of their double-sided stone fireplace set in the center of the Sea Lion's common room. He thought of his faro table, and Chap circling the hearth with sharp eyes, and Magiere in her leather vest — or perhaps her blue dress — behind the long polished bar.

'This place doesn't compare, does it?' Magiere said.

Leesil looked up to find her watching him intently. Apparently he'd slipped up, his thoughts obvious to read on his face.

'No, I suppose nothing would,' he answered. 'Who'd ever think I'd be homesick?'

There was long moment's silence before she replied.

'Home remains a long way off, if today is any measure. We should ask Chetnik to call for us when another attack is reported. If we can get Chap there quickly, he might pick up a trail.'

Leesil frowned. Chetnik was the last person he wanted involved.

'You mean *if* another attack is reported, and there are two undeads out there, by our best guess. Lanjov's grief and arrogance are eating up his patience, so if it's about getting paid, we need to find the nobleman from your vision first, and quickly. We've no clues, and what little we've found points to this roaming female.'

'So what do you propose?'

'I don't know.' Leesil shook his head. 'But I've been thinking about the fight eventually to come and preparations to make. Also, we're on our own. No townsfolk to organize, so we can't particularly lay a trap and draw them in. That means hunting them down while remaining undetected.'

'We already know this,' she argued. 'What about your little excursion to a weaponsmith?'

'It's more than just the hunt,' Leesil answered, shaking his head. 'And you'll see – I hope soon – what's coming from the smithy.'

Magiere appeared about to press with more questions, but Leesil continued before she could get in a word.

'We have to get to these creatures while they're unaware and off guard. If they're working together, we need to take them separately. I want the advantage, and I want them outnumbered. That means quick changes in tactics and proper supplies.'

Magiere stared at him silently from across the small table. The hearth's light painted her white skin with amber, and set off crimson glimmers in her black hair. In the moment's distraction, Leesil didn't quite catch the suspicion growing in her eyes. Her face, drawn and fatigued, was still beautiful.

'Just like your old times, yes?' she said, but with no warmth in her voice.

Leesil stiffened. 'What?'

'You've done this before.'

Leesil assumed she was jesting with him. 'We both have done this—'

'No,' she cut him off.

He was completely confused. 'What are you talking about?'

'I never realized how cunning – even sly – you were until Miiska,' she began. 'You've always been nimble, and I've seen you take down someone twice your size. But there's more to it, isn't there? Maybe something to do with all those mornings you disappeared into the woods.'

Leesil's nerves hummed with tension. Now wasn't the time to explain things she wouldn't want to know.

'And lately, you've been . . .' She stopped, and he saw determination settle on her face. 'Leesil, were you just a thief before we met?'

She'd never asked him this, never even come close to it. The crux of their life on the road had been to leave the past well enough alone. There was only the day at present and perhaps the day ahead, and nothing else had mattered.

'I was someone else living another life. Someone you wouldn't want to know,' he said finally. 'Now I'm someone who needs to find a good crossbow.'

Magiere slumped on her stool.

'All right. We'll try to pick one up tomorrow.' She gazed vacantly toward the fire. 'We prepare what we can and, once we locate the undeads, if possible, we do exactly what we did before: track them down and take them before sunset. It would have worked last time had we found them more quickly.'

Leesil felt his tension ebb but not completely. There were only so many times he could evade her, and he was using them up.

'Yes, if we do this right,' he offered, 'there may not even be much of a fight.'

'Or need to burn anything down,' she snapped without looking at him.

Her tone wasn't truly accusing, but even if it had been, it wouldn't have mattered. She'd been unconscious and bleeding to death with her throat slashed open. Rashed was after them, and there was no other option. So he'd burned Miiska's largest warehouse down – and he'd do it again without a second thought. There was no argument as to what came first as he sat there watching her.

Leesil folded his hands on the table and looked down at the scar of teeth marks on his tanned wrist.

'If there's a fight, if you're cut again,' he said, trying to reassure her, 'I'll be there for you. I know what to do now.'

When he raised his head, Magiere glared at him, eyes wide. Her words came out in a hiss of breath.

'Don't ever say that to me again.'

Her hands pressed hard into the table, and Leesil thought he heard a creak from the wood. Teeth clenched, her expression was caught between fear and anger, and she looked at him as if he were an undead.

'Magiere, I just meant—'

'I know what you meant.'

She pushed back from the table. Leesil saw her anger fade, to be replaced by something painful in her blinking eyes.

'I'm tired,' she whispered. 'I'm going up to sleep.'

'You need to eat. I was trying to offer assurance. This isn't the old game. I just wanted you to know I will be with you, no matter what it takes.'

'Don't be such a dolt,' she said, and her voice returned to its familiar, bad-tempered tone. 'I could never do any of this without you – and Chap.'

Leesil's heart pounded in his chest as he nodded. He was uncertain what had just happened, but now was obviously not the time to press for answers.

'I have an idea,' he said. 'Bela's a large city, the biggest port on this end of the continent, and all we've done is work. Let's forget the mutton stew and find a bit of some-thing special. There's bound to be a high-class inn or an exotic eatery around here. We can't do anything else until tomorrow, so why not enjoy ourselves?'

'Aren't you tired?' she asked in mild disbelief.

'Exhausted. My feet are going to fall off any moment.' He grinned. 'But let's go anyway.'

He watched her expression relax, and though he rarely tried to charm her as he did with others, he knew his expressive moods were infectious.

'We don't know how long we'll be here.' She shook her head. 'Our coins have to last. I think we've enough to keep us for a while if we're careful.'

Leesil collapsed upon the table with an audible groan.

'All right, enough dramatics,' she said. 'You said you bartered for whatever that smith is making, and there are still the coins you took back on the schooner. So I suppose we can afford what you have leftover.'

Leesil's breath caught in his throat, and he tried not to let his checks flush as he raised his head with an inno-cent look. 'Oh, didn't I tell you? I—'

'Did you lose it?' she asked. 'Not all of it? To those sailors?'

'Well, I had to pay for my share of their grog, and then I lost a few hands of Jack o' Knives, just to be polite. I was about to start winning when Chap sounded the alarm and—'

'You were too drunk to fight!' Magiere shouted, and slammed her hand down so hard that the table bounced. 'I've seen you fight with your face slashed open, but you're a second-rate gambler even when you're sober.'

'I am not!'

'I can't believe you didn't tell me this sooner,' she con-tinued. 'You lost it all to a bunch of drunken deckhands?'

'I think there are a few pennies left,' he offered.

Magiere tried to utter words that simply wouldn't come out, and then she stood up too quickly, knocking her stool over. As she headed for the stairs, she didn't even look back.

'Then you have enough for your evening out,' she snarled. 'Next time, trust me enough to confess before you're pressed to it.'

Magiere took the stairs two at a time, and Leesil heard a door slam. He looked at Chap.

'Oh, yes, I should trust her because she responds with such kind understanding,' he said sarcastically.

Chap rumbled at him. Before Leesil could guess at the hound's complaint, Chap got up and gingerly trotted up the stairs as well.

Leesil stared up the stairs in bewilderment. He should have told her, but she would have shouted at him no matter when he'd chosen to speak up. Well, let her pass on the wonders of Bela's nightlife. Now more than before, he deserved a respite.

The innkeeper came back with their tea.

'The stew is coming,' he said, and looked around. 'Where's your woman and dog?'

Leesil grunted, refraining from any unpleasant explanation.

'Have supper sent to her room. I won't be eating here tonight. Can you recommend someplace in the city that shouldn't be missed?'

The innkeeper frowned. 'I suppose maybe the Rowanwood. They've one of the largest gaming rooms in Bela.'

'Perfect,' Leesil said.

Chane waited upon the steps, his satchel bulging with acquisitions, as Toret unlocked the front door of their house. It had been a tedious evening, with his master's constant complaints still ringing in his ears.

They had wandered the lower markets and shops after dusk, as Chane judiciously acquired what he would need. All the while, Toret continued with the same irritable questions. Why had Chane left all of this to the last possible moment? Why hadn't he gone by himself and left his master at home in comfort? Why hadn't Chane ordered the materials ahead of time to be delivered or picked up as needed?

Each time, Chane patiently – or less so – explained it again. Some of the acquisitions needed to be fresh, while others required that he gauge appropriateness by feel, hence the necessity of Toret's presence.

The first reason was true enough. In addition, it was best to acquire supplies in short order from diverse sources, leaving no obvious trail to find or connection to make. Some apothecaries might become suspicious if asked for certain combinations of goods. Conjury was not outlawed like sorcery, but it was not as welcome as thaumaturgy or as revered as theurgy.

The second reason was, of course, a lie. In truth, Chane did not need Toret's presence, but the subterfuge served a purpose. Still uncertain as to precisely how, Chane intended to find his way free of his maker's control. It was worthwhile to stretch Toret's nerves and keep him off balance, and feed the puzzling disquiet growing in him ever since that night the mysterious note had arrived. Chane was still exasperated that he had not eavesdropped on Toret that evening. Something happened after he'd left to escort Sapphire. Upon Chane's return before dawn, Toret was waiting for him in a frenzied state, though he would not speak directly of the cause. Instead, he gave Chane two tasks: to plan for this evening's work, and to use his resources to hunt for two people – a woman of black hair and pallid skin, and her half-blood companion.

Additionally, this evening's outing, however stressful and tiresome, served Chane's future options. A later mention of another such venture would be enough for Toret to quickly give him leave to go alone.

Chane followed Toret into the foyer of their home. As they removed their cloaks, a piercing squeal of delight scraped across Chane's nerves. He looked up and choked.

Descending the stairs was Sapphire, a vicious spark in her overadorned eyes above an unrestrained smile of white teeth between wine-colored lips. But it was not her face that held attention for long.

'Am I not delicious!' she exclaimed.

The gown she 'wore' – for Chane did not care to speculate how it stayed on – was charcoal velvet trimmed in scarlet lace, the whole of it fitted smoothly to her ample form. The skirt dropped from her hips to the floor in wrapped layers hanging loosely around her legs. Strapless, the bodice rose in two points to just below her collarbone on either side of her throat, and its center split down to her sternum, passing between her breasts. As she descended the last step with an extended leg, the skirt's folds rolled apart like an ebbing black tide to expose a slender death-white ankle and calf.

With an obvious undulation of her torso, she stepped up to Toret, draping her arms across his shoulders.

'Well, tell me how much you love my new dress,' she said.

'You . . .' Toret answered with a swallow, 'are not going out in that.'

For a moment, Chane was stunned. Could it be that his slow-witted master understood that she looked like a trolling prostitute?

Sapphire's expression altered to a glower.

'You don't appreciate anything I do for you,' she snapped at him. 'I've been stuck in this place all day and all evening, while you wander about just so Chane can get his smelly little its and bits for . . . whatever. I'm bored . . . bored! What good is a new dress if no one appreciates it?'

'I'm not letting you out like that,' Toret repeated. 'There's a limit to how much attention we can risk. Now go change into something less . . . obvious.'

In place of jealousy's ire, Toret now spoke sensibly – too sensibly, and Chane began to wonder. Since the night Toret had received the note, he had become wary and agitated. Perhaps someone already had taken notice of them, and that was why Toret wanted to move quickly ahead with tonight's task.

Sapphire spun about and headed upstairs. At the first landing, she cast a sullen glare over her shoulder before continuing upward.

Chane kept silent as Toret ran a hand over his face, for anything he might say on the matter would simply make him the alternative outlet for his master's frustration. It was more useful to let Toret seethe.

A flutter of wings passed through Chane's consciousness, casting a false impression of shadow across his vision. He stepped through the parlor and straight to the front window.

'What is it?' Toret asked, following him.

'Tihko,' Chane replied.

Toret's voice became urgent. 'Has it found something?'

'In a moment, we will know.'

Pulling aside the curtain, Chane flipped the latch and the two halves of the window opened inward like the doors of a portal. He opened the outer shutters as well and, right before him, a large black raven landed upon the windowsill.

Shifting from foot to foot, flexing its wings, it tilted its head. Chane reached out the back of his hand, and the raven hopped onto his wrist.

'What did it see?' Toret asked.

'One moment, master, if you please.' Chane turned his full attention upon the bird.

Its name meant 'silence.' With Tihko close, Chane felt tingling warmth from the small brass urn hanging upon its chain beneath his shirt. He closed his eyes, blotting out all awareness as he cleared his thoughts. Tihko's return signified that his familiar had accomplished something of the task given to it.

The bird's feet tightened on Chane's wrist.

Chane felt the air rush around him, and in the dark of his closed eyes, a slowly moving vision came into sight. He forced Tihko's small mind to focus until a glimmer in the shadows of its memory began to appear.

Seeing through Tihko's eyes was still novel, though a bird's memory was not particularly organized or clear. Bela always looked so small from above. Soaring over the night-shrouded rooftops, Chane watched the empty roads and streets through Tihko's vision. There were few people about, and even so, he looked down from a great height that rendered them as little more than isolated spots of color and movement among the pools of light from street lanterns.

Recognition . . .

The city lunged upward toward Chane and his stomach lurched.

He floated in the soft breeze at twice the height of the tallest building. In his mind, Chane saw the central castle walls upslope and to his left. It was enough for him to know he glided over a lower-southside merchant district inside the middle ring wall.

From above, he saw pale hair, too pale for that of most humans. Chane's field of vision passed above the figure striding down the street. There was a golden tint to the figure's skin, and it was male. The man lifted his hands and began tying something around his head that hid his hair from view.

The vision lurched, and Chane's view pointed briefly toward the starlit night sky before leveling off again into the northern distance of the city. This was all Tihko had seen and why the bird had returned.

Chane opened his eyes, and Tihko shifted fitfully on his arm.

'Well?' Toret asked. 'Did it find anything or not?'

'Perhaps,' Chane said quietly. 'It may be the half-elf, or perhaps another full-blood. Their kind are scarce in the land, but there is an elven ship moored on the harbor's far side. Perhaps this one came with it. Nothing is certain, other than that it was a male with elven blood.'

'Where was he?' Toret insisted. 'What was he wearing? What was he doing?'

Chane shrugged. 'In the lower-southside merchant district. The man was walking down a main street. I did not see where he came from or was going, or what he was wearing. He tied something around his head, perhaps a scarf, and that was all Tihko saw.'

Chane watched Toret walk aimlessly about the room, the brow of his slightly wide head furrowed. He suddenly stopped and passed one hand lightly over the side of his chest as if feeling for something.

'It has to be,' Toret muttered. 'That damn half-breed . . . but how did they know I was here?'

'How did who know?' Chane asked.

For a moment, Toret seemed not to hear, and then he looked up at Chane.

'I'll explain,' Toret answered. 'But right now, get that bird back out there before dawn, and have it find where that half-blood is sleeping.'

Chane opened the window again and settled Tihko on the ledge. The bird cocked its head, watching him with one eye. Chane focused his thoughts into its mind, reinforcing the image of the white-haired man and urging the bird out again to find and, this time, watch until dawn drew near.

Tihko lifted from the ledge in a black flutter of feathers. Chane barely resecured the window when the clop of pouting footsteps came from the parlor's archway.

'Well, I'm changed,' Sapphire exclaimed. 'Now will you take me out of here?'

She now wore lavender silk of a plainer cut, and though the bodice was not cleaved quite as severely as before, there was still an ample display of elevated flesh. Toret hesitated as if he could not tell whether the change was an improvement.

'That's better,' he finally announced. 'But you'll have to wait. Chane and I have work to do, and neither of us can escort you right now.'

Sapphire's mouth dropped open. Before she could screech another word, Chane cut in.

'Perhaps if I acquire a coach,' he suggested, 'to take her directly to a chosen place, Mistress Sapphire could take her ease.' Chane turned a firm glance toward Sapphire. 'Provided she does not leave the establishment until we join her later.'

Toret appeared about to disagree.

'We must focus on the task at hand,' Chane interjected. 'And the mistress cannot assist us.'

He raised one eyebrow with intent, hoping his master had enough wits to take the hint.

Toret looked confused for a moment and then hesitantly nodded. 'Yes, I suppose that's all right.'

Sapphire lunged across the room to drape herself around Toret, but she cast Chane a coy glance.

'The Rowanwood. I want to go to the Rowanwood,' she said as she bit gently on Toret's ear, though her gaze never left Chane.

Chane returned a curt bow of his head. One dull wit at a time was enough to deal with.

As Toret sat upon the cellar's dirt floor holding the palm-sized brass urn Chane had placed in his hands, a constant, subtle shiver ran through his small frame. It wasn't the cold, nor the large gray wolf that lay muzzled, bound, and chained to the floor in front of him, nor even the impending spell, ritual, or whatever Chane would perform upon him and the animal. Clinging to his own new existence made him quake.

Somewhere in the city were the half-breed and that pasty-skinned bitch of a dhampir.

He was certain of this, regardless that Chane's familiar hadn't gotten a clear look at the white-haired man. But what could have possibly led them to Bela to hunt him down? He'd been careful, though Sapphire was sometimes hard to restrain. She was still young in this afterlife and would learn in time. He was sure of it. And Chane was far too exacting and elitist to have done anything to attract attention. Now the hunter and her companion had come to track him down and send him into dust and ashes with Teesha and Rashed.

He wouldn't run again, as he had from Miiska. He had too much to lose. It'd been over two moons since his last fight with the half-elf, and still he felt the lingering bite of a broken stiletto blade cutting away at his insides.

One good turn for another.

Toret remembered the sharp thrust of thin metal at both his sides, as the half-blood's blades jammed up into his chest cavity. He felt and heard the snap of his own ribs, as both weapons were wrenched downward and the right one broke off inside his body.

'One good turn for another,' Toret whispered.

'What was that?' Chane asked. He was grinding something with a mortar and pestle.

'Nothing,' Toret answered. 'Let's finish this. We have more preparations to make.'

After Sapphire's departure, Toret had explained to him the nature of these people for which the raven now searched. Chane listened carefully to every word. Toret tried to impress upon him the dhampir's strength, the dog's savage nature, and the cunning of this half-blood with his hidden blades.

The cellar was as wide and almost as long as the house above it. To one side were stone steps leading up, and the opposite supported the weapons rack for training. Beside this, they'd removed masonry and excavated a passage directly into the city's sewers. At the cellar's back wall behind him was the door to Chane's private room. Toret's tall servant preferred this lower, dark and dank quarters to either of the free rooms on the second floor.

Toret had little interest or even liking for the magical arts, though Chane's skills proved useful. He'd seen a few thaumaturges in his time, from an eclectic hedge mage to a blithering old alchemist still chasing after the secret for creating gold. Conjury, however, was a different matter. He knew nothing of it.

'Time to begin,' Chane said, and he crouched before

Toret with a bone-handled silver dagger in his hand.

Toret looked down at the tiny brass urn clutched in his hands. 'What do I do?'

'Exactly what I tell you,' Chane answered. He turned toward the wolf, dropping to one knee. 'Nothing more or less.'

He grabbed the scruff of the wolf's neck. The animal jerked and thrashed, snarling through the leather thongs binding its muzzle. Chane thrust the dagger point into the furred skin clenched in his hand and withdrew the tip slowly. He held the blade flat and level, careful not to spill the blood pooled on its tip, and turned back to Toret.

'Give me your wrist,' he ordered.

Toret held out one arm. Without tilting the blade, Chane drew the tip's edge along Toret's wrist, cutting into the skin. Black fluid seeped from the shallow wound to touch the red already on the blade. As the fluids mingled, Chane tilted the tip slightly so the mixture seeped partially back into the cut. Toret felt the tiniest tingle of life creeping up his arm.

'With the living, this would be enough for the binding ritual,' Chane said. 'But our existence would merely consume the animal's spirit instead of holding the part of it I will conjure. That is why we must use the urn as container and conduit. Lose the urn, and you will lose the familiar.'

He leveled the blade again, lifting it, and then dipped its point into the mouth of Toret's tiny urn. The mixed fluids dripped from the blade into the vessel.

Chane stepped back to his crate table and picked up the lit candle there. He carried it to Toret and held it over the urn to let wax drip until it welled to the vessel's top. As he replaced the candle, he retrieved the pestle he'd been working with and a narrow-necked bottle of glass too dark to see through.

With the silver blade, Chane cut a double-bordered triangle in the dirt floor around Toret. Between its borders he carved tangled strings of symbols and characters, which he filled with a viscous, olive green fluid poured from the bottle. The liquid soaked in, making the marks swell into raised, glistening ebony lines. He stepped back and cut a wide double circle and more markings in the floor around himself and the wolf, and dusted them with the powder mixed in the pestle.

Chane picked up the candle and settled cross-legged on the floor with the wolf between himself and Toret.

'Do not move from the space marked around you,' he said, and stretched out his arms, resting them upon his knees with palms up. His gaze focused upon Toret's eyes.

Toret remained still. He felt his own body rigid with the exertion not to move. Chane's eyes were still upon him, unblinking, as Toret saw the barest movement of Chane's lips in a silent but continuous chant.

Toret began to ache inside, as if half the night had passed, until the tall undead's eyelids drooped closed.

The wolf began to struggle.

The animal thrashed, chains rattling as it growled. It wrestled as if to escape some torment beneath its own skin. Saliva leaked through its muzzle onto the floor as its head rolled sideways.

Chane's hands slapped together, enveloping and smothering the candle's wick, and the sound hammered through Toret's bones. He clenched the urn.

Its metal burned hot, but Toret's attention was now on . . . the wolf's open eyes staring back at him . . . his own open eyes staring back . . .

The room flickered before him. He saw both ends of it at the same time. He felt the still air around him, and the press of chains wrapped tightly across his body. He opened his mouth freely, but felt the press and smell of wet leather binding his jaws.

'It is done,' Chane stated.

Toret looked down at the wolf. Its eyes looked back at him, and his vision began to spin and flicker. He looked at the wolf and through its eyes – at himself. His head throbbed. Nausea overwhelmed him, until he collapsed.

Prone upon the floor, he found himself looking up into Chane's wry, smiling face.

'Never watch yourself watching your familiar through its eyes,' he said. 'Contact of gaze in such a state is most disorienting. It is the first lesson we all learn the hard way.'

Toret sat up and looked for the urn. Chane handed it to him, and he hung it around his neck. The wax was dried and sealed solid within it.

'Do not lose the urn,' Chane admonished, 'or you lose control of the familiar. And if the urn is out of your possession for too long, the familiar may break free permanently. Also be aware that the death of the familiar can be dangerous to its master.'

Nodding in comprehension, Toret climbed to his feet.

The wolf was already unbound and stood shifting upon its paws as if uncertain of its own actions. Toret tried a brief attempt to will it to sit, but nothing happened. Chane seemed to guess what he was attempting.

'Exerting control comes with time and practice,' he explained. 'Think of it more as a suggestion rather than a command, and remember the sensation of being inside the creature's awareness yet not linked to its senses. Do not overcontrol a familiar, or its resistance will grow, making it more, rather than less, difficult to deal with over time.'

'Enough for now,' Toret said. 'We have other servants to acquire.'

'Not yet; you are already taxed from the bonding. You need to feed.'

'No,' Toret answered. He needed to feed, but he must continue to fast for the moment to come. 'I must be able to absorb a life quickly enough to drag my victim beyond death.'

'As you wish.' Chane collected his equipment from the makeshift table. 'Then perhaps we should go to join your lady.'

He headed toward the door to his chamber with his belongings in hand.

Toret slowly placed a hand on the wolf's head, the first of his new minions yet to come. The animal growled low in its throat but did not resist. When Toret found the half-blood and his white-skinned dhampir, they wouldn't believe what they faced. The final days in Miiska would be a tavern brawl by comparison.

8

Leesil wasn't easily impressed by grandeur, but as he stepped into the Rowanwood's wide entryway, he slowed his pace.

Large oil paintings hung on white walls, and all archways, windows, railings, and other fixtures were made of aged and polished wood suitable to the place's name. Carpets depicted patterns of ivy and forest scenes. Men and women in rich dress floated about. To the left was a dining chamber, and to his right was an elaborate gaming room, with tables for cards, dice, a fortune's wheel, and some oddity concerned with sliding marked tiles around a grid of squares. Ahead was a wide hallway of forest-green carpet that flowed up a staircase. Leesil imagined sumptuous rooms above that he could likely never afford.

Among the patrons were occasional servers and a few tall and solidly built men of moderate but clean dress. The latter moved about the room or stood near archways watching the rooms. They wore no uniforms and carried no visible weapons, but each was similarly dressed in white shirts and colored vestments of fine fabrics.

Leesil felt painfully underdressed and yet again out of place. Before the nearest guard turned around, he slipped into the gaming room.

A few patrons cast him curious or disapproving glances, but most were preoccupied with their pursuits. He counted seven at the faro table, and sounds of ecstasy and despair carried to his ears. Most of the players were middle-aged elites, and odds at faro favored the house too much for the few coins that he carried.

The scent of pipe smoke drifted to his nostrils, and he turned to see a game of Two Kings at a table near the short bar at the room's front. A handsome woman in her mid-forties caught his eye and smiled. He smiled back. There was no need to be impolite. Leesil approached the table, and her expression grew more welcoming.

Her auburn hair was piled up in elaborate coils, and she wore a rich, mute forest-green gown that made her appear part of the establishment's own décor. The dress was sashed about her torso with a long olive scarf. Something about the gown puzzled Leesil. It had a high collar, rather than the open-topped bodices most of the women wore.

'Are you searching for a game, sir?' she asked.

'If you have space at your table, it would be my honor,' he answered.

The other players were mostly well-to-dos and old wealth. The dealer was an ashen-faced man wearing a badly fitted wig, who seemed appalled by the woman's suggestion.

'My dear madam,' he sputtered.

Leesil knew he'd stepped too far across some social barrier and was about to be escorted briskly into the street. After Lanjov, the council, and the other nose-in-the-air nobles over the last few days, he'd had quite enough snobbery for one lifetime.

A younger gentleman to the woman's right appeared embarrassed by the dealer's manner. He reached out and pulled over an empty chair from another table. But there were scowls, and a couple of worried glances from other players as Leesil settled cautiously into the offered seat.

'I am Madame Lenska,' the woman said. 'My husband and I are in Bela on trade.'

'What trade would that be?' Leesil asked.

Madame Lenska laughed, whispering in a conspirator's tone, 'Snails.'

The young gentleman to her side blinked in surprise. 'Snails?'

'Yes,' she went on. 'It sounds appalling, but the demand for this delicacy is almost insatiable. We've been settling contracts with the better establishments.' She leaned toward Leesil. 'Personally, I can't stand the disgusting little things.'

Leesil chatted politely while the cards were dealt. Two Kings was a relatively simple game. Though the odds favored the house, as always, the stakes tended to be low. Winning meant coming as close to twenty points as possible without going over, and anyone dealt two kings in the first round won automatically. With a queen of spades and nine of diamonds on the first pass, Leesil decided to stay the hand and bet everything in his pocket – which amounted to three copper pennies. He won, and the small pile of coins grew.

Several men looked at him in displeasure, but Madame Lenska laughed again.

'I've heard beginners are fortunate company, and I'm feeling generous toward the lucky. Would you like a goblet of wine? The burgundy from southern Droevinka is quite excellent.'

Leesil's attention wavered. How long since he'd tasted it? He'd sworn to himself, never again, but the image of Magiere storming up the staircase rose in his mind. She thought him nothing more than a gambling drunk, and a 'second-rate' one at that.

Well, why not have just one goblet? He could live up to her low expectations, and enjoy himself at that.

'Thank you,' he replied. 'You are most kind.'

Madame Lenska snapped her fingers, murmured to a

serving girl, and moments later, a large pewter goblet brimming with burgundy was placed beside Leesil.

He forgot to watch the dealer while taking a long, slow sip, and the wine slipped dry and sweet down his throat. He made small bets, lost two hands and won four, and realized his goblet was empty. Studying his amassed coins, he saw there was enough to purchase one refill and still continue playing. He signaled to the serving girl.

The wine was strong and made him light-headed, but he wasn't drunk. He knew well enough when 'drunk' was approaching, and it was a long way off. He made a larger bet on a new hand.

As he absently stacked his coins, one toppled and rolled off to the floor, and he leaned down to retrieve it. Under the table, Madame Lenska's legs were crossed, exposing a bare ankle and a touch of calf, and he froze. Her boots were weatherworn, and a king of diamonds peeked from the top of one.

Leesil sat up slowly, fingering his cards with a sidelong glance at the woman.

Madame Lenska's gown was very traditional. Too much so, now that he thought about it, worn only by women from old houses he remembered from his days in the Warlands in service to Lord Dartmouth. The dress was in a fine state but unlikely to be worn by a lady out for a little leisure. He suddenly realized why she'd been so inviting to him.

If the players and dealer were watching an under-dressed lowborn, no one would pay attention to her as she slipped in a card or two. She'd even bought him a drink to keep him at the table.

At the draw of the cards, the dealer exceeded twenty, and Leesil won again.

The house should win Two Kings at least two thirds

of the time. If someone became suspicious, who would they point to first – an old-world lady or a half-blood outside his place?

Leesil stood and gathered his coins. 'Well, I'm off to supper.'

Several gentlemen looked openly relieved, and the one who'd offered him a chair gave a polite nod of farewell. Madame Lenska frowned.

'So soon? But you've only just started. Let me buy you another goblet.'

The server walked over with the wine he'd ordered, and he quickly paid for it himself.

'You're most kind,' he said for the second time. 'But I've won a few coins and need to refresh before continuing.'

With a slight bow, Leesil left the room carrying his goblet.

An entryway guard gave him an appraising look but no more. Entering the dining chamber, Leesil watched lavish trays of seafood and roasted birds sweep by in the servers' hands, and he realized even his winnings might not cover the price of a meal. Several polished stools by the room's bar were empty, so he perched to watch the people as he sipped his wine.

Then she walked in.

Leesil was certainly light-headed now, but his vision was still clear, and the flash of lavender silk burst through the archway without warning. He spared little attention for rich, useless women, and only Magiere filled his heart, but he couldn't help staring.

The low-cut neckline exposed mounds of creamy, pale bosom pushing up from a tight bodice. Ringlets of perfectly curled hair hung across her shoulders and back, and her neck and fingers shimmered in jewels. Like the game room, she was an infectious sight. With eagerness in her eyes, she looked about. Then she noticed his attention and smiled.

Leesil grew mildly uncomfortable. He returned a polite smile and spun around to face the bar. As light steps approached from behind, she floated up beside him.

'Have we met before, sir?' she said. Her gazed moved almost hungrily over his face. 'You look very familiar to me.'

He raised one eyebrow. 'I don't think so. I believe I would remember you, miss.'

'Was that a compliment?' She tilted her head slightly. 'May I join you? I'm without an escort at the moment and would be so much more at ease in good company.'

His guarded surprise increased but so did his reluctance. He didn't wish to encourage her. Neither did he wish to be rude and attract further attention.

'Please,' he said finally, and gestured to the stool on his far side.

'Wouldn't this be more splendid?' She raised one hand toward an empty table nearby with a coy drop of her lashes.

As Leesil stood up, he noticed her eyes resting on his half-open shirt, across his collarbone and chest. Again, he wondered how to politely escape the situation as they settled at the table.

'I'm Sapphire,' she said, with a touch of fingertips to her throat.

'Leesil,' he replied.

'Are you just visiting Bela?' she asked.

'Yes, on business,' he answered shortly. After a moment's silence, he cleared his throat. 'And you?'

'Oh, no. I have a lovely three-story home in the city. For anyone interested in real society, I think Bela is the only place to live.'

He nodded politely.

'Your eyes – so unusual,' she said. 'Where are you from?'

'I don't know.' He hesitated, then added, 'My mother was elven.'

'An elf?' she replied with interest. 'Ah, but I think your father was human, yes? You're half-elven?'

'Yes,' he answered flatly. 'I'm a half-blood.'

'Oh, I didn't mean that. It's just . . . I've heard elves live a very long time. That their life force is much stronger than humans. Is that true?'

For the first time, he smiled. 'Where'd you hear such a thing?'

She laughed, but it was forced, as if she were embarrassed by her own bluntness. 'If all half-elves look like you, I should be glad to meet more of them.'

The second those words left her mouth, Leesil tensed in his chair.

'Well, thank you,' he said. 'But if you're a wealthy man's daughter or wife looking for a unique diversion, I don't think I'm your man.'

He stood up, took his goblet, walked toward the game room, and didn't bother looking back to see her expression.

The game room was hectic, but it didn't take long to find a seat at an empty table. He settled to sip his wine and watch the faro game.

Another flash of lavender caught his eye. Sapphire had followed him.

He began to stand, but she stopped him with a delicate hand on his shoulder. Before he could blink, she pressed him back into his chair and settled sleekly into his lap.

'I just wanted to know you better,' Sapphire said. Looking down at him, she made a show of stretching her torso upright as she brushed her hair back.

Now it was his turn to stare at her – or whatever ample features hung right before his eyes.

Magiere sat on the bed's edge, ignoring the bowl of mutton stew on the bedside table. Chap shoved his nose into her hand, and she petted his head a few times, but her thoughts were elsewhere.

'Was I too hard on him?' she said.

Chap sat down with a low whine, eyes intent.

'Just when I think he's improving, he gets drunk and loses our money, and then he's too cowardly to admit it.' Throwing up her hands in disgust, she looked at Chap, wishing he could speak. 'You make more sense than he does.'

Chap trotted to the door, scratched at it, and looked back at her.

'You have to go out . . . now?'

He woofed once, tail swishing.

'Fine,' she muttered. 'It's not like I have anything better to do.'

Taking Chap out to do his after-meal business was now Magiere's high point for the day. It wasn't enough that they'd gotten nowhere with their search. Now Leesil was playing some idiotic gallant, offering up his . . . blood . . . as if she'd ever again let that happen. What was the fool thinking? Out of habit more than need, she snatched up her falchion, preparing to strap it on as she opened the door. Before she could finish, Chap bolted out and down the stairs.

'Chap, stop,' she shouted, rushing after the hound, but he quickly left her behind.

Loud exclamations came from below in the common room, followed by a raucous clatter and a string of curses in a high-pitched voice.

When Magiere descended, she looked about for the dog. The common room was empty, except for one old man still smoking by the front door, who now stared wide-eyed toward the bar. She followed the gaze, noticed the curtained doorway behind the bar that most likely led to the kitchen, and her eyes narrowed.

'Chap, you glutton!'

She headed for the kitchen, intending to chase the hound down, but then slid to a stop.

Sticking out along the floor from the bar's end was a small booted foot with an overturned tankard stuck on the toe. Magiere peeked around the corner.

There sat – or rather sprawled – young Vàtz, an over-turned bowl in his lap and a pile of scraps, garbage, and leavings all over him and the floor. He looked up at Magiere with an egg-boiling heat in his little face.

'Oh, Vàtz . . . no,' she said. 'I'll get him out of the kitchen. And I promise, when I'm done with that mongrel, this will never happen again.'

She was about to step over him when he growled, 'No!'

Vàtz looked down at the mess of himself and back up to Magiere. Mouth open, he heaved a couple of exas-perated gasps in place of whatever words he couldn't get out, and then stabbed a finger toward the inn's front door.

Magiere frowned and then cringed. Vàtz must have been on his way out with the garbage when Chap had bolted through.

'I see,' she said, reaching down to help the boy up. 'He . . . he must have really needed out.'

Vàtz swatted her hands aside, letting out an incom-prehensible series of grunts and exclamations, and then violently waved her off toward the door.

'Yes, well, again, I'm sorry about this,' Magiere

stammered, and twisted about, muttering under her breath, 'Chap, you're going to be pig's slop when I'm done with you.'

Strapping on her falchion, Magiere opened the door and stepped outside.

There sat Chap in the middle of the street, staring at her, wide-eyed and ears perked.

'You!' Magiere snapped, lunging at the hound to snatch him by the scruff.

Chap darted away up the street, turned about, and sat down to look at her again. Magiere glared at him, dumbfounded.

'The alley – that way!' She pointed around the side of the inn. 'Now get. And you'd better hope I don't leave you out all night.'

Chap's tail slowly swept the cobblestones. He barked twice at her, wheeled about for two more hops up the street, and sat to stare at her again.

'What is wrong with you?' It took Magiere a puzzled moment to realize what the hound was up to. 'No! No Leesil. Now get.'

She pointed toward the alley again. Chap was immediately up on all fours, barking continuously, hopping about and turning circles.

'Quiet. Stop that.' She took two steps toward him, but Chap again spun farther up the road. 'I'm not going after your sot of a master. Now quiet.' With that she threw up her hands in disgust and turned to go back inside. 'You can stay out here the rest of the night.'

When she reached for the door's latch, her fingertips barely touched it as a strange tingle ran up her spine.

Leesil? She held an image of him in mind, seated at his faro table, watching her behind the Sea Lion's bar as if she weren't aware of him.

Magiere looked back over her shoulder, as if expecting to see him. There was no one there but Chap.

Had she been too hard on Leesil? He was an irresponsible dolt, and had no idea what he was really saying this evening. But was it asking too much to let him have his way just a little? It hadn't been that long since they'd left the game, and, in his own way, he was doing his best – wasn't he? It hadn't been his idea to quit and settle, and she certainly hadn't given him much choice.

Magiere's hand hung near the door latch. She looked back at Chap waiting in the street.

'Stay,' she said, and pushed the door open.

Inside, Milous was helping Vàtz clean up. He gave her a disgusted glower.

'Did my partner tell you where he was going?' Magiere asked.

'He wanted someplace special,' the stout innkeeper answered. 'So I told him to go to the Rowanwood. Any coachman in the city can take you there.'

Magiere sighed. Leave it to Leesil to choose someplace they couldn't afford.

'Thank you,' she said, and stepped back out.

Chap now sat so close behind it startled Magiere.

'I told you to stay.' She stepped into the street with the hound pacing beside her. 'You get more like your master every day. I'd better find him, before he cheats his way into a cell at Chetnik's barracks.'

She walked up the street until spotting a passing coach. Hailing it, she gave the coachman her destination while Chap climbed in and stretched across one of the seats. The ride wasn't long, and soon the coach came to a halt as the driver called out 'The Rowanwood!' Magiere paid him and looked up with mounting apprehension at the elegant inn.

Richly dressed patrons walked in and out, and here she stood in breeches, high boots, and a leather vest. She decided to just go in, pull Leesil out – and, maybe, see if he wanted go someplace a little more suitable.

'Come on,' she said to Chap. 'But I don't think they'll want a dog in this place.'

A woman in a cream lace gown looked at them in shock as they walked through the front doors. A few other heads turned as well. Magiere began doubting her decision and wondered if she shouldn't quickly leave. A tall man approached her, wide shoulders filling up his white shirt and embroidered vestment.

'May I help you?'

'I'm searching for a friend,' she explained. 'Soon as I find him, we'll be on our way.'

The guard nodded politely. 'You'll need to leave your sword with me. Food is served in the chamber to the left. Gaming is on the right. Rooms are also available, and you can ask any of the staff to assist you.'

Magiere felt her stomach turn hollow.

'You have a gaming room?'

'Yes, miss,' the house guard replied. 'Your sword?'

A faro table was one thing, but a whole room of chance? The thought of Leesil in there was too much for her. She unstrapped her blade and handed it to the guard, and suddenly Chap growled.

'We try to be accommodating,' the guard added sternly. 'But you will keep your animal under control or leave immediately.'

Chap inched toward the archway to the game room. A low rumble began in his throat and slowly grew to an eerie high-pitched whine. Several nearby patrons stepped away in alarm. It was a familiar sound, and Magiere's attention fixed on the archway.

She looked down to her chest. The topaz amulet glowed brightly.

'You've got bigger problems than the dog,' she said, and turned to Chap. 'Go!'

Chap lunged into the archway as Magiere followed. She scanned the room for Leesil but couldn't find him, and a bright spot of color grabbed her eye – the back of a shapely woman in a lavender silk gown sitting in a man's lap. Dark-blond ringlets fell down past her shoulders.

Chap let out a series of savage, snapping barks that startled even Magiere.

And the room burst into turmoil.

The nearest patrons rushed, lunged, stumbled, and fell over one another and their chairs while trying to get away from the animal. A dice table overturned. Two men in vestments rushed forward to help patrons, all the while keeping their attention on Magiere and Chap. At the commotion, the blond-haired woman looked back, shifting in the man's lap and exposing him to view.

Leesil? Magiere mouthed, but no sound came out.

He sat alone, except for the woman he held, with a stack of coins on the table next to a large pewter goblet.

Chap's attention was fixed directly on Leesil's companion.

Magiere snatched the edge of a table in her way and jerked it over and aside. Leesil looked at the woman atop him with a strangely baffled and annoyed expression, and then he caught sight of Magiere.

He took a deep breath, amber eyes widening, and his tan complexion appeared to pale.

As Sapphire nestled onto his lap, Leesil had no idea how to respond. The rustling silk and the plump mounds of her breasts filling his view put him at a momentary loss. Blinking, he looked up at her with what he hoped was adequate annoyance. He grabbed her upper arms and was about to hoist her off when he noticed her eyes. He hadn't looked at them closely before.

They were bright blue, her pale face framed by long curls of dark-blond hair. There was something familiar about her, as if he'd seen her once before. Then came a strange, unnatural howl more familiar than the woman's face, and people began shouting.

Patrons clamored and shoved their way toward the room's back. Tables, chairs, and bodies toppled one over the other. Two house guards waded in, trying to disentangle bodies from furniture. But everyone's attention was fixed toward the bestial sounds coming from the archway. His uninvited companion turned in his lap as well, opening his view.

There stood an enraged Chap.

And Magiere.

He was in a gaming room. He was drinking. He had a silk-clad blond in his lap with her chest in his face. Magiere's infuriated expression sent a numbing chill through Leesil that sank through to the seat of his breeches.

There wasn't anything that could save him from Magiere long enough to explain all of this.

Chap snarled, inching into the room, and Leesil tensed in alarm. The reasons for Magiere's ire were plain enough, but what had gotten into Chap?

Magiere looked at Sapphire, and Leesil had a moment's concern over what Magiere might do to the woman. Grabbing a table in her way, Magiere slung it aside, and Leesil winced, trying to figure out how to get both himself and Sapphire out of harm's way until Magiere calmed down. Then he saw the topaz amulet in the room's softer lamplight.

It glowed. His eyes rolled up to Sapphire once again.

Dark-blond ringlets. Bright blue eyes – like gemstones. Pretty and eager. With smooth, pallid skin. Like Magiere's.

Leesil stiffened, a coin's toss between mortified and horrified, and choked back a curse before it could escape. The slim chance of explaining anything to Magiere faded. He'd be lucky if she ever spoke to him again, if he lived through this.

His right hand dropped slowly to his side, and he flicked the sheath strap to slip a stiletto into his hand.

Sapphire's hand clamped around his throat, nails biting into his skin.

'Try that and you're dead,' she hissed without looking at him. Her attention was on Magiere, confusion in her voice as she spoke. 'Hold that dog off, or this one dies!'

Magiere stopped. 'Let him go, or you won't reach the door.'

The two guards in the room stood still and uncertain. Leesil spotted a third poised in the entryway behind Magiere, eyes shifting, as if wondering whom to deal with first. Such a disturbance was probably rare in a place like the Rowanwood, and they clearly had no wish for a patron to be killed inside the establishment. But they also appeared more anxious over Chap than the sight of Sapphire's fingers on his throat.

In one movement, Sapphire slipped out of his lap and spun around, pulling Leesil to his feet with his back toward Magiere and Chap. She retreated toward a side exit used by the staff.

Leesil still believed he could remove her fingers with little damage to himself, but there were too many people inside the game room. She might simply grab someone else. He decided to let her to pull him outside.

Chap raged somewhere behind him, and he wondered what Magiere might do next.

Sapphire pulled him through the side door into a narrow, plain passage and kicked the door shut behind them. Her fingers tightened as she backed hastily toward the hallway's end and another door.

'Now, I'll never be able to come here. And this is my favorite place,' she hissed, pulling him along. 'You might have mentioned you were married, but your kind rarely does on an evening out. Maybe she won't even care if I rip you apart.'

Leesil couldn't believe what he was hearing. Not only was she completely vapid if she thought Magiere was some enraged wife, but her main concern was that she'd not be able to patronize the Rowanwood again. When Magiere caught up to them, this idiot corpse had a few surprises coming. How had such a creature survived on her own?

He still gripped the hilt of a stiletto in his right hand, the blade up his sleeve. Sapphire had been so preoccupied she hadn't told him to drop it. The blade wouldn't kill her, but perhaps he could get free at the right moment.

A young house guard stepped from a side door down the passage, blocking Sapphire's way. He looked uncomfortable, as if he should be asking Leesil to release the woman and not the other way around.

'Miss, please, we can't have this sort of thing here. Let the man go.'

Saphire's head twisted so sharply toward the guard that Leesil was unprepared.

Her free hand shot out.

Nails split the man's throat as her fingers drove deep into his neck and then jerked out again. Dark red liquid coated Sapphire's fingers and ran down the back of her hand. The guard crumpled, choking on blood overflowing his gasping mouth.

Leesil punched upward with his right hand, slashing the stiletto's blade against the underside of Sapphire's wrist. He grabbed her outstretched forearm and spun to his left, twisting her arm.

She lost her grip on his throat and screeched in surprise. As she jerked herself free of him, Leesil slashed downward across the top of her wrist. They stumbled apart, Leesil clutching only a severed sleeve cuff where he'd tried to take her entire hand.

Chap and Magiere burst through the door behind them. Fright replaced the fury on Sapphire's face. Clutching her slashed wrist with her bloodied hand, she fled down the passage toward the end door. Chap shot past and out the door as well. Leesil started after them.

'No!' Magiere yelled. 'Let me.'

He ignored her and shoved the piece of fabric inside his shirt, bolting after Sapphire.

Magiere's anger increased when Leesil ignored her order. She didn't even have her falchion, and all he carried were his stilettos. Fury fed her speed as she ran after him. She felt her eyeteeth elongate as the night around her brightened in her sight. The topaz amulet's light actually felt warm on her chest. Beneath rage, she remained focused – almost aware, almost controlled.

Leesil gained distance ahead of her, and she heard a crack and a snarling yelp echo down the alleyway. Chap must have reached the undead harlot first.

Magiere forced herself to run faster, anxious to reach the dog, and her body obeyed. Leesil reached a corner in the alley and was about to round it, when he suddenly threw himself to the ground in a roll, head over heels.

From around the corner, a wood timber struck down and smashed into the empty space he'd just occupied.

Leesil's roll continued toward the far alley wall. Magiere reached the corner, and the timber rose again. She snatched the protruding end.

Holding the other end was the woman who'd been sitting in Leesil's lap. With a screech of frustration, she jerked the timber, but Magiere held on. Surprise and fear registered in the creature's bright blue eyes.

Leesil came off the far wall, body whirling across the alley floor. Scarf fallen away, his hair was a wild cloud moving across the ground. His right foot hooked the undead's ankle, and his body twisted over with both hands slapping hard against the alley floor. His left leg shot up.

The kick struck the woman's breastbone and ground its way up into her face. Magiere blinked as she felt the wood jerk harder in her hands. The undead arched backward, falling. Magiere toppled forward and threw her weight behind the timber.

The timber's splintered end struck the woman's sternum. A muffled snap of bone sounded from inside her chest as ribs gave way and a dark stain raced through her silk bodice around the wood. She screamed louder than Chap's hunting wail.

The sound pierced Magiere until she felt it inside her head. Heat and hunger answered it to rise up her throat. She shoved hard, and the timber drove through. When it struck the cobblestones beneath the undead, wood splintered in Magiere's grip.

The creature sprawled limp and silent on the alley floor.

Magiere dropped to her knees on top of the corpse, panting and regaining self-control. It came quickly this time, the ache washing from her jaw. She didn't have to slide fingers into her mouth to be certain.

Leesil rolled to his feet and ran to where Chap lay against the alley wall. Magiere got up to follow him. He had a lot to answer for, and there would be no more evasions.

Leesil gingerly touched Chap's legs and head.

'Anything broken?' Magiere panted.

'I don't think so, but he's still dazed. She must have hit him hard.'

Chap groaned – and then growled. Magiere took a deep breath of relief.

This was what they did – always. They would speak of matters at hand and push aside all else. She was sick of it.

'Are you sober?' she asked bluntly.

'Yes, I . . .' He looked at her, amber eyes so sad that he seemed on the verge of pouring out words, but he simply looked away and said, 'I am.'

Anger drained from Magiere. What good would lecturing him do? What good had it ever done? Leesil lived in the moment and did whatever he wanted at the time, never realizing what his own lack of awareness could cost him.

Chap lifted his head with a rumble still in his throat. Magiere stroked him once and then rocked back on her heels.

'I doubt anyone can dismiss this,' she said wryly. 'We have proof enough even for the council.'

They both turned toward the corpse. Leesil got quickly to his feet again.

'What . . . ?'

Magiere stood as well, panic taking hold as she looked both ways down the alley.

The body was gone.

9

Along, wailing cry rang out in the distance, and Toret's fingers dug into the coach seat. The sound brought a flash of memory.

He'd fled through the woods outside of Miiska from the half-blood and the dhampir, with a silvery hound leading their hunt. No other animal ever made such a sound.

Sapphire was out there alone. There couldn't be anyone else the beast hunted.

'Stop the coach!' he yelled at the driver.

The instant his feet touched cobblestone, he bolted, hearing Chane close behind. They wove through the streets faster than harnessed horses pulling a burden and neared the Rowanwood, but the hound's cry seemed to come from several directions.

'Which way?' Toret demanded.

Chane closed his eyes to listen, but the wailing had stopped.

'Chane!' Toret demanded. Helplessness mounted inside him, seeding anger within it.

'I hear nothing. She went to the Rowanwood. We will start from there.'

'You don't know what that dog can do,' Toret said, and reflexively touched the scars on his face as guilt and fear muddled his thoughts. 'She doesn't know what's happening. I didn't even warn her.'

'We will find her,' Chane insisted, 'but we must slow down. Gentlemen do not run through the streets attracting attention. She will try to get out of sight, taking to back roads and alleys.'

'No!' Toret shouted. 'She could get trapped in a dead end, or penned in some narrow way.'

'I did not say it was wise,' Chane answered, reaching out to pull Toret back. 'I said it was what she would do.'

For a moment, Chane sounded so much like Rashed that resentment passed through Toret. Always so calculating and focused, coldly thoughtful. Did Chane feel anything? For all Toret's immortality and cunning, he would never be tall and imposing like Rashed or Chane. But he had Sapphire, who loved and needed him, and now she was hunted.

Toret pressed on, but the drag of Chane's grip reduced him to a hurried walk. Peering into each empty side street and alley, he hastened to the next.

'Wait.' Chane's grip tightened on his shoulder. 'Can you feel her?'

Toret stopped, casting about for any hint of Sapphire's presence. When opened wide, his senses were more powerful than those of most of his kind. And he'd made Sapphire, so he could always feel her presence when she was near.

'Nothing,' Toret answered. 'It's like she isn't . . .' He couldn't bear to finish the thought as he looked to Chane.

His companion scanned about quickly and returned Toret's own puzzled expression. Neither Chane nor Sapphire was developing anything close to the mental abilities Teesha or Rashed had possessed. But Chane had other powers natural to him.

'Get that damn bird of yours,' Toret commanded, 'and find her.'

Chane closed his eyes and stood still as a statue poised upon the street corner.

'Hurry up!' Toret urged.

'Be quiet,' Chane said, only his mouth moving. His eyes snapped open, and he drew his sword.

'Did you find her?'

'Perhaps,' he said, and he headed down the nearest side street at a trot.

Toret followed, so angry now that he wanted blood. He wanted to find the half-elf or the dhampir, or even the dog trying to get his Sapphire – something to take the brunt of his panicked rage. As they passed an open alleyway, he heard sobbing and shuffling footsteps.

'This way!' he shouted, not caring who might hear.

As he bolted down the alley, Chane turned back to catch up. The narrow way was cluttered with refuse, crates, and other odds and ends left behind the shops that the alley served. Toret darted around obstacles or kicked them out of his way.

A shadow wavered to his right. What he saw wrenched a moan from him.

Sapphire struggled along a side alley wall, supporting herself with her hands. One hand was coated in red blood. The right sleeve of her gown was sheared away below the cuff. Her own fluids trickled from a circle around her wrist, and also leaked from her mouth, down her chin and throat, to blacken her bodice and chest.

But the worst of it made him hesitate as she lifted her eyes to him.

A long, splintered timber protruded from the center of her chest. Her expression twisted up in fear and confusion.

Toret rushed forward to grab her as she collapsed. He lowered her to the alley floor, supporting her shoulders.

'Sapphire! Stay with me!' he ordered, his tone vicious with demand. 'Chane!'

Chane already knelt beside him, studying the timber through Sapphire's chest with cold composure. Sapphire mouthed something, but all that came out was a gargled choking.

'Again,' Toret urged. 'Say it again, slowly.' He watched her mouth this time to read the words from her lips.

Can't get it out.

Toret grabbed the timber.

'No,' Chane said, catching his wrist and pulling his hand away. 'She's weak and half-drained.' He paused. 'It's in her heart.'

Renewed panic gripped Toret. 'I won't lose her!'

'She still moves,' Chane whispered in puzzlement. 'A wooden stake through the heart should destroy one of our kind.'

Help me, Sapphire mouthed.

'What do I do?' Toret pleaded.

Toret's dread mounted as Chane remained passively contemplative.

'Tear your wrist open – down to veins,' Chane instructed. 'As I pull the strut out, you must feed her. There is no life in our fluids, but perhaps it will keep her body whole long enough to take her back to the house. Then we must find her blood as quickly as possible.'

Toret hesitated. 'I haven't fed for days. I can't . . . you feed her. I'll pull the timber.'

Chane jerked upright with an expression close to revulsion. Just as quickly, his features smoothed back to calm indifference. He put the edge of his sword to his wrist and sliced deeply, and his own fluids began dripping to the ground. Dropping the sword, he forced the base of his hand into Sapphire's mouth.

'Bite down,' he ordered, and then to Toret, 'Now.'

Toret wrenched the timber out, wincing as it ground

against the bones of Sapphire's rib cage. Her eyes and mouth opened wide as she tried to scream. Chane held fast, forcing his wrist between her teeth, smothering any outcry.

'Quiet, and drink,' Chane ordered.

His words cut through to Sapphire, and she bit down, swallowing mouthfuls. Chane's upper lip trembled once in a snarl, but he neither recoiled nor cried out. Toret felt a strange rush of gratitude and was ashamed of the emotion.

The seepage in Sapphire's chest slowed and stopped. Finally, Chane put his free hand on her forehead and jerked his wrist away with effort.

'More!' she wailed at him.

'No,' Toret said. 'We must get you home. I'll bring you life to feed on.'

Sapphire grabbed Toret's shoulders and snapped at his throat, but he held her down until she calmed and simply lay in his arms, twitching.

Chane tore a strip of silk from the hem of Sapphire's dress and bound up his wrist. He shredded more fabric to wrap her torso.

'I will find us a coach,' he said. 'Once back on the open street, we must get her out of sight quickly.'

Without further comment, he headed down the narrow side alley.

Toret rocked Sapphire gently, understanding for the first time exactly how Rashed had felt and why he refused to run from Miiska.

'It's all right,' he crooned. 'I'll have you home soon.'

He wouldn't wait for the hunter and her minions to find one of them alone again. He would find her first.

'I pierced its heart,' Magiere whispered.

Leesil watched her pace in his room at the Burdock,

her falchion leaning in the corner. He'd waited in the coach with Chap while she'd gone back into the Rowanwood to retrieve it. Sooner or later, they were going to catch hell for what had happened there tonight, but he couldn't imagine it would be any worse than dealing with Magiere at the moment.

'That timber went right through her,' she insisted, clenching her hands as if she still felt the wood in her grip.

'I know,' Leesil said. 'I saw it.'

Chap rested on the bed as Leesil's mind worked over what had happened – and what hadn't happened, it seemed. At the very least, his idiocy at the Rowanwood was put aside. He carefully ran his fingers through Chap's fur, feeling for injuries. His fingertips passed across a swelling on the side of the dog's head. There was no blood, but Chap had been struck down too hard for him to track tonight, so they'd returned to their rooms. On the small table near Magiere's sword rested two burning candles and a tin basin of water they'd procured from the innkeeper.

Leesil pointed to the basin. 'Hand me that.'

Startled from her thoughts, Magiere passed him the basin as she sat down on the bed's far side. Leesil dipped a folded rag in the water to make a cool compress and placed it gently against Chap's head.

'How could that thing have gotten away?' she asked.

Uncertain, Leesil shook his head. 'There are only two possibilities. One, you missed the heart.'

'I didn't.'

'Then . . . it's not the first thing we've tried that turned out to be nothing but superstition.'

'Fine,' Magiere grumbled at him. 'That means we're back to taking heads.'

'Or ashes,' he added.

'Don't get any ideas,' she warned.

An edgy silence passed that left Leesil wondering if it was now time for her to turn on him. She sat quietly, watching him refresh the compress for Chap's head.

'Besides,' she continued, 'ashes won't prove anything to the council. We've nothing to show for tonight. There's no way to track this thing, unless Chap heals fast enough to pick up a trail. I didn't get anything from her for him to smell.'

Leesil hesitated. 'I did.'

Maigere's eyes narrowed as her lips pressed into a flat line, but she didn't look up at him.

'Well, you had more opportunity, didn't you?' Her voice held a cold bite. 'Perhaps this is how we should hunt now. Turn you loose in the nearest brothel with a card table and a goblet of wine, and just wait for the first undead slut to drop into your lap.'

Leesil tried not to flinch and failed. He actually bit his tongue, knowing anything he said now was just fuel for her fire. For that matter, he'd no idea what to say.

He felt as if he'd been unfaithful – but unfaithful to what? Everything he'd done, every gentle ploy he'd tried to get close to her, had failed. She pushed him away again and again. So why feel ashamed? Well, there was the drinking and gambling. But he wasn't drunk, and he hadn't lost, and that left one thing to be ashamed about, and that he hadn't even wanted. He hadn't even thought of such things since settling in Miiska.

He'd thought only of Magiere.

And the worst, most infuriating and confusing part was that of all the things he'd done tonight, the one she fixed upon was that *thing* sitting in his lap.

A deep sigh from Magiere caught Leesil's attention.

When he looked up, she was gazing at his white hair hanging past his shoulders.

'You lost your scarf,' she said. 'We'll have to get you a new one.'

Leesil reached into his pocket and pulled out an entire handful of coins, which he poured onto the bed in front of her.

'Here. I won back most of what I lost on the ship, but I doubt the scarf makes much difference anymore.'

He felt thankful for the change of topic. But when she saw the coins, he realized too late that it was another mistake. He quickly rambled on before she could cut into him.

'A scarf won't hide my eyes or skin. It seems my people are more of an oddity here than I realized.'

Her attention pulled from the coins. 'Your people?'

'You know what I mean.'

'No, I don't,' she answered with an abrupt shake of her head that whipped wisps of black hair about her pale face. 'I didn't forget what you did back in the alley. You didn't learn that in a month of mornings out in the woods.'

Leesil busied himself with Chap again. This wasn't what he'd expected. Now was not the time. But she leaned in toward him across the bed.

'Look at me!' she snapped. 'We're in a bad way, and I don't know what to do next. The only two things I've ever counted on besides myself are you and this dog. You changed when we settled in Miiska, for the better, but now . . . now you're starting to act like the old Leesil from our days on the road – or worse. Drinking, gambling, and—'

'And nothing,' he cut in. 'That wasn't what it looked like.'

'This isn't about that whorish little monster you let dazzle your wits.'

'I wasn't dazzled!'

'I don't want to fight with you – but I will. Now, tell me, what's wrong?'

His jaw tightened. This was going to be bad, and worse for the timing – worse than being caught with an undead trollop in his lap.

'I promise I'll never touch a drop of wine again. I will always be sharp, in control. And I'll stay that way.'

Candlelight flickered upon Magiere's face, and Leesil could see his response wasn't enough. Chap's breathing deepened into a light snore as he rested comfortably between them, and Leesil set the basin out of the way on the floor.

'I need more than promises,' Magiere said.

'What do you mean?' Futile as it was, Leesil still hoped there was a way out of this.

Magiere let out a sigh. 'I don't talk about my past because there's little to tell and even less that I know for certain.' She looked him directly in the eyes. 'But I would tell you anything of it . . . anything you asked, if I knew the answer. So why won't you tell about your life before we met?'

'There's nothing you want to hear, and it doesn't matter anymore.' For all his usual guile, this came out as a blatant evasion, and she ignored it.

'Where did you learn to fight like that? What is that long box of strange tools you carry, and where did it come from? It never mattered before, because you kept it hidden away until two moons ago. It matters now.'

Leesil closed his eyes. If he told her, what would she do? What could she do but walk away and never look back?

'*Anmaglâhk,*' he whispered.

'What's that supposed to mean?'

'It's an elvish word my mother used. I never learned its meaning, but after a while it wasn't hard to guess with the way we lived. She used it rarely for herself. And once for me.'

Magiere settled back to the bed's edge, staring at him.

'She was an assassin,' Leesil said, his voice flat and emotionless. 'So was my father. So was I.'

Wariness – or was it revulsion? – replaced the anger on Magiere's smooth face. She looked briefly about the room, perhaps wondering where his 'tools' might now be hidden, then down to his arms. His cuffs were loose and unbound, and one hilt of a stiletto in its wrist sheath protruded. Leesil slowly pulled his hands back into his lap and closed his sleeves.

'Your mother – an elf – was an assassin.' Her voice was barely a whisper. 'You murdered for money?'

'You know of the Warlands far up north,' he continued. 'Provinces, not even true countries, where rulers hold power by military force. Ever heard of a Lord Darmouth?'

'Yes,' she answered hesitantly.

'My family served him. We were his slaves – his spies and assassins.'

Magiere turned away toward the far wall.

Leesil was afraid now, and few things frightened him anymore. There was little else to do but finish.

'Rulers like Darmouth have enemies, not only outside their borders but within. And if they don't, they still think they do anyway. I was raised to deal with those enemies – proficiently. By the age of five, my parents were already training me. At first it was just a thin dagger I held, wielding it like a sword while pretending to be a warrior. I didn't know we were property to be owned. But in the years after, I wondered about the purpose of the strange things they taught me, until I no longer had to wonder.

When to move silently, unnoticed. How to lie convincingly. Who and what to watch for in the dark. Which places on a body afford the quickest kill.'

Magiere peered back over her shoulder. All Leesil saw was one eye watching him.

'The toolbox,' she said. 'That's what it's for?'

He nodded. 'From my mother. Probably made by her people, though I don't know how or why. I learned to use everything in it, and I was a good slave, for a while. Some days I can still remember every person I've killed.'

'And now you need new tools? You bartered with the smith for them.'

'No, that has nothing to do with my past,' Leesil added, his own voice suddenly harsh. 'I can't keep trying to take vampires with stilettos. I need something else. But I've no time to learn any standard weapon, so I'm having ones made to fit the skills I have.'

Magiere shook her head, holding up a hand to ward off his words.

'Even a slave can think for himself,' she said. 'So why didn't you run before it was too late? Why didn't all of you run?'

Such a simple choice, Leesil thought. If it had only been that simple. And he laughed.

Magiere spun about to glare at him. 'What's so funny?'

'Nothing,' he answered, no smile on his face. 'Absolutely nothing. We were never allowed to work together. There was always at least one – mother, father, or son – who stayed behind under a watchful eye to ensure the job was done, and the one at work came home again.'

He watched her eyes for any hint of understanding. When it didn't come, he simply went on.

'I was forced to betray a kind old teacher falsely accused of treason, and he was hanged. That was when I ran. I lived on the road with Chap, drinking myself to sleep to forget – until I met you, and we began a whole new round of killing.'

'Killing?' Magiere shook her head. 'We've never killed anything together besides undeads.'

Leesil took in her puzzled expression and hated himself even more. But as long as it was all coming out, she might as well face the whole past.

'The peasants?' he asked. 'You're thinking too simply again. How many peasants starved because we took their seed coin? Or died in the stocks from exposure, or were worked to death in indentured service because they couldn't pay their taxes?'

Her head hung low. 'Now at least we try to make up for those years. But what we did wasn't the same as being paid to take a life.'

'You can never make up for it,' he argued. 'It doesn't work that way.'

There was no bitterness in his voice, for this was simply how things were.

'Now we save people,' he continued. 'We do what we can to help. It's a better life, for the most part, than the ones I've lived before.'

Magiere sat there for a long time. Leesil kept quiet as well, waiting.

'It wasn't your life,' she whispered. 'Just the one forced on you by birth.'

As Leesil watched, her gaze became empty and hollow. Her words came from somewhere other than this moment. She shook herself, clenching her eyes briefly as she did.

'Your mother married a human,' she said. 'Do you know how strange that sounds? Elves keep to themselves for the most part, and I've never even heard of one working for a human lord. Not as an assassin, let alone a slave.'

'My parents never talked about that, though a few times I tried to ask. I don't know much beyond what I've told you.'

'So they're still there and . . .' – she stopped and then spit out the words – 'killing for Darmouth. Why didn't they leave as well? They no longer needed to protect you. Or is there something else they stayed for?'

'Magiere . . .' he began, and then dropped his head, frustrated.

She'd never fully understand the world he'd come from. He kept his words quiet and detached.

'Slaves, remember? And always under a watchful eye – hostages. That was the chain Darmouth used to bind my family. You don't think about what you do. You just do it, and stay alive, and keep those who depend on you alive. But I couldn't kill anymore, and I ran.'

This time he was the one to turn away, sitting on the bedside with his head down and eyes closed. For all the lives he'd taken, the last two were the ones he locked away so carefully they'd not even entered his nightmares.

'You did the right thing,' Magiere offered.

'The right thing?' Leesil spit without looking at her. 'They're dead, Magiere! My parents . . . I ran. And so now they're dead.'

That was the end of it. He'd never spoken this to anyone, yet he'd told the one person who should have never known. Where would he go, now that this life with Magiere was at an end?

He sat with eyes closed, not wanting to see her leave. It was better that when he opened them again, she was simply gone.

The sound of tapping metal reached his ears, and he

realized she'd picked up her sword. He listened to her footsteps around the bed as she headed for the door. There came another soft tap of metal on wood, closer.

Fingers slid lightly up his cheeks to comb through his hair until palms settled upon his temples.

Opening his eyes with his head still down, Leesil saw the tin basin resting on the floor at Magiere's feet between her crouched legs. He heard her breath close to his face as her forehead touched his.

'Thank you,' she whispered. 'Thank you for telling me.'

With his wrist bandaged tightly, Chane stepped from a coach into one of the poorer areas of the outer ring. He preferred not to be announced by the clatter of a coach rolling through a district where no one could afford such luxuries. Paying the driver, he walked down the street toward what Domin Tilswith and Wynn referred to as Hovel Row.

Only a short while ago, he'd left the house to find sustenance for the wounded Sapphire. She had related small parts of what happened to her, how a half-elf had out-maneuvered her through sheer speed and ability, and a white-skinned woman had shown more strength than was possible for a mortal. Toret's face had nearly glowed with anxiety.

More questions formed in Chane's mind as Toret ordered him out into the night on this errand of mercy. These two old enemies of Toret's might indeed be the key to Chane's freedom. He decided a brief detour was in order, but he must hurry. If he was gone too long, Toret would not only be infuriated over Sapphire's prolonged suffering but might become suspicious. Still, with Toret's recent erratic behavior, there was no telling when he would have another opportunity.

The hour was late, and Hovel Row had been aptly named. Street gutters smelling of rot and decay, the shabby dwellings pushed against one another. There came an infant's cry of hunger and a man shouting obscenities. A woman's answering shout turned to defeated weeping.

Chane sped on toward his destination.

Wynn had told him of an elf living in the secluded squalor of Hovel Row. Strangely, she had interacted with elves in her homeland and spoke their language fluently. She had heard of one here in Bela, somehow, and was eager to meet the elves of this continent. But upon her visit, she'd met with quiet hostility and hadn't gotten past the front door.

Chane was not aware there were elves anywhere other than the far northeast, past the Warlands over the Venjètzí Rozpàtjè – the Crown Range. He'd heard through his father's friends of how the elves were reclusive to the point of paranoia. Now he had questions concerning them, or at least pertaining to one half-blood. He wanted answers, and he didn't really need to get past a front door.

He never forgot anything, and Wynn had kindly told him where to look. Six streets in, he found the correct abode. It was old, but some of the planking and roof shakes had been replaced or repaired in recent years. The place looked completely sealed up.

He'd asked Wynn why an elf would live in such a place. She grew thoughtful before answering.

'I cannot say, but I had the strange feeling he was waiting or perhaps just watching. For what, I do not know.'

Chane felt oddly calm when remembering her oval face. It had been many nights since she had sat next to him, speculating upon the ancient parchment sent for translation. He glanced at his bandaged wrist, remembering the feel of Sapphire's mouth upon him. If it had been Wynn . . . but the thought that he had given of himself to save Sapphire swelled an angry revulsion amidst his thoughts.

He approached the oak door and knocked hard and let his senses open fully, though the smell of the district instantly assaulted him for it. No one answered, but he hadn't expected an answer right away. He knocked again and kept on knocking.

There was no sound of movement, but he heard the heartbeat approach from within even before a soft but bitter voice called from behind the closed door.

'Go away.'

'I have information,' Chane replied, 'regarding one of your kind newly arrived in the city.'

After a moment, the door cracked.

Chane stared at a loaded crossbow held by a man standing back in the doorway's shadow. He was thin with sharply peaked ears and sand-colored, tangled hair. He wore a long cloak of faded dun-colored fabric that hid the rest of his attire. His tan skin looked unhealthy, as if he ate poorly and had not seen daylight in some time. His long face was triangular, and he was taller and more slender than the man Tihko had seen.

'I am the only one of my people living in this city,' he spit out. 'Now stop pounding on my door and go away.'

'You are mistaken. There is another.'

'Nonsense,' he rebuked, and was about to slam the door.

'If you won't share information, then I will, for there is a half-blood here in the city. Younger, agile, with exceptional fighting skills. Stilettos are his favored weapons, and he travels in the company of a woman warrior and a dog. I have questions. Do you have answers?'

The crossbow did not waver, but Chane saw the barest

widening of his bloodshot amber eyes, and heard his pulse quicken briefly.

'You are mistaken,' the elf said quietly.

The door slammed shut, and Chane heard the metal bolts slide home.

Chane was anxious now. Too much time had passed since he had left to find blood for Sapphire. Toret would be pacing in fury by now, but there was still more to be learned here, and he might not have a chance to come back. He would contrive some story of delay and deal with the consequences later. Turning back down the road and around the nearest corner, he settled into the shadow of a wattle and daub hut to wait and watch.

A short while later, a soft and faint rhythm reached his ears. Footsteps.

Chane carefully surveyed the hovel. The door and all windows were still closed. He focused on the sound until it nearly resounded in his hearing, and then he faced down the street, separating the shadows with his sight.

Something moved quietly along the buildings, and Chane slipped across the street to follow.

The cloaked figure avoided the few dim pools of light from street lanterns, heading out of the city. He was stopped by the guards at the outer gate. Under the gatehouse's bright lanterns, Chane saw the elf's face inside his gray cowl. The elf exchanged brief words with one guard, opening his cloak for inspection, and then moved on his way.

Waiting a moment more, Chane stepped out and followed.

There was actually a mix of men at the gate. In addition to four surcoated Sträzhy-shlyahketné, there were two armed men in plain clothes, likely from the local constabulary.

'And where might you be going at such an early hour, sir?' asked one of the guards.

Chane remained polite, but gave the man a slow and appraising glance that made the guard shift uncomfortably.

'I was visiting the home of some workers of mine and simply stayed too late,' he answered. 'And with the night almost gone, I thought to walk for a while until one of the local inns opened. Too little night left to return to my bed.'

The guard made a cursory appraisal of Chane, glancing back down the street, and nodded.

'Very well, sir,' he said stepping to one side. 'But best keep to the main streets and well-lit ways. A good night to you.'

Chane moved on, staying as close to the buildings as he could, slipping into a side street now and again just long enough to let his quarry stay ahead of him. It was actually easier to trail his target outside the city, as the buildings and huts became sparser, giving way to small fields and groves of trees. The elf moved furtively, finally stepping off the road and heading into the thick woods. Chane followed from tree to tree, watching as the elf wove his way.

The forest grew dense. Chane crept forward, low to the ground, working his way wide to the right of where the elf had passed, but he could not find an alternative path through the brush. Crawling under the lowest branches of a tree, he carefully cleared the earth in front of him so as not to make more noise than necessary.

The elf stood near an old fir rising high into the night. Its lower limbs were sparse and sheared away, exposing its trunk. The elf dug within his cloak and withdrew a simple object. An oblong shape ending in narrow points, it was no longer than the man's palm, light yellow in color, and its surface shimmered, polished smooth.

Placing it against the tree's trunk, the elf flattened one

hand over it to hold it in place, and appeared to whisper to himself, over and over. Then he spoke, and a stream of words in his own tongue came out in a halting pattern.

Chane grew more intent. It appeared the elf now held a kind of conversation with the tree. No, his eyes were turned aside, staring vacantly through the woods.

The elf spoke through the tree – to someone else.

Chane knew a little of the elvish tongue from scant texts he seen over the years but had rarely heard it spoken. He tried to listen carefully, wishing he possessed Wynn's gift for language.

'Bithasij fuile letheach ag'us âg méanna, gye sapâjasij Anmaglâhk colhtaseach!'

The words jumbled in Chane's mind as he tried to pick out what he could recognize. Part of one word, *lethe*, meant 'half' in the masculine form, but half of what? The half-blood perhaps. *Âg méanna* meant 'not of us.' But most curious was one emphatic word – *Anmaglâhk* – which seemed to be a name or title. Perhaps the person to whom the elf spoke? Several phrases slipped by before Chane focused again.

'Triâlhina lhos âg mé. Urkharasej tù aonéc.'

The best Chane could guess was 'not depart plan or purpose' – and an emphatic 'send one more,' but one more of what?

'Leanave faodeach âg â bithéana ahk bith so cúishna. Vorthasej so trúe!'

The stream of words stopped suddenly, and the elf slipped the polished sliver back into his cloak. He turned and headed back the way he came. The last thing that Chane could make out was about someone's parent, a mother perhaps, and taking the life of a 'traitor.'

It seemed there was much more to this half-elf that Toret feared.

Gray streaked the night sky as Chane crept out from under the tree to trot back to the city, slowing briefly as he passed through the gatehouse once again. Instead of traversing Hovel Row, he swung toward the waterfront, reaching the low-end merchant street where a few coaches could be found. He could not arrive home empty-handed.

Urgency was always dangerous, but there was no time for cautious selection. Walking the side streets, he watched for signs of movement in the alleys and listened carefully for heavy breathing. He found a drunken sailor behind a tavern, curled soundly asleep against the building's side. Chane walked purposefully over and struck the man hard enough across the jaw to be sure he would not awaken anytime soon.

He flagged down a coach while supporting the sailor with one arm.

'Too much ale,' he said to the driver. 'I must get my friend home.'

He gave an address two city blocks away from the house. He would walk the rest of the way and not risk the driver seeing his destination. As the carriage wheels clattered away, he rolled one word over in his mind.

Anmaglâhk.

10

Near dawn, Magiere and Leesil still sat on the bed next to Chap's sleeping form. Their talk strayed from past to present and to more comfortable topics like strategy or any possible way to find the nobleman in her vision. In spite of all that happened this night, Magiere wasn't dismayed by Leesil's confession. His obvious guilt and self-revulsion for his earlier life made her want to comfort him, but she didn't know how. One phrase kept ringing in her ears.

Until I met you, and we began a whole new round of killing.

Guilt was an emotion she'd rarely experienced, but in the last few months, enough of it had poured through her for one lifetime. Perhaps this was a cord that bound them together no matter how much she feared accepting a deeper bond.

'How is the swelling?' she asked, watching Chap.

'Better – he's a quick healer,' Leesil answered. He lifted the cold compress to inspect Chap's head. 'A good night's sleep and some breakfast will put him right. Oh, that reminds me.' He pulled the ripped scrap of lavender silk from inside his shirt. 'This won't help find your nobleman, but it may help us find our wayward undead from last night. If the two are somehow connected, so much the better.'

Looking at the silk scrap, Magiere felt a moment's ire return, but she knew it was poorly placed.

'You really didn't know that doxy was an undead?' she asked, trying to keep venom from her voice.

'I didn't even look at her enough to notice she was

somehow familiar,' Leesil answered defensively. 'Not until she dropped in my lap two breaths before you and Chap burst in.'

Magiere felt her face flush. She was about to change the subject, when a knock sounded at the door.

'I don't remember ordering breakfast in bed,' Leesil quipped.

Magiere saw his right wrist tense slightly, ready to slip a stiletto into his palm. Now that she knew where and how he'd learned such things, the movement sent a chill up her spine. He got up, cracked the door, and then opened it all the way.

Standing in the hall was the gray-robed young woman who'd addressed Leesil in the corridor of the council hall. She was small, with a long brown braid hanging forward across her shoulder.

'Excuse me for this early intrusion,' she said. She had a soft, almost guttural accent to her voice that Magiere couldn't place. 'My master sent me to speak with you.'

'Who are you?' Magiere asked.

'I am Wynn Hygeorht, apprentice in the Guild of Sagecraft under Domin Tilswith, my teacher and head of our branch here. We reside in the old guard barracks of the inner ring. The domin was playing Hounds and Foxes with Councilman Lanjov last night when word of the disturbance at the Rowanwood reached them.'

'Well, that was quick,' Leesil mumbled, and he stepped back to allow her in. 'Thought we might at least make it through breakfast before anyone caught up with us. So who brought word? The city guard?'

'Yes,' she answered. Her attention was diverted by Chap's sleeping form. When she saw the water bowl and rag, her expression became instantly concerned. 'Is your dog ill?'

'A thump on the head, but he'll be all right,' Leesil said.

'I might be able to help. We have medicines of many types at the guild.'

She knelt down next to the bed, eyeing Chap curiously, and then put her hand out. Leesil was about to stop her, when Chap opened his eyes, lifted his muzzle, and lapped her fingers once before settling himself again. Wynn took her hand back with a smile.

'He appears well enough,' she said. Her brow wrinkled slightly as her smile faded, and she stood up to face Leesil again. 'The day in the council hall, when I . . . spoke to you . . .'

She appeared embarrassed and briefly dropped her eyes before returning her gaze to Leesil's tan face.

Magiere felt a sudden flare of ire again. How many strange women were going to fawn over Leesil before they got out of this cursed city?

'I was surprised that you do not speak Elvish,' Wynn said. 'One of your parents was of that race, yes?'

'I was never taught,' he answered flatly.

Again Wynn appeared embarrassed, and then confused.

'I see. I was only commenting on how beautiful your dog was and wondering what breed, as I have never seen his like before.'

Leesil merely shrugged. 'My mother gave him to me when I was boy and he was just a pup.'

'You mother, she was your elvish parent?' Wynn asked.

'Yes.' Leesil leaned down and stroked Chap's back. 'He's probably just a mutt of some kind. We mixed-breeds tend to be the smartest.'

Chap rolled his head at Leesil's touch, shifting for comfort on the bed.

'There was this loon of a man in Miiksa,' Leesil added, 'who called him a *majay-hì*.'

Wynn's head tilted. '*Majay-hì?*' she asked, the word smoother and more rolling than Leesil's pronunciation.

'Yes, that sounds about right.'

'Perhaps a colloquial reference or a regional nickname for the breed.' She shook her head in what appeared to be quaint amusement. 'In the Elvish dialect that I know, it might mean something like 'fay hound' or 'hound of the elementals,' though I have never seen his kind before. He seems a very amiable creature.'

'You don't have to hunt with him,' Magiere said under her breath. 'Now, what was Lanjov's reaction to what he heard?'

The barest hint of disapproval surfaced on Wynn's face as she looked at Magiere.

'Councilman Lanjov was quite upset. He seems to think the creature that killed his daughter is to be found among the common folk and cannot understand why you keep plaguing respected members of society.'

Magiere rose and sighed. 'Did he mention dismissing us?'

'I do not recall this,' Wynn answered. 'But my domin was interested in the event. A woman dressed in silk' – she faltered, and swallowed hard – 'speared a house guard through the throat with only her fingers. And your dog was reported as turning savage toward the woman and frightening the patrons. Then all of you pursued her into the back alley.'

Magiere grew more uncertain as to what this young woman wanted.

'Do you believe in undeads?' she asked.

'I've read of such,' Wynn answered politely, 'though only in my homeland's legends. Having heard Councilman Lanjov's story, I looked into what little I could find of this land's folklore, though we have yet to begin setting up a proper library and collecting texts. In my tongue there are fables of the *àtheldéth*, which surprisingly means almost the same as Noble Dead in your language.'

'So you do believe,' Magiere said.

'To study a concept is not same as believing it,' Wynn continued. 'Domin Tilswith considers Lanjov superstitious, but we have learned more since meeting him, and I began searching for what I could learn. The Noble Dead are accounted as the highest forms of the undead. Unlike lesser forms, they retain all memories, consciousness, and self-awareness from their mortal life. Among them are your vampires, high revenants found in our legends, some wraiths, and the like.'

'What about methods for destroying these Noble Dead?' Magiere asked, turning the conversation to her own agenda. 'We know most of the myths and superstitions, such as a wooden stake through the heart, which we now have reason to doubt.'

Wynn shook her head and returned Magiere a dubious but polite scowl.

'Most works on the subject are legends, fables, and stories. Some accounts involve staking the creature in its burial place and beheading it. Perhaps the stake was intended to pin the creature, keeping it from escaping, and that became a further superstition as a way to destroy them. There really is no way to be certain . . . if one believes any of this.'

Magiere fell silent. All their skills in battling undeads had been learned through trial and error, along with the cryptic advice of Welstiel Massing back in Miiska, who seemed obsessed with the Noble Dead. But this young woman appeared to know a bit and was far more open than Welstiel had ever been. Magiere pulled out the stool.

'Please sit. Would you like some tea? The kitchen folk are probably up and about by now.'

Wynn smiled openly and shook her head.

'I cannot stay, but the domin and I are interested in your experiences. In return, we offer the support of the guild's resources, though our materials are scant compared to the main branch in our homeland. I will help translate any document I can.'

'We don't have time for schooling,' Leesil put in. 'And it won't help track . . . unless you can access recent deeds on houses purchased in Bela, those of middle to upper quality.'

'This information should be available,' Wynn answered with hesitation. 'If the local city government keeps such records.'

Leesil smiled. 'Oh, I'm fairly certain this city does.'

'What are you up to now?' Magiere asked.

Leesil settled on the bed next to Chap. 'The woman we chased last night said she had a three-story house. Chetnik's reports of her go back only a few moons. There's a great deal of old money in the city, so buying and selling that kind of dwelling won't be too common.'

Magiere quickly caught up to where Leesil's thoughts had turned.

'We find recent purchases,' she added, 'and pick up a trail or even locate this woman's exact hiding place – if she wasn't lying.' She looked at Wynn. 'Can you help us with this?'

'Yes, but I must speak to my domin first. He is interested in your exploits in Miiska and seeks an exchange of information.'

A thought occurred to Magiere. 'This domin of yours was at Lanjov's last night? Lanjov told us he never has visitors.'

'Oh, Domin Tilswith visits now and again to play Hounds and Foxes with the councilman. But I believe Count Lanjov discourages other visitors.'

Magiere glanced toward Leesil, who now wore an irritated frown.

'What does Domin Tilswith look like?' she asked. 'Is he noble? Does he wear black gloves?'

Wynn laughed. 'No, he dresses as I do. Why do you ask?'

'We believe Chesna knew her killer,' Leesil answered. 'So if no one besides your domin visits, and he doesn't fit the description, then where and how did Chesna meet this man?'

At that, the young sage's oval face grew puzzled.

'Most nobles acquainted with Count Lanjov would be on the council as well. Perhaps his daughter went with him to the hall or to his bank.'

The scope of events was changing, and it did little to ease Magiere's mind. This young scholar was open and unbiased, and appeared to have no hidden agenda. It might pay to keep her around.

'Tell your domin we'd be glad to talk,' Magiere said, and then turned to Leesil. 'We should sleep awhile and then have a visit with Lanjov at his bank.'

Leesil nodded and got up to open the door for Wynn.

Magiere waited for the young sage to leave before discussing anything further with Leesil. She caught Wynn Hygeorht glancing back as the door closed. At first Magiere felt another tinge of ire, thinking the glance was for Leesil, but instead the woman's eyes dropped briefly toward the bed and the sleeping dog.

After too brief a rest, Leesil found their plans changed slightly. A note for Magiere from Captain Chetnik had been left with the innkeeper. It simply read, *I need to speak with you about the incident at the Rowanwood.*

They both decided to put off that meeting as long as possible. Leesil was anxious to check on the progress with his new weapons, but Magiere wanted to stop at the sage's guild to provide Wynn with as much information as possible regarding the type of dwelling to search for. Stone constructions with cellars would be foremost. To Leesil, Magiere seemed a bit too relieved by the young sage's apparent willingness to help. The girl could prove useful, but they knew nothing about these supposed scholars from across the ocean.

He agreed to meet Magiere at Lanjov's bank by noon, and then he headed out for Balgaví's smithy, Chap trotting at his side. As they approached the smith's shop, Chap slipped in ahead toward the scent of burning forges and the noisy clang of metal.

The sudden hiss of steam from the forge room filled Leesil's ears upon entering the outer stall. To his surprise, he found Chap dancing along a row of weapons on the west wall. An assortment of spears and swords and even metal quarrels hung in plain view, and the dog was determined to sniff every one of them. The bear-sized smith in his leather apron looked up to see Leesil and the prancing hound, but instead of showing annoyance, Balgaví grinned.

'He yours? A hunter breed?'

'Something like that,' Leesil answered. 'Chap! Leave those alone and come here.'

'Knows his weapons,' the smith said. 'Keeps coming back to that boar spear. Could skewer a full-grown bull with that.'

'Come here, Chap,' Leesil insisted.

There were times Chap's presence was a blessing. At other times, the dog's behavior was embarrassing. Chap bounced over, but sniffed everything along the way. He looked up at the smith and wagged his tail.

'Fine animal, rather tall,' the smith said. 'I've never seen fur like that. My father kept wolfhounds, but their coats turn coarse as they grow up. What breed is he?'

'I don't know. He was a gift,' Leesil answered coldly. 'Are my weapons finished?'

Balgaví was slightly taken back by his tone. 'One's done. Still working on the other.'

'You told me you'd have them done in a matter of days,' Leesil snapped. 'That stiletto I traded is worth ten times the amount of two punching blades.'

The smith's face, shiny with steam, clouded over, and he turned on his heel. Walking to the blackened worktable, he picked up an odd spadelike shape in a matching sheath.

'I took two journeymen off paying work to get this done for you. If you can find better than this in two days, take your stiletto back and be my guest.'

Pulling the blade from its sheath, Balgaví held it out.

Leesil took it from the smith's hands, examining it carefully. The forward end was shaped like a flattened spade, though slightly elongated to the tip. At its base was a crosswise, oval opening, allowing the blade to be gripped by the backside for punching. The oval's base was the handle, painstakingly wrapped in woven leather for the grip. When held, the blade's outside edge continued in a gradual curve that extended the full length of Leesil's forearm, ending just past his elbow.

Gripping it, Leesil swung his arm slowly.

It was heavier than he'd expected, and he'd have to compensate for loss of speed. It wouldn't be the same as infighting with short blades, but it was exactly what he'd envisioned.

Chap wagged his tail and barked, staring up at Leesil.

Balgaví watched them both curiously, his annoyance slipping away.

'What do you plan to fight with that thing?'

Leesil realized he was being a difficult patron and changed his manner.

'You wouldn't believe me if I told you, but this is everything I'd hoped for. How long on the second one?'

'Another two days, perhaps. You mentioned staying at the Burdock? Vàtz passes by often enough, so I'll have him bring you word when it's ready.'

Leesil nodded. 'My thanks.'

He feinted forward again, punching straight outward at an imagined pale-skinned throat.

Magiere paced in front of the bank. It was no surprise that Leesil was late, as his sense of time was annoyingly flexible. Her frustration nearly had the better of her when a small coach pulled up, and out hopped Leesil with Chap at his side, tail in the air with a cheerful countenance.

'Sorry,' Leesil offered. 'One of my weapons was finished, and I stopped by the inn to store it. I'd rather not wear it, as we already make Lanjov nervous enough.'

Passersby cast them an occasional wary glance, and Magiere realized that Lanjov wasn't the only one they made nervous. Leesil had a dark red scarf tied around his head.

'I thought you weren't going to bother with that anymore,' Magiere said.

Leesil just shrugged. 'Habit. The eyes are obvious, but my ears and hair are a dead giveaway from a distance.'

Magiere turned toward the bank doors. 'We don't exactly fit in this part of town. We could put a scarf over your face, and people would still stare at us. I miss Miiska.'

'We'll be headed home soon enough,' he said, but his words brought Magiere no comfort.

The bank's interior wasn't as lavish as the council hall, but the floor was polished speckled granite, and two narrow pillars of the same stone framed the large entryway, more as ornament than support. A few uniformed, armed men in gray tabards stood along the side-walls. To the right was a row of clerks upon a long raised platform lined with a polished cherrywood counter. All were busy with parchments and quills. On the left was a matching wood partition rising chest-high, and to Magiere's surprise, Doviak, the foppish council secretary, sat at a desk in the walled-off space.

As Lanjov's main occupation was running his bank, serving on the council being only proper for a gentleman of his station, Doviak must serve as secretary for both the council and Lanjov's business.

The wispy little man looked up and locked eyes with Magiere, and disbelief turned to dismay. He scurried around the partition's far end with his shoes clicking upon the floor like a cricket.

'Mistress Magiere . . . I . . . how . . . may I assist you?'

Magiere wavered at the poorly hidden distaste in his voice. In the council hall, she'd been summoned as 'the dhampir,' assuming her familiar role of convincing village or town elders that she was their only salvation. In this place, amidst a faltering investigation, she was as lost as a peasant among old-blood nobility. She remembered the hatred and distrust from her home village and suddenly felt swallowed by uncertainty. She blinked and summoned her mask – her dhampir persona – once an illusion but now a reality.

As if sensing her struggle, Leesil stepped forward.

'We've come to speak with Councilman Lanjov.'

Doviak's lips parted slightly, and his perfectly curled hair swayed forward as he pretended to check the appointment log he carried.

'Oh, he does have a full schedule. Perhaps if you make an appointment for another day, he can fit—'

'This won't take long,' Leesil cut in. His politely disarming manner vanished. 'We'll see him now.'

Whenever Leesil's voice turned threatening, most people backed down. Rather odd, since he was neither large nor imposing. Doviak straightened his spine without even a flinch, either brave or merely stupid.

'No one,' Doviak said coldly, 'not even the king, would expect to see Councilman Lanjov without an appointment. His duties serve the city, and his schedule is set well in advance.'

Leesil smiled and took one step toward Doviak.

'I'm not the king, you little dandy. I was hired to investigate a murder. And where were you the night Chesna was killed?'

Doviak sputtered, two dainty fingers over his mouth. He took his fingers away and shouted, 'Guards!'

Magiere snatched Leesil by the shoulder, their roles suddenly reversed in who held who back. She raised her empty hand, open palm toward Doviak.

'We meant no offense. We simply need to—'

'What is going on out here?' a deep voice called out.

As gray-clad guards closed in from around the room, Lanjov stepped out from a side door.

'That's more like it,' Leesil said with satisfaction.

Lanjov scanned the room over the partition's top. His gaze finally rested upon his secretary and the new arrivals, and his eyes widened as his mouth closed. Waving the guards back, he came to join them.

'Mistress Magiere,' he greeted her with cold formality.

'What are you doing in my place of business?'

'Our apologies,' she said, as this wasn't at all what she'd had in mind. 'We need to speak with you urgently . . . regarding the situation.'

Before Lanjov could reply, a second figure appeared at his chamber door. Lord Au'shiyn, the Suman merchant who'd opposed her presence at the council meeting, exited Lanjov's office, striding through the room to stand behind the councilman, dressed in a floor-length russet robe open in the front. His head was wrapped in folds of beige cloth mounted in layers. His shimmering white shirt was of strange design, with clasps of satin cord stitched in curling, looped patterns.

'Ah, the dhampir,' he said. 'Come to make a deposit? Or perhaps a withdrawal?'

The last person Magiere wanted to mince words with was this arrogant outlander. She ignored Au'shiyn and spoke directly to Lanjov.

'This won't take long.'

Chap growled low, and Leesil slowly crossed his arms. Magiere only hoped it had the proper effect, now that this visit had fallen to such displays. Lanjov's choices were either to see them in his office or to have them 'escorted' out, and it was clear that at least two of the visitors would make a scene. One thing a man like Lanjov couldn't endure was a scene.

Forcing a welcoming expression, Lanjov motioned them toward his office. 'Of course, come in.'

Magiere put aside all self-doubts and strode past Lanjov and Au'shiyn and around the partition to the chamber door still ajar. Leesil and Chap followed.

Lanjov's office was austere compared to the sitting room at his home. A window facing the street was hung with opened plain burgundy curtains that exposed iron bars on the inside and heavy oak shutters on the outside. Narrow bookshelves lined the walls to either side of the door, and a stout desk sat on the room's opposite side.

To Magiere's surprise, Au'shiyn followed Lanjov in and closed the door.

'Our time here is actually the end of my scheduled appointment,' the Suman said. 'This is council business, and I am a member of the council.'

Lanjov appeared about to protest and then thought better of it. He sat down tiredly behind his desk.

'What is it you need?' he asked Magiere.

'We're more convinced the killer is noble,' she said, 'or at least masquerading as an elite. And I believe your daughter knew him. We've since learned that Domin Tilswith is a regular visitor at your home. He doesn't fit the description, so Chesna may have met her killer elsewhere. You said she rarely went out, and I'd guess most people you know well are either on the council or connected to your business. Since the killer is also an undead, he can't go out during daylight hours. That narrows things down considerably. Who do you know who prefers night meetings and finds excuses to avoid mornings or afternoons?'

It was all blunt and unproven, as Magiere had little evidence beyond her vision, but Lanjov didn't need to know this.

'Have you been talking to Domin Tilswith?' Lanjov asked in surprise.

'How dare you?' Au'shiyn interrupted. 'Chesna's murderer was not noble, and you will not harass council members and the patrons of this bank. The council has been patient with Chairman Lanjov out of respect for his grief, but you will cease this at once. Am I understood?'

Before Magiere could cut into Au'shiyn, Leesil grunted

in disgust, crossing his arms again, and spoke directly to Lanjov.

'Is there any way she could have met someone who fits the description either at the council hall or through the bank?'

Lanjov dropped his head. Magiere almost felt sorry for him – almost.

'Some evenings,' Lanjov answered, 'she came with me to read aloud my dispatches for the following day. My eyes get tired and certain material is too delicate to leave the hall. But she was in my company at all times, and the few men she ever met were proper gentlemen.'

'Who also happened to be in the courthouse at night,' Magiere said, trying to make her meaning clear. 'We need their names.'

'You need no such thing!' Au'shiyn roared, apparently not caring who heard him in the outer chamber. 'Cease this immediately. I will not have the council accosted by the likes of you. Leave now, or I will call the guards and have you thrown into the street.'

Magiere appraised him in silence. Could he be that elitist, or was he hiding something? Perhaps both. His outburst leaned far beyond snobbery.

Chap whined and trotted toward the chamber door. Magiere found herself agreeing with the hound's sentiment. She turned again to Lanjov.

'If you want Chesna's true killer found, you'll assist us. If not, find someone else to waste their time. You know where we're staying.'

Motioning to Leesil, she turned and left.

11

That night, Chane climbed the stairs to Sapphire's room shortly after a message was delivered for Toret. Feeling some trepidation about entering her room, he knocked on the door.

'What is it?' Toret called from inside.

Chane cautiously opened the door but remained in the hallway. Toret sat on the satin-covered bed next to his beloved, along with a half dozen shimmering night-gowns of varied hue he'd ordered, so she would have choices of attire for her convalescence. Sapphire reclined against a mountain of pillows in a sea-foam-green dressing gown.

'I can't do my own hair like this,' she complained. 'You must hire me a girl.'

'That's not safe, my sweet,' Toret replied, as if to a child.

'But my curls are fading. Just look at my curls.'

Indeed, Chane noted without sympathy that her sculpted ringlets hung half-coiled in a dark-blond mass down her shoulders.

'A message was delivered,' Chane said. 'Do you wish me to read it to you?'

Toret's neck craned around and then he reached out. 'No, I'll take it.'

Unfortunately, this required Chane to actually enter the room and hand it to him.

'Are you listening to me?' Sapphire demanded.

Toret opened the message, looked at it for several moments, and then folded it again.

'Chane, stay and entertain your lady awhile.'

'In here?' Chane asked.

'Of course in here. You and I are going out later, and I don't want her alone all night. See to her wishes but stay out of the parlor. I need some time to myself.'

Toret left, closing the door, and Chane fought down his revulsion as he looked at Sapphire. He had been reduced to a houseboy.

Sapphire smiled with the wide, glassy eyes of a cat spotting a mouse. 'What can you devise for my amusement?' she asked.

Chane wondered if snapping her neck would qualify as a suitable diversion.

'I'm bored,' she said. 'And my ribs hurt, and Toret promised to bring me a pretty girl to satisfy me. You make sure he remembers that.'

'Yes, some nobleman's daughter. A trifle, I'm sure. Where should we look for such a treat, my lady?' He bit off the last two words. 'Young people from proper families are safely ensconced in their homes at night.'

'Toret and I found you, didn't we?' Her smile widened. 'Not so proper then, are you?'

Her bright eyes dropped to his half-open shirt. When the message arrived, he'd been alone in his cellar room, preparing to change clothes for Toret's errand later this evening.

'And not proper at all tonight,' Sapphire added.

Revulsion turned to mild fear. If he walked out, she would begin screeching. Toret would come up and simply order him to stay − or worse if he suspected something illicit had occurred. It would be his fault either way.

'What about a game of cards?' he suggested quickly.

She blinked, honest surprise washing over her round features.

'You would play cards with me? Really? I haven't played cards in a long time.' She pointed at something in the corner. 'We can use that little white tray if you set it on the bed.'

'I must find a deck,' he said. 'Unless you have one?'

This was a gamble, but the chance of Sapphire's having a deck of cards in her room was minimal.

'No, I . . . don't think I do,' she answered.

'I have one in my room that I use for scrying experiments. It is old, but will do. If you give me a moment—'

'How long will you be?' she asked, slightly suspicious now.

'Not long, but it may take me a few moments to find my cards.' He handed her a pewter comb and picked up the small mirror next to her. 'Best comb your hair and put it up. Fallen curls do not become you.'

At those words, she grabbed the mirror and gazed into it with serious concern. 'Oh, my. Go find those cards.'

Chane slipped quietly out as Sapphire fussed with her curls.

He could not use the main stairs for fear Toret might hear him, so he walked quietly to the hall's end and the staircase landing. He pressed down with his booted toe against the corner of the floor, and the wall pivoted outward just enough to grab its edge. He opened it and slipped inside the wall. At times he wondered why the original owner had wanted this parallel passage between all four levels of the house. Closing the hidden door behind him, he crept downward. There wasn't enough light even for his eyes in this narrow space. At the bottom of three steep flights, he pressed against the wall until it grated open, and he stepped into the cellar.

He liked to keep this outer area sparse. Slim long swords, small bucklers and shields, and one short sword lined the opposite wall. This was where he and Toret did most of their training, and he practiced by himself if time allowed. A sharp mind with a dull body was useless. He hurried to his own room.

'Sparse' would hardly describe it. Rows of books lined the walls inside of old shelves. The narrow iron bed with a thin mattress and no blankets seemed to be an afterthought. The focal point of the room was his desk, covered in feather quills, faded parchments, crystal orbs, tiny wooden boxes, and whatever tome he happened to be studying. At the back of the desk was a cage with a large rat.

Chane opened the cage, hoping Sapphire still worked on her second or third curl. Whisking up the rat, he carried it to the bottom of the main stairs and focused his mind, absently touching the small urn around his neck as he did so.

He felt the animal's scattered thoughts at the edge of his awareness. He would need to guide it, but it would not hurt to implant an impression in its thoughts first. The small creature wriggled its long whiskers and stretched. Chane took it to the top of the cellar stairs, pushed the door slightly ajar, and set it down. The sleek rat slipped out.

Chane shut out his awareness until only the rat's senses filled his mind. It scurried past the kitchen and dining room, along the short hallway toward the edge of the parlor. Two sets of booted feet stood in the room. The rat darted quickly under and to the forward edge of a divan.

'She drove a stake through my mate's heart! I will take this fight to her.'

Toret's voice was the first that Chane heard through the rat's ears. But to whom was he speaking?

Chane turned the small creature's attention upward.

A stranger stood across from Toret. Middle-aged, dressed like a gentleman in well-fitted clothes, the man had a dignified bearing, except that his crafted high boots were dull and scuffed as if well traveled. Dark brown hair, combed carefully back, was marked with a stark white patch at each temple.

'Of course,' the stranger agreed. 'That is why I warned you.'

'Why would you care?' Toret retorted.

'It's merely fortunate – for you – that our objectives are compatible. How would this play out if you were unaware she was even here?'

Toret stepped closer, and Chane now saw both men through his familiar's eyes. How ridiculous Toret appeared next to his visitor. He was small and lowborn, and his deep purple tunic and black polished boots made him look like a houseboy playing dress-up.

'Very well, what do you suggest?' Toret asked finally, relenting.

'She and her partner stay at the Burdock in the southern merchant district. You know she can stand against a swordsman. Rashed was skilled and strong, but to no avail. She's never fought magic, and she dealt with Rashed one-on-one. Force her to deal with your conjuror. Increase your numbers. Give her more than one opponent to face.'

Toret nodded. 'I've already been preparing for this.'

Chane wasn't sure how he felt about greater numbers in the household. He wanted to be free of Toret but remembered how weak his master had been in Chane's early nights as an undead. Making more than one new minion might weaken or disorient Toret enough for Chane to take advantage.

It appeared the conversation would soon come to a close. As much as Chane wished to hear all that was said, he needed time to reach the third floor before Toret returned there. He pulled his awareness back and summoned the rat. When it reached the cellar door, he carried it back to his room and its cage.

He rummaged through his belongings, opening small boxes and satchels until he found a deck of cards. Once back at the cellar's hidden entry, he slipped into the wall and up the narrow hidden passage to the third floor.

Why did Toret not further question this stranger's willing assistance? The man had hinted at an agenda. Were Chane in his master's place, he would take no advice, follow no suggestions, until he was certain what this man stood to gain. Toret behaved as if he were more accustomed to taking orders than giving them.

Chane slipped out onto the third floor and moved down the hall to Sapphire's room. As he entered and closed the door, she was still combing out her curls and looked at him expectantly.

'Did you find some?'

He held up the deck, and she clapped her hands.

'What should we play?' she asked.

'Two Kings. And I deal.'

Welstiel sped by coach from Toret's house directly to a modest but respectable inn called Calabar's inside the second ring wall. Lanjov had sent for him, and he did not wish to keep his acquaintance waiting. He found the councilman sitting at their usual table, but Lanjov's face had changed much in recent weeks. Lines around the man's eyes made him appear weary.

But more seemed to weigh upon the councilman tonight, for Welstiel noted a strange apprehension in the man. He fidgeted, glancing about as if not wishing to be discovered. Then his eyes focused on Welstiel.

'Your message sounded urgent,' Welstiel said in a calm voice.

Lanjov offered a half smile tinged with relief, followed by a look of reluctance. 'Yes, my friend, please sit and have a drink with me.'

Welstiel settled quietly across from him. 'What troubles you?' he asked.

Lanjov signaled to the innkeeper for two tankards of wine before answering.

'Tomorrow, I will dismiss the dhampir. I wanted to tell you first. You were so helpful to me in finding her, and I did not want you to mistake this as ingratitude.'

'Dismiss her?' Welstiel leaned back, surprised by this sudden turn. 'You have given up on bringing Chesna's killer to justice?'

'No, of course not. But the dhampir has some mad idea the killer is a nobleman who . . . who knew Chesna. It is ridiculous that such a creature could pass for one of us.'

Welstiel folded his hands upon the table. 'What brought her to this conclusion?'

'Some vision she apparently experienced while she and that half-blood were at my home.' Lanjov paused and shuddered with apparent revulsion. 'The point is, she is not only incorrect but invading the privacy of our best citizens. Only last night, there was a distasteful scene at the Rowanwood, and now the council must pay for the damages. Today, she came to my bank, stood in the lobby, and demanded to see me. I was thankful there were no patrons of note present. Lord Au'shiyn was with me, and we had no choice but to take her into my office. She plans to question any dignitary or council member who had contact with Chesna, and demanded a list of names! Lord Au'shiyn was supportive in this matter, and I hope you, too, see the need to stop this nonsense.' Lanjov became almost manic in the moment. 'This cannot happen. I would lose my place on the council.'

A serving girl brought their tankards and set them on the table. Lanjov paid her quickly and waved her off.

'If you dismiss the dhampir, who will destroy the creature at large?' Welstiel asked.

'Please,' Lanjov continued. 'We cannot have council members questioned in this manner. It is pointless and only creates outrage and disarray. Captain Chetnik understands how these things work. He may not be a dhampir, but at least he'll search in the right places.'

'And what happens if he finds it?' Welstiel asked. 'Can he fight an undead? Can any of the city guard? If you dismiss the dhampir, it could further endanger Bela's citizens.'

Lanjov ran a hand over his face, and then held it over his mouth. He leaned closer across the table.

'Councilman Batak is our legal adviser,' he whispered through his fingers. 'His wife is niece to the queen, but Batak keeps a mistress. If he was with the woman on the night of Chesna's death, how could he provide an alibi? Councilman Amrogovitz is a sixth-generation lord of a southern province, but he has also lost much of his fortunes in the gaming rooms, and few beside myself know this. It does not hinder his voice on the council, but we have no wish for his . . . pastime to become public knowledge.'

Welstiel stared at him, and Lanjov shifted again in his seat.

'If you dismiss the dhampir,' Welstiel said, 'you are a fool, and more will die. What does it matter if a few men are embarrassed in comparison to the safety of your city?'

Lanjov tensed, and his voice hardened in return. 'I explain my reasons out of respect for your kind efforts thus far. Lord Au'shiyn's counsel to dismiss her is the correct course of action, whether you agree or not.'

Still, Welstiel did not blink, and for just a moment Lanjov's face expressed a suspicious fear as he stood up.

'I'm sorry you are cross with me,' he said. 'But my mind is firm on this. She leaves tomorrow.'

Welstiel realized he had lost his own composure, and held up one hand.

'Forgive me,' he urged. 'Sit and drink, and we will speak more. Perhaps there are other ways to put an end to this matter.'

'It is late, and the day was long,' Lanjov stammered. 'Another time. Enjoy your wine, and thank you for meeting with me at such a late hour.'

Lanjov hurried out into the night, and Welstiel sat alone.

Although Sapphire's protection often drove Toret's actions, as he and Chane wove through the back alleys of Bela's coast-side outer ring, he pushed all thoughts of her from his mind.

He'd starved himself since this stranger had first appeared on his doorstep with word of the hunter. For all of Rashed and Teesha's abilities, he'd done something neither of them ever attempted: He had created his own minions. He didn't like to think of Sapphire as a servant, but in truth, she was bound to him. Chane certainly was a servant, and a valuable one at that. Toret enjoyed the irony of raising a wealthy noble as his slave. Now, he needed muscled fodder to provide the dhampir with an exhausting fight from all sides.

He would surpass even himself, and raise two from death in the same night.

'You understand what to do?' he asked Chane, as they peered from an alley across a filthy street to a shabby tavern. Prostitutes, who'd seen more prosperous days, shuffled in the doorways, trying to entice a few pennies for services rendered.

'Yes, but you need to choose carefully,' Chane replied. 'Men armed with swords, or at least visible fighting blades, are the best probability. Choose men who have been drinking but are not drunk. A true fighter seldom falls too far into his cups.'

Months ago in Miiska, if Rashed had given him such a cavalier lecture, Toret would have hissed back with seething resentment. He'd changed since then in more ways than simply improving his station. Now, he carefully listened to Chane's advice.

'Did you ever help your father choose guards?' he asked.

Chane's jaw twitched. 'Yes.'

Toret didn't press the matter and looked back to the street. They were both dressed as poor merchants in order to blend in, should they walk on the streets or enter a tavern. Toret wore a faded blue tunic and green cap made by winding a thick scarf into coils and fastening the ends. For the first time in months, he felt comfortable. He liked the loose tunic and how the cap hid his constantly unruly hair.

He was starving for life, for blood, but he still felt anticipation as Chane watched for possible candidates.

'Anyone?' he asked.

'Not yet. Do you wish to find both men and have me incapacitate them before you begin?'

Toret hesitated. He wasn't exactly certain what 'incapacitate' meant but grasped that Chane wanted to know if they should secure both subjects before Toret began — as opposed to turning one and then beginning the process again.

'Yes, both,' he answered, and leaned his hand against the stained bricks, feeling strangely comfortable. 'I've never been in this part of the city. Have you?'

'No.' Chane quite often used as few words as possible. He had his functions, but conversation wasn't his strong point.

Several men passed in and out of the tavern, but Chane showed no interest in anyone. Then, unexpectedly, he spoke. 'Sapphire wants a pretty young girl to feed on. Did she tell you?'

'Oh, she told me, all right.' Toret sighed. 'I've no idea where to find one, and we've other matters to worry about right now.'

'When we finish, I will go into the second ring. An attractive merchant-class girl in a decent dress should do.'

Toret gave him a sidelong glance. Chane had never offered on his own to do anything for Sapphire.

'Yes,' he answered, still puzzled. 'That'll do.'

'There.' Chane nodded toward the street. 'Look.'

Two tall sailors with weatherworn skin emerged from the tavern. One wore a hook-tipped sword on his belt, and the other wore two heavy daggers strapped crosswise over his lower back. They were sober enough to bypass a large and obstinate prostitute without causing a scene.

'They are together,' Chane said. 'Convenient, and I doubt we will find anyone more likely down here.'

Toret agreed. 'Stay back.'

Once again, Toret became Ratboy the street urchin, who knew how to survive, disappear, and remain forgotten. He'd always despised this part of himself, and yet now slipped effortlessly into his old ways. Pulling off his cap, cloak, and purse, he messed up his hair. Chane faded back into the alley shadows. As the sailors passed, Toret stepped out and dropped the purse behind them.

'Sirs,' he called, drooping shoulders and bent knees making him look even smaller. 'One of you dropped a purse.'

Both turned at once, instantly on guard. Upon spotting the thin, dusty-brown beggar boy, they relaxed.

Toret picked up the fallen purse and stepped toward them, but only as far as the alley's near corner. He held out the purse.

'I think you dropped this.'

'Not me, lad,' answered the one with the sword. 'It's not mine.'

'Are you sure? I saw it fall as you passed.'

Curiosity crossed their features. They stepped closer, and Toret settled back slightly, as if wary of their approach, forcing them to move in front of the alley's mouth. The leader approached without fear and looked down.

'No, lad, you're an honest fellow, but that isn't—'

Toret sprang at him, clamping down with one strong hand over the man's mouth and wrapping his other arm about his throat. Before the sailor could reach for his sword, Toret wrenched him sideways into the alley and dragged him farther into the darkness.

The instant Toret had moved, Chane lunged from the shadows and lifted the second one off his feet, the sailor's mouth equally stilled by an iron grip. A quick spin into the alley, and the second sailor struck the brick wall and slumped.

'Chane!' Toret called, holding his struggling victim.

In a flash, Chane swung hard with one fist, catching Toret's sailor in the jaw with a sharp crack. The sailor slumped unconscious.

'Not so hard,' Toret snapped. 'You'll kill him.'

The sailor moaned, and Chane shook his head. 'He is still alive.'

Toret knelt atop the sailor, hesitating for a moment. He was starving but couldn't allow himself to fail, no matter what it cost him. His actions were all based on what he'd heard from his old master and maker, Lord Corische. He'd never actually seen Corische raise an undead, but he'd heard enough over the years to piece the process together.

Gripping the back of the sailor's head, he bit into the man's throat and drank without caution, feeling life and strength slam into his body like an overwhelming wave. He had fasted in order to take in more life than usual, and he took in as much as he could hold. This was the gluttonous gorging of the starved, with no pleasure in it as his body seemed to tear inside under the pressure of so much filling him up all at once.

He slowed immediately as he heard the sailor's heart-beat falter. His victim had to die so fast and hard, with a full leaching of his life energies, that it pushed him beyond the point of death before it actually occurred. He was guessing at what came next, but it had worked with Sapphire and Chane.

Toret pulled his teeth out of the sailor's flesh, slashed open his own wrist with his nails, and forced the dripping wound into his victim's mouth. Trying to keep from choking with his last breath, the sailor swallowed down Toret's dark fluids.

The man's heart stopped beating.

Toret fell, writhing in pain.

The alley darkened before his eyes, and sounds of his own body convulsing on the alley floor faded in his ears. Perhaps this was why there were so few of their kind.

Awareness died in Toret as he suffered the sailor's death as if it were his own. In this moment, he and his new creation were connected as one.

The first time with Sapphire had been horrifying, experiencing death again. What would have happened if he'd given in, sinking to the bottom of the darkness? Would he have truly died?

His own flesh felt like it would split and rupture from the inside. He forced his senses to widen, open, and then slammed his fist against the alley wall. Pain shot up his arm, but he didn't dismiss it as any undead could. He let it stab him. He struck the wall again. And again. Finally he flopped down on his back.

The hard cobble ground into his shoulders, and he let the irritation goad him. Any sensation to stay aware and pull him back up away from death was welcome.

As his vision returned, he found Chane staring down at him curiously.

Toret tried to speak but couldn't and simply held up a wavering hand. Chane obeyed, pulling him to his feet, and Toret staggered deeper down the alley to disgorge.

He'd not taken in all of the sailor's blood, for that was physically impossible. But he'd taken in so much to kill so quickly, that he couldn't feed on the other man if he was already glutted. His abdomen clenched as he heaved, and like an overturned bucket, blood poured from his mouth to splash on the ground, collecting in a dark pool around his feet.

Toret's vision jumped and twisted in vertigo as he stumbled back down the alley, one hand on the wall to steady himself. The first sailor's body lay still and unmoving, eyes open and mouth frozen wide in shock. Chane's expression remained casually curious.

'He is dead?' Chane asked.

'Yes,' Toret managed to answer, resting for just a moment more. 'The body will flush all waste, and perhaps by the end of the night he'll rise, but he must rest for tonight. Tomorrow evening, he'll be ready to serve our family.'

Chane studied Toret. 'You do not look like you can do this again.'

Toret ignored him, and straddled the second man. Gripping the back of the sailor's head, he gorged again. As life slammed into his already sated body, he gagged. When he heard the heart falter, he pulled back, but the alley spun wildly around him.

'Help me!' he hissed.

Chane gripped his wrist, jerking it toward the sailor's mouth.

Darkness erupted in Toret's head and swallowed him whole.

Pieces of memory thinned and drifted from him like blood in tepid running water.

A clay-walled hovel in the beggar's quarters of il'När'Sähkil, where his mother lay sick as he scavenged and stole food from the markets, wondering always where and who his father was.

Teesha's eyes, softly stern but warmly admonishing as she tended his wounds.

Sapphire's cool body next to him while the sun burned through the sky over their roof.

Cold panic seized Toret like frost crystallizing around him to hold in the memories.

He opened his eyes to find himself lying facedown in the alley, his cheek to the cobblestone, and he convulsed until blood poured again from his mouth. He pushed himself up on his elbows as his abdomen clenched over and over, even after nothing more would come up.

By the time Toret finished, he was too weak to walk, and Chane lifted him to his feet, leaning him against the alley wall. He looked down at the bloodied cobblestones.

'I see now why you did not want to take them back to the house first,' Chane commented dryly.

Toret ignored him, both hands flat against the wall to keep himself from sliding to the ground again.

'Search the alleys,' he instructed weakly. 'Find barrels, crates, tarp, or whatever is useful to hide the bodies. Then hail a carriage. I must get them back to the house.'

'Very well,' Chane answered. 'I'll get them loaded. While you take them home, I will find your lady her young girl, perhaps somewhere in the upper districts. Will you be strong enough to unload them by the time you reach home?'

Toret nodded, and Chane slipped down the alley.

A visitor waited patiently outside Lord Au'shiyn's home in the inner wall ring. He remained in the shadows, and no one in this wealthy neighborhood had even seen him arrive. In little time, his patience was rewarded, as a coach pulled up to the outer gate.

Lord Au'shiyn stepped out and walked toward the front steps of his home as the coach pulled around behind the house. In a city that had grown faster in population than in physical size, space for a personal coach and driver was a luxury even among the wealthy. Lord Au'shiyn lived well indeed.

As he reached the front door, the visitor stepped from the shadows to follow him up the walk, and called out softly, 'A word, if you please.'

Au'shiyn turned in mild annoyance, looking tired and uninterested in a late chat, but then recognition crossed his features, and he stopped.

'Oh, good evening. What brings you here so late?'

The visitor stepped up to front porch as if to convey information, and his gloved hand seized the back of Au'shiyn's neck.

Before the Suman elite could cry out, the visitor bit into his throat with elongated canines, not to drink but to tear. He ripped flesh open to expose raw veins, crushing his victim's windpipe in the process.

Lord Au'shiyn died quickly, with panic in his eyes.

The visitor shook the body until blood ran free to soak the white shirt and russet robe. The layered cloth wraps about Au'shiyn's head fell to the porch. Pausing, the visitor shredded the shirt's front for savage effect and then dropped the corpse upon the steps.

12

The sun hadn't yet risen, and Leesil lay sleepless in his bed.

Upon leaving Lanjov's bank the day before, he, Magiere, and Chap had gone to the alley behind the Rowanwood. Chap smelled the piece of lavender silk Leesil had cut from Sapphire's gown, sniffed the ground, and, with a bursting cry, took off down the winding back ways. Only a few streets away, the hound raced into an open road and stopped, turning about in confusion. The trail was gone.

After this disappointment, they journeyed to the sages' guild to check on Wynn's progress, but she was still awaiting delivery of records. With nothing further to follow up, they returned to their inn for supper and much-needed sleep. Except that Leesil had not slept well at all, and now lay on his back, eyes closed, unable to quiet his thoughts.

How would they spend yet another day with no further hint of where to look? He had no answer.

Predawn darkness finally overwhelmed him in his frustration. Rolling to his feet, he leaned the bed up against the wall on its side to give him a small space of open floor and lit the candle on the bedside table. He slipped his new weapon from its sheath. The blade had been well beveled and sharpened, ready for use.

He began with slow feints as he tested its weight. At times he felt unbalanced, for it was heavier than expected. The blade itself was stable in his grip, but he needed its twin as a counterweight on his other arm. He executed a series of straight jabs with the blade's point, alternating with sweeps of his leg. Each time he tried a swinging chop with the weapon's outside edge, he felt an unnerving imbalance in his step.

In the sleeping inn's silence, booted footsteps in the hall were easier to catch, and he paused, perfectly still. Who would be walking around the upstairs guest quarters at this early hour? Then a short rapping sounded at his door. Slipping the blade behind his back, he cracked the door open.

One of the white-surcoated city guards stood outside. A few steps down the hall stood Captain Chetnik in full uniform, pounding on Magiere's door as well.

'It's Captain Chetnik,' he called out. 'Don't be alarmed.'

'Don't be alarmed?' Leesil said, sticking his head out. 'Yes, why would she be alarmed by someone beating on her door before sunrise? If this is about the Rowanwood, we'll talk later at the barracks.'

Chetnik barely glanced at him, and Magiere opened the door, rubbing one of her eyes.

Her long hair was completely black in the dim hallway and hung loose down past her shoulders, making her pale face stand out like a specter. She still had her shirt on and was wrapped up in a blanket from her bed.

'Chetnik?' she said. 'What's wrong?'

Magiere was tall for a woman but looked vulnerable standing next to the towering captain. Chetnik looked her up and down, and Leesil's grip tightened on the blade hidden behind his back.

'Lord Au'Shiyn of the city council was found dead on his front steps this morning,' Chetnik said. 'Looks the same as Councilman Lanjov's daughter.'

Magiere stared at him without speaking.

'There's more,' Chetnik went on. 'The constabulary of the Westside mid-district found a body two days ago in an alley but just notified me. It's a young woman who was reported missing, and her condition appears to fit the pattern. I assumed you'd want to look at both immediately.'

Magiere rode in silence to Au'shiyn's manor.

Leesil sat in the military wagon across from her, equally quiet, with Chap resting between his feet. Chetnik sat beside her, and the single guard who'd accompanied the captain drove the wagon. As they pulled up to a house, Magiere wondered at the display of wealth all around them.

Nearly every house was three stories tall and constructed of crafted stone or cast brick. Fences and gates were solid iron or stained timbers carved with ornate patterns. The street was impossibly clean, and dwarf trees and shrubs were planted in the small front spaces of many houses. Chetnik leaned toward her.

'I had the woman's body brought here, before it was taken to the funeral house, so you could look them over together. The constabulary couldn't identify her, but one of the guards saw the similarity to Lord Au'shiyn's death and brought it to my attention. I won't contact her family until I hear your thoughts on this.'

'My thoughts?' Magiere asked.

'I want to know if you think the killer is a madman or . . . or something else, and if the deaths are truly connected.'

She climbed out the wagon's back. What could any of this matter to the woman's family?

The sun was rising. Magiere felt it on her back as she spotted the weary figure of Lanjov standing on the house's front steps. She passed through the open gate and up the walk toward him.

'I'm sorry,' she said and meant it.

He simply nodded, his expression guarded and beaten at the same time.

'Thank you for coming so early. I was not sure what else to do, so I asked the captain to bring you.'

'Is it the same?' she asked.

'Yes, both of them,' Lanjov answered, and then added as an afterthought, 'but the young woman was found in an alley.'

His steel hair looked limp and simply gray as dawn began. Magiere couldn't help feeling pity.

Leesil came up quietly beside her, and she was grateful for his presence. He often picked up details that she didn't. Chap sniffed around on the porch, drawing close to Lanjov, who didn't pull away this time. The council chairman motioned them inside, past a sobbing middle-aged maid, through a fair-sized dining room, and down the servants' hall to a back part of the house Lanjov simply referred to as 'the kitchens.' Magiere entered the macabre scene.

Both bodies were laid out on the large center table with pots and knives hanging above them. Peasants did this for visitation, having no better place to wash the dead before burial, but Magiere was jarred by their lying on a table used for chopping meat and other foods consumed by the wealthy.

'Nothing has been changed or removed from the bodies,' Lanjov said, flat and emotionless. 'The captain wanted you to see them as found.'

'You found him on the front steps?' Leesil asked. 'Like Chesna?'

Lanjov nodded. 'Yes, across the stairs. The door was

not open as with my daughter. His coachman came inside from the rear stable and, not finding Au'shiyn present, stepped out front to discover the body.'

Chap reared, placing both paws on the table to sniff at Au'shiyn's body. At this, Lanjov winced and closed his eyes.

Leesil reached out to his dog. 'Down, boy.'

Magiere winced as well when she looked at Au'shiyn.

His eyes were still open, and one side of the man's throat had been torn away. There were no clean punctures or teeth marks to be seen. The flesh had simply been ripped to veins, and blood covered his clothing all the way to his abdomen.

'His windpipe is crushed,' Leesil said, examining the unwounded side of Au'shiyn's throat. He didn't appear remotely squeamish or even moved by any of this, and pointed below the man's chin. 'There's a pattern of bruises running around the back of the neck. Fingers. And look at the dark blotch running around front – a thumb.'

Leesil walked around the table, his attention turning to the woman's body.

Her grayed, mottled flesh suggested it had been days since her death. She wore a well-made red cotton gown, now soiled with grime from the alley in which she was found. The front was shredded and the shift showed through, but it was spattered rather than soaked with her blood. A tiny red velvet cap was partially pinned to her disheveled hair.

She was small with black hair, and likely of fair complexion when alive.

Magiere looked to Chetnik back in the doorway.

'It's the merchant's daughter-in-law, isn't it?' she asked. 'That one in your office the day we came to the barracks.'

'I think so,' he answered. 'I won't be sure until the family identifies the body.'

'The wound is different,' Leesil broke in, as he leaned against the table's edge staring at her throat. 'The teeth marks are clean, no tearing of flesh, and there's less blood on her. This was a feeding. Look at her hair and the bruises on her wrists. At the least, she had time to struggle. Or the creature played with her a bit.'

Lanjov averted his eyes, and even Chetnik scowled at that final remark, but Leesil gave them no notice.

'It's unfortunate,' he said, 'that we don't know more about Chesna's state when she was found.'

His gaze skipped back and forth between bodies, and he shook his head ever so slightly. Something bothered him, and Magiere stepped closer.

'What is it?'

'There are no other bruises or marks from a struggle on Au'shiyn, and from his color, the amount of blood on him, and the type of wound, it wasn't a feeding. He died fast, before he could even defend himself.'

'They're unconnected?' Chetnik asked with some doubt.

'I'm not certain,' Leesil answered. 'There's something else wrong here.'

'We already know we've been hunting two separate prey,' Magiere added.

'Three,' Leesil said. 'Maybe.'

Magiere looked over the bodies again, but couldn't see how he'd come to this conclusion.

'Why three?' she asked.

Leesil remained locked in contemplation.

'These two weren't killed in the same way.' His voice was quiet, as if he merely spoke aloud to himself. 'Chesna's dress was shredded as if she were . . . well, ravaged. But then why is Au'shiyn's shirt ripped? The woman had time to struggle but was used as food. Au'shiyn died quickly and wasn't fed upon.'

He reached out with two fingers to carefully pull aside the shreds of shirt.

'Look at his chest. No wounds. Though his skin is spattered, it isn't thoroughly coated in blood. The shirt was ripped after the kill . . . likely after he was dead.'

Lanjov stayed back, but Chetnik stepped closer. Magiere looked at the details Leesil pointed out, though it made her throat dry. She saw what Leesil described but still didn't see what it meant.

'Someone wanted a connection between Chesna and Au'shiyn's deaths,' Leesil explained. 'But was it the same attacker?'

'Perhaps it was the woman you chased out of the Rowanwood,' Chetnik suggested.

Magiere looked at Leesil's face, now beginning to catch up.

'No,' she answered to the captain's suggestion. 'Undeads as a whole are viciously strong, but that woman couldn't take a large man this quickly, not before he could defend himself.'

'The bruises on his throat are too large for her hands,' Leesil added.

'And I doubt brute strength is her way to snare victims,' Magiere finished.

Leesil lifted his gaze to Magiere and nodded toward Au'shiyn's body. 'Are you up to trying again?'

For a moment, Magiere was uncertain what he meant. Then she felt sick as she realized he wanted her to have another vision.

'I'm right here,' Leesil whispered. 'I won't leave your side.'

Nausea still threatening, Magiere reached out and

touched Au'shiyn's cold, stiff hand. She closed her eyes and waited, anticipating the shock of the world suddenly shifting around her as it had before.

Nothing came. Magiere exhaled, suddenly aware she'd been holding her breath.

Reaching across to the woman, she tried again. The result was the same.

'Maybe it's the place they died,' Leesil suggested.

As Magiere turned to leave, Leesil pulled out a stiletto from his sleeve. In the same movement, he sliced a blood-soaked strip from Au'shiyn's shirt and turned toward the kitchen door. As they stepped out the front door, Chap sniffed yet another set of dark stains on stone steps. Lanjov and Chetnik had followed, but Leesil motioned them both to stay inside as he pressed the bloodied cloth into Magiere's hand. When she flinched, he held her hand closed around it.

'It might take both the place and object,' he said.

She nodded and stepped down onto the front walk.

Magiere closed her eyes and felt herself walking to the side of the house. She opened her eyes again.

Dawn's light had vanished, to be replaced by the cold dark of night.

A coach pulled up, and she watched as Lord Au'shiyn stepped out. Along with the sights and the smell of damp night air, there was something more inside of Magiere. She could feel anger. Perhaps frustration of some need or desire unfulfilled.

She stepped from the shadows and followed Au'shiyn as he approached the front door, and felt her hands flex inside leather gloves. In the bottom of her view, the cloak she wore swirled around her, and she felt sharp canines inside her mouth. It wasn't the same as the familiar aching change of her own teeth.

'A word, if you please,' she said as she stepped close.

Magiere heard the sound this time, but before she could focus on the deep voice that issued from her mouth, Au'shiyn turned in annoyance and recognition crossed his features.

'Oh, good evening. What brings you here so late?'

Magiere's right hand shot out and grabbed his neck so hard she felt her thumb crush Au'shiyn's windpipe. She tore the left side of his throat open with her teeth, and warm blood ran into her mouth. As with Chesna, she didn't drink.

Au'shiyn choked, unable to breathe. Magiere shook him and blood flowed from his neck to soak into his clothing. She reached out to shred his shirt and—

'Stop it!'

Strong hands gripped her arms, and she spun around as Au'shiyn's image whirled away. She felt herself jerked backward against something hard, as wiry arms wrapped around her. She thrashed to get free.

'Enough!'

The grip around her remained as light poured into the darkness.

Magiere found herself sitting on the porch with her back up against Leesil's chest. Remembering Au'shiyn's fight for air, she choked.

'Leesil?'

'Shhhhhhh,' he said. 'It's over.'

Chetnik now stood in the walk, watching her suspiciously. Magiere curled away from him toward Leesil, leaning her head against the steps' railing.

'It's all right,' Leesil said from behind her. 'She'll be fine in a minute.' Then he whispered in her ear, 'Was it the same creature?'

Magiere relaxed at his familiar voice. 'Yes . . . the same one . . . I think.'

She breathed deep and, while hidden from Lanjov's or Chetnik's view, slipped her fingers into her mouth, making sure her teeth were normal. She rose out of Leesil's arms, bracing against the railing as she turned toward Lanjov. He looked embarrassed or revolted by her.

'It's the same one, Lanjov,' she said. 'Dressed like a noble with black gloves. And it's not a masquerade.'

It took a moment to quell the lingering vertigo before she could continue.

'He moves and speaks like one of you, and you're the only connection I can see. Why would any noble want to kill Au'shiyn and your daughter . . . anything, no matter how far-fetched or minor?'

The councilman looked utterly at a loss. 'I don't know any reason. Au'shiyn was strong-willed, but respected by all.'

'You're sure of all this?' Chetnik asked Magiere.

'Of course she's sure,' Leesil snapped. 'We need the name and home address of everyone on the council.' He looked directly at Lanjov. 'As well as anyone you've worked with through the bank who knew your daughter.'

The pain that flashed across Lanjov's face brought Magiere another flicker of pity, but not nearly enough to overcome her frustration with the man's arrogant obstinacy.

'Captain Chetnik will take you to the council hall,' Lanjov answered softly. 'My aide will provide the information you require.'

'Not enough,' Leesil added, and he turned on Chetnik. 'Shut the city down. Close it off.'

Chetnik scowled, hands on his hips, but it was Lanjov who cut in first.

'We cannot do that!' he shouted. 'This is the kingdom's main port. Thousands, no, tens of thousands here and elsewhere depend on daily trade through Bela.'

Magiere's head swam with afterimages of her vision, making it hard to clearly follow what was being said. With a quick glance at Leesil, his words resurfaced in her mind, and she understood.

'We can't let these things out of reach,' she said. 'Will your precious trade continue if more bodies are found? What ship's captain would harbor here? And there won't be a farmer or merchant in the region who'd risk coming to market.'

'So you'd lock us all in?' Lanjov retorted in panic. 'This cannot be done.'

'Yes, it can,' Chetnik cut in.

Lanjov looked at him in stunned disbelief, but the captain continued.

'If any of these creatures escape, they'll move on to another town or cluster of villages. And the killing starts all over again.' He looked at Magiere sternly. 'But we're not doing this your way.'

'How then?' Magiere insisted.

Chetnik cast one last glance at Lanjov, as if fed up with political influences.

'These things move only at night, correct?' he asked.

Magiere nodded. 'We've never heard of or seen one move in daylight.'

'Then night is the only time they can leave,' Chetnik said. 'Commerce continues for the day, and there's little or no business done past dusk. I'll double the watch by day and night, but we'll lock the city up only before dusk.'

'Except the sewers,' Leesil added. 'Seal the bayside spill-ways and keep them guarded at all times.'

Chetnik became immediately disagreeable. 'If it comes to that, better to send my men into the sewers and flush these things out.'

'If you want to lose half of them,' Magiere replied. 'You don't know what you're dealing with, and we don't have time to teach you, so stay out of it. Just tell your men to keep the bayside grates locked down.'

Lanjov ran his hands over his face and through his hair. Chetnik finally nodded agreement.

'Take us to the courthouse. We need that list,' Magiere said more calmly.

Chetnik didn't answer for a moment. 'We still need to talk about the Rowanwood.'

Magiere indicated the councilman with a lift of her chin. 'They can pay for it.'

When the captain looked up the steps, Lanjov nodded without a word. Chetnik stepped purposefully down the walk toward the wagon.

Magiere tried to follow but lost her balance, and Leesil caught her. This vision had been quick but more intense than the last.

'Looks like we're the villagers this time,' Leesil muttered, as he half supported her down the walk.

'What?' Magiere replied.

'Au'shiyn's body . . . that mimic killing, even if it is the same creature,' he said, but then saw that his answer still mystified her. 'We're the ones being played. Someone's on the game here, and it isn't us this time.'

The coach rolled up to the next house on their list, and Magiere kept her emotions in check. Flickering images of Au'shiyn's death and the little velvet cap hanging by a thread from the dead woman's hair drifted through her mind. Two more deaths, and they still had no clear idea where to find the undeads of this city.

Leesil believed the woman's blood had been consumed, but what if he was wrong about the third Noble Dead?

Her visions were both of one, from what she'd could tell, and what if Sapphire had killed the young woman?

'I shouldn't have given up my sword at the Rowan-wood,' she said to Leesil, bitterness in her voice. 'I could have taken her head.'

He turned from gazing out of the coach window.

'Forget it. You can't change the past – only alter the present and future.'

His words pulled her out of her guilt. 'Are you trying to spout wisdom?'

'It's true.' He shrugged. 'We can never change what's passed, no matter how much we might want to.'

Without giving him the satisfaction of knowing it, Magiere felt a little better, though still somber. He was right, once again, and it was wasted effort to think otherwise.

'I want something to fight,' she said.

He grinned. 'I'm contagious.'

'Sure,' she muttered under her breath, 'fleas, laziness, vices . . .'

'I don't have fleas.'

He pushed open the door and stepped to the ground, pulling out bits of fabric from Sapphire's and Chesna's clothing.

'They're both lavender,' he mused. 'I never noticed that before.'

'It doesn't mean anything' – she looked briefly at the scraps – 'except they both had a great deal of coin to spend. Chap, come on.'

Armed with a list of Bela's council members, but not ready to start pounding on the doors of the elite, they were counting on Chap. He'd tracked Miiska's undead to the warehouse, so they hoped he might sense something if they stumbled upon one here. One by one, they worked through half the list, moving from house to house as Chap sniffed his way around each building. But nothing had come of it.

Chap stepped to the coach door, eyes taking in the street.

'Come on,' Leesil said. 'To the house.'

Leesil held out the cloth scraps, but the dog ignored them, hanging his head as if he had no further interest in their scent. He stepped out and walked up to the house's front gate, sniffed the iron bars a few times, and then trotted back to the coach and jumped in.

'Get your mangy backside out of there!' Magiere scolded. 'This is important.'

The coachman glanced over his shoulder as if they were all mad, and settled back in his seat.

Inside the coach, Chap dropped his haunches to the floor with a low, grumbling whine.

'This isn't it,' Leesil said, the words spoken slowly, like a gradual realization. 'He knows this isn't it – and he wants to move on.'

'He's just a dog,' Magiere answered in exasperation. 'Smarter than most, I'll grant, but he can't possibly know what we're doing. He's merely tired of this, probably more than you or I.'

But the moment those words left her mouth, she looked into Chap's translucent blue eyes and felt certain Leesil was right. This was indeed not the house.

She climbed back into the coach, snatched the list off the seat, and handed it to Leesil.

'Give the driver our next stop.'

Chap crawled upon the seat opposite her, panting softly.

Au'shiyn's dying face peered back at Magiere each time she blinked or closed her eyes. And behind the Suman's sagging head, Chesna watched her with an ashen face.

13

Again, Leesil sat alone in his room unable to sleep. Perched on the bed's edge, he stared at the burning candle, watching wax drip into the baked clay holder.

Neither he nor Magiere could find a solid link between Sapphire, Lanjov's daughter, Lord Au'shiyn, and the young woman they'd examined that morning. Instinct told him if he found that link, the question of location might be answered. Completing their duty would simply be a matter of hunting down undeads. He knew how to do the latter, but the former still eluded them.

Chap's behavior became more troubling by the day. The dog was obstinate, as if nothing they did interested him at all. They'd covered most of the houses on Lanjov's list, and Chap showed mild to no interest, often jumping back into the coach and refusing to get out again until they reached their next destination. Leesil didn't know what to make of this, but the search had proved fruitless. The last thing he wanted to do was investigate one more house, and that was Magiere's agenda for the coming day. There might be a limit to how long Chap would cooperate.

He sighed and arose, picking up his punching blade and lifting his bed against the wall.

Dressed only in loose breeches, he maneuvered around the small room in his bare feet. He almost never took off his stilettos, so he practiced with those strapped to his forearms as well. It would do no good to adjust to his new weapons, and then have to compensate midbattle for additional weight on his arms.

He spun around, kicking up swiftly behind a swipe of the blade. He repeated this several times and then shifted the weapon to his other hand, preparing to go again on his other side. The door to his room swung open.

'What in the seven hells are you doing in here?' Magiere asked, rubbing her eyes.

Leesil froze, legs slightly bent from a finished spin and his arm straight out with the new blade.

Magiere blinked, half-awake, but her eyes fully opened as her gaze slipped along his bare arm and the weapon.

'Sorry,' Leesil said quickly, lowering the blade to his side. 'Didn't mean to wake you.'

Magiere didn't seem to hear him as she stepped into the room. She still wore her faded white shirt from the day. Except for her amulets, she wore nothing else that Leesil could see. Her bare feet seemed small for her height, and her legs were the same pale, near-white of her face and hands, from ankles across smooth, muscled calves to just above . . .

'Is that what the smith made?' she asked. 'I was wondering when you'd get around to showing me.'

Leesil faltered a moment before catching her question.

'A punching blade, of sorts,' he answered. 'With some changes of my own.'

He lifted the weapon, holding up the wing that extended back along his forearm.

'Stand back and watch,' he said, and Magiere returned to the doorway.

He spun again and kicked and then shot out throat-high with his bladed hand. A quick punch with his free hand followed, and he whipped around again. The blade scythed an arc through the air at neck level.

'Might not decapitate on the first strike,' he said. 'But it'll get the job the done. Wait till the twin is finished. Heads will fly.'

Magiere stepped close again, studying the bright steel more closely. A soft smile on her face was barely visible beneath the shadow of her hair.

'Soon you won't even need me,' she said.

'Nonsense, I'll always need you,' he answered instantly.

A brief and embarrassed silence followed. Again, Magiere's gaze followed the blade along his arm, and this time continued up along his shoulder.

Leesil had a sudden urge to touch her face and caught himself halfway to reaching for her cheek. He pushed his white hair out of his eyes instead.

'I'll be quiet now. You should get some more sleep.'

Magiere stepped back to the door.

'It's all right if you need to practice. I don't think anyone but me would hear, but you should get some sleep yourself.'

She reached for the latch to pull the door closed.

'Good night,' he said.

She looked at him a moment longer and then closed the door, saying, 'Good night,' in return.

Leesil set his blade on the table and jerked the bed back down with both hands. Dropping on it, he puffed the candle out and lay in the dark, eyes closed, trying to clear his thoughts. He lay quietly for a long time – how long, he didn't know – and listened to the *click-tick* against his window.

Late night to early morning in Miiska always brought a coastal breeze through the trees. Large firs and pines out back of the tavern were old and long limbed, occasionally fingering the tavern's rear walls and shutters. He'd listen to the settling sound reminding him that they'd made a place in the world away from the cold outside. *Click-tick*, they whispered.

He wasn't in Miiska.

And there were no trees in the back alley behind this inn.

Someone was trying to break into his room.

Toret hung down from the roof to the window's edge and opened his vision to its full extent. The crescent moon provided enough light for his undead eyes, but when he peered into the inn's small room, the bed to the left was pushed too near the window's wall for him to see it clearly.

Using hardened fingernails, he hooked and pulled the window's frame outward just enough to slip a blade into the crack. An early-evening visit by Chane to the Burdock had revealed that it boasted four private guest rooms and only the first two were occupied. Although still shaky from the previous night's events, Toret could wait no longer. The dhampir and her sly half-elf would be caught in their beds tonight and quickly killed.

The newest members of his 'family' were Tibor and Sestmir, both of whom showed him a good deal more respect than Chane ever had. They treated him as they would a captain at sea, and this was a benefit he hadn't expected. Chane wasn't accustomed to orders or to looking after anyone but himself. Tibor and Sestmir expressed confusion and fear regarding their new existence, but once taught to feed and given their orders, they had adapted and even shown a dutiful attention to their master's welfare.

Tibor, tall and lanky with close-shaven brown hair and clear brown eyes, was skilled with the hook-tipped saber, and now waited while Toret worked the latch. Sestmir had gone with Chane to the next window down the inn's alley side.

'Don't forget about the dog,' Toret whispered to Tibor. 'It's fierce and unnatural. And its bite burns like fire and leaves scars.'

The window latch gave and he paused, listening for any sound inside the room. Nothing.

'Let me enter first, master,' Tibor whispered.

'No,' Toret answered. 'Whichever one is in here will die quickly in bed. But if a fight breaks, you watch for any chance to kill from behind. Do you understand?'

'Yes.'

Toret swung the window open and slipped down lower along the wall. He pivoted his grip on the sill and let his feet settle quietly on the ledge. Slipping his long sword out, he stepped down into the room.

The bed's blankets were wrinkled but flat. The bed was empty.

From his right, he caught a glint in the dark arcing toward his head.

Toret lifted his long sword and felt the resounding clang of steel against steel as a foot slammed into his side and propelled him across the small room. He hit the wall near the door and pushed off, swinging the sword back to force his opponent away. Legs slightly bent, sword straight out, Toret faced his skulking attacker.

Out of the corner came a slender man wielding a strange blade along one arm, naked to the waist. His skin was golden brown, and white-blond hair hung to his shoulders.

Toret hesitated as recognition flowed into his mind.

'Elf,' he whispered.

The half-blood's eyes widened. His jaw dropped ever so slightly in disbelief.

'You?' he hissed.

Tibor dropped in through the window, saber in hand.
'Magiere!' the half-blood shouted. 'Get up!'
And Toret charged.

Chane saw Toret slip through the window and knew he
had to move quickly. He hoped the half-elf would be
waiting inside the room he would now enter. As much
as Toret feared the half-blood, Chane preferred to have
his master battling the dhampir. Chane wasn't remotely
afraid. He could handle almost any kind of fight, but he
felt potential freedom lingering close. The dhampir had
a better chance of finishing Toret.

'Stay here unless I call for you,' he said to Sestmir.
The mindless minion nodded. Although pleased that
the creation of these new slaves had weakened Toret, Chane
found them almost as annoying as Sapphire. It was sickening the way they groveled so before their maker. He
dropped through the window and landed without a sound.

A low, rumbling growl filled the room.

Chane turned to lock gazes with an enormous blue-
gray hound glaring at him with crystalline eyes. Its coat
almost shimmered in the dark room.

The bedcovers shifted, someone turning beneath them.
All Chane could see was dark hair around a pale woman's
face as she groaned in annoyance.

'Chap . . . ?'

The dog leaped, wailing, and struck Chane hard at the
waist.

Its teeth sank through his cloak into his sword arm.
Shock and pain hit him as his forearm began to burn as
if ignited from the inside.

A loud thud came through the wall from the next
room, and a voice shouted, 'Magiere, get up!'

Blankets flew off the bed into the air. From behind

the flurry of cloth, the woman scrambled for the near corner of the room. This was happening too fast.

Chane punched the dog in the head, and it tumbled away and rolled back to its feet. Its snarling and wailing pounded in Chane's ears.

The black-haired woman stood near the door, an unsheathed falchion in her hand. Dressed only in a loose shirt, she had pale skin like one of his own kind. A light below her throat pulled his gaze to a small stone on a chain that glowed brightly, casting her features in yellow tones. He had not expected her to be lovely.

Thumping footfalls and scraping metal sounded from the next room, and the dog's attention shifted. It looked quickly at the woman. Without taking her eyes from Chane, she flipped the door's latch and flung it open, and the dog raced out.

Saliva filled Chane's mouth, and he willed himself into tight control. If she was the dhampir, then Toret now faced the half-blood. Chane needed to make this look like a true fight, without killing her or allowing her to kill him. No small feat.

She was poised, blade at guard, waiting and watching. Grunts and cries and the dog's wail sounded from the other room, and then another loud thud, but the dhampir remained fixed upon him.

'Come for me,' he said, throwing his torn cloak off.

She took in the sight of him, and her gaze settled on his leather gloves.

Chane felt unsettling confusion as her dark brown irises flooded to pitch black. She hissed at him, her mouth lined with elongated canines among sharp-edged teeth.

Cold wrath coiled inside Leesil. Ratboy? How was that possible?

He'd seen the little undead vanish into Miiska's woods with a wooden branch through his chest. Now he was somehow in Bela? The sly little creature looked different, well dressed and groomed, and brandishing a crafted long sword fit to his size. But it was indeed Ratboy, and he wasn't alone.

Leesil wanted to rush the door and get to Magiere, but Ratboy stood in the way, and an armed sailor dropped through the window. No doubt some undead was slipping into Magiere's room as well.

If two faced him, how many had come for Magiere?

Ratboy hesitated, and Leesil feinted with his blade at the sailor, keeping him at bay. He was about to call out to Magiere again, when the door slammed inward as the jamb splintered. The snarling mass of Chap charged past Ratboy and into the sailor.

Leesil quick-stepped toward Ratboy. He slammed the arm blade down hard against the undead's lunging thrust, and then spun and kicked Ratboy in the face. The scrawny undead grunted as his head whipped to one side, and Leesil stepped in tight, driving his blade's point at Ratboy's throat.

The space in front of Leesil was empty. Steel flashed down from his right.

A quick twist of shoulder and arm, and Leesil blocked. The long sword screeched along his blade's edge. Snarling and the sound of a man's painful cry filled up the room. Chap had gotten past the sailor's guard and connected with his teeth. Ratboy settled back into the room's center, blade out.

It struck Leesil as bizarre that this creature, who'd fought so viciously with teeth and fingernails, now relied on a weapon.

With a wrist flick, Leesil slipped a stiletto into his empty left hand.

'Remember these?' he said, holding the thin blade out in plain sight. 'I think you still have one. Been bothering your guts much lately?'

Ratboy hissed and charged. Someone had taught him to wield the sword, but a man with a sword was just that and nothing more, if he didn't keep his wits. The second Ratboy lunged, Leesil spun again, low beneath the thrust.

His foot caught the inside of a knee, and Ratboy's balance faltered.

Leesil hooked the long sword's crossguard with the stiletto blade. He didn't need to hold it off but only guide it away on Ratboy's momentum. Rising up, he pushed off the floor with his legs, snapping his arm blade forward.

At the last moment, a sudden lurch by Ratboy made Leesil's blade point miss its mark at the undead's throat, and pierce just below his collarbone. Leesil drove forward and up with his entire weight.

Ratboy stiffened as his slender body was slammed against the wall and his feet left the floor. Unable to cry out, he stared in shock at the blade buried nearly to its grip in his upper chest.

Mundane weapons might not even slow down an undead, but a gaping wound in any creature's body would cause confusion if not outright panic. At least that was in Leesil's mind when he'd first conceived his new weapons. Now he only wished he had the second blade to take this little vermin's head. His left hand arched up, driving the stiletto through Ratboy's left eye.

The small undead screamed this time and dropped his sword. He slashed with his fingernails, catching Leesil across throat and shoulder. Pain burned Leesil's skin, and he retreated, losing hold of the stiletto, but keeping his grip on the punching blade.

Ratboy dropped to his feet and jerked the stiletto out,

flinging it away as he stumbled along the wall to the corner, dark trails running down his cheek from his mangled eye socket. Leesil clutched at his own throat, but saw the surprise on Ratboy's face as the undead looked down at himself.

Black fluids poured from his chest wound, soaking his split tunic and dripping down to the floor.

Leesil hesitated in shock. Had his blade gone so deep?

Chap and the undead sailor toppled to the corner beyond the window, the sailor's saber lost in the scuffle. With Chap's teeth clamped around his wrist, claws tearing at the man's face, the sailor resorted to his own teeth and nails.

Before Leesil could move, Ratboy reeled toward them and kicked the hound in the side. Chap tumbled back against the foot of the bed with a yelp, and the sailor snarled as he tried to seize the dog. Leesil started to rush in.

A snap and hum sounded behind him, and something whipped past him through the air.

The sailor lurched back on his knees. The feathered end of a quarrel protruded from his throat, its metal head sticking out below the back of his skull. He clutched at it, as his throat began to smoke.

Leesil glanced back to see Vàtz in the doorway with an empty crossbow in his hands. He was trying to recock the string, his face scrunched in determination.

'Run!' Ratboy shouted, clambering through the window. 'Now.'

Chap lunged after the sailor, but his front leg gave way. Ratboy suddenly reached back through the window from outside, grabbed the undead sailor's arm, and they both were out the window and gone.

'Vàtz, stay with Chap,' Leesil snapped.

He pushed the boy aside and dodged into the hallway. Magiere's door was half-open, and the room inside burst into flames.

Too many impressions spilled into Magiere's awareness at once.

She didn't need to look down, for the topaz amulet's glow filled the space in front of her. Leesil had shouted and was likely under attack as well. She felt relief when Chap charged out the door, and inwardly willed Leesil to stay alive until she could get to him. A tall undead with a long sword, dressed like a nobleman, stood in her room by the window. He was broad-shouldered and clean-shaven, his red-brown hair tucked behind his ears. She didn't know him, but marked him as someone of means.

And his black gloves fit well.

A gnawing began in her stomach and raced up her throat as the ache spiked through her jaw.

'Come for me,' he said, throwing his cloak off.

Instinct flooded Magiere, and the room lit up in her sight until she could clearly see its darkest corners. A hiss escaped her throat, followed by hunger rising from her stomach.

His cold face was void of emotion or thought. He simply stood, waiting as she charged.

Magiere swung the falchion for his neck. He blocked and turned his own sword at the point of contact, trying to slide hers away. She shifted and pulled her slash to the right. His long sword's tip cracked down on the bed's end, and Magiere rammed her knee into his rib cage, sending him tumbling over the bed and his own sword. She sidestepped to the room's center to go after him, but he'd already righted himself with his sword at guard.

Emotion now registered on his face. Hunger. Arousal.

Flickering sensations passed through Magiere. She'd felt this enough times before that it was now familiar.

His desire to feed on her slipped inside her head. When she'd fought Rashed or Teesha, the only impressions she'd felt were hatred and the wish to see her dead. But this creature hungered for her.

Magiere fought down the answering desire to tear him open with her teeth. She matched his stance, blade at ready, and her wits returned.

She had to get back inside his guard and take his head, but a flesh wound might give her an opening. Her falchion had proven painful to undeads in the past, though she didn't understand why. If she could just slice his chest or sword arm . . .

He made a fast slash, slipping over the top of Magiere's sword before she could counter, and she was forced to retreat. At that he circled near the window again. He straightened slightly, his features smoothing to a calm, calculating expression.

His hunger faded from Magiere's awareness, leaving nothing in its wake.

Instead of the impressions themselves, the instant loss of them broke Magiere's concentration. A small panic set in. She could no longer feel what drove him.

She feinted to his right, and when he moved to block, she reversed and slashed him across his upper left arm. He didn't cry out but reared backward in shock, and she swung at his throat.

His swiftness surprised her as he dropped and crab-stepped back to her right, and her falchion cleaved through empty air. He kicked out, and his booted foot caught her in the side and stomach. Magiere's bare feet slipped, and she fell back against the wall beside the window.

'Sestmir!' he shouted. 'Now.'

Someone dropped feet-first through the window, landing on the floor between her and the undead nobleman. His eyes were bright, and his open mouth showed jagged teeth between elongated canines. Point downward in each fist, he held long, triangular daggers.

He lunged, stabbing down at her chest.

Magiere rolled right, coming to one knee. She clenched the falchion's hilt with both hands as she reversed her twist and brought the blade down on the back of his neck. As the edge hit, he jerked upward in panic, and the blade cleaved through.

His body toppled backward. His head struck the sill and bounced down between his legs. Dark liquid pooled on the floor around the corpse.

Before the head had even stopped rolling, Magiere was on her feet. She felt something cool and wet flowing around her left foot as she faced her first opponent again.

For the first time, he looked uncertain. He'd moved like a much better swordsman than his actions portrayed. Why the toying, and why the loss of bloodlust she'd felt from him? He no longer showed an interest in killing her, yet he also made no overt move to flee.

She still felt her own hunger, and stepped away from the cold wetness around her feet.

The tall undead began whispering, the movement of his lips quick, and his eyes rolled up once before he made a flashing gesture with his hand.

The clothing of the headless corpse upon the floor burst into flames.

The heat was blinding, and Magiere shielded her face with her free hand. When she looked back a moment later, the nobleman was gone. The fire climbed the wall around the window.

'Magiere!'

Leesil burst through the door and held one arm up at the sight of the flames. He looked about frantically, until she reached out and grabbed his arm.

'I'm here.'

Something metallic brushed against her, and she saw his new blade still clenched in his fist. It was stained black, and fluids smeared on her forearm as he turned toward her. Shallow, jagged cuts ran along his throat and shoulder, bleeding down his chest.

'You're cut,' she choked through the smoke.

Leesil crouched, shielding his face from the blaze, and he reached out to grab the nearest handle of their chest across from the bed. He jerked it toward the door. The fire now lapped across the ceiling, and its crackle grew deafening in Magiere's ears as the air became painfully hot in her chest.

'Grab the other end,' he yelled. 'We have to get out of here.'

She spun around the chest and grabbed its other handle. Leesil had never been one to care much for possessions, but hauling on the chest, he pulled it and her out into the hall. As she passed through the frame, Magiere snatched her sheath by the door where she'd left it.

Leesil dropped his end of the chest, leaving his blade on top, and ducked inside his room. He picked up his sheath from the bedside and tossed it to her. Magiere slapped it down on top of the chest with his blade.

Magiere was stunned to see young Vàtz kneeling next to Chap, an empty crossbow in his arms and quarrels tucked through his belt. His overlarge hazel eyes watched the animal in either worry or anger. Leesil scooped up the hound in his arms.

'Hurry up,' Magiere said. 'Vàtz, where's your uncle?'

'He's out,' the boy answered, and followed Leesil to

the door. 'I take care of things when he's with his lady friend, and he . . .' His mouth dropped open and his eyes widened as he looked back down the hall. 'What the hell did you do?'

Smoke rolled along the hallway ceiling from out of Magiere's room.

'Not now,' she snapped, and shoved him toward the stairs.

Leesil hurried after Vàtz, Chap in his arms. Magiere tucked their weapons under one arm and dragged the chest behind her. It suddenly occurred to her why Leesil wouldn't leave the chest behind: His box of tools was inside. She shuddered at the thought of what he'd wanted to save as she glanced back at the smoke-shrouded hallway.

Ashes and fire, as well as blood, seemed to follow wherever they went.

14

As the light of the Burdock's flames faded in the southern merchant district of Bela, a different light shimmered unnoticed near the north point of the Outward Bay.

A large ship skimmed the water, rounding the point, long and sleek, its iridescent sails reflecting the crescent moon's light. Sails began to fold, and it slowed well away from the harbor to slip as close to shore as the bay's depth allowed. A small shape bobbed upon the water, moving away from the vessel.

Slender as its parent, the longboat glided into shore with four cloaked forms aboard – one to the stern, two at the oars, and the last at the bow. As the boat drifted to a stop, the forward passenger leaped out upon the gravelly sand.

His cloak was colored between charcoal gray and forest green. He wore a scarf around the lower half of his face and a cowl covering his head. Large amber almond-shaped eyes gazed back at the longboat. He raised a slender gloved hand.

His companion in the stern returned the gesture and called out, '*D'créohk.*'

'To an end,' he repeated back in the language of the land he now stood upon.

'And good hunting, Sgäile,' his companion added.

The longboat drifted back toward the ship, and Sgäile fled into the shoreline trees.

A light rustle of autumn leaves and pine needles on the forest floor followed in his path, with no thump of footfall or crack of twig. When the nearest of Bela's out-erlying villages was in view across the fallow fields, he settled upon the mulch carpet between the trees. He would wait and enter the city by daylight amongst its populace on the streets.

Sgäile sat still in contemplation. Word had passed to the homeland from the city's watcher, and then to the ship where he'd been assigned.

'A half-blood?' he whispered.

So few such aberrations existed in this world. He was mystified why this particular one distressed the watcher enough to call through the trees across the continent. Sgäile had never met a half-blood. Traitor, this one had been labeled, and in that there was possible sense. For the only one he heard of had been born years ago to another traitor to his people . . . a traitor to her people.

Aoishenis-Ahâre – Most Aged Father – was wise beyond comprehension in ancient memories, and as leader of Sgäile's people, knew more reasons than his descendants why they should fear the humans. It was not Sgäile's place to challenge such wisdom, though it concerned him that he did not know how or why his target had been judged.

He untied the cloth strap running crossways over his chest and pulled its end until the narrow bundle it held to his back slipped from under his cloak and into his lap. He unfolded the cloth, arranging his belongings with care, and made sure each piece was in proper condition.

Picking up a tube of silvery metal and two double-curved lengths of polished, tawny wood, he assembled the short-bow and strung it. Five arrows with teardrop points also lay on the cloth. His stilettos were strapped to his forearms beneath his shirt.

Setting the bow across his lap, he reverently picked up his last possession, a plain but finely crafted wooden box as long as his forearm, wider than his palm, its depth less than the thickness of his wrist. When he opened it, he carefully inspected each item within, from the strangling wire to the bone-cutting blade, to the delicate struts, hooks, and implements hidden beneath a second panel in the lid.

Traitor, this half-blood had been called. The only other Sgäile knew of who'd borne such judgment was now dealt with. And her child, if that was truly who this one was, would not receive the mercy she had been granted by her people – or by her kind, the *anmaglâhk*.

Magiere and Leesil trudged through the late-night streets to the front door of the sages' barracks. Lanterns to either side were extinguished, but Magiere banged upon the door anyway.

By good fortune, her breeches and boots were in the chest, so she hadn't had to walk the streets half-naked waiting for some guard to arrest them for indecency. She was certain her hair was a wild mess. Her shirt hung loose, black smears and spatters across it. There were no marks of her own blood, but her ribs and hip ached where she'd been kicked. She was about to pound on the door again when it cracked open.

To Magiere's relief, Wynn Hygeorht peered out, clutching her robe closed. She held up a lantern, its light somehow brighter than any Magiere had seen.

'Oh,' she said, 'it is you.'

She took sight of Leesil's state of undress and his gashes, and the massive gray form of Chap in his arms. Magiere knew she didn't look much better. Wynn's eyes widened in alarm.

'Spare a little bread for a few beggars?' Leesil jested.

Wynn jerked the door open. 'Come – come inside.'

It was then that Vàtz stuck his head out from behind Leesil. Wynn's surprise grew, but she motioned the boy in as well.

'What happened? Why are you carrying Chap? Is he all right?' Wynn asked all at once.

'He's alive,' Leesil answered, 'but can't seem to walk on one front leg.'

Without another question, Wynn ushered them down a hallway, then along another passage that emptied out into a kitchen. Magiere imagined the room probably looked similar to when it served the city guard, but now narrow wooden poles hung from the ceiling with a variety of harvested herbs arranged there to dry.

'Lay him on the table,' Wynn said. 'I must find Domin Tilswith. He has more medicinal knowledge than I.'

Setting the lantern on the table next to Chap, her hand hesitated, about to touch the hound lightly on the head. Instead, she hurried away back down the passage.

Vàtz walked up to Chap but didn't touch him either. 'He won't die, will he?'

There was a bit of concern in the boy's voice beneath his general fuming. For half the walk to the barracks, he'd spouted a never-ending barrage of angry questions and foul exclamations over the fire at the Burdock. Magiere had bitten her tongue more than once. As much as Vàtz had every reason to be upset, it wasn't helping matters. They could only apologize so many times in one night.

Leesil shook his head adamantly at Vàtz. 'No, absolutely not. You won't believe how soon he'll be up and around again.'

'Good. I thought that vampire was gonna kill him.'

At the word 'vampire,' Magiere closed her eyes for a few breaths. Small for his age, probably due to poor diet,

Vàtz couldn't be more than ten years old and yet spoke so matter-of-factly about something she'd only recently come to accept.

'Well, you saved him,' Leesil said. 'A good shot.'

'I was aiming for the bastard's eye.'

Leesil roughed up the boy's already frayed hair.

'Knock that off,' Vàtz snarled. 'I'm not your dog!' But he remained at Leesil's side.

Magiere felt a stab of loneliness and the desire to see little Rose at the Sea Lion again. She'd never really paid attention to how children so easily attached themselves to Leesil – even those who didn't show it openly. Though in all honesty, Vàtz didn't behave much like a child.

After they fled the inn, the boy roused the locals, and a fire brigade was organized faster than Magiere thought possible. The local constabulary arrived, and Leesil gave them a story about brigands raiding the inn. The Burdock's bottom floor was lined on the outside with stone, and one-story buildings bordered it. With enough people at hand, the fire was kept from spreading, and a portion of the ground floor might be salvaged.

So far, no one had located Milous, the innkeeper, and Magiere dreaded facing him. She planned to ask Lanjov for council money to rebuild the Burdock. If he refused, then the cost would come out of her and Leesil's final payment. Milous and Vàtz couldn't be left homeless and without a livelihood.

Leesil knelt and took the crossbow from Vàtz. Smaller than most, its length was two-thirds of the boy's height.

'How did you load this?' Leesil asked.

'I didn't,' answered Vàtz. 'My uncle loads it for me whenever he leaves for a night.'

'We're safe here,' Magiere said. 'You shouldn't need it anymore.'

'Course I will,' he answered. 'I'm gonna help you fight vampires.'

Leesil looked at Magiere.

'I don't think so,' she said, putting an end to the subject.

'It probably pays better than sweeping floors or packing some fop's baggage,' Vàtz added.

Leesil frowned and sat on the floor next to the boy, showing him how to put his feet against the bow and use his legs to help pull the crossbow's string back to the catch.

The sound of trotting feet flooded in from the hallway. Wynn reappeared, followed by an older sage of medium build and close-cropped silver hair and beard with a few hints of black remaining. His bright green eyes appraised the room's occupants. Like Wynn, he wore a simple gray robe, and his expression was somehow calm and concerned at the same time. Magiere guessed this was the head of Wynn's order, Domin Tilswith.

He stepped close to Chap and said something to Wynn, though Magiere didn't understand the words he spoke. Wynn retrieved a small jar from a shelf behind the table and handed it to the domin, but her gaze was locked upon the dog.

'Can you fix him?' Vàtz asked in a challenging tone.

The elder man smiled down at the boy. 'Yes, but not know he need me.' The accent of his broken speech was like Wynn's but thicker. He turned toward Magiere. 'I Domin Tilswith, head of new branch of guild. Your dog heal now.'

Magiere peered to where the domin gently fingered Chap's fur. A narrow cut along the hound's right shoulder was no longer bleeding and had closed. Wynn also studied the wound, and her lips parted, speechless.

'What about his front leg?' Magiere asked. 'Is it broken?'

Tilswith felt gingerly along the limb, and Chap let out a low whine.

'Bone feel right, but . . . ?' He paused to speak again to Wynn in their strange, guttural tongue.

'Fractured,' she added for the old man. 'It might still be cracked.'

She quickly poured a liquid like brewed tea from the jar onto a large wooden spoon. She was about to lower it to Chap's muzzle but stopped. Looking to Magiere, she held out the spoon.

'This will help the pain and allow him to sleep. Perhaps you should try. He seems to listen to your words most.'

'Not lately, he hasn't,' Magiere said, but she took the spoon.

Putting one hand under Chap's jaw, she tilted his muzzle up. Leesil put his hands around the dog's shoulders to hold him steady. Oddly enough, Chap didn't struggle and lapped the fluid from the spoon.

'Good boy,' Leesil praised.

Chap licked his jowls and laid his head down.

Domin Tilswith looked from Magiere to Leesil to Vàtz and then chuckled.

'We not see visitor at night much. I have . . . salve? Yes, salve for wounds.' He stopped suddenly and examined Leesil's cuts more closely. 'Claws?'

'Fingernails,' Leesil answered.

The domin raised one eyebrow and picked up another jar. Wynn fetched a bowl, filling it with water from a clay pitcher, and began washing Leesil's throat and shoulder with a clean cotton cloth. She worked gingerly, but Leesil still flinched, and Magiere tried to see how deep the cuts were.

'They're not bad,' he assured her.

Once Wynn finished, the domin liberally applied white salve to Leesil's wounds.

'Good stuff,' Leesil remarked with a soft smile. He rolled his wounded shoulder a little, but didn't wince at the movement.

'May I take that with me?' Magiere asked, pointing to the jar. 'I may need some myself . . . later, in private.'

The domin merely nodded and handed her the salve.

'What happened to all of you?' Wynn asked. She glanced up briefly from stroking Chap's back.

'Blazes and bloodsuckers is what happened,' Vatz grumbled.

Before Leesil could add anything, Magiere presented a less colorful and somewhat sketchy account of the night's events. When she finished, the domin spoke with Wynn. The elder had some trouble with the Belaskian tongue, and it was annoying not knowing exactly what he now said. With a nod to her elder, Wynn turned to Magiere.

'You must be tired, and we have a room for you.'

'A room?' Magiere asked, somewhat startled. 'We just needed to get inside and didn't know anyone else in the city. We'll stay in the kitchen until sunrise and then find an inn.'

'We know Lanjov,' Leesil suggested dryly. 'Perhaps he could put us up?'

Tilswith chuckled again. Wynn tried to scowl disapproval at him but couldn't hide her own smile. The two knew the council chairman well enough.

'Domin Tilswith says you should stay here,' answered Wynn, 'with us – for the remainder of your time in Bela. We have quarters set aside for scribes or visitors. You will be safe here and able to save your coins for other needs.'

Magiere was uncertain but relaxed a bit more. These sages reminded her of Karlin back home, who still thought his own generosity of spirit was commonplace. She looked to Leesil to see if he agreed.

'Thank you,' Leesil said to Wynn. 'We do need the rest.'

He picked up Chap, and Wynn grasped her lantern to lead them back through the passages to the far end of the building. Along the way, Wynn assisted Magiere in retrieving the chest. She showed them to a simple room with no door and two identical sets of stacked wooden bunks. Blankets had already been laid out, and another of the brilliant lanterns rested on a table at the room's rear.

'Will this do?' Wynn asked, as she led them inside.

'It'll do fine,' Magiere answered.

Leesil laid Chap on the lower bunk to the left and gestured to the bed above it.

'Up you go, Vàtz. We'll find your uncle tomorrow.'

Vàtz stood outside the doorway. His normally dour and serious expression had given way to worry as he glanced up and down the dark hall at the row of openings to similar rooms. Perhaps he'd expected to be placed in a separate room. At Leesil's words, he appeared openly relieved and scrambled into the bunk above Chap.

Leesil pulled a blanket over the boy and added, 'Hunters of the dead stay together at night.'

With a grunt of acknowledgment, Vàtz pulled the blanket under his chin and closed his eyes. Magiere wondered how often the boy was left on his own and what had happened to his parents.

After helping Magiere to settle the chest, Wynn placed her lantern on the table, sliding the one there closer. She removed its tin cap and frosted glass, and as she reached toward the exposed light, Magiere almost called out. The sage's slim fingers closed about it and were stopped firmly before pinching out the illumination. When she lifted her hand, the light came with it, perched between her fingertips.

'What are . . . what is that?' Leesil asked, stepping closer.

Wynn smiled. 'It is a cold lamp.'

Opening her hand, the light rolled down her fingers and into her palm, and though it was still painful to the eyes, Magiere saw the glimmering outline of a clear crystal against Wynn's skin. It was no longer or thicker than one joint of her finger.

'With all that we keep here – scrolls, books, and other precious knowledge – open flame is a risk we cannot tolerate,' she explained. 'Some of our people are thaumaturgical artificers, mages of making, and create the crystals we use in our lamps.' She held it out. 'Here, feel it.'

Magiere set down the salve jar on the chest and took the crystal with some hesitancy. It was cool to the touch.

'Now rub it between your hands,' Wynn instructed.

She did so gently, and when she opened her hands, the light was indeed too bright to look at.

'That is all you need do if it dims,' Wynn explained. Taking the crystal again, she returned it to the lantern, replacing both glass and cap. 'Sleep as late as you wish and come to the kitchen when you wake.'

She slipped out and back the way they had come.

When Magiere was certain the sage was gone, she whispered, 'Vàtz?'

The boy only grumbled and shifted, seemingly lost in slumber, and Magiere turned to Leesil.

'It was him, the one in my vision. He was the one in my room tonight.'

For a moment, Leesil appeared uncertain what she meant. But then, instead of eagerness over finding their prey, he closed his eyes and slumped on the edge of the bunk across from Chap.

It was Magiere's turn to wonder in confusion.

'Are you certain about this?' Leesil asked.

'Dressed like a noble in a well-tailored black cloak,' she answered. 'He wasn't in the council chambers that first day we arrived.' Her voice grew firm. 'But he wore black gloves, well fitted. How many other undeads do you think we can find like that?'

'Oh, this is more twisted than even I can deal with,' Leesil muttered.

'What?' Magiere asked. 'I've seen him now. This is what we're here for.'

'No, it isn't,' he whispered.

She crouched down with some effort, the side of her chest aching even more. When she looked into Leesil's narrowed eyes, he stared back at her, unblinking.

'It was Ratboy . . . in my room,' he said.

His words washed all else from Magiere's thoughts. 'Ratboy?'

'He was different . . . dressed like a wealthy elite,' Leesil went on. 'And wielding a sword this time, like some half-pint warrior. But it was him.'

This was far beyond anything Magiere had anticipated. She shook her head slowly. 'Please don't tell me he was wearing black gloves as well.'

Leesil shook his head as well. 'I don't recall.'

Confusion and fatigue snuffed the last of Magiere's fury at seeing the nobleman's black-gloved hands. Sly and cunning, Ratboy, Rashed, and Teesha had concealed themselves among townsfolk – but in an out-of-the-way place, not the king's city. So why would Ratboy now keep company with a demented dead nobleman murdering the city's elite citizens . . . and not even for their blood? She tried to stand again but doubled over halfway, pain slicing through her side.

Leesil snatched the side of her shirt and lifted it. In reflex, she swatted his hand aside.

'What are you doing?'

'Oh, stop playing the prude,' he growled. 'You didn't get out as unscathed as you look. Now sit down.'

Magiere was too tired to argue. It wasn't the first time they'd tended each other's wounds. She settled on the bunk's edge, and he lifted the side of her shirt again.

'Ah, I see you're finally getting some color,' Leesil said with a frown.

Magiere pulled the shirt up enough to see for herself. A large patch of her pale torso was mottled and yellowed. There was still a hint of black and blue beneath the skin, but the bruise looked days old instead of a quarter night.

'You and that dog.' Leesil sighed, and reached behind her on the bed to gather the folded blanket against the wall. 'Still, the salve should take away some pain. Lean back.'

Magiere reclined, and if she had any reluctance at being tended like an invalid, she lost it in another aching stab.

Leesil unbuttoned her shirt to the base of her breastbone. She suppressed another urge to push him away and do it herself. He lifted the shirt side to expose her ribs and then dipped his fingers into the salve sitting on the chest. She winced hard as he gently worked the salve into her side, but her thoughts were still on the puzzle that had grown more baffling this night.

'What is Ratboy doing here?' she asked. 'He's more savage than Rashed or Teesha were, but that's not the same as butchering bodies without feeding. It's not his way.'

'I told you when we left Au'shiyn's home, someone's on the game here.' There was a hint of exasperation in Leesil's voice. 'I just didn't know it was that little wretch until now.'

His fingers worked along the edge of her rib cage

around her white stomach. It was possible she'd cracked a few ribs, but the pain began to dull. She felt numb beneath the salve, which made the occasional brush of Leesil's hand against her stomach more acute.

'Make some sense, please,' she said tiredly.

'Put it together,' he answered. 'The killer left Chesna dead on Lanjov's doorstep but never contacted Lanjov or the council. So why? Intimidation? Fair enough, but for what reason? And what did Lanjov and the council do?'

'They sent for us,' she answered.

'All the missing people, a few bodies, and then Chesna . . . as if someone felt he wasn't getting enough attention and needed to be a little more obvious.'

Magiere hesitated, not even wanting to believe where he was leading her.

'Bait,' she whispered.

Leesil nodded.

'Yes, and we walked right into the snare, no better than the peasants we fooled all those years on the road. Tonight was Ratboy's worn-out way of throwing a welcoming party, complete with his new family.'

'But why Au'shiyn?' she asked. 'That doesn't fit, if murdering nobles was just to get us here. He died after we arrived.'

'I don't know.' Leesil shook his head. 'It's a large city, and perhaps they couldn't find us either and needed us to show ourselves. Even in daylight when we went to Au'shiyn's, Ratboy could have found a way to track us.'

As Leesil finished a stroke of salve down her side, his wrist brushed the crest of her hipbone. Magiere flinched more from pain than the flurry of nerves she felt inside. Leesil pulled away and frowned again.

'Looks like he grazed the hip as well.'

'No, it's fine,' she said, and began to sit up.

'Stop being a child,' he snapped. With one quick hand to her shoulder, he shoved her back. 'We hunt tomorrow, and even your rapid healing needs all the help it can get.'

Resentment got the better of Magiere's nervous discomfort. She leaned back on her elbows, as he uncinched her belt and carefully peeled the side of her breeches down enough to expose her hipbone. Discolored like her side, the skin was also scraped raw from the nobleman's boot.

As Leesil worked the salve in, she refused to flinch and give him an excuse for another remark. But when the numbness settled in, it was followed by the same mix of uneasiness and contentment that spread from Leesil's fingertips.

Magiere watched him, still naked to the waist, and their conversation slipped from her mind.

'We need to find you shirt,' she said quietly.

'You don't look so neat and tidy yourself,' he replied. 'Unless those black stains are some new badge of honor for dhampirs. Guess you finally got me out of my old rags.'

Every nerve in Magiere's body tightened in a rush of panic, and she stood up, buckling her belt with some difficulty.

'Thanks . . . it's better now,' she said.

Leesil sat tight-lipped, as if she'd just insulted him.

'You'd better take the bottom bunk, in case you need to get up in the night,' he said.

With that, he hauled himself into the top bed and flopped back to stare at the ceiling.

Magiere settled on the lower bunk. It didn't matter how much she might want Leesil closer, because the closer he came, the more danger he would be in. She was still a dhampir, and nothing would change that.

'Leesil?' she asked, wondering if he were still awake.

'What?' he said from above.

'If it's a trap, why are we playing into it?' She didn't really expect an answer, and just wanted to hear his voice. 'Shouldn't we wait?'

'No, not on my life,' he said harshly.

The pause that followed was so long, Magiere was about to speak when Leesil abruptly continued.

'He's mine. That filthy little whelp is mine. I'm going to finish what I should have . . . what I couldn't that night outside of Miiska.'

This was no time for vengeance, and Magiere felt an angry rebuke rising in her throat. Then she remembered her rage upon seeing the nobleman in his black gloves.

'With the four who attacked us,' she said, 'there should be a clear trail to follow. Except Chap is too injured to track.'

'We may not have to search anymore,' he whispered. 'They're coming to us now. And that suits me.'

'We have to find the lair,' she insisted. 'This won't be over until we're sure we've gotten them all.'

He didn't answer, and in a little while, his breathing deepened.

The cold lamp burned brightly from the table. Magiere wasn't certain she'd be able to sleep. She lay listening to Leesil's deep, slow breaths and the occasional creak of the bunks when he shifted. She closed her eyes against the light.

Blind in one eye, his body trembling with exhaustion and lost fluids, Toret shoved open the front door of his house, and he, Chane, and Tibor staggered into the foyer.

Sapphire sat in the parlor in her mustard silk gown. Her jaw dropped. Toret knew they were an ugly sight.

Tibor had long gashes all over his arms and face. There was a blackened hole in the middle of his throat, and his dirty clothes were a shredded mess. Chane wasn't wearing his cloak. Something sharp had slashed through the shoulder of his vestment and shirt, leaving a black oozing mess down his sleeve. The wound wouldn't close.

Toret was the worst of all. In place of his right eye was a gore-seeping cavity. His upper chest was split open, his ribs and severed breastbone exposed in the wide wound. The whole front of his split vestment was soaked black like Chane's sleeve. But he was home now, and Sapphire was waiting. Toret stumbled toward her.

'My sweet,' he managed to say.

Her horror grew as he closed the gap between them and put his hands on her shoulders for support. She stepped back and pushed him away.

'Toret! This is real silk.'

Toret leaned on the divan in confusion, sending fresh black fluids trickling down one arm. Why didn't she comfort him?

'That's a velvet divan,' she said. 'Chane, do something! And don't you dare let that sailor in here.'

Toret stared at her through his one good eye. 'Sapphire . . . my love. We're in a bad way. We need your help.'

She frowned, as if this scene were simply too much, and whirled out of the room without a word.

Toret watched Sapphire's departing yellow-clad backside in disbelief. He could order her to stay. He could order her to help him, but he didn't. She should be caring for him, as Teesha had cared for Rashed, yet now she walked away in disgust because he was bleeding.

Lacking his usual grace, Chane stumbled in to assist him.

'You need rest,' he said flatly. 'So does Tibor.'

'I need to feed,' Toret answered. 'Can you find me something?'

Chane moved to the window, lifted the curtain aside, and looked out.

'Dawn is too close, but rest will help, and I will go out the moment the sun sets tonight.' He looked at his own open wound. 'This is not closing. What do you know of the dhampir's sword?'

Toret sank upon the divan and leaned back. 'Enchanted – or cursed,' he replied. 'I've felt its sting myself.'

Chane pointed to Tibor standing in the foyer. 'What about his throat? A quarrel should not do that to one of us.'

'Simple trick. It was soaked in garlic water . . . poison to us.' Toret closed his eye. 'Send Tibor up to rest and then assist me.'

It shouldn't be Chane helping him but Sapphire. Through the nightmare of making their way home unseen, Toret's mind was filled with images of Sapphire's concern for him, of how she would care for him as he had cared for her.

He felt strong hands pulling him up, but he pushed Chane away.

'Go downstairs and rest.'

'Yes . . . master.'

Toret walked to the stairs and grabbed the railing. As he climbed, he hoped feeding later would restore his mutilated eye. The half-blood had used mundane weapons, not like the dhampir's sword, so time and life force should heal his wounds completely. But when he saw Sapphire's closed door, he wondered if all wounds would heal.

He went to his room alone.

Welstiel sat at a small table in his room, thinking. At the bedside in the frosted-glass globe on its plain iron pedestal, the three dancing sparks dimly illuminated the small room.

It was the oldest thing he possessed, having been the first thing he'd ever created in his long studies. That seemed so very long ago.

His fingers laced, and he absently traced the stub of the severed smallest finger with his other hand. His plan was not proceeding smoothly, and he was troubled. Lanjov was ready to dismiss the dhampir, and this was not a contingency Welstiel had considered. Magiere was an excellent hunter. This alone should outweigh any of her social shortcomings, even in Lanjov's world. Or so he had thought.

In addition, the pathetic Ratboy – or Toret – was not proving the challenge Welstiel had hoped. Magiere required practice and training. She needed to learn to handle multiple opponents, and to expect that older prey might have additional skills at their disposal beyond the varied abilities and strengths of the Noble Dead. Ratboy's lackey, Chane, was obviously a conjuror, and perhaps more, and yet for all Ratboy's efforts and resources, he bumbled about like a fool.

Welstiel leaned back, exhausted. He had used his own methods to keep the dreams at bay for several days now – to keep himself from the coils of his dream patron. But he had to rest, at least a little while, before anything further could be addressed. He rose, made sure the door was tightly locked, and collapsed on the bed.

He barely noticed the room. A typical inn, and suitable for the kind of man who frequented the Knight's House, but he had seen the inside of too many inns. In recent years, they'd all begun to look the same. He reached into his baggage under the bed and pulled out a pewter vial, sipped its content lightly, and murmured a soft chant. Willing himself not to sink into dreams and merely to lie down for a while, he closed his eyes.

But it had been too long since he'd rested.

The world around him shifted and rolled like tall desert dunes, the countless grains of sand threatening to bury or pull him under. But there was no sand. The dunes were black. Movement sharpened slowly into clarity and sand grains became the glitter of light reflected upon black reptilian scales. Scale-covered dunes became a mammoth serpent's coils, circling on all sides of him. They slowly writhed with no beginning and no end and no space between.

'Where?' Welstiel asked. 'Where is it? It has been so many years. Am I closer?'

They were the same questions he always asked.

High . . . to the cold and ice, came the whispered answer that penetrated his thoughts. *Guarded by old ones . . . oldest of predecessors.*

'How do I find it?'

As always, he tried to peer beyond the black coils to find what he sought, but he still did not know what it looked like – only what the coils promised it would do for him.

A jewel or gem – something unique and long forgotten to the world. It would be endowed with a divine essence able to free him of his current existence. He let his mind roll with the coils around him.

The old ones.

He did not know for certain, but he suspected what the coils tried to tell him. And to battle these guards was why he needed and prepared Magiere. She would be the most useful tool for his task.

The constantly roiling coils of his patron exhausted him, but he languished amid its dream. Words slipped like an echo through his mind. He could not tell if they came from his own thoughts or his faceless, scaled patron.

The sister of the dead will lead you.

15

Sgäile neared the end of the district outside of Bela's third ring wall. He slipped off his cloak and reversed it. The inner lining, now outward, was evening blue and, though as dark as the rest of his gray-green raiment, broke the conspicuous monotone of his attire. His features would be eye-catching enough. He disassembled his shortbow, lodging the pieces in the back of his belt.

Humans moved about the street, but with his cowl up, few took notice of him. He slowed has pace as he approached the gatehouse through the outer ring wall.

Beneath the raised portcullis were four white-surcoated city guards, watching each passerby, and several other armed men in plain dress. Upon the wall top, more guards paced the rampart in both directions into the distance. There were more than expected, and he wondered what had forced an increase in the day watch.

A guard lowered a prong pike across his path. 'What's your business here, master treeborn?'

The man was tall for a human, almost as tall as Sgäile, with a close-cropped beard spiking from his chin and small eyes beneath the ridge of his plumed helmet. Human facial hair had always been somewhat repugnant to Sgäile.

'I am delivering a letter to kin,' he answered.

After a moment's appraisal, the guard held out his gloved hand. 'Let's have a look.'

Sgäile withdrew a folded paper from his vestment. The guard took it and roughly snapped it open with one hand, squinting as he stared at the inked scrawling upon it.

It was merely a letter from Sgäile's brother on a journey down the coast. As it was scripted in Sgäile's own tongue, it was doubtful this simple guard would know the difference.

'There has been a death in our clan,' Sgäile lied. 'I am here as the bearer of sad tidings for a kinsman.'

The guard shook his head, trying to read the letter, and then handed it back.

'Move along,' he ordered.

Sgäile gave a curt nod and passed through the gate-house archway.

In this lower district, few people moved about the filthy streets. The denizens of the city called this place Chatrù ché Zästup – Hovel Row – and its packed stench confirmed its name. Little was given attention in such a place, which was why the one he came to see would be found here.

Upon arrival he ignored the dwelling's shabby appearance and directly approached the front door. His knock was light and sharp, and he hoped the occupant was at home.

The door cracked ajar, and it was dark inside. A figure appeared back in the shadows through the opening.

Thin, with sharply peaked ears and long, sand-blond tangled hair, the man hid his attire beneath a faded dun-colored cloak. His large amber eyes windened, and there was the barest hint of joy in his soft smile for the visitor upon his porch.

'Kinsman,' he whispered.

The door opened fully, and Sgäile quickly stepped inside.

Something tugged Leesil's bare foot. He opened sleepy eyes to see Vàtz hanging on the bunk's edge, glowering at him.

'You all right?' Leesil mumbled.

'I got to find my uncle,' Vàtz answered. 'And tell him about the inn.'

'The whole district knows by now,' Leesil said, coming fully awake. 'I'll get you back. He's probably worried, wondering where you are.'

Vàtz slowly blinked hazel eyes too large for his face.

'Naw, but he'll be mad about the inn, and I got to tell him what happened. And you shouldn't be there when I do.'

Leesil heard Magiere stir, and she rolled out of the bunk below him.

'Of course we should,' she said. 'You don't have to deal with this. None of it is your fault.'

'No, he'll take it better from me,' Vàtz said, shaking his head adamantly. 'Just stay and help that Wynn girl track down the vampires from all that stuff she's reading. I'll be back soon to help fight. I've a notion what you might be getting paid, so I ain't working cheap.'

'Now you hold on,' Leesil growled.

The boy's ardor for his fancied new trade was getting out of hand. Before Leesil could tell Vàtz to put such ideas out of his head, Magiere turned the subject aside.

'Tell your uncle I'll request that the council pay to rebuild the Burdock, and if they refuse, we'll take care of it somehow.'

'Good enough.' Vàtz nodded in satisfaction. 'You're okay . . . though I still should have charged you more on the pier.' He strode out of the room on his short legs.

Leesil's yawn ended in a sigh. 'Have we inherited a child?'

'He won't take no for an answer,' Magiere replied. 'So we make sure he gets no opportunity for trouble.'

'Ratboy.' Leesil leaned back again. 'He knows quite a bit about us. That may change the way we handle this.'

The sight of Ratboy had been unsettling, to say the least. Of all possible places across this land, it seemed nearly impossible that Ratboy should reside in two places that he and Magiere were called to for different reasons. But the pieces slid together in his mind last night while he'd been ministering to Magiere. It bothered him that they'd been played so easily into this blood-soaked mess. Taking Ratboy's head would end that problem, much to his pleasure.

Magiere leaned down to check on Chap. At her hesitant touch, the dog yawned deeply, and then rolled off the bunk, limping but surprisingly able to hobble about. She roughed up the fur on his head.

'He heals even faster than I do.'

Leesil watched, unnoticed, as Magiere lifted the side of her shirt enough to inspect her ribs. The yellowed mottling was still visible, but no black and blue remained beneath.

'Chap can't track yet,' Magiere added. 'So we might as well look in on Wynn. I don't read well, but you do, and perhaps we can narrow down what she's looking for.'

Leesil looked down at himself. 'We need to find me some clothes. Boots and a shirt, at least.'

Her expression seemed troubled, as if in looking at him she was now uncertain of something. Did it bother her that much to look at him?

'Stay here,' she said, 'and I'll see what I can find.'

The only clothing Magiere found was a shabby gray hand-me-down sage's robe and a guard's old, faded surcoat. Leesil chose the surcoat, which he sliced off just below the belt and sashed around his waist with the remaining strips. It didn't cover the stilettos strapped to his smooth brown arms. The soldier's boots were too large, so he wore a pair of sage's sandals instead.

Once he was decent, of course, Leesil gave little thought to his attire. Magiere found the effect worse than his previous shabby shirt, as he would stick out wherever they went. There would be no more arguments about new clothes. She was reoutfitting him at the first opportunity, including some additional raiment she had in mind.

Magiere led them back to the old sergeant's chamber now used as the sages' study. She liked it, with its glowing cold lamps, shelves and tables, parchments and books. A peaceful place of thought, even if she couldn't read most of what was stored here. To her mild surprise, the place had changed. Casks, crates, and stacks of parchment were piled around the far table, and Wynn was shuffling through documents. She smiled widely at Magiere.

'It would appear both the city guard and the local constabulary consider me part of this investigation. I've received almost everything I asked for in the way of records.'

Magiere sat down on a stool. 'They're finally listening to us. Hopefully, this will all be over soon, but we're still uncertain how many undeads we're tracking. The number keeps growing.'

Leesil followed more slowly with Chap, looking over the room with mild surprise, taking in the sight of rolled parchments and a few leather- or wood-bound sheaves and books. He glanced out one of the small windows in the room with concern.

'I hope Vàtz gets himself back here before nightfall or stays in with his uncle. Ratboy and his little horde have seen him. It's not going to be safe out there, especially near the inn.'

'How many are you hunting?' Wynn asked.

'At least four,' Magiere said thoughtfully. 'Assuming Sapphire wasn't destroyed. There were two in Leesil's room, and one of them we know. He escaped us in Miiska. I took down the second one entering my room, but not the first. He is a more serious problem.'

Wynn set down a handful of parchments, attentive as Magiere shifted upon the stool and continued.

'He's a mage, or some such, and ignited his dead companion's body from across the room. The place burned down and left me with no proof – no head – to show the council.'

Wynn's nose wrinkled. Magiere had related some of this the previous night, but without mention of a headless corpse.

'That last one was dressed as a noble,' Magiere went on. 'With a cloak and black gloves. I've never seen him before, but he could be the one we are after . . . who murdered Chesna, and possibly Au'shiyn.'

Wynn lifted a teapot from a side table and poured two steaming mugs, dropping a tiny green leaf into each. She handed one to Magiere. It smelled slightly of mint.

'I will arrange food shortly,' Wynn said. 'Tell me what this nobleman looked like. I've seen many of the council and their staff on royal grounds.'

'Tall, well built, not much older than me,' Magiere said. 'Handsome, I suppose, with hair to about the chin and tucked behind his ears. Good with a sword but . . .'

Magiere hung on the thought for a moment, but still could not understand what had happened in the room with the nobleman.

'When I fight one of their kind, at times I pick up impressions – feelings, intentions, or occasionally a name or identity. There were strange flashes from him, as if he wanted to bleed me slowly, toy with me rather than kill me. And then everything wiped away, and I felt nothing from him.'

Wynn's head tilted; then she shook it. 'Your description

does not match anyone I have seen on the council or at their hall.'

Magiere shook her head as well. 'I'm not certain of his voice, as I didn't hear much of it.'

'You've heard the killer's voice?' Wynn asked in surprise.

'A few words . . . in a vision. Which means we may be looking for five.'

The mention of visions gave Wynn pause, though she did not seem surprised, which in turn made Magiere wonder.

'I will return in a moment with food,' Wynn said quietly, and left the room.

She returned shortly with a wooden tray carrying three bowls of steaming soup made from yellow beans, potatoes, and assorted vegetables. She passed one each to Magiere and Leesil, set the third upon the floor before Chap, and gestured to the crates around them.

'Perhaps these will help us,' she said. 'They contain records, some of which are for dwellings purchased in the half year. It is further back than you asked for, and not all are deeds and bills of sale, but I wanted to be thorough. The one you call Sapphire, or some of the others, could have existed in the city before the death of Lanjov's daughter.'

'Where do we start?' Magiere asked.

Wynn looked at her. 'You wish to sift through records?'

Leesil pulled off the top of a crate, fingering through its contents.

'Chap needs more rest, so there's little else to do,' Magiere explained.

At these words, Chap growled and loped toward the door, but he stumbled three times, halting in frustration.

'Get back here. You can't hunt like that,' Leesil said without looking up. He piled parchments and a few scroll cases onto a table. 'We're looking for a three-story dwelling; that's what Sapphire told me. Knowing Rashed's past arrangements, if Sapphire is with Ratboy, the little butcher will want underground access. Sing out if you find any cellars in the descriptions.'

Magiere knew he was speculating, but it made sense.

'Oh,' Wynn added, 'And if Magiere's theory of a connection to Lanjov is correct, be sure to check any deed you find against the names of the council members.'

Chap growled again.

'What's wrong with him?' Magiere asked.

'He'd rather be hunting.' Leesil scowled, and then his expression became troubled at some thought. His voice became hesitant. 'I lost my shirt.'

Magiere shook her head. Since he now resembled a refugee soldier, his lost shirt was rather obvious. 'We'll get you another one.'

'No, I mean, I lost my shirt. The shreds of cloth from Chesna and Au'shiyn and Sapphire's dress were inside it. Chap may not be able to track without them.'

'Oh, Leesil . . .' Magiere sighed, and sank back down on a crate. Another setback wasn't what they needed. 'There's nothing you could've done. We barely got out of the fire with most of our belongings.'

Wynn shuffled and organized parchments into new stacks, separating what appeared to be recent deeds from older ones and other papers they didn't need.

'It does not matter,' she offered. 'You told me Chap can smell the presence of an undead. All we need do is find the right dwelling and bring him near it.'

The young sage was right, and Magiere opened another crate.

'Start with the properties purchased in richer districts about three months ago,' she instructed. 'Or at least what sold for a substantial sum.'

Wynn nodded and continued sorting, while Leesil stopped to stir his soup with a spoon.

Chap limped back, ignoring the bowl on the floor, and, without warning, reared up to place both paws on Wynn's table. He sniffed at the parchment stacks, and then suddenly began clawing sheets off the table as he pushed his nose deeper in the piles.

'What is wrong with him?' Wynn asked, voice rising above its normal calm.

She grabbed at papers as they flew or were knocked from the table. Magiere dropped the stack she held, about to go after the hound and the parchments spilling everywhere around the table. Leesil reached out first, setting his bowl aside.

'Get down. Stop that.'

Chap turned his head and snarled at Leesil, partially baring his teeth. His growl faded to a low, continuous rumble. Instead of dropping down, he shoved his muzzle into another stack, knocking half of it across the table. Wynn made a quick grab for the teapot before it toppled.

'Chap, please!' she said in frustration.

Just once the hound glanced at Wynn with an extra rumble.

'All right, that's enough,' Magiere snapped.

Wynn sat back in fright, but watched as Chap continued digging through the parchments. 'Wait,' she whispered. She hesitated a moment longer, and then she whispered again, this time to the hound. '*a'Créohk, mâthajmé.*'

Chap froze, almost appearing startled, and looked up at her.

Magiere stepped closer. 'What did you say to him?'

Everyone's attention was now fixed on Chap, ignoring even the disarray he'd created. The hound lowered his head as if aware he was the center of attention. Muzzle on the table, he glared at the young sage with a low grumble in his throat.

Wynn's breaths were quick and shallow as she stared back at the dog. '*a'Créohk, mâthajmé,*' she repeated.

Chap dropped down, rumbling still in his throat, and belly-crawled under a nearby table.

As suddenly as Chap had attacked the parchments on the desk, Wynn bolted across the room and began rummaging though the contents of other tables. She didn't seem to find what she was after and turned instead to the room's rear shelves.

'What are you doing?' Leesil insisted. 'Just what is going on here?'

'He understood me.' Wynn gasped. Shoving books roughly aside, she dumped small boxes out on the table and sifted quickly through their contents.

'So he understands Elvish,' Leesil said in confusion. 'My mother gave him to me and likely got him from her own people. He's heard it before.'

'No,' Wynn said. 'I requested that he halt what he was doing.'

'So you told him to stop,' Magiere added. 'He's smart enough to know that, though I don't know why he listens to you now instead of us.' But she still stepped to the side, trying to see where Chap had gone.

'No!' Wynn shouted this time, and both Magiere and Leesil were taken back by her tone.

Wynn tried to compose herself and panted as if out of breath.

'It was not an order,' she continued more calmly, 'and he could not have . . . should not have known, even if raised hearing your mother speak some of the language.'

'Make sense,' Magiere snapped at her.

Wynn took several more deep breaths. 'I requested – not ordered – that he end what he was doing . . . formally.' She paused, then held up a hand before anyone could interrupt. 'I formed it in the Elvish that I speak. Any one root word in Elvish can be transformed into an action, thing, or rather verb, noun, and so on. The little Elvish I've heard or read since arriving in Bela is not formed the same way as from my region, though I'm not certain why.'

Magiere was utterly confused now and only barely followed what the young sage was saying. Wynn gasped in exasperation.

'I formed the request in the Elvish I know, not what Chap would have heard. And even so, a dog would not have understood without interpreting the differences of dialect, let alone the formality of phrasing.'

Finished, she waited for the words to sink in.

An unsettling chill crept over Magiere as she began to comprehend the explanation, though it didn't quite explain much. Leesil crouched down to peer through the legs of the room's furniture.

'Chap?' he said, half-voiced.

Magiere crouched down as well.

The dog hunkered in the shadows beneath the table in the farthest rear corner of the room. His glittering eyes sparked, shifting between her and Leesil. He looked in Wynn's direction with a slight show of teeth, as if she were a threat he wouldn't even come out to face.

Wynn returned to her frantic search and then suddenly stopped, snatching up an item from a box of quills, styluses, and charcoals. She scurried to the middle of the room between the dog's hiding place and Leesil and dropped to the floor.

'Please stay behind me,' she instructed. 'I think he knows what we are saying . . . and is very upset.'

Chap twisted about beneath the table, eyes fixed on the young sage. He snarled at her with exposed teeth.

'Chap, stop it,' Leesil ordered, but the dog barely glanced at him.

'That is ridiculous,' Magiere muttered, but readied to jerk Wynn back if Chap lunged at her.

Wynn held a lump of white chalk, and she poised it on the floor.

'Call to him,' she said to Leesil.

Leesil looked at her suspiciously, and with a sigh of resignation, did as she asked. 'Come on, boy.'

Chap growled at him, and dropped his head low to the floor.

'Come out,' Leesil insisted.

The hound inched forward, gaze shifting between the three of them, but mostly still glaring at Wynn. When he'd crossed half the distance, Wynn began drawing on the floor with the chalk. She scripted two sets of symbols a hand breadth apart, but Magiere couldn't read either of them. Wynn pointed to the first and then the second.

'*Bithâ . . . na-bithâ*,' she said, looking to Chap.

She scrawled a second set of words below the first, this time in Belaskian.

'Yes . . . no.'

Chap immediately backed away with a pathetic whine.

'Come here,' Magiere ordered him.

The hound dipped his muzzle to the floor with a loud, resistant rumble. He limped forward again, stopping before the chalked words and wrinkling his jowls at the young sage. It took another moment before Wynn could speak.

'*Majay-hì?*'

Chap turned slowly toward Leesil, staring at him for a moment. His paw reached out to the first set of words on the floor.

Yes.

'Oh . . .' Wynn whispered, sitting back upon her folded legs. 'Oh . . .'

Chap hung his head.

Leesil dropped hard to sit on the floor and ran a hand across his face. He looked like a peasant mourner in a dank Droevinkan burial ground, lost and abandoned.

Wynn's hand, still holding the chalk, was shaking.

'Fay,' the young sage whispered, gazing at the dog.

'What?' Magiere asked, but when no answer came, she shook Wynn by the shoulder. 'What do you mean, "Fay"?'

Wynn looked back at her.

'He is Fay,' she said, and swallowed hard. 'An elemental spirit.'

Magiere shook her head with a grunt of disgust. 'That's just something that loon Welstiel called him. You told us yourself it was probably a folk term for his breed, even if he's a rare kind at that.'

Wynn regained some of her composure, her attention split between Magiere and the hound.

'He senses death and life, has intelligence, understands language as well as dialect, heals miraculously . . . and his injuries are slight compared to what they should have been. I know of no breed such as his, and he does not have the look of mongrel or mix. You both have told me how powerful he is in battle, enough to face an undead.'

She looked back to Chap, leaning down and trying to catch the dog's attention, but Chap swiveled away.

'Possession cannot change an animal's innate intellect, not that I know of,' Wynn continued. 'So his intelligence is part of his nature. I know of no way such could be created through magic.' She fingered the chalk markings on the floor. 'And when asked, he confirms it himself.'

Magiere was on her guard now. Chap had been with them for years – had been with Leesil most of his life. In all that time, the hound had understood everything they'd said and done? True, Chap displayed uncanny intelligence for an animal, but this was nonsense.

'How is this possible?' Magiere demanded. 'Even if he is capable? Leesil's had him since they were both young . . . and why are we only now finding this out?'

Wynn swallowed hard and shook her head.

'I don't give a damn,' Leesil muttered. 'I'm sick of every day revealing more . . . *things*' – he looked suspiciously at the dog – 'pulling and pushing us around like unwitting puppets.'

Magiere couldn't help but share Leesil's suspicion. Years ago, she'd stepped from a tavern into the dank, cold night of a Stravinan town so far inland and remote she no longer remembered its name.

A trembling itch had run up her spine as her senses came alive to the smallest sound and scent, followed by an urgency that told her to turn about. Something approached from behind.

It was the barest, tiniest rustle she shouldn't have *heard*, but she had heard rather than felt the hand digging in the cloth sack over her shoulder.

When Magiere whirled, ready to deal with this thief, she halted with his wrist in her grip. They stood there, she and he, staring at each other. Neither tried to move away. There was complete surprise on the thief's tan face.

Leesil's face.

Now, in the sages' barracks, Magiere looked into Leesil's amber eyes.

Something had prompted Leesil to steal from a well-armed woman. Something had piqued her awareness of a thief. After all the skill and cunning Leesil displayed over the years, she shouldn't have caught him. And somewhere nearby had been a dog.

If any of what Wynn concluded was true, then why of all people did this creature choose to keep company with a couple of peasant-cheating rogues?

Magiere shivered at the sudden recollection of the night she'd chased Chap into the street from the Burdock. There had been an urge to find Leesil, built upon her memory of their first meeting. Why was she recalling these two events now?

Leesil's eyes widened at her, and a sickening knot formed in her stomach.

'What . . . ?' she asked hesitantly. 'What're you thinking?'

'The first night . . .' he said, uncertainly. 'I remember the first night we met.'

Leesil's face turned hard and cold as he looked upon Chap.

'You . . .' Leesil whispered.

Magiere's muscles clenched at the thought of what had happened that first night she looked into Leesil's eyes – and neither of them had known until now.

'You son of a bitch!' Leesil snarled, and he lunged at the hound.

Chap skittered away as Wynn fell backward, caught between the two of them.

Magiere grabbed Leesil by the waist and, crouched as she was, threw herself backward, toppling them both across the floor. Wynn spread her arms out like a barrier, with Chap nervously peering around her side.

Clinging tightly to Leesil, Magiere pulled him along as she backed across the floor up against the legs of a table.

'You did that to me!' Leesil shouted at the hound. 'Stealing from a wandering woman with a sword – it was lunacy – but I couldn't leave well enough alone.'

'Stop it,' Wynn shouted back. 'From all you have told me, he has never harmed you . . . never done anything to hurt you.'

'Leesil, calm down,' Magiere whispered.

He wrestled out of her grip and rolled to his feet. Backing toward the hallway entrance, he wouldn't even look at Chap.

'I can't be here.'

He left without another word.

Gathering her gray robes and pushing her braid back, Wynn clambered to her feet. The young sage was obviously at her wits' end.

'I do not understand,' she said, looking to Magiere for an answer. 'Why is Leesil acting this way?'

Magiere had no answer for her. There was too much behind all of it, too little time, and so much more they were now facing. All these years, Chap had been hiding from them, following them silently. And telling Wynn anything meant revealing her and Leesil's past livelihood to someone who wouldn't understand it.

'Stay,' Magiere finally managed to get out. 'Stay with Chap and try to find out why he was digging through those parchments.'

Betrayal and revelations aside, their immediate needs hadn't changed. She couldn't allow Leesil to turn away now. As she backed toward the hallway, Chap peered again around Wynn's long gray robe.

Canine crystal blue eyes looked at Magiere, watching her carefully.

The moment the sun set, Chane slipped from the house to find Toret sustenance. He felt the hunger himself, and his wounded shoulder troubled him. It burned.

He traveled the alleys and side ways into a lower district

until coming upon a derelict woman resting behind a stack of crates, half-conscious, an empty brown glass bottle in her hand, the air around her smelling of cheap liquor.

Her flesh reeked of sweat and filth and urine, but Chane gorged himself on her blood, soaking in her life. He was careful not to shed a single drop on his clothing. Eyes closed, he settled back and focused inward, awareness sifting through his flesh, driving the woman's stolen life into his shoulder.

Pain decreased, but the wound did not fully heal.

He let the woman's body lie where he had found it. As he walked away, it occurred to him that Toret had abandoned all rules concerning prey. Before this hunter's arrival, they killed infrequently and always disposed of the bodies with discretion — or rather, Chane made certain that was what Toret believed. Now, no question were asked.

The hunter.

She was the key to fit the locks and chains upon him. All he need do was to bring Toret and this dhampir together. All previous schemes tossed aside, he stepped onto the main street of the inner ring wall, heading for the sages' old barracks. Toret waited to be fed, and time was limited.

Upon reaching the barracks, Chane stepped inside, not bothering to knock. It was still early evening, and likely Wynn would be about. He headed straight for the large study area, relieved to find her inside poring over a stack of parchments.

He paused upon entering.

Across the floor were scattered scribblings. Chalked words were everywhere, and only a 'yes' and 'no' were in Belaskian, the rest scrawled in what appeared to be Elvish script in odd groups at all angles.

He stepped in, and Wynn noticed his arrival. She looked

perfect sitting there in her neat gray robes and long brown braid, surrounded by piles of parchment in the glowing light of the cold lamp upon her desk. Her calm olive face was lovely, and her knowledgeable counsel was always welcome. He could see that she was attracted to him, though her intellectual nature blinded her awareness of this. She was a little sparrow of a scholar, and he would never play with her.

'Good evening, Wynn,' he said politely.

For some reason, she appeared mildly agitated and not particularly glad to see him.

'Oh, Chane . . . did we plan to meet this evening?'

He crossed the room and pulled up a vacant stool to sit by her. 'No, but I need information and thought to stop by. I hope that is all right?'

She nodded absently, preoccupied, and began scooping up parchments into neat stacks. 'Yes, you are always welcome. There is simply a great deal happening right now.'

'What is this?' Chane asked, glancing down at the chalked symbols on the floor and indicating the general disarray of the room.

'Assisting some friends,' she replied, and sat back on her stool. 'I am glad to see you, but I am a bit scattered at the moment. A change might clear my mind.'

Wynn rubbed her eyelids; clearly she had been at her task too long without pause. Chane felt momentarily reluctant to burden her further. Mortals on the whole meant nothing to him, but Wynn was unique.

She reached out with small and perfect hands to straighten up the table. 'Tell me what you are seeking.'

'First, can you translate an Elvish word for me?'

'I can try. What is it?'

'*Anmaglâhk*,' he answered. 'Something I read recently, but I have no idea what it means.'

Wynn's brows knitted. 'I do not think it is a real Elvish word, Chane. Where did you see it?'

'In a history text on this continent's elves,' he lied.

She appeared thoughtful for a moment. 'My best guess . . . would be "thief of lives." That is the closest I can surmise.'

'Thief of lives?' he repeated. 'That sounds like a killer – or an assassin.'

'Perhaps,' she replied with a frown, likely finding his interpretation unpleasant. 'But the elves do not use assassins, so the word must have been used in reference to other races.' She offered him a tired smile. 'Now, what did you really come to research?'

'As long as you promise not to laugh at me,' he chided.

'Why would I ever laugh at you?' She blinked, not quite catching his humor.

'I want to know about a legend called the "dhampir," rumored to be the offspring of a vampire and a mortal. A mere superstition, but curious.'

Wynn did not laugh. In fact, she stared at his hands and hair and, for a moment, Chane thought he saw fear pass across her pretty features.

'Where did you hear that word?' she asked.

Her reaction confused Chane enough that his senses began to open. Carefully casual, he spread his hands, palm up, in a carefree gesture.

'A passing fancy,' he said. 'I think it was in a tavern, a rumor I overheard.'

She nodded, outwardly calm, but he heard the quick-ened beat of her heart and the slight tremble of her breath. Was she afraid . . . of him?

'Domin Tilswith is the expert on lore. If you will wait here, I will find him.'

As she stood up, Chane felt an urge to prevent her

from leaving, to find out what had suddenly frightened her. Such an action would certainly frighten her further and, strangely, that bothered him.

With a quick bow and a shaky smile, Wynn left the room.

Something was amiss. Then Chane heard the sound of quick footsteps coming toward him from the far end of the barracks. Instinct took hold, and he bolted from the study toward the front door.

Magiere paced the short path between the bunks in their barracks room and the open hallway. Every time she reentered the room, she saw Chap perched next to the table, his expression somehow sad.

She understood little of what Wynn had explained throughout the afternoon and evening, as the young sage worked to speak with the dog in their halting manner. The study's floor was now covered in chalk marks.

Fay were as old as the world itself, so legends said, and for the most part they were considered to be myth and superstition. Varied religions had their stories of how life began, but older still were the tales of the world's making.

Earth, water, air, fire, and spirit.

Mountain, wave, wind, flame, and tree.

Solid, liquid, gas, energy, and essence.

Perhaps divine by some faith's standards, these elemental intelligences had been the Fay, whose mingling brought the world into existence.

The sages believed humans were the oldest race, and the mingling of the first humans with these Fay, when the world was young, gave birth to new beings. In turn, these beings mingled among themselves and from them, down through the ages, descended the new races. The Elvish word for these Fay-derived races was *Úirishg* –

which meant either 'Fay-blooded' or 'Children of the Fay.'

Amongst the trees and forests were the elves. The people of earth and mountain were the dwarves, though Magiere had never seen nor heard of any in this land. The Fay-descended races of wind, wave, and flame were not known to Wynn.

In the far-forgotten past behind all of them were the Fay, the elemental beings.

Magiere looked up at Leesil lying in the top bunk. One arm thrown over his face, he ignored both her and the hound.

'Wynn told you,' she said. 'He doesn't control us. It's more a touch of thoughts, an urge built upon a memory – nothing more. That we weren't aware of what was happening' – she glanced at Chap – 'is why we never ignored or dismissed it.'

'And how many times have we been unaware?' Leesil asked. 'How many turns in our lives were made because he wormed into our thoughts?'

Chap barked twice.

'Quiet!' Leesil snapped. His arm dropped, and he rolled his head enough to look at Magiere.

'I don't know,' she finally answered.

'And what else is he concealing?' he asked in a snide tone. 'Why are we so privileged to have his company?'

Magiere shook her head. 'I don't know,' she repeated.

'Well, I should be used to living in the dark by now,' he muttered.

His words made her pause, as if he spoke of something else, but there was no time for it.

'We know Chap . . . thinks . . . the murderer isn't part of the council,' Magiere offered, hoping to divert Leesil's attention to more immediate matters.

In truth, she didn't care to contemplate the mystery

of the dog any further. The reasons for, and the implications of, Chap's hidden nature following them all these years were too overwhelming.

'The best Wynn can make out,' Magiere continued, 'is that Chap was looking for scent on the parchments. If an undead signed for the purchase, there might have been a lingering trace, but he found nothing. It's probably been far too long and the scent is gone.'

Chap stood up on all fours and yipped at her, tail switching.

'I told you to be quiet!' Leesil shouted at the animal.

'That means "yes,"' Magiere said tiredly. 'It's something Wynn arranged with him.' She let out a deep sigh. 'One for "yes," two for "no," three for "maybe" or "uncertain."'

Leesil's head flopped down on the pillow again.

'Think you can do better?' Magiere asked. 'She's done the best she can, considering she's trying to talk with some . . . one . . . who can't write or speak. She says his thoughts or way of thinking – as Fay or what have you – isn't the same as ours, making it hard to communicate with him.'

A cold, wet lump prodded her hand, startling her.

Chap had inched to her side, shoving his muzzle into her hand with a soft whine. His tongue whipped between her fingers.

'How much of our lives has been shaped by him?' Leesil said, and leaned on one elbow to peer down at them. 'Would we even have met if he hadn't forced it that night?'

'Does it matter?' she asked. 'We're here, together, for a purpose. And I have to believe we'd still be here, whether or not he had anything to do with it.'

Leesil's amber eyes narrowed and sent an ache through her chest. She wanted to comfort him but was uncertain how. Then a high-pitched voice filled the room.

'What's the problem? You burn something else down already?'

In the doorway stood young Vàtz in fresh oversize pants and shirt, his frazzled hair only slightly tamer than when he'd left this morning. A small relief spread through Magiere.

'Did you find your uncle?' she asked.

'Yup. Kept switching between moaning like he'd lost his mama and wanting to skin you for supper, till I told him about the money. Then he started growling about lost income while the place is being rebuilt.'

Magiere sighed again.

'Had supper yet?' Vàtz asked. 'I ain't eaten much since last night.'

'I'll find Wynn and get you something,' she answered. 'Stay here.'

Perhaps the boy's presence and his ignorance of the evening's events would provide a safeguard between Leesil and Chap.

Magiere headed for the study, her mind filled with questions concerning the hound that refused to be dismissed. It was too much coincidence that an animal born to hunt undeads – though perhaps that was just a consequence of his true nature – should end up in the company of a dhampir, let alone a reluctant and retired assassin. When more immediate concerns were met and their task for the council completed, she hoped Leesil would gather himself enough that they could turn to finding answers.

When she entered the study, there was no sign of Wynn. A cold lamp sat on the desk where the young sage had been working.

She headed for the side passage leading to kitchen. In the dimness of the entryway, a soft light called her attention, and she glanced down.

The topaz amulet glowed brightly.

Magiere spun about.

There was no one in the room. The sound of booted footsteps echoed from the main hallway, and she started to run.

'Leesil!' she shouted. 'My sword!'

She passed the front entrance but saw no one. Before she headed down the hall toward their room, Chap came toward her with Leesil close behind. The dog still limped, but he dashed past as Leesil tossed her the falchion. His punching blade was in his right hand. Vàtz came running behind, loaded crossbow wrapped in his little arms.

'Get back in that room!' she ordered him.

His expression clouded, and his angry little mouth opened.

'No arguments,' she snapped. 'Move!'

A wail echoed down the hall behind her as Chap burst into full cry, and Magiere whirled to follow without waiting to see that Vàtz obeyed.

As she reached the study again, Wynn and Tilswith scurried in from the side hallway to the kitchen. Leesil and Chap entered behind Magiere, and the hound circled the room with a continuous rumble as he sniffed about. He let out a growl as he passed by Wynn's table, and then turned and trotted back into the main hallway.

Magiere hesitated before going after him. The two sages hung back.

'Who was just here?' she asked.

'Our friend, Chane,' Wynn replied, out of breath and her voice unsteady.

'Good scholar, but . . .' The domin paused, gripping Wynn's arm, his voice touched with sadness. 'He is tall, noble look . . . red-brown hair behind ears.'

'Oh, merciless saints!' Leesil snapped, and he bolted after Chap. 'Come on. They've been inviting an undead for tea and studies.'

Magiere followed. As she rounded the corner to the front door, she saw it already ajar. Leesil ran into the night ahead of her, and Chap's wail echoed from the street outside.

Sgäile tied the corners of his cloak about his waist to keep it out of his way and hold his cloth bundle of equipment snug against his back. With the shortbow hung over his shoulder, he slipped into a space between buildings close to the inner ring wall and searched for a way to the rooftops.

It had been a long day's wait, and his brethren in Hovel Row had informed him of the strange, well-dressed human who had come with questions. The city was being locked down at night because of a string of unexplained deaths, and movement would be difficult. He stepped out before dusk to give himself time to enter the city's wealthy inner districts before the gatehouses were closed for the night.

Ascending the rough buildings was easy for Sgäile, and he soon perched at the apex of a three-story structure. Leaping to the next rooftop, he landed silently and worked his way along. Out ahead and above, he could see a white speck atop the wall and settled still as a shadow next to a clay chimney. A guard in white surcoat and feather-crested helm strolled along above. When the guard passed down the other way, Sgäile continued along the roofs.

It would be difficult to locate his target with little to guide him but the secondhand description given by his brethren. He reconciled himself to a long night of silent searching. Then a wail carried through the air.

Sgäile froze again, dropping low.

There had been mention of a dog.

The wail sounded again, long and savage, and Sgäile sprang to his feet, leaping across the rooftops.

Chane ducked through a doorway, out of sight, as he heard shouting in the hall. He did not stop to listen and slipped out the front door once the footfalls passed by toward the study.

When the explosive wail burst from behind him, it startled him. He had heard that sound twice now – once from a distance and once close by – and knew the dhampir's dog was inside the barracks.

What could the dhampir possibly be doing among the sages?

As he ran through the street, the wail shifted to a high-pitched tone that cut through the night air, and Chane knew the hound was outside. Looking back, he saw far behind two gleaming pinpricks like diamonds in the dark. Its silhouette loped oddly. Chane's own legs were long, and he ran swiftly, but he heard the hound gaining ground.

He searched about for refuge, someplace to make a stand, and spotted the shabby frame of a large storage shed between two buildings against the ring wall. The door was broken but three walls were intact, so he dodged inside, stepped to the back, and began chanting softly.

In his mind, he drew lines of light, slowly crafting symbols in his thoughts. First the circle, then around it a traingle, and into the spaces of its corners outside the circle, he scrawled glyphs and sigils, stroke by stroke. The mesh of lines in his mind overlay his sight of the room wherever he looked, and he aimed through its center at the ground before the door.

Still wailing, the hound slammed into the broken door,

smashing it open, and its voice shifted to an elongated snarl.

In the shack's darkness, the animal's blue-gray fur stood on end around its neck and along its back, its sharp teeth exposed beneath wrinkled jowls. It was so tall that its back would reach Chane's thigh. And the dhampir could not be far behind.

Chane focused upon the floor before the hound. A shifting warp twisted his vision of the room.

Spirals of flame shot up in front of the hound.

Without looking back, Chane dashed through the shed's broken side, scanning the street for the nearest sewer grate.

Leesil ran at full stride out the guild's front door. Chap wasn't far ahead, but for running on only three legs, the dog covered ground at a rapid pace.

His slender legs pumped wildly to catch up. The hound had sustained too many injuries on this exploit from throwing himself into every battle. More than once, he'd been outnumbered or flanked before Leesil could get to his side. They knew little of this undead that Chap pursued, other than that he was a swordsman and perhaps a mage as well. This was more than Chap had faced before.

Hound . . . Fay . . . or both. Anger flared inside Leesil, a mix of resentment toward Chap and ire at the undead who'd walked right through the building when they weren't paying attention. He pushed harder to catch up, knowing Magiere wouldn't be far behind. Out ahead, he caught sight of Chap's loping form. He peered farther down the gradual arc of the road.

There was the dim outline of a fleeing form. Then it was gone.

Chap turned, heading toward a large but shabby three-sided shed at the far end of the barracks grounds. Why would the undead run there? It offered no protection.

As Leesil followed, he saw Chap standing just inside the shed's doorway, snarling loudly. A breath later, fire erupted like a fountain inside the shed, and the doorway quickly ignited into flames behind the dog.

A shadow flickered away out of the shed's broken side.

Leesil wanted to scream. He ran headlong through the door, leaning forward to grab Chap by the chest, and threw himself forward.

He felt heat like the pressure of water closing around him, as if he'd leaped from a height into a boiling sea. Rolling across the ground with Chap clenched tight to his chest, he smashed them both against the shed's back wall. Leesil scrambled up and shoved Chap ahead of him out of the shed's broken side.

Once in the street again, he grabbed the hound, running his hands over the gray-blue fur, checking for burns. His heart thrummed against his ribs. To his relief, the fire had mainly scorched Chap's tail and singed a few patches of fur on his haunches, but that was all. A moment more among the flames, and the result would have been more than Leesil cared to imagine.

Chap tried to lunge away down the street again, but Leesil held tight.

'No,' he said. 'You wait.'

'Leesil!'

Magiere's shout came from the front of the burning shack.

'Here,' he called back. 'We're over here.'

She ran toward him, falchion in hand. 'Where's the undead?'

'I don't know.' Leesil shook his head and looked to

the burning shack. 'Should we sound an alarm? This one enjoys his little fires.'

Magiere looked to the shed as well and shook her head. 'This shack isn't connected to anything.' She dropped next to Chap. 'Did that bastard burn him?'

'No, not really.' Leesil allowed relief to flood him.

Chap turned and licked his face once before growling, struggling to be released. But Leesil hesitated.

'You ready?' Leesil asked Magiere.

'Let him go,' she answered.

Chap lunged down the street, slowing now and again to sniff for a trail. Leesil had no idea how the limping dog kept his pace, but they ran after him along the open street.

Anger mounted again, and Leesil felt the sweat in his hand gripping the blade as he pictured this undead's head rolling on the cobblestones. He shifted the blade to his other side and wiped his palm dry on his breeches. Street lanterns partially lit the way, but there was no one in sight.

The guard patrolled near the city walls in greater numbers, but he hoped this undead wouldn't run into them. They would likely get themselves killed.

Chap pulled up short at a sewer grate and circled it, nose to the ground, and then looked at them. He clawed at the grate with his good front paw. An anxious rumble issued from his throat, but Leesil saw the slight shake of his legs. The dog panted in exhaustion.

Magiere kicked at the grate. 'He went down.'

The light glow of her topaz dimmed to nothing as Leesil watched. He knelt down next to Chap, and Magiere crouched as well. She looked at the grate and then at Chap.

'We've no lantern or torch, and Chap's done in,' she said.

Leesil peered down through the grate. She was right, but the image of Chap circled in flame still burned in his mind. He put his hand on the dog's back and felt the tremble of fatigue beneath the rumbling vibration of his growl. He reached down to grab the grate.

Magiere put a hand on his shoulder.

'Not like this,' she said. 'We stick to the plan. Find the lair and go in during the day when we're all well prepared and at our best.'

'He can't have gotten far,' Leesil argued.

'We'll find them,' she insisted. 'It may take a bit of time, but we will. They can't get out of the city, at least I hope not, now that Chetnik has all the gates locked down after dark.'

Breathing slowly, Leesil nodded, but Chap continued to growl, looking downward through the tight mesh of iron bars.

'And I know you can understand me,' Magiere said to him. 'So don't pretend otherwise.'

Chap quieted but glowered at her.

At another time, when he'd been just a dog, Leesil might have found Chap's expression humorous. Now it gave him shivers. Movement in the street pulled his attention, and Leesil rose and turned in one movement, blade at the ready.

Vàtz stepped up behind them, crossbow loaded and a determined look on his face.

'We going down?' he asked.

Magiere's jaw dropped. 'I told you to stay inside with the sages!'

'I ain't hiding behind that bunch of gray skirts.'

She was about to grab for the boy with a vicious glint in her eye, when Leesil pushed Vàtz back down the street the way they'd all come.

'Let's get inside,' he said. 'We can talk about this later.'

'What!' Vàtz growled. 'I thought you two were—'

'Move,' Leesil ordered.

The boy reluctantly obeyed, with Magiere following him, and Leesil turned to call for Chap.

The dog was gone.

Fire in the night. A wail in the air.

Sgäile focused upon the glow ahead rising up between the night silhouettes of the rooftops. He barely caught the sound of running feet and indistinguishable voices. When he landed upon a shaked roof with twin chimneys, front and rear, he saw the flames across the way against the city wall. Scanning the barrier's top into the distance, he saw the far-off guards in white making their circuit around the wall's top. None appeared to have spotted the waning blaze. Perhaps it was tucked too close to the wall to be seen from such a distance.

What burned was little more than a lone abandoned shed, and it already collapsed upon itself, the fire dimming. Scattered sparks wafted upward and extinguished before they crested the wall's top. Firelight impaired his night sight, and the wail, footfalls, and voices had all faded. He crept closer to the roof's edge over the street and looked along the line of buildings.

Walking away to the far right was a small boy, crossbow hefted over his shoulder. Behind him was a tall female, back turned, with long black hair and loose-hanging shirt. He could not make out much of this person, except for the heavy-bladed sword in her hand. A flicker of white in the dark pulled his attention left and up the street.

Standing near a street grate was a figure with long white-blond hair, a ragged white sleeveless vest or shirt lashed sloppily around his waist. The only other feature Sgäile could make out was a strange blade gripped in his hand.

The figure turned slowly about, looking all around

with seeming concentration, and Sgäile saw his face. He focused his vision.

It was man of tanned skin like his own, but the face was not quite right. The eyes were not as wide or large as his own, and the feathered brows not quite as arched and high. His chin was more the squarish end common to humans.

Half-blood.

Sgäile glanced quickly at the woman and boy farther down the street's gradual arc. His target stood still and in plain view, and he could not let such a chance pass by.

He slipped an arrow from the back of his belt and fitted it to the shortbow. Taking aim, he drew the string back.

Leesil looked up and down the street and between the nearest buildings, trying to spot where Chap had gone. He was about to call out when an odd tingle scurried across his back. Wariness overtook him, and he peered about the dark as if there were something else nearby that he couldn't see.

Had the undead come out through another grate and doubled back? He listened carefully as he peered into the shadows of the buildings.

One shadow moved, low to the ground, and he tensed.

Chap ambled out from between two silent shops, nose to the ground as he followed the line of buildings. Leesil relaxed in annoyance.

'Get over here,' he called. 'It's gone already.'

Chap looked up and paused again to the scan the street. With reluctance, he hobbled toward Leesil.

Sgäile fixed his gaze upon the half-blood's chest just right of center and at the man's heart. He took a slow, deep breath and released half of it.

A gray flicker bobbed from a building to the left and along the cobblestones toward his target. Sgäile paused, releasing the rest of his inhale.

It was a dog or hound approaching the half-blood at a slow, limping gait. Sgäile settled again with another breath, in and halfway out. The dog circled the target as the two moved slowly down the street, and Sgäile pulled tighter on the bowstring.

The angle was no longer what he needed, and he raised his focus to the half-blood's temple.

The sheen of the dog's coat caught the glimmer of a street lantern.

Sgäile paused again, and this time his breath caught in his chest.

The hound limped along next to the half-blood, and Sgäile looked carefully at it.

The dog was blue-gray in color and taller than the forest wolves, its head narrower and muzzle longer than those wild beasts. Even from a distance, Sgäile caught the glitter of its crystal-blue eyes as it intently looked about. He lowered his bow, slowly releasing tension on the string, and sat in silence, watching the two figures recede down the street.

'*Majay-hì*,' he whispered in disbelief.

16

Toret sat alone in the parlor, waiting for Chane to return with a mortal for him to feed on. His ruptured eye socket had closed up. He'd shut out any pain from his chest wound but loss of fluid had drained him, and he felt empty in more ways than simple hunger. In each passing moment he found the illusion of 'Toret' more and more a ridiculous joke, and the reality of 'Ratboy' welled up inside him.

The previous night's fight played out in Toret's mind, again and again, as disquiet crept into his thoughts. He was stronger than the half-blood, yet for all Chane's sword training, the mongrel had still outclassed him.

Tibor walked into the parlor, his appearance severing Toret's thoughts.

'Pardon, master, but there's a man here to see you.'

The sailor's throat wound had closed, but the flesh around the hole was still seared. His undead existence made his gaunt, hawklike features stand out. His skin looked weathered and tight but was losing its dark, ruddy tan in his undead state. His brown eyes seemed distant and sad.

'Sestmir was your friend for a long time?' Toret asked.

'My brother.' Tibor paused. 'I suppose he was my friend too.'

A brother? Toret should have realized. The two looked so much alike.

'Who is at the door?' he asked. He wasn't in the proper condition to conduct any type of business.

'Fancy gentleman,' Tibor answered.

Toret tensed slightly. 'Dark hair with white patches at his temples?'

'Yes, master, that's the one.'

The last person Toret wanted to see now was this stranger who kept appearing from nowhere with warnings about the dhampir.

'Tell him I'm not here.'

Tibor turned to go back to the door, and a cold voice rose audibly from the foyer.

'I think you should see me.'

The stranger entered, impeccably dressed in a long black cloak and well-fitting gloves. Toret felt a small flare of righteous resentment.

'This is my home,' he said. 'I'm not well and wish to be alone.'

'Yes,' the stranger responded in the same cold tone. 'From what I understand, you were wounded by the half-elf. That is hardly befitting someone of your station.'

His station? A sickly, humorous comment. Toret looked at Tibor.

'Wait in the dining room. This won't take long.'

Tibor nodded and left, and Toret stood up.

'Where are the dhampir and her half-elf now?' the stranger asked. 'Even with my resources, I cannot locate them.'

Toret wondered about the man's age, though he looked to be in his mid-forties. He also appeared a bit haggard and tired, perhaps from a lack of sleep – quite different from his last visit. Why was he so interested in the dhampir, and why did he expend all this effort with warnings? Suddenly the answers didn't matter.

'I've no idea, and I don't care. I am taking my family away from here tomorrow.'

'Away?' The stranger appeared stunned. 'Where? Destroying her is the only way to ensure your survival.'

Toret almost smiled, but not quite. 'I once knew someone who thought like that. His bones are dust under the dhampir's tavern. Vengeance is expensive.'

Open anger slipped into the stranger's voice. 'The guards now lock up the city at dusk. No one gets in or out. Even the sewer gates into the bay are sealed both day and night. And scaling all the city's walls would be difficult at best.'

Toret turned away, and the hollow hunger of his existence became acidic.

'If you think I can't find my way around a few mortal guards, you have no idea what I am. Get out. You're no longer welcome here.'

He heard footsteps coming toward him and spun about. The stranger stood close. His expression was intense, watchful, an unknown decision being made.

'Should I call Tibor to escort you?' Toret added.

The stranger's lips parted and then closed quickly. His mask of composure returned as he stepped back.

'As you wish.'

He turned and left. Toret followed and bolted the door behind him.

'Tibor!'

The undead sailor came to the foyer. 'Yes, master?'

'When Chane returns, let him in, but no one else. If that man appears, send him away. Understand?'

'Yes.'

Toret climbed the stairs to the top floor. He was tired and drained, and badly needed to feed, but he was finally seeing his world clearly. At the top floor, he walked into Sapphire's room without knocking. She was dressing in front of her oval mirror.

'Oh, Toret,' she said, as if surprised at his presence. She looked him up and down.

He knew he appeared paler than usual, and his one eye was crushed closed, but in his fresh tunic, no one could tell his body was damaged. She was lacing herself into a red velvet gown, and the sight of it touched him. Teesha had worn red velvet at times, though not as brilliant a shade. Sapphire's round face shifted between pouty and indignant. In a flash, she smiled and came to put her arms around his neck.

'You look better,' she said, petting his shoulder. 'I simply couldn't abide all those wounds and mess last night. I'm much too delicate.'

Yes, perhaps she was, and he drank in the sight of her. She might not be Teesha, but she was his.

'You must feed,' she said. 'I'll finish dressing, and we'll go find you a treat. You should have anything you want.' She smiled again, perhaps thinking herself quite generous to consider his desires.

'Chane is out,' he said. 'He will bring something back for me.'

'So we're staying home?' she asked, a pout returning. 'I've been trapped in here since that horrible hunter attacked me.'

'You're going to be busy all night – packing,' he said softly. 'We leave Bela at dusk tomorrow. I'll make the arrangements tonight.'

It took a moment for his words to sink in, and then she laughed.

'You can't be serious. I'm not leaving Bela. This place is paradise. There's nowhere in the country with better inns.'

'We're leaving,' he repeated. 'If we don't, the dhampir will track us down, douse the place with oil as we sleep, and light it on fire in broad daylight. Still sound like paradise?'

His seriousness slowly dawned on her, and for a moment she didn't even speak. Then a scream burst from her ripe, snarling mouth, and she grabbed a porcelain vase off the wardrobe and threw it.

Toret ducked as it shattered on the wall behind him.

Welstiel sat in Calabar's inn, waiting for Lanjov. The last dream had been suffocating, and he felt weary. His carefully woven web was being cut apart thread by thread. He had lost track of Magiere after the fire at the Burdock, and now Ratboy planned to flee. He sipped at his tankard of wine and willed calm into his thoughts. Lanjov would come soon, as requested by messenger. If anyone knew where Magiere now hid, it would be Lanjov.

Possibilities remained, if he could only delay Ratboy and unobtrusively assist Magiere in her hunt – but not too much assistance. If she found Ratboy's home before nightfall, she would have the advantage of daylight and not be forced to engage multiple opponents and the conjuror as well. Her training must proceed.

A stout woman with graying hair came up to his table.

'Are you Master Welstiel?' she asked. 'A boy just delivered a message.'

When he nodded, she held out a small folded paper, and he took it. His own name was addressed upon it. The woman glanced at his missing finger.

'Thank you,' he said, not taking his eyes off of her as he waited.

She grunted and left.

Welstiel turned over the paper. A wax seal held it closed, and he split it, opening the letter.

To my dear friend:

I regret not joining you tonight at our favorite inn. Events in Bela demanding my attention grow ever more pressing. I fear my own time has become so limited I will have the leisure to meet you at neither the Knight's House nor Calabar's inn.

By now, you may have learned of Lord Au'Shiyn's death. I have reconsidered your counsel and retained the dhampir's services, so there is no need for us to discuss this matter further in my offices.

Rest assured she has both the services of the city guard and the sages to assist her. Thank you again for your guidance. I do not know when we will be able to meet again.

I remain your humble friend.
Alexi Lanjov

Welstiel read the note again, though every word was clear the first time.

In the polite manner of a gentleman, Lanjov had just informed him that he was no longer welcome at the council hall, and any relationship outside of there had also ended. Lanjov had severed their acquaintance.

The calm in Welstiel's mind withered. He read the note again, this time pausing at the mention of the sages. Lanjov had spoken of them ensconced in a decommissioned barracks.

Welstiel placed a silver penny on the table, not waiting to have his change returned. He stepped into the street and hailed a passing coach.

'Do you know of the new sages and their location?' he asked the coachman. 'Take me there, now.'

★　★　★

Chane emerged from a sewer grate somewhere in the city's second ring. He had lost the dhampir back at the sages' barracks, but much still troubled him. Wynn, as well as Tilswith, would now know what he was.

He had emerged in one of the poor districts west of the moderate merchant area and still needed blood for Toret. A trio of prostitutes hung together upon one street corner near a tavern, but Chane never chose anyone from a group. Across the way stood one lone young woman outside an alley. She was small, with limp, dirty hair. Her muslin dress was threadbare but mended. Her eyes were clear and unclouded by ale.

He walked up to her.

'Lookin' for company?' she asked. Her voice was defeated and cheerless, and she was missing several teeth.

'Yes, but not here. Come home with me?'

She hesitated and took in the cut of his cloak and boots. Men dressed like Chane did not often patronize the poor side of the lower merchant district.

'I got a room. Not far from here,' she suggested.

He held out his purse. 'I'll pay for the entire night.'

She wavered, captivated by the click of coins and yet still wary. She moved closer to him, nervous but determined, and slipped her arm into his.

Finding a coach was difficult in this part of the city, so it was several side streets later before he called one to a stop. To Chane's relief, the girl neither offered nor expected conversation during the ride. When it ended, they walked to the house together, and Chane was surprised to find the front door bolted.

He knocked, and Tibor cracked it and looked out. At the sight of Chane, he opened it fully and stepped back.

Chane motioned his companion in and said to Tibor, 'Tell the master I'm home.'

The sound of Sapphire screeching and glass objects shattering floated down from upstairs. The woman looked up and glanced warily at Chane.

'You got a master? I thought you was the master?'

Chane didn't answer, and she began backing toward the door.

'I changed my mind,' she said. 'I'll just walk back. You don't owe me nothin'.'

Chane grabbed her upper arm.

She didn't scream but quickly lifted one leg to jerk a fish knife from her boot. Slashing across the back of his hand, she surprised Chane into releasing her. But when she turned toward the door, it was already closed. Tibor stood silently in front of it.

Chane snatched the back of her neck with one hand. Though he'd fed earlier, the slash on his hand drove him to salivate. She swung back blindly at him with the blade, and he grabbed her thin wrist as well. Sheer will kept him from setting his teeth to her throat.

'Is that for me?' came Toret's voice from behind.

Pulling his captive toward the stairs, Chane saw his pale little master descend the last steps, his one good eye fixed on the woman.

'Yes . . . of course,' he answered.

He was loath to offer such a delight to Toret. This woman, as tiny as she was, brimmed with life and survival instinct. It was like serving a vintage wine to a drunkard gone too long without ale.

Chane held her out like a gift as she struggled. He closed his hand on her wrist until the muffled crack of bone was heard. She dropped the knife in a whimper of pain.

Toret enveloped the woman in his thin arms and bit into her throat so rapidly that Chane lost his grip on her neck. He let her arm drop, as he suppressed a sneer of disgust.

Such a waste.

Above in the house, a door banged open or closed, followed by hammering footfalls on the upper stairs. Sapphire shortly appeared at the top of the stairs to the foyer. Her normally perfect curls were disheveled, and she appeared beyond one of her usual tantrums.

'Don't you walk away from me, you little rodent!' she shouted. 'I'm not going anywhere, do you hear me? Anywhere!'

Toret dropped the dead girl and opened his tunic. The gaping rent in his chest was closing. The sunken eye socket was now full, and when he opened it, a clouded orb filled it. He turned toward the staircase.

'Close your mouth,' he ordered Sapphire. 'Go and pack, now.'

Sapphire's mouth snapped shut as she twitched, one hand coming to her head as if a sudden pain struck her behind the eyes. She turned around to shuffle back up to her room.

'Pack?' Chane asked.

'We're leaving.'

'The house?'

'The city. We're going home, to my home. We'll bribe smugglers to get us off the docks tomorrow evening and sail south to the Suman Empire. It's been too long since I've been home.' He paused. 'If we stay, the dhampir will find us. We survive only if we leave. You'll like the desert – it's clean.'

Toret climbed the stairs, leaving the prostitute's body on foyer floor.

'If a man with dark hair and white temples comes,' he added, 'don't let him in.'

Then he stopped and turned.

'It's a slim chance in a city this size that the dhampir will find this place before we leave, but we should take no chances. There's one more day to get through. Set up a ward or a trap, or something, in case anyone breaks in. Anything simple that will slow her down and warn us.'

Holding his composure, Chane nodded obediently. 'Leaving Tihko and your wolf loose on the main floor should provide warning, and I will arrange another suitable deterrent.'

'Nothing with a tripwire,' Toret said. 'Use your craft. I think that half-blood can spot a trigger from a league away.'

'Very well,' Chane replied. So much for simplicity.

This turn of events was disturbing. If Toret's new plan came to fruition, they would all be bound for the Suman Empire by the following night, living among camels, nomads, and who knew what else. It could take years or decades before he found or arranged another opportunity such as this dhampir offered.

Something had to be done. But what?

Although Welstiel had never visited the sages, he had met several through Lanjov at the council hall. The aging Domin Tilswith showed up at odd times to badger the councilman about improving their arrangements. Seeing the barracks firsthand, he better understood the domin's perspective. One intact and weather-aged building was not large enough for a library, as well as housing a handful of sages.

He knocked on the door. A female voice called from the other side.

'Who's there?'

'My name is Welstiel Massing. I believe some of your

people know me. I have assisted Councilman Lanjov on occasion.'

The door cracked open, and a young woman in a gray robe with a long braid peered out.

'Young Wynn, isn't it?' he asked. 'Do you remember me? We met once in the council hall.'

'Yes, I remember you, but it is quite late.' Her oval face was marred with worry, and she glanced furtively in both directions along the street. 'Do you have a message of some kind?'

'No,' he said reassuringly. 'But after speaking with the council chairman, I thought to offer you my assistance. I have some experience with the dhampir's current pursuits, and I understand you are working with her.'

She paused in consideration, and then stepped back so he could enter.

'Please come in. I am sorry if I seem overly cautious, but we have had an eventful evening.'

He stepped into the entryway and offered a polite bow of thanks.

She led him to what appeared to be an old officer's chamber. It had been transformed into a common study room, complete with all the trappings and fixtures of sequestered scholars.

'Have you seen the dhampir of late?' he asked. 'I assume she found new lodging for herself and her companion. Councilman Lanjov was concerned.'

'Oh,' Wynn said. 'He has not heard? I meant to send word but so much has happened. I thought Domin Tilswith had informed him, but if not, please tell the councilman that Magiere and Leesil are safely housed with us.'

Welstiel stopped. 'She's here? Now?'

'Yes, would you like to see her?' she asked. 'I believe

she and Leesil are tending to Chap in the kitchen. He is fine but received a few burns earlier.'

Welstiel did not wish for Magiere to see him yet. That would create even more complications than he already faced.

'The kitchens are far?' he asked.

'At the back of the building.' She pointed toward a side entrance in the study.

'Then do not bother her. How was the dog burned?'

Again she did not speak, and he suspected that whatever weighed secretly upon this young sage was connected to Magiere. Focusing his will, he gently poured a suggestion into her thoughts.

He was a kind older man, like-minded and knowledgeable. A good listener to whom she could talk.

She dropped her gaze in sadness.

'I have a friend,' she whispered. 'Also a friend to Domin Tilswith, with whom we have spent many hours in study here. He was trusted and . . . his name is Chane. And when he came tonight, the dhampir's hound exposed him as a Noble Dead.'

The news of Toret's conjuror frequenting the sages' guild did not surprise him. But it was quite curious how preoccupied Wynn was with Toret's vassal.

'He ran . . .' she continued, 'and Chap chased him. But he threw fire at Chap and vanished into the sewers.'

Welstiel patiently watched a scatter of emotions play across her delicate face.

'He is polite, well educated, considerate . . .' Her voice broke. 'If you knew him, you would not believe what has been uncovered. I can barely accept it myself.'

How intriguing. Still, if Magiere was nearby, Welstiel could not stay any longer.

'I am sorry, my dear,' he said. 'But if some mistake has

been made, the truth will come out. We should focus on assisting the dhampir to find this truth.'

Wynn straightened, possibly embarrassed by her brief outpouring.

'Of course. You are most kind.'

She walked to a table and showed him a stack of unrolled parchments.

'Leesil believes at least one of the Noble Dead purchased a three-story house. But this one is female, and I found no dwelling recently deeded to a woman. That means little, though, as he also says they tend to live in groups.'

Welstiel's eyebrows arched. 'What makes him think that?'

'I assumed it was experience.'

Welstiel sifted through the parchments one by one. At the fifth he tucked his finger into the stack above it and kept paging at an even pace. That one deed had been for a three-story stone dwelling near the inner wall ring purchased two moons ago. The signature at the bottom read *Toret min' Sharrêf*.

How close the little sage was to what she sought.

'Well, I assume,' he said, 'you'll begin looking at the most likely possibilities in person.'

As Welstiel reversed his paging through the stack, he began pulling out selected parchments. When a dozen or more were in his other hand, he slipped the one he'd marked to the bottom of the stack and handed her the selections.

'These might be the best,' he said.

She took the parchments. 'On what basis did these seem best?'

'Look at them . . .' he said intently.

Westiel let his voice drop low, and focused upon its

sound, its vibration. It became a thrum in the young sage's ears. 'See the connections. Think of what you know of all that has happened.'

Wynn stared into his eyes a moment, and then her gaze dropped to the parchments.

Welstiel kept the hum of his voice steadily slipping into the back of her awareness.

'They are within a reasonable distance of the most recent deaths and disappearances. It will take all day to work through them, the last to be approached near dusk. You will go with the dhampir tomorrow and visit all of them. She will need your counsel, no matter how much she objects.'

Wynn's gaze remained on the parchments without blinking. Her breath came slowly and evenly. She was lost in his words, his voice, and if not for her open eyes, she might have merely been asleep on her feet.

'Wynn, look at me,' he said evenly.

The young woman's eyes drifted up.

'Forget what you now see,' he said, voice still steady in the silence of the room. 'Forget I was here. And remember only what is in your hands, what you must do. Visit the last house at dusk.'

He stepped from the study and left the barracks, in control once again.

'You're lucky I got there in time,' Leesil growled at Chap. 'Or you'd have been scorched bald as a plucked goose.'

Magiere stood in the kitchen doorway watching her partner examine the dog once again. A tuft of his tail and some spots of fur were singed, but Chap was otherwise sound. Now knowing the hound understood language, she had words for him about these stupid, headlong rushes at undeads before help arrived. And Leesil, ready to dive into the dark sewer, wasn't much better. Such a pair these two had become.

'What are you smirking at?' Leesil asked.

Magiere hadn't been aware of her expression. He looked ridiculous in the torn-off surcoat, though it had certainly made it easy to follow him in the dark.

'We need to find you a shirt tomorrow. Maybe something more as well.'

'Oh, not the clothes again,' he said. 'This will do just fine. But I could use some boots, and hopefully my second blade is finished by now.'

Yes, he'd left his boots in the fire at the Burdock, but had thought enough to grab the chest with his toolbox inside. Magiere wondered about his priorities.

'Besides such exciting errands,' Leesil asked, 'what is our plan for tomorrow?'

'Wynn has a stack of deeds for houses we'll look at. Hopefully one of them will be what we're looking for.'

Chap whined loudly at the mention of more houses.

'These aren't members of the council,' she added.

He barked and struggled in Leesil's grasp, his voice excited and eager.

'We'll have a fight soon enough,' she added. 'We handle it the same as in Miiska. Enter in daylight and take them before they know what's happening – and without burning anything down.'

At that, Leesil shot her a belligerent scowl. 'I'm not the one setting fires in Bela.'

'Small miracle,' she answered, and crouched down next to him and Chap.

In spite of her mocking him, Leesil remained serious.

'I had no choice back in Miiska. You were dying, and I had to cut off all pursuit.' He reached out to touch the bone amulet dangling below her throat. 'I would have died after the cave-in if you hadn't breathed air back into me, and once we were out, you would have died if I hadn't fed you.'

For once, his words didn't trouble her so much. Extreme actions had been required of them both over this past season of their lives. She understood his intention, even if he still neither comprehended the full meaning of his own words or the consequences of his actions.

She didn't pull back or take the amulet from his hand. Her concern was that he seemed to live for extreme actions, and she saw them merely as a necessary misfortune.

'When this is over, Leesil, what do you want?'

'To go home. What kind of a question is that?'

The fire from the kitchen hearth burned cheerfully, and under the soft scent of wood smoke was the aroma of dried herbs hanging beside pots and cookware. Beneath that, she could smell Leesil. He needed a bath, but then so did she, and his thick, musty scent wasn't unpleasant.

'And you'll be happy? Living in Miiska and running the tavern? That will be enough for you?'

Magiere felt the bone amulet bounce against her shirt. Leesil dropped cross-legged on the floor.

'Is that what you're worried about? That I'll get restless?'

'Among other things,' she said carefully.

'Listen to me,' he said with equal caution. 'We're sitting in a strange kitchen in a sage's guild and sleeping in an old barracks. This is most likely going to be our life. We'll have quiet seasons, possibly years at the Sea Lion if we're lucky, but this won't be the last time we're called.'

She wasn't certain of his meaning.

'I'm bound to you,' he continued, 'as you are to this

path. If we try to deny or avoid it, it will catch us unaware. Why do you think I was in the woods all those mornings outside of Miiska? To stay sharp. Of course I want a life at the Sea Lion, but it's never going to be that simple.'

She let his words sink in. He was right, though she wished it otherwise.

Whatever hope she had to live a quiet and secluded life had been taken away, bit by bit. If their exploits in Miiska caused their current call to service in Bela, how much more would she lose of the life she wanted once they were done here?

Magiere felt a small shame for part of her judgment of Leesil. He'd been willing to settle with her in the tavern but knew they couldn't. Not with the consequences of the path they now traveled. In Miiska, when she'd received the letter from Bela, she'd tried to hide from it, but he had not. He'd already known what was coming, and he was still here with her.

'The path I walk seems to narrow every day,' she whispered, 'and so little would matter if you weren't here to share it.'

'It's the same for me,' he said.

Magiere felt her mouth go dry. 'But once we're in the hunt, I fear what could happen to you.'

Because of me, and because of you, she thought.

At first he said nothing. Magiere felt an old, chill fear within the lingering salt memory of his blood in her mouth, his flesh in her teeth, his life seeping away into her.

'Nothing's going to happen to me,' he said. 'I'm not that easy to kill.'

They sat in silence a long time by the fire. Chap licked the singed fur on his haunch.

'I think he's got a little more than scorched fur there,' Leesil said.

The change of subject brought no relief. 'Do we still have any of Tilswith's salve?'

Leesil climbed to his feet. 'I should check on Vàtz anyway. When I put him to bed, he was still hopping mad at you for ordering him to stay behind.'

'Isn't his uncle worried about him?' Magiere asked. 'Have you asked him anything about his family?'

'I don't think Milous cares where he is. I assumed his parents were dead or otherwise long gone. Vàtz is strong. He can take care of himself.'

Magiere wondered, if such were true, then why was Leesil tucking him in and checking on him?

'I'll be back,' he said, and headed out the kitchen door.

Magiere had become fond of this odd tenderness in him, strange as it was when mixed with the cold-blooded nature of his past. She petted Chap's head and suddenly realized the dog was watching her intently, ears perked up.

He'd been listening to every word and yipped softly before butting his head against her side.

Leesil strolled back to their room trying to fathom what had – and had not – just happened. Magiere assumed he was unsatisfied with their life in Miiska. It was true he enjoyed being out and about, but mostly because he wouldn't let her face the future alone. Between the two of them, he better understood the consequences of their actions and the future that lay ahead. In this, at least, now she was perhaps more at ease, but there was more to her distance than the fear that he might want to leave. In fact, knowing he clearly wished to stay seemed to distress her as much as the alternative. The whole thing was worse than a hangover.

Down the hall came a glimmer of light from the open

door of their room. He'd heated up the cold lamp's crystal before leaving Vàtz to sleep. The boy acted tough enough, but he was still just a boy in the midst of nightmares come to life.

A softer light came from a doorway two openings closer than their room, and Leesil slowed his pace, curious as to who was there. It might be just another guild apprentice. He peered inside.

It was much like the room they'd been given: two sets of bunks on either side, with a small table and stools at the far back, but with no bedding or blankets. Instead of a cold lamp, a single, stubby candle was placed on the table's edge and burned dimly.

Leesil stepped in. Then he remembered.

The sages were terrified of open flame anywhere in the building. No sage would have lit a candle here, let alone without a holder.

A glinting line flashed down past his eyes and weight slammed against his shoulders.

Two knees struck his lower back, and he felt feet kick in behind his knees. He crumpled facedown on the wooden floor, and a wire cinched about his throat before he could get one of his hands inside of it.

As he curled his left hand to release a stiletto, something struck his elbow, and his hand went numb. Before he could try again with his right, the same blow landed again, and both his hands lay limp.

The wire closed tightly enough to press against his throat without constricting his breath.

A garrote wire.

'Cântasij tú äiche so aovar!'

The voice behind him was muffled. Leesil had heard this rhythm enough to recognize the words if not their meaning.

'I don't understand,' he answered. 'I don't speak your language.'

The wire cinched slightly tighter, and a long silence followed.

'Tell me why you are here . . . in Bela,' the man asked more softly this time.

Leesil felt knees press down his upper arms just above the elbows, pinning them to his sides. Feet hooked across his thighs, the man's weight evenly distributed. It was a very familiar arrangement, though he'd never fallen prey to it himself. He'd used it only to subdue others. There was a scent about his attacker – a strange mix of wild grass, pine needles, and sea salt. Leesil realized *what* if not who now held him at this severe disadvantage.

An elf – and assassin, trained as his mother had taught him.

Feeling began returning to his hands. As much as Leesil believed he could dislodge his captor with some effort, he couldn't escape the wire around his neck. If he told the truth, would this man even believe him?

'Hunting undeads,' he answered.

The wire jerked tighter around his throat.

'You lie!' the elf hissed. 'And what would the *majay-hì* want with the company of a traitor?'

'What . . . are you talking about?' Leesil managed to choke out. Traitor? And how did Chap fit into this? 'Ask the hound yourself. He's not telling me much.'

A familiar thrum sounded from the wire as it whipped free from Leesil's neck, leaving a hot, burning line. All weight lifted instantly from his back.

Leesil spun over and reached for the stiletto he'd lost, but it wasn't on the floor. When he scrambled to his feet, a dark figure stood beyond the doorway in the hall.

From cowl to cloak, hauberk to boots, and shirt and

pants beneath, the figure was colored between char and forest green. The cloak's lower corners were tied around his waist, and his cowled face was masked below the eyes with a scarf or wrap. Beneath high, feathery eyebrows of dusty blond, two large and slanted amber eyes stared back at Leesil.

The elf held Leesil's stiletto in one hand, the handles of the garrote gripped in the other. When Leesil freed his remaining stiletto, the elf didn't even blink.

'Who taught you our ways?' the elf asked.

'First, tell me what you mean,' Leesil replied. 'Whose ways? The elves?'

For an answer, the elf flicked his wrist, and the stiletto spun through the air.

Leesil sidestepped and snatched the handle midflight. Before he'd righted the blade in his hand, the cloaked figure leaped through the door at him. He slashed crosswise with both blades to ward off his attacker. But the elf instantly ducked and rose up inside the arcs, palm striking out toward Leesil's face.

Leesil collapsed to the floor, and his right leg shot along the left of the elf's feet. He swirled his arms over himself, blocking the elf's descending fist, and slashing with the blades. Something lashed sharply across his right hand, tangled around the stiletto, and ripped it from his grasp. Leesil hooked his right foot behind the elf's ankle as his other leg shot up.

There was no impact.

Though Leesil's foot connected, it was more a touch than a strike, and the elf merely arced backward into the hallway. He landed, watching Leesil intently. The same stiletto he'd thrown a moment ago was now snared in the garrote wire's loops between his fingers.

'Who taught you *Map am'a Fiar*?' he asked flatly.

On his guard, Leesil stared blankly at him. 'What?'

'Cat-in-the-Grass,' he said. 'The ground fighting.'

'My mother,' Leesil replied cautiously. 'And my father. But I don't know what you're talking about.'

The elf slowly pulled Leesil's stiletto from the wire loops.

'You mother is a traitor. No outsider is taught the ways of an *anmaglâhk*.'

Leesil stiffened. Before anger came, the word settled in his mind.

'What does that mean?' he asked. 'What is *anmaglâhk*?'

The elf's eyes widened, and Leesil saw puzzled suspicion in that gaze. The elf then relaxed upon the realization Leesil truly didn't understand the word.

'You are no more than a renegade who cannot even speak his own language. Finish your task and leave here.'

'Leesil?'

Magiere's voice came from down the hallway. And with it was the low, rumbling growl of Chap. Leesil had been gone too long, and they'd come looking for him. He inched forward toward the figure beyond the doorway.

'Touch them, and I'll gut you right here,' he warned. 'Whatever it takes.'

With but a side glance, the elf bolted down the hall, and Leesil ducked out the door behind him.

A flash of metal flew toward his legs.

Leesil threw himself toward the hallway's far wall as his own stiletto, snatched from him by the elf's garrote, struck home into the doorjamb. Chap lunged forward, snarling. The elf merely leaped over the dog and against the right wall.

For a blink, the man seemed to cling there like a spider, hands and feet flat against the surface with his head near the ceiling. He pushed off into air and arced to the floor behind Magiere, who whipped around to follow his movement.

Chap tried to reverse and Leesil grabbed him and held fast, arms slipping around the dog's chest.

'Shhhh,' he said. 'Stop it.'

Chap's struggles ceased, but he continued growling. Down the hallway past Magiere, the 'visitor' had vanished. Magiere looked back and forth in confusion and then dropped to Leesil's side.

'What's going on?' she asked. 'Was that an elf? Your neck – did he attack you?'

Leesil instinctively touched his throat, still burning from the wire's slip.

'The wire in his hand . . .' Magiere added more calmly. She looked at the blade stuck in the door frame, and recognition that it was Leesil's spread across her face. 'And he moved like you.'

Leesil dropped his gaze.

'He's a hired killer, like you were. Isn't he?' she insisted.

Leesil hesitated. '*Anmaglâhk*,' he whispered toward Chap.

The dog looked down the hallway, and his growl became a low rumble. As he looked back to Leesil, he yipped once.

'That's a "yes,"' Magiere said, hard and angry. 'Why does a supposed Fay react viciously to an elf, if they're supposed to be related? And what's that word?'

Leesil felt her eyes upon him now.

'That word, Leesil,' she repeated. 'Assassin?'

When Leesil couldn't even understand the word, the elf had seemed astonished at his ignorance. He had called Leesil a traitor, then the same for his mother. One could only be a traitor to a service, a cause, a nation, or a people. The fact that the elf hadn't killed him because he wasn't acting as part of the man's own people meant that fealty wasn't the issue. That ruled out nation or people. This was about the skills his mother had taught him – for which she'd been marked as a traitor? Skills of an assassin and spy not to be taught except to an *anmaglâhk*.

'I think it's a caste,' he said quietly. 'The *anmaglâhk* are some caste among the elves. And my mother was a part of it.'

Magiere shifted around in front of him. He saw on her face the pieces coming together, and like everything else in their lives, the revelation brought more questions than answers.

'Why would elves have a caste of assassins?' she asked. 'And even so, why did one come after you? We have nothing to do with them.'

Leesil had no answer for her.

His mother had taught him their ways, but nothing of their kind, made him one of them but wholly apart from them. She'd kept all other aspects of her people a secret, down to the very language they spoke. The elf's judgment of her had been a broad statement, condemning her for all time, even though she was now dead.

But the *anmaglâhk* had said his mother was a traitor. Not *had been*, but *was*.

Sgäile watched the old barracks from a rooftop across the street. He had let the half-blood live. He had questioned the wisdom of his elders and *Aoishenis-Ahâre*, Most Aged Father. To take the life of one of their own people was forbidden, and a half-blood, though polluted, was still part of them in a twisted way. To break their law meant a grave and serious issue was at stake.

It was true this one had been trained in their ways, though not as well as most. Still, the half-blood knew nothing of his kind, not even the language of his mother's people. How and why could this be?

Aoishenis-Ahâre foresaw so much, so why had he not spoken of the *majay-hì*? Did he not know? The Fay so seldom appeared anymore, even to his own people, so why here and now to this misbegotten child of a traitor? It had taken flesh in one of the old forms not seen since ancient times, as told to Sgäile in the tales of his grandmother.

The *majay-hì*'s presence troubled Sgäile as deeply as his own failure to obey, and he sat upon the roof long into the night, watching.

17

Any preconceptions Magiere had of how the day would unfold crumbled at breakfast. Wynn was convinced that the day's search held great promise for finding the undeads' lair, and so Leesil insisted they be fully prepared.

By breakfast's end, several sages had finished boiling garlic. Leesil prepared short torches, wineskins of garlic water and oil, fresh tinder, and one large and one small quiver of quarrels soaked in garlic water. Domin Tilswith donated a light crossbow. Leesil strapped Vàtz's larger one across his back, and then stunned Magiere by handing the smaller bow and quiver to the boy.

'We can't leave him,' Leesil whispered to her. 'He'll just follow on his own. This way, if things go awry, I can stuff him in a coach and send the driver off before he can get out.'

Having Vàtz in tow wasn't among Magiere's considerations, but she reluctantly conceded that Leesil was correct about the troublesome little whelp.

Leesil stowed his toolbox inside the back of his surcoat, strapped on his sheathed punching blade, and announced that he was ready. However, Wynn provided two more surprises.

Rummaging through what the city guard had left behind, she'd found a pair of soft leather boots for Leesil. The young sage then announced that she was coming along.

Before Magiere or Leesil could refuse, Wynn waded in with more vehemence than either of them thought her capable.

Several deed signatures were foreign names, and thereby a translator might be needed. Neither of them had spent as much time as she in paging through city documents and were far less likely to fathom any quandary that arose. Lastly, she was adamant that no other choice was acceptable. She wouldn't give them city records, for which she was responsible, unless they agreed.

Magiere stewed silently as the motley band stepped into the street. Glancing back at Wynn with her parchments, and Vàtz waddling along with a crossbow conspicuously hoisted over his too-small shoulder, she turned on Leesil as if this were all his doing.

'Don't say it,' he warned. 'Just get us a coach before half the city sees us coming.'

Leesil looked no better than their two tagalongs, with his torn surcoat, quiver, crossbow, stilettos, and punching blade. He looked like a vagabond making a poor attempt to sell himself as a mercenary by mere show of arms.

With the hope that Leesil's other blade was finished, their first stop was at the weaponsmith. As their hired coach rolled into the area, Magiere scanned the passing shops, watching for one in particular. With relief, she spotted what she sought. A bit of misdirection was now needed, for which the boy and sage would prove useful.

As all of them except Chap climbed from the coach, and Leesil headed directly into Balgaví's smithy, Magiere grabbed Wynn by the arm and handed her some silver pennies.

'When he's done, have Vàtz take all of you to the nearest clothier and get Leesil a shirt. Durable and as dark colored as possible. I'll meet you back at the coach.'

Wynn nodded hesitantly. 'Where are you going?'

Magiere glanced toward Leesil. To her relief, he held

his second blade up, inspecting it before the bear-sized smith.

'There's more he's going to need,' she said quietly. 'Whether he likes it or not.'

She left a puzzled Wynn behind and headed up to the shop she'd spotted along their way.

Built of dark, weathered wood with a narrow doorway, it was a tiny place. The carved sign swinging gently above the door read *Shartek's*, and below the worn letters was the shape of a hauberk crossed with a pair of gloves. Magiere stepped inside.

The shop was thick with the smell of acrid oil and a hint of iron, and the scent of cured leather she could practically taste in the air. A little old man in leather apron sat at a table working stain into an uncut hide. He nodded to her and continued with his tasks.

Goods were lightly piled on crude tables, from gloves and vests to skullcaps and craftsmen's aprons. The shop-keeper's bench was strewn with tools, scraps of hide, thongs, and bits of metal. She soon found what she sought hanging from a peg on the back wall.

The leather hauberk had a diamond pattern of iron rings woven to the chest with leather laces. Battle damage could be mended by reweaving instead of sewing. Of clever design, it was lightly padded without being too thick for flexibility. However, the sleeves were near elbow length and the skirt dropped too low. She pulled it down and took it to the old man.

'This'll do,' she said, 'but I need changes, and they must be done now.'

The old man nodded, and she proceeded to tell him what she required. When finished, the skirt was tapered front and back, and split at the sides to just below the waist. The sleeves' were similarly shortened. It was not as 'covering' as it had been, but Magiere judged the changes would accommodate Leesil's ways.

'How much?' she asked the old man.

'A silver sovereign,' he replied without pause.

Magiere's breath caught, but it was a fair price. She counted out four silver shills, each a fifth of a sovereign, and the remainder in silver pennies. What was left might see them through two or three days about the city. She headed back with the hauberk bundled under one arm and found the others already waiting at the coach.

Wynn smiled as she appraised Leesil, which gave Magiere a sudden surge of irritation. Leesil now wore a heavy linen shirt of chocolate brown that suited him quite well, and his hair was covered with a charcoal scarf. When he spotted her, he threw up his arms.

'Are you content now?' he asked in challenge.

'Not quite.' She tossed the hauberk to him.

Leesil unfolded it. When it hung open in his hands, he gaped at her, eyes wide in fury.

'Not on your life!'

'Put it on,' she said.

'I can't fight in this.'

'Leesil, you put it on' – her voice grew louder as she pointed to the smith's workshop – 'or I'll hire four of their biggest men to pin you down – and I'll put it on you myself!'

Wynn backed against the coach in frightful embarrassment. Vàtz watched eagerly, likely hoping Leesil would refuse just to see what would happen.

'Fine and well,' Leesil snapped.

He climbed into the coach, and Chap scuttled out of his way. Wynn gave the driver their first destination, and Magiere waved her and Vàtz inside. When she climbed in, Leesil was trying to remove his shirt.

'Over the shirt, you half-wit,' Magiere growled.

Leesil glared at her though the neck of the shirt halfway over his head, and Chap shifted away from him to the seat's far end. He jerked the shirt back down and fussed with the armor long enough to make his resentment apparent. Magiere offered no assistance, not about to give in to his little fit.

Once finished, Leesil tugged dramatically at the hauberk's collar and sullenly stared out the window. Instead of an overarmed vagabond, he now looked like a walking armory, but at least he was protected. Her gaze flickered to his right wrist, the open sleeve cuff not large enough to close across his stiletto hilt. The scars were just visible.

Yes, protected. But not from her – or himself.

Leesil sensed Magiere watching him. So she feared for his safety, but now that she'd taken it all into her own hands, why the worried glances? With her clashing moods and complications leaping upon them at each turn, he was getting fed up with everything – including her. Beneath the hauberk's leather, the shirt felt itchy, as if he'd slept all night upon an anthill.

Throughout the morning, the coach traveled most of the city's inner ring and the wealthier districts of the middle ring, only to have Chap jump out, sniff about once, twice, or not at all, and jump back into the coach. Past noon, Leesil's overtried patience was nearly depleted.

Suddenly, Chap sat up and sniffed, eagerly pushing his head out of the coach door window. Everyone looked up with anticipation, and Leesil leaned over the dog to look out as well.

They passed a small open market near a gatehouse, and several roving vendors had stopped their carts full of prepared foods at the busy crossing.

'Exactly what have you done to be hungry?' Leesil asked, about to pull the hound back inside the coach.

'A brief pause,' Wynn suggested.

She leaned against the coach's sidewall, strained and tired. Riding around in the jostling coach appeared to have caught up with her.

'Yes,' Magiere said. 'I think so.'

Leesil signaled the driver to stop. He'd barely stepped out, when Chap leaped clear and bounded down the street toward the makeshift market.

'Get back here!' Leesil shouted, but the dog disappeared into the crowd.

'We'll catch up to him,' Magiere said. 'It's not like he's going to buy any food on his own. Or he'll beg his way into a handout again.'

The noontime street was crowded with people on their way to or doing business in the market. Nearly all paused at a cart to purchase a skewer of roasted beef or hot pastry. Leesil idly wandered, ignoring them, until a sudden shout caught everyone's attention.

'Thief! Stop!'

The crowds were too thick to see what the fuss was about, so after briefly craning his neck, Leesil continued on his way. Little caught his attention among the peddlers and rickety rolling carts, and finding that he was not particularly hungry, he wove his way back toward the coach.

There was Chap, sitting on the cobblestones and desperately trying to tear a bite out of an oversize sausage.

Leesil closed in on the dog. 'What did you do?'

Chap ignored him. There was no telling how long that sausage had been in some vendor's cart, but it proved as tough as rolled sailcloth. For all Chap's wrestling, he couldn't break off a mouthful. The others had already returned and sat inside the coach. Vàtz chewed at a stick of grilled beef while Wynn nibbled a potato pasty. Magiere sat quietly with nothing in her hands.

'Not hungry either?' she asked him.

'Let's move on while they finish,' Leesil suggested, shaking his head and turning to Chap. 'Get in, you gluttonous little thief.'

Chap whined in frustration, the sausage still whole between his jaws, and hopped into the coach. Leesil followed, signaling the driver to continue.

Squatting on the floor between the seats, Chap pinned one end of the sausage under a forepaw and began pulling on the other end. He shook his head, gnashing his teeth as he tried to grind a piece loose.

'Serves you right,' Leesil grumbled at him. 'Next time wait until I can buy something edible.'

Vàtz finished his own repast and grabbed the sausage's end from under the dog's paw. 'You stupid mutt, you're never going to get a bite that way.'

Leesil was caught unaware as the boy snatched a stiletto right out of his wrist sheath.

'Give me that,' Magiere said, grabbing for the blade.

'I can handle this,' Vàtz growled back, evading her.

Chap backed between Leesil's legs, growling and refusing to release his would-be meal. Vàtz laid hold of it with both hands, unable to cut off a piece with the stiletto. Leesil grabbed the dog to get the sausage out of his mouth while Magiere grappled with Vàtz again for the stiletto. Wynn leaned away, protecting her potato pasty from getting smashed in the four-way flailing until it all ended quite suddenly.

The sausage snapped.

Chap lurched back against Leesil, muzzle flung up, and grease and ground meat spattered across Leesil chest.

Magiere grabbed Vàtz's wrist as the boy recoiled against her, and his half of the sausage was slung into the air.

It smacked against the coach's roof, slopped down on Chap's head, and spattered sausage guts all over Leesil's sleeves.

Everyone fell silent as Leesil stared down at himself in disbelief.

Wynn dropped her pasty out the window, apparently losing her appetite. Magiere merely wrinkled her nose in disgust before hailing the driver to stop the coach.

'You're supposed be a Fay?' Leesil hissed at the hound.

With a whine, Chap snapped his jaws once and the sausage stump vanished with a gulp.

Leesil held out his hand to Vàtz.

The boy made a hurried attempt to wipe off the stiletto's handle on his pants and only managed to smear the blade with grease before handing it back hilt first. Leesil stepped out of the coach to brush himself off and scrape the remaining mess from the coach floor. Chap whined again.

'You disgusting pig,' Magiere muttered. 'Get up on that seat and stay there.'

Chap gave Vàtz a quick snarl before doing as ordered.

'What?' Vàtz asked, looking at Magiere. 'I was trying to help.'

'Move,' she answered with a swat across the top of his head, and pointed to the coach corner farthest from Chap.

Leesil shouted to the driver to move on. His new shirt was ruined, though he didn't know why that bothered him, as he hadn't wanted it in the first place. He rolled up the grease-covered sleeves, picking off sausage bits along the way.

Once again, he caught Magiere watching his every movement. Trying not to alert her to his awareness, he let his arm drop to his lap and her gaze followed again. He looked down, thinking perhaps he'd missed some smear on his arm, but it was clean right down to the scars.

Leesil traced the white line where he'd slashed his wrist open, and then the jagged arcs made by her teeth. Magiere shied away to stare out the window.

Cold awareness raced through Leesil.

The prey they sought, her uncertainty of their future, or even the *anmaglâhk*, weren't the reason for her distance or fear for him.

The danger that Magiere feared most was herself.

Magiere watched the stone houses of the quiet, wealthy street pass by outside the coach.

'We only have one more,' Wynn said. 'Then we are done, if it is not the lair.'

Leesil glanced out the window, then turned to Magiere. 'Sun's going down. You want to leave it until morning?'

'No, we still have time,' Wynn added. 'We are near enough.'

Leesil was correct, but as much as the sage's insistence surprised Magiere, she preferred to have it all over and done. The day was wasted and, by midafternoon, she'd given up hope of finding what they sought.

'All right, the last one,' she agreed.

Wynn called out the final location to the driver, and they rolled on. The young sage stayed at the window, leaning out for fresh air. The smell of sausage still lingered inside the coach. Vàtz grumbled a bit, but otherwise had remained quiet for the rest of the day. And so had Leesil, strangely enough.

When he'd touched the scars, her mouth and throat turned dry. Perhaps they still itched or ached.

Chap suddenly raised his head and sprang up on the

seat to stare out at the passing houses. A low rumble began in his throat as the fur along his back rose. Vàtz tried to climb out of his seat to get to Chap's window. Magiere pushed the boy back and crouched on the coach floor at the hound's side.

Leesil swung out the other coach door and spoke softly to the coachman. 'Don't stop yet.'

'We should be right in front of it, I believe,' Wynn whispered.

Magiere watched Chap closely. The hound's eyes shifted back and forth as he sniffed the air, and then settled on one house.

It was a three-story, solid stone structure with arched windows and a wide front door, much like many along the street. Chap's rumble grew as his jaws opened and his jowls pulled back. Magiere closed her hands over his muzzle.

'Don't!' she ordered. 'No noise. The sun is almost down, and we don't want to warn them. Understand?'

Chap rolled his eyes toward her and let out a muffled yip.

Magiere shivered and released him. She still wasn't accustomed to the idea that Chap understood her words and even responded intelligibly in his own fashion.

The coach continued another four or five houses down the street, then rolled to a quiet stop. As Magiere opened the door, Chap leaped out. He didn't run toward their destination but stood waiting, fur bristling.

Magiere glanced down, but the topaz amulet wasn't glowing. Perhaps she needed to be closer. As Leesil came around to join her, Wynn and Vàtz stepped out as well. To Magiere's surprise, Wynn reached up and handed the coachman some coins.

'What are you doing?' Magiere asked.

'This is the correct house, is it not?' Wynn answered.

'Wait . . .' Leesil started.

Before Magiere could respond as well, Wynn waved the driver off. The coachman cracked the reins, and the horse stepped into a trot down the street.

Leesil put a hand over his face, and Wynn looked completely perplexed at his reaction.

'You and Vàtz can't be here for this,' he finally added. 'We don't even know what we're dealing with.'

Vàtz's little face flushed. 'I didn't sit in that damn coach all day for nothin'. I'm here to earn my share of the coin.'

Magiere's voice dropped to a deep menacing tone.

'When exactly did we agree to that?' She turned on Wynn without pause. 'And you . . . you can barely keep you food down when facing a stale sausage!'

Wynn pursed her lips at the insult. 'I am no true mage,' she said as if it were a confession, 'but all sages learn the simplest things in their general studies. Domin Tilswith has trained me in the principles of thaumaturgy. Though we do not know the kind of magic you faced, I may be able to help, perhaps, if such arises again from . . . Chane.'

As she spoke the name, her oval face flushed slightly, but her back remained straight.

'You're no more than an idle dabbler,' Magiere scoffed. 'Whatever Chane is, he's far beyond what you could deal with.'

'Oh, for the love of mutton,' Leesil spit out. 'This is madness.'

'You two are staying outside,' Magiere said. 'And that's the end of it.'

'That won't work,' Leesil said. 'We can't protect them if anything gets out of the house. And if we wait to get rid of these two, any undeads inside might sense we've been here already. By tomorrow morning the place would be empty . . . or worse, they'd be waiting for us.'

Leesil was right, again, and Magiere found it intensely annoying. If only they'd come to this house first. Catching their prey in daylight was now hopeless, and they couldn't afford to wait.

'All right, we may yet have surprise on our side,' she said with disgust, and then turned on the sage and the boy. 'But you two do as you're told and keep silent.'

She led the way slowly along the row of stone and timber houses, all the while watching for signs of movement or life. She stopped one dwelling away from the one they sought and dropped down on her haunches.

Built of heavy, mortared stone, it wasn't what she'd expected. At least not compared to the warehouse backrooms and underground chambers used by Miiska's undeads. Leesil slipped forward to crouch beside her.

It sat sedate and respectable amongst its neighbors in this quiet and well-to-do street, front door to the left atop three steps. There was one wide window with heavy shutters closed over it. The next two floors up each held two windows evenly spaced but similarly protected.

'We can't do this out in the open,' Leesil said. 'For that matter, we may have already attracted attention we're not aware of. Best look for a rear entrance.'

He moved out ahead, peered along the building's front, and then scurried back to Magiere's side.

'There's an access way on the far side,' he said.

Leesil reached behind himself and pulled out the thin box he'd slipped up into the back of his hauberk. He glanced at Vàtz and Wynn, and then Magiere.

She waited, expecting him to say something, but he gripped the box under his arm and dashed along the front of the house. Magiere unsheathed her falchion and followed him.

★   ★   ★

The rear door wasn't as wide as the front. Leesil removed a thin silvery strut from inside his toolbox's lid as he inspected the door handle again for anything notable.

'No lock, so it's latched or bolted from the inside,' he whispered to Magiere.

He pressed slowly and firmly against the door until he could slip the tiny strut through the crack at its frame. Closing his eyes, he slid the strut upward until it reached and raised a latch. He pulled the strut out and placed it into its slot in the box's lid.

'Too easy,' Leesil whispered. 'Everyone stay clear of the door.'

Leesil tugged the crossbow's strap over his head and set the weapon upon the ground. He cocked and loaded it, signaling to Vàtz to do the same. The boy plopped onto the ground and braced his feet against the bow, working its string into the catch.

Again, Leesil examined frame and door but found nothing. He leaned against the wall on the door's hinged side. Then he pushed the door open with his right hand and quickly pulled back.

Nothing happened.

'If anything, and I mean anything, comes at you or Wynn,' Leesil instructed Vàtz, 'you fire first and both of you get out of the way. Don't get fancy. Aim for the center of its body or the first part you can sight. Pain from the garlic water might buy you a moment, but that's all. If one of these things gets hold of you, it'll snap you in half.'

Vàtz blinked, suddenly very still and quiet. He nodded, tight-lipped and determined. Chap rumbled softly, and Leesil grabbed his jaw.

'You keep your head and watch out for them.' He pointed to Wynn and Vàtz.

Chap offered an offended look and growled at the door.

Wynn suddenly dug in her robe pockets and pulled out a small crystal much like one from a cold lamp. She rubbed it furiously between her hands, and it began to glow.

'Keep that covered until I tell you otherwise,' Leesil admonished.

Wynn nodded, closing the crystal tightly in both hands. The light muted to a dull orange glow between her fingers.

Leesil motioned to Magiere, and she slipped around to the door's far side, falchion in hand.

In close quarters, any target would be near enough that little aiming would be necessary. The crossbow was heavy, but Leesil could still point and squeeze the firing lever with one hand. He gripped it in his left and slipped his right punching blade out of its sheath.

There was no turning back now.

Magiere appeared composed, but he knew better. She was the dhampir and played the council with cavalier confidence and mystery for their benefit. But in reality, this was only the second time they'd hunted undeads. He slipped through the door ahead of her.

As expected, they entered a kitchen, everything neat, clean, and in place. Only a few items of cookware hung on the walls, and most looked old and untouched, having probably been left behind by a previous owner. An immaculate hearth free of ash or char was on the right with a line of rough cupboards to the left. In the room's center was a solid, thick-topped scullery table, yet there were no knives, cleavers, or preparation implements in its block or hanging from its side hooks. There were neither dishes nor food. No bread, no tea, not even a shriveled carrot.

The kitchen hadn't been used in a long while.

Leesil led them across to the far side doorway, Magiere close behind him. He stopped long enough to check the entry for anything suspicious and then pushed it open to scan the room for any movement or presence.

This was the dining chamber. Stone walls were hung with simple tapestries, and an oval cherrywood table and matching chairs filled the room. Two silver candelabra rested upon the table. The candles were all new, having never been lit. Pulled to the ceiling upon its chain was a chandelier, dripping with an array of cut crystals.

An earsplitting caw filled the dark room, and Leesil crouched low. He felt Magiere's hand clamp on his shoulder from behind as a tinkling sound pulled his attention upward.

A large raven hopped about the crystal chandelier, flexing its wings, and its black beady eyes stared at them. It cawed again, louder, and Chap growled.

'Ssh,' Leesil warned the hound. He had to quiet the bird quickly.

A snap and twang came from behind Leesil, and the crystals in the chandelier jangled loudly. The raven dropped with a hollow thump in the middle of the table, impaled through the body with a quarrel.

Leesil looked back over his shoulder.

Vàtz's crossbow was empty. The boy shrugged. 'It was loud.'

'Reload,' Leesil whispered back, and rose from his crouch.

At the room's far end was an open archway, and he stepped around the table toward it.

Another low growl filled the room, but before Leesil turned to admonish Chap again, two glittering eyes came into view around the side of the entrance.

A gray wolf as tall as Chap stood in their path, a low rumble issuing from its throat.

Chap leaped to the tabletop beside Leesil, knocking both candelabra to the floor in a clatter. He answered the wolf with a snarl of his own, jowls back to expose flexing jaws.

Before Leesil could fire, Chap lunged off the table, and the wolf launched himself forward. They slammed together, knocking the end chair over, as the room filled with sounds of snarls and snapping teeth.

Leesil shifted back in panic. So much for the element of surprise.

Chane lay fully clothed upon his bed in the cellar's back room, listening for any sound. Though he heard nothing, his nerves were tightly alert.

Someone was in the house.

His consciousness slipped upward through the building until it touched avian thoughts somewhere upon the main floor.

At first the perspective was disorienting. His raven, Tihko, looked downward from a height, its vision partially obscured by tiny reflections of light in the dark dining chamber. Yes, Chane made out the table clearly now. Tihko was in the chandelier, crystals blocking parts of the room, but why were those crystals sparking softly with light? Twinkling reflections began to move.

Dim light spread from one side of the room where the half-elf stood.

It was the first time Chane had truly seen this man. Hair hidden beneath a dark scarf, he was of average height. Surprising, considering his mixed blood, as most elves were taller than humans. Now armored in a leather hauberk, he carried in one hand a loaded crossbow, and the other gripped a strange, wide-pointed blade extending from his fist, the outside edge arching back along his arm.

Beside the half-elf was the blue-gray hound, its shining eyes peering about the room. Directly behind them was the hunter. At the sight of her, Chane experienced a surge of hunger.

Back in the kitchen doorway was a young boy clutching a crossbow. A puzzling thing. Chane wondered why the hunter would bring a child into this. The light dimly illuminating the room came from the hands of a young woman in gray robes.

Chane stiffened on his bed, and in response Tihko thrashed his wings, making Chane's vision through the bird's eyes waver.

Wynn was in the house.

Her appearance rattled Chane enough that he nearly lost contact with the raven. He watched the half-elf carefully enter the room, knees slightly bent.

Tihko's loud caw filled Chane's head. The half-elf dropped low and looked up. Behind him, the boy raised the crossbow, and aimed at the raven – at Chane.

A shaft of pain pierced Chane through the chest and his vision went black.

Chane convulsed sharply into a ball, the pain stabbing through to his back. When he thrashed over the bedside, his tiny urn jangled on the floor stones. He pushed himself up to his knees, as the cellar back room snapped into focus.

Tihko was dead.

Sounds of snarling and crashing pounded down through the floor from above, and Chane's thoughts tangled. He could slip through the passage into the sewers and let Toret and Sapphire face the hunter and her minions. But what if Toret survived and realized he had run? As long as Toret lived, Chane was his slave. And then there was Wynn.

He cleared his mind, and reason presented the only possible course of action.

Chane pulled his long sword from its sheath and headed for the opening to the hidden passage at the base of the cellar stairs.

'Don't shoot,' Leesil ordered Vàtz. 'You might hit Chap.'

'I ain't stupid,' the boy answered.

Leesil dropped the crossbow on top of the dining table. He heard Magiere pick it up and follow behind him as he inched toward the whirling tangle of hound and wolf battling in the archway. Chap could handle a wolf, but the fight made enough noise to wake the dead, literally.

When the wolf twisted away from Chap's lunge, Leesil kicked out hard at it.

The wolf slammed against the archway's side and lost its footing. Leesil stepped in, swinging his blade downward across the animal's neck. At the last moment, the wolf righted itself, head turning toward Leesil's forward leg.

Chap darted in, jaws snapping closed over the wolf's snout, and he jerked, pulling its head away. Leesil's blade struck the animal's throat, sinking through fur and flesh, and nearly severing its head. The wolf dropped to the floor, motionless. With one last thrash and snarl, Chap released his grip.

Magiere slipped past Leesil through the archway, and he saw the yellow glow of her topaz.

She groaned. 'Anything in this house with ears is certainly awake now.'

'Wait,' he said. 'Let me.'

She stopped and let him lead. When Leesil looked

THIEF OF LIVES 385

back, he found Vàtz pulling his quarrel out of the raven's body and Wynn, her brow furrowed in apprehension, staring at the wolf's corpse.

This was not going well at all.

Alone in the room he usually shared by day with Sapphire, Toret opened his eyes to a distant cawing. His sluggish thoughts cleared.

Chane's raven was loose in the house, and its racket echoed up from the main floor. Toret remembered his wolf.

He tried to do as Chane had taught him, tried to see through its eyes, but he caught only bizarre flashes of images passing through its mind. The view through its eyes was disorienting, misty, and kept shifting about.

Something black dropped from the ceiling, and he barely heard its thud upon the table through the wolf's ears. Then the blue-gray hound appeared on the table, glaring at him with crystal-blue eyes as it snarled.

To the table's side was a man in leather armor he couldn't see clearly. Then he made out the curved blade along the man's arm.

Leesil.

The hound lunged at Toret from the table. He flinched and lost contact with the wolf.

Toret panicked. The half-blood had found him. Was it still day – or night?

He forced himself to stay calm. If Leesil was here, then the hunter was with him, and Sapphire might still be dormant.

She'd been so angry with him as dawn came that he said nothing when she'd stayed in her own room. He rose quickly from the bed. His sword leaned in the room's west corner. Part of him wanted to leave it and return to Ratboy's ways of tooth and nail, but upon leaving the room, he picked up the blade.

Leesil stepped into the parlor, with the other close behind, and felt the mood inside the house instantly change.

Colors here meshed in a warmth that surprised him. A tan-and-russet Suman rug covered the floor, and thick brocade draperies enclosed the windows. Mauve velvet divans were placed around the room below paintings of open glades and forests hung upon the walls. As Wynn stepped into the parlor's archway, the light of her crystal further enlivened the room, and Leesil's gaze passed to the back wall. There was a life-size portrait of Sapphire in a rich red gown.

Wynn examined the portrait. 'Someone lives in this space. Can you feel it?'

This room felt different. The inhabitants never went to the dining chamber or kitchen, but they spent time in here. Down the hallway were only the foyer and front door, and a stairway beginning there led up to the next level. Beneath it was another set of stairs leading below.

'Up or down?' Magiere asked.

She still held the crossbow atop her falchion, and her topaz appeared slightly brighter. Chap growled toward the front foyer, lowering his head.

'Up it is,' Leesil said.

He sheathed his blade and held out his hand to Wynn. She handed him the crystal, and he began working his way down the hall, watching for anything unusual. The last time they'd invaded an undead's lair, he'd tripped a wire and been buried under a rigged cave-in.

When he reached the foyer, he turned to the stairs leading up. In place of the usual knob on the bottom of the staircase's oak railing was a softly glowing orb. It cast light like that of the sage's cold lamps, only dimmer, and appeared to serve no other purpose than illumination. Leesil turned his attention to the stairs themselves. Again, he found nothing, and that unnerved him.

'Is it safe?' Magiere asked.

'I can't find anything,' he answered, and it sounded uncertain even to him, but they had to move on. 'Step back into the foyer while I look farther up.'

He stepped up the first stair, and a thought occurred to him.

What would undeads, who saw clearly in the dark, need with a light in the stairwell? He looked down at the orb as his foot touched the next step.

The orb's light flashed like lightning, and Leesil raised his hand too late.

Brilliant white stabbed through the backs of his eyes into his skull. He jerked away and his foot slipped. As he fell, his hands clamped over his eyes and he cried out, unable to stop himself.

His back collided with something that stopped his fall, and he felt arms wrap around him and lower him to the floor. Someone gripped his wrists and pulled his hands away.

'Leesil?' Magiere's voice asked sharply. 'Are you all right?'

He felt the floor at his back and below his head, and he opened his eyes. Above him wasn't Magiere's pale face but only an oily blackness sparked with swirls of blurred, mute colors.

He was not all right. He was blind.

Toret peered out of his door. There was no one in the hall. He hoped Chane had been awakened by the noise below. He crept down the hall and slipped into Sapphire's room, closing the door quietly.

She was still dormant, lying atop her peach velvet

comforter, and he paused at the sight of her creamy white face and dark-blond ringlets resting upon her cheeks. Adoration swelled inside him. Toret put his fingers over her soft mouth.

'My dear,' he whispered. 'You must get up.'

Her sapphire-blue eyes opened in surprise. But when she saw him, they darkened in temper.

'If you've come to beg for love, you can get out!'

'Shush,' he said, touching her mouth again. 'Quiet, my sweet. The hunter is in the house.'

The expression on her face shifted to shock and then cunning. Indeed, it gave him some relief. It meant she understood their situation.

'How could she find us?'

Toret shook his head. 'You need to escape. Chane, Tibor, and I will take care of this.'

'How can I get out if she's already here?'

'The passageway behind the stairs, remember?' he answered, waiting for her realization. 'Go down to the cellar and into the tunnel we made that leads to the sewers. I've heard the exits to the sea are closed, but you can travel a safe distance in that direction and climb out a grate in the city streets. I will find you later.'

She blinked at him as if he spoke a foreign language.

'Drag one of my gowns through a sewer? My feet? Through that filth and stench?'

A pained cry echoed up through the house.

'What was that?' she asked.

'With luck, one of our trespassers was caught in Chane's trap. Now you must get out of the house.'

She wore only a silk nightgown, so he hurried to the closet and grabbed the nearest gown.

'You can't attract any undue attention in the city now. Put this on and leave quickly.'

'I'm not wearing that. You bought that; I didn't. Midnight blue makes me look sallow.'

'Then you won't care if it gets dragged through a sewer,' he said, and tossed the gown on the bed.

He needed to make sure Chane was awake and couldn't waste any more time. He was on the verge of outright ordering her into the sewer when she smiled.

'Of course, you're right,' she said. 'I don't mean to be difficult. How will you find me later?'

'I'll find you. Now get dressed and go.'

'I'll need some coin,' she stated with a stubborn look.

Toret sighed deeply. 'There's a purse on my wardrobe.'

Magiere caught Leesil as he fell. Her eyes hurt, and everything she looked at was speckled with spots of light, but otherwise she could see.

'I'm blind,' Leesil said in a wild tone. 'Magiere, I'm blind.'

Leesil had caught the globe's full flash in his face. Vàtz seemed tense and on guard, rubbing his eyes, but he was unhurt, as was Wynn. Chap had been closer. He whined, shaking his head and pawing at his face, but from the way he looked about, responding to the movement of the others, he was able to see.

Magiere pulled Leesil up to sit and kept one arm at his back for support. She didn't know what to do and hated the uncertainty.

'Hold on,' she whispered to him, and turned to the young sage. 'Can you help him?'

Wynn picked up the crystal that Leesil had dropped and stood examining the globe more closely now.

'It's still intact,' she whispered.

'What is?' Magiere asked.

'The globe. I do not know how it is triggered, but it

could be almost any of the magics . . . conjury, thaumaturgy, maybe even alchemy by artificing.'

'Is it safe now?' Magiere asked with more insistence.

'I do not know.'

Vàtz jerked the globe free from the railing with both hands, dropped it, and stomped on it. The globe shattered like a mere eggshell upon the floor.

'It's safe now,' he said.

Wynn sighed and knelt down beside Leesil.

'Wynn, can you help him?' Magiere asked.

'Blindness from a flash is usually temporary and passes in little time,' the sage answered. 'Apprentices have suffered similar accidents during first works of magic.'

'We don't have a little time,' Leesil growled. 'If you can do something . . . then do it!'

Wynn slipped her hand around Leesil's back and nodded to Magiere that she had him supported. Magiere stood up. She reversed the falchion in her grip so she could still hold it and aim the crossbow.

'Vàtz, watch the hallway,' she said. 'Shoot anything that moves.'

The boy settled himself in next to Wynn, crossbow aimed down the passage toward the kitchen door.

Wynn set the crystal on the floor and took a pouch of water from Leesil's belt. She shifted around and pulled him back to lean against her.

'We simply need to speed up your body's ability to heal around your eyes,' she said. 'I am not a healer, but perhaps I can stimulate the process. Lean your head back upon my shoulder. I am going to rinse your eyes first.'

Leesil did as she instructed. Wynn carefully poured the water across his blinking eyes.

'Now be still and quiet,' she said. 'I must concentrate.'

She placed her palms like a mask over his face. As she

closed her own eyes, she began chanting softly.

Magiere waited, impatient and anxious, as she watched Leesil. She couldn't finish this without him, and even if she could, she wasn't about to have him remain in this lair if he was blind. If Wynn failed, they would flee immediately.

Wynn ceased chanting, and Magiere forget to watch the stairs. She wasn't certain what the sage was doing or how such magic worked, but there had been no light, sound, or other sensations. No sign that anything had happened at all from the sage's actions. Wynn lifted her hands from Leesil's face.

'Open your eyes,' Wynn said. 'Is it any better?'

Leesil pushed up to sit on his own. He blinked twice, squinting, and Magiere quickly crouched in front of him. At that he looked directly at her face, and she took deep, long breath.

'Yes . . .' he said uncertainly, then nodded. 'It's a little clearer.'

His voice was calmer now, but Magiere still heard the strain in it. Blindness was probably the worst thing Leesil could imagine. He was a fighter. He turned his head and squinted at Wynn.

'Thank you. I don't know how—'

'How well can you see?' Magiere interrupted.

Leesil climbed back to his feet, and she grabbed his arm to steady him.

'Better,' he answered. 'It's getting better quickly now. That's all I need.'

She nodded, uncertain whether he was completely truthful. 'Then we go up.'

Chane emerged on the second floor, long sword in hand, and moved quickly to Tibor's room. It contained only thick curtains and a mattress on the floor. Tibor was deeply dormant, and Chane knelt next to him. He reached out and touched Tibor's shoulder.

'Wake now,' he said, his tone urgent. 'The hunter is in our house.'

Tibor jumped slightly and opened his eyelids. He pulled back away from Chane with a startled expression before recognition dawned.

'The hunter?'

'Get your sword. We must protect the master.'

At mention of Toret, Tibor grabbed the blade lying next to him upon the mattress.

'You lead,' Chane said. 'Head for the hidden passageway, and we'll slip upstairs.'

Without question, Tibor headed for the bedroom door with Chane close behind. As Tibor stepped into the hallway, Chane raised his blade. On some hidden instinct, Tibor looked back.

Chane's blade cut a path through the darkness into Tibor's neck and cleanly through it.

The sailor's head tumbled off, striking the floor and rolling down the hall. The body crumpled with a heavy thud, black fluids seeping into the hallway rug.

Chane wiped his blade clean on the body and stepped over it, hurrying to the concealed entrance of the hidden second stairway. Inside the small space of cobwebbed stone, he took the narrow steps two at a time and emerged quietly in the third-floor hallway.

He saw Toret peer from Sapphire's room, and Chane tapped lightly on the wall. Toret looked up at the sound and saw him. The small undead pointed back toward a spot behind the railing at the top of the stairs. Chane nodded and motioned for Toret to head for the far end overhanging the stairwell.

Toret shook his head and pointed back into the room as he mouthed, *Sapphire*. He then pointed at the passage Chane had exited and downward.

Chane understood. Sapphire was still in the room, and Toret wanted her in the passage so she could escape. He motioned for Toret to send her down the hall. Then he heard voices from below in the house.

His small master pulled the struggling form of Sapphire from her room and pointed at Chane, but clearly Sapphire wasn't ready to leave. Could she possibly be any more vapid? With an angry expression, she scurried down the hall. To Chane's amazement, instead of coming straight to him, she ducked into Toret's room.

Chane looked at Toret in disbelief, and saw his little master clench his jaw with frustration. The hunter could come up the stairs at any moment. But before Chane took a step to go after Sapphire, she slipped back out of Toret's room with a purse in her hand.

She'd wanted money. She wore a midnight-blue gown and a gold pendant with a sapphire, and carried a large matching bag with a drawstring closure. She dropped the purse into the bag. As soon as she was close enough, Chane grabbed her arm and pushed her into the passageway so he could close it.

'I'm not climbing into some sewer!' she hissed, swatting at him.

Chane's anger flared but realization presented an opportunity. Perhaps Toret was not the only annoyance he could be rid of this night. He peered over his shoulder at Toret hiding above the stairwell at the hall's other end, then pitched his voice low to Sapphire, making sure his little master would not hear.

'Then just go to the exit for the second floor and wait,' he instructed her. 'Toret and I will take care of the hunter. When all is finished, I will come for you.'

She mulled over his suggestion. 'If I hear the fight move upstairs, couldn't I just slip out onto the main floor and out the front door?'

'No, wait behind the second floor's entrance and do not come out until I open it.'

Chane pushed her inside and closed the passage entrance.

He would never come for her and, eventually, Sapphire's impatience would be too much. She would try to sneak through the house. With luck, she would also join Toret in a second death.

Chane opened his senses as wide as possible.

Soft growling and the barest footfall upon stairs sounded from far below. He crouched in the hallway behind the railing near the landing. Toret was at the far end of the railing over the stairwell, examining his sword for a long moment. To Chane's astonishment, he put the blade down. What did he plan to fight with?

Where's Tibor? Toret mouthed without sound.

Chane drew a line across his throat with one finger and pointed down the stairwell to the sound of approaching steps.

Toret looked blankly down over the railing's edge. He crouched, angry determination on his face. Chane settled low, waiting.

With a little luck, Toret would find himself very suddenly alone against the dhampir and the half-blood. Not the best plan, but it was all that Chane could arrange in the moment. Freedom was perhaps only moments away.

18

Leesil let Magiere lead the way up the staircase. Her slightly blurred form was silhouetted by the glow of her topaz amulet, an unsettling sight. Hopefully, the orb was the last surprise they would encounter. Although he could see enough to fight, he couldn't clearly make out the carpet's pattern. Spotting any fine detail of warning was impossible until his vision cleared further, and they didn't have time to wait. He feared little in the world, but the prospect of blindness had never occurred to him.

Chap snarled softly as he mounted the stairs beside Leesil. Wynn and Vàtz followed behind, the sage now carrying her cold lamp crystal and the crossbow Magiere had given her. Nearing the second floor, Magiere stopped with one foot on the landing and looked back at Leesil, her dark eyes troubled and uncertain.

Leesil unsheathed his second blade, one in each hand, and took two steps up to peer through the stairs' railing along the hallway floor.

A headless body lay there, and a pool of dark fluid was already soaked into the rug. Leesil reached out to touch the stained spot – it was still freshly wet.

Magiere stepped onto the landing and into the hall, and Leesil followed. Halfway down the passage lay a decapitated head. A gasp came from behind Leesil, and he looked back.

Wynn's eyes were wide and round, fixed on the corpse. He waved a hand at her several times before she looked up, and with a scowl, he put one finger to his lips. She nodded slowly.

Vàtz sidestepped the body at Leesil's feet. He glared at it as if someone had stolen a dockside fare out from under his wrinkling nose.

Leesil gave Magiere a questioning glance, but she merely shook her head in confusion and moved down the corridor. They passed by the head and reached the base of the final flight of stairs.

Creeping upward, Magiere led them. As they stepped beyond the halfway point, Chap snarled loudly.

Magiere shifted back against the wall and Chap inched another step upward. Fur on end, the hound looked up toward the floor above. Leesil followed that crystal gaze.

Somewhere above were undeads.

Chap cut loose a wail that shattered the silence, and the world around Leesil became a flurry of motion.

A tall figure appeared above the railing along the third floor and slashed down at Magiere with a long sword. The clang of it colliding with her falchion rang in Leesil's ears, and he missed a grab for Chap as the hound bolted past Magiere to the landing.

Magiere slashed the sword out of her way as she climbed upward. The sword's wielder stepped into full view as he brought his blade back to swipe at Chap's lunging form.

He was tall, with brown-red hair, and dressed in a simple but finely tailored tunic. As Leesil took two more stairs, he heard Wynn cry out.

'Chane!'

That single word made the swordsman falter as he looked down the stairs past Leesil. Indecision broke the cold determination on his pale face.

A quarrel sailed past Leesil's head and struck the tall

undead in the chest. Smoke welled around the embedded shaft. Leesil glanced back to see that it was Vàtz who'd fired. Wynn stood petrified beside him with her crossbow clutched at her chest. Vàtz was already reloading.

As Leesil rushed upward, he glimpsed a form leaping over the railing along the back of the hall and down into the stairwell. It landed on his back and crushed him against the stairs. Wiry hands like skin stretched upon bone snatched both of his wrists to pin them down.

'You're dead, half-blood,' hissed a familiar voice in his ear.

Leesil felt the chill of Ratboy's grip on his wrists as if the cold burrowed into his flesh and spread through his body. Burning pain shortened his breath as teeth clamped against his hauberk's collar.

Not again.

The teeth closed hard on Leesil's neck, but his collar took the brunt. As shock finished its rush through his blood, he folded his left leg and kicked against the stairwell's left wall.

The thrust threw him into the right wall, crushing Ratboy behind him, and the wiry undead lost his grip. Leesil jerked his left elbow back and felt the rearward point of his blade sink into Ratboy's side. The teeth upon Leesil's neck released.

Leesil slipped down two steps and chopped back with his right blade. It bit into the empty steps. Ratboy already stood upon the landing.

The eye that Leesil had stabbed was now a mottled white orb in a bruised socket. There was only a dark, circular stain where the iris should have been.

Leesil followed carefully, both blades out in front of him. 'Chap!' he yelled.

The hound spun from Magiere's side to face Ratboy.

A quarrel struck the small undead above the right eye and pierced the top of his skull. His head recoiled off the wall as smoke rose from the wound. Ratboy screamed, slapping at his face, and Chap slammed into him with both forepaws, sending him back hard into the landing's corner.

Leesil couldn't look away to see where Wynn and Vàtz were, or which of them had fired. He rushed upward and made a backhanded swing with the left blade directly at Ratboy's neck.

Ratboy jerked the quarrel from his forehead as he ducked, and Leesil's blade scraped along the wall. The shock shuddered through his arm, and Ratboy ducked under toward the stairs.

Leesil turned.

Wynn stood down the stairs, an empty crossbow in her hands. She swung it at Ratboy as he drew back a claw-shaped hand to slash at her with his fingernails.

Time slowed to a crawl in Leesil's vision. The undead's nails could rip open throats. A twinge passed through the faded scars on his jaw.

Chap leaped down the stairwell.

The hound struck with his forepaws and full weight against Ratboy's back. Dog, vampire, and sage all tumbled down the stairs together in a rolling heap. Vàtz grabbed the railing with one hand and barely avoided getting entangled.

A low male voice called out, 'Wynn!'

Leesil couldn't help following the sound in surprise.

Magiere's eyes were black, canines bared, as she swung at Chane with her blade. It had been Chane who'd called out in panic to the young sage.

There was no time to puzzle over this, and Leesil rushed down the stairs after Ratboy.

*   *   *

Chane was furious. Everything that could have possibly gone wrong had before he could react. He had planned to momentarily engage the half-elf while pushing the dhampir off on Toret, but his little master's eagerness for revenge fouled everything.

He had not given due consideration to the hound's involvement. The beast's teeth were more than an annoyance. The gashes on his legs burned. In avoiding the dog, he had ended up fighting the dhampir after the boy shot him in the chest. The wound still smoked, even after he'd jerked the quarrel out.

And now Wynn was somewhere below, trapped between Toret and the hound.

Chane roared and swung at the dhampir. When she snarled back, he saw her extended canines. Unlike the crystal shimmer of an undead's eyes fully opened to the night, her irises were black pits that swallowed all light. She forced him back down the hallway. The wound in his chest hindered his sword arm, and to make matters worse, as he blocked another swing, he saw the boy near the stairs re-loading his crossbow. If he did not do something quickly, this could end in his second death.

Chane feinted and stepped back.

'Toret will gut your half-blood,' he said. 'Tear him from throat to groin.'

The dhampir hesitated. Chane feinted again, and when she moved to block, he followed with his left fist.

The blow struck her jaw. To Chane's surprise, the impact sent a jar up his arm. She was far more solid than he anticipated, but her head still whipped to the side.

She stumbled back, striking the door frame of Sapphire's room and spinning along the wall. Before she hit the floor, the boy with the crossbow stepped into the hall. Chane grabbed the railing and leaped over it, the hiss of a quarrel passing behind him as he dropped into the stairwell.

Wynn huddled on the floor at the stairs' bottom, with the snarling hound guarding her. Chane heard small footsteps on the upper landing, and turned to see the boy again trying to recock the crossbow. He lashed out with the long-sword. The blade tip cracked against the top stair, and the boy skittered back to fall against the wall.

Chane leaped down to the second floor landing. Before the hound could turn on him, he swung the flat of his blade into the side of the animal's head. It tumbled across the floor.

Wynn looked up at him with terror in her eyes.

It was an expression he never thought to see upon her face when she gazed at him. He bent over to grab her wrist with his free hand and pulled her up.

'Chane . . . no!' she cried out.

There was no time to explain, and he hoisted her over his shoulder. Wynn's body was so small she seemed to weigh nothing. She struggled, but with little effect.

Toret scrambled to his feet, and the half-blood kicked him in the side. The small undead toppled against the closed door of the empty spare room. As the elf closed in, Chane kicked him in the back, sending him careening into Toret.

Chane took two long steps down the second-floor hall, grabbed the railing, and leaped into the next stairwell. As he raced down the last flight of stairs and out the front door, he heard the half-blood yell out Wynn's name. He sped off into the street without a backward glance.

As Toret struggled out from under Leesil, he caught only a glimpse of Chane leaping over the railing with the robed young woman over his shoulder. Then he saw Tibor's head upon the floor.

Toret was alone.

Of all the ways he had thought this would play out, facing the half-blood and the dhampir on his own had never entered his thoughts. The hound as well was on its feet, inching forward. Leesil gripped two curved blades directly in front of himself.

Leesil's eyes shifted briefly to the railing where Chane had just fled, and Toret knew the half-blood wanted to run after the abducted woman.

'Why don't you just lie down and die for good,' Leesil snarled at him, and rushed forward, clearly trying to force his way farther down the hall.

Toret dodged and slashed at Leesil's face as one of the blades dropped too low, but he was buying time, and he knew it.

He was going to be destroyed, and Sapphire was in the sewers, fleeing to escape. What would happen at the moment of his second death? These intruders might go after Chane, but they might also use that wretched hound to find the passageway Sapphire had followed. They could hunt her down or even separate to go after both her and Chane.

Toret glanced quickly about for some advantage, but he saw only Tibor's head. He backed another step, and his foot bumped something on the floor.

The body.

He waited for Leesil's next advance, and when it came, he dropped low under the blade's swing.

Toret dropped his blade in midcrouch and grabbed Tibor's headless corpse with both hands. As he rose up, he pushed with his legs and flung the body forward.

The half-blood's eyes widened as the corpse collided

with him. Living and dead limbs sprawled backward toward the hound, and the animal retreated. Toret leaped over the railing into the stairwell and ran down to the foyer.

The front door remained open from Chane's flight, but Toret didn't follow in his servant's footsteps. He pressed upon the wall at the stairs' bottom to release the catch and the hidden entrance popped open. Slipping inside and slamming it shut, he heard the padded footfall and snarl of the hound beyond the wall.

Toret headed downward as he heard the thud of the dog battering against the wall where the entrance had closed. He quickly exited into the cellar.

Several practice swords lined the walls. He grabbed the stoutest blade that looked manageable and headed into the open passage they'd dug down into the sewers.

Sapphire couldn't have gone far. He would catch up to her, and together they would escape from Bela to the Suman Empire. He no longer wanted revenge. Now, all that mattered was survival.

'Get up! Get up!' Vàtz shouted, pulling on Magiere's arm.

She sucked in air and struggled up to all fours. She felt as if she'd been struck with an iron cudgel. Her head ached, but the worst was her jaw. Then awareness took her, and she realized Vàtz was looking at her.

Magiere closed her lips tight with a quick pass of her tongue, and relief came at the touch of reverted teeth that closed smoothly together.

'Hurry,' Vàtz said. 'He took Wynn, and Leesil's on the next floor fighting the other one.'

Magiere pulled herself up, grabbing her falchion from the floor. Before she could stop him, Vàtz rounded the railing's end and headed down the stairs, crossbow in hand. She followed quickly, regaining clarity with each step. When she reached the second floor, Leesil was dislodging himself from under the corpse they'd passed earlier, and there was no sign of Chap. She helped pull Leesil up.

'Where's Wynn?' she asked.

'He took her,' Leesil called out as he headed around the railing down the next flight of stairs. 'That butchering undead we've been after – he has her.'

Vàtz tried to get ahead of Magiere, but she pushed him behind. 'You stay back.'

At the bottom of the stairwell, she saw Chap repeatedly throwing himself at the wall next to the landing in the foyer, ignoring the open front door. His snarl was broken only by yelps on impact. Wynn's crossbow lay at the foot of the stairs.

Leesil ran out the door onto the front porch, looking up and down the dark street.

'Stop it,' Magiere yelled, grabbing Chap before he lunged again.

Spinning out of her grip, the hound turned and snapped at her. Magiere backed away. Vàtz took a step up the stairs, not about to get near either of them.

'What is wrong with you?' she shouted at the dog.

Chap circled back around, glaring at the blank wall next to the base of the stairs.

'Pay attention,' Magiere said. 'Where did the tall one go? Find me a trail, damn you!'

Chap glowered at her for a moment and then backtracked to the stairs. He sniffed the floor and whirled about to rush outside and down the steps. Magiere trotted out next to Leesil and watched as the hound worked the street's cobblestones, back and forth.

He stopped, head low, facing the way they had first

come, and his rumble shifted to a vicious growl that carried in the night air.

'Chane is panicked,' Leesil said. 'I'm betting he heads into the sewers again.'

Chap darted back to them, clearly wanting someone to follow him. But he also kept looking through the front door toward the wall he'd been insanely battering himself against.

Leesil followed the hound's gaze, and for a moment the anger on his face turned to puzzlement. Magiere put it aside and turned to Vàtz now standing in the doorway.

'Do you know the new guard barracks, just inside the inner ring wall?'

The boy nodded uncertainly.

'Run to Captain Chetnik,' Magiere said. 'Tell him what's happened, and that there is at least one vampire in the sewers. Have him double the guard on the bayside openings, but no one goes in. Can you do that?'

Realizing the task was important and real, Vàtz nodded. 'Yes, I'll be fast.'

She tossed him her pouch of remaining coins.

'Find a coach if you can. Do what you have to.'

As the boy scurried into the street, Magiere stepped back inside to pick up the abandoned crossbow.

'Leesil, give me your remaining quarrels.'

He unstrapped the quiver across his back and handed it to her from the doorway. A number of the quarrels' feathered ends were splintered or snapped off, but three were still whole. Leesil remained fixated upon the foyer wall.

'Let's go,' she said.

'No,' he replied.

He stepped inside to study the wall Chap had assaulted and ran his fingertips slowly across its surface. Then he stepped out the door again, this time looking at the left side of the building beyond the front door's frame.

'Leesil!' Magiere said angrily.

He lifted the tip of his left blade across his lips as if it were a finger, signaling her to silence.

'It's too wide,' he whispered, and pointed to the left side of the building.

He reached his hands into the doorway's left side, extending one blade on the inside and the other outside. When he pulled them back, she could see the doorway wall's width was less than the length of his arm. Then he stepped out, looked to the left side of the building, and spread his arms, widening the measure he'd just shown her.

She stepped out with him to stare at the left side of the building.

Although the door's wall on the inside ran directly to the left side of the foyer, the outside wall was three or four times wider by the measure Leesil had just shown her. She could think of no reason why one stone wall of an old house would be so much thicker than the others.

Magiere looked to Leesil in puzzlement. What was he was trying to tell her in silence? He carefully pointed the tip of his blade at her chest, and she looked down.

Before she even saw the growing glow of the topaz, Magiere felt twinges of burning hunger roll in her stomach.

There came a soft grating of stone from inside the foyer. The wall at the bottom of the stairs slowly inched outward.

Dark-blond curls and the profile of a round face peeked out of the exit. The one called Sapphire scanned the parlor room across the hall. She smiled with relief and stepped out.

As she turned to the front door, Sapphire sucked in air and screamed out in panic: 'Toret!'

Magiere flinched, almost turning about at Sapphire's cry, suddenly wary. She assumed Ratboy had run out the door in search of a sewer, but perhaps he was still in the house as well. Why else would this painted doxy wail for help?

Sapphire lunged back for the opening, and Magiere kicked out against it.

The hidden door slammed closed on Sapphire's arm, and Magiere leveled her falchion as she swung for the woman's neck. Squealing, Sapphire ducked and wrenched her hand free. Magiere's blade clanged against stone.

This was the little harlot who'd been sitting in Leesil's lap.

'Search the upper floors,' Magiere snapped at Leesil. 'She's not alone in here.'

'But Chane—' Leesil began.

'I want no one at our backs,' she shouted, and rushed after Sapphire fleeing down the hallway.

The undead scurried along the railing of the stairs leading below. Magiere slashed at her from behind, but she ducked aside and the falchion shattered through the railing. Sapphire darted into the parlor along the far wall around a velvet divan. Magiere followed rapidly and swung down. The blade split through the back of a divan.

As she wrenched her blade free, Sapphire tried to dash out the parlor archway, but Magiere kicked her in the stomach. Sapphire stumbled away in her heavy gown. She grabbed a cream porcelain vase from an end table and threw it.

Magiere side-stepped, as the vase shattered against Sapphire's own portrait, and steadily closed in on Sapphire with purpose. The undead squealed again and ran behind another divan. Magiere smashed this one as well, sending Sapphire scurrying to the far corner of the room.

The familiar ache grew in Magiere's jaw, but she swallowed down the pain. There would be no mindless rage this time, no loss of self to hunger. She wanted full awareness of every moment. She let hunger creep into her head just enough so that her night vision sharpened.

This creature had been sitting in Leesil's lap.

Sapphire looked around wildly.

Magiere swung down, the falchion shattering the light oak table to Sapphire's right as she cringed back, crying out.

Magiere felt no pity. For certain, Sapphire felt no pity for her victims. She'd killed an unarmed house guard at the Rowanwood without a thought. Now she pleaded for help as her victims had surely done. How had this pathetic creature survived in the night?

Sapphire kicked up the table remains at Magiere, but the gown fouled her attempt, and Magiere swatted the fragments aside. As Sapphire made one last dash toward the parlor entrance, Magiere snarled her free hand in the woman's hair. Sapphire's head snapped back as she was jerked to a stop.

'Turn around,' Magiere demanded. 'Look at me.'

Sapphire stared into Magiere's black irises, sobbing with quivering red lips. And yet, strangely, no tears fell from the dead woman's eyes.

Magiere let the falchion pendulum down in front of her and up under her other arm, her grip tight in Sapphire's hair.

No! Sapphire mouthed, as she raised a hand to shield herself.

Magiere slashed crosswise, pulling on the woman's hair at the same time. As her arms scissored outward and apart, the falchion swung level through the dark room.

One final sob from Sapphire ended halfway as the blade

passed cleanly through the forearm of her raised hand — and then her neck. The hand spun and dropped to the floor first.

Magiere's gaze never left the pale, painted face as the body collapsed and the head hung suspended in her grip, draining black fluids onto the carpet.

She stood a moment longer before realizing she was panting. Her grip had tightened so severely that the dark-blond hair began to tear out between her fingers.

This thing had tried to take Leesil.

The room dimmed around her, though her settling vision still picked up details in the dark. She looked down to see the topaz dim and lifeless against her hauberk.

Magiere dropped the head onto the rumpled folds of the corpse's gown.

Running footsteps on the stairs broke her fixation as Leesil hurried into the room with Chap close behind. He crouched down immediately by the corpse, stared but a moment, and reached for the head.

Magiere was about to stop him. It wasn't time to collect proof for the council, but he waved her off.

'I may need this,' he said simply.

He took a dark blue drawstring bag from the corpse, placed the head inside, and tied it to his belt. Taking out flint, he struck it several times with his blade until he ignited the torches he'd brought with them. He handed one to Magiere.

'Find Chane and get Wynn back,' he said. 'Chap's already tracked him to the first sewer grate up the street. I know where Ratboy has gone.'

Before she could ask, he stepped out of the parlor toward the foyer. Magiere followed him to the opening in the wall. Inside were narrow stone steps leading both up and down.

'Chap's already confirmed it,' Leesil said, staring at the steps leading downward. 'Ratboy is mine.'

'Take Chap,' Magiere told him. 'And this.'

She unhooked the topaz amulet's chain and went to fasten it about his neck. Leesil was about to stop her, but she shook her head.

'I don't think I need it anymore,' she explained with a glance back toward the parlor. 'I can feel them now when they're close. If we can't find each other later, we'll meet back at the sages' barracks.'

Leesil nodded and motioned Chap into the passage. As Magiere was about to head for the front door, he grabbed her by the arm.

When she looked at him, all the warmth and wry humor she'd become accustomed to finding in his face, his eyes, his smile was gone without a trace.

'You stay alive,' he said.

Magiere felt cold inside.

Leesil wasn't just hunting anymore. This was vengeance. Or some fool's need to rectify what he thought was a failure from the past. Somewhere in the back of her mind she'd probably always known this, and now there was no time to stop him.

'And you,' she said.

Magiere slipped out the front door, down the steps, and into the cobble street, running for the first grate she saw.

From the shadows between two houses across the street, Sgäile watched the unfolding events with an unsettling ambivalence. He had followed the renegade and *majay-hì* all day as they looked at houses in the city's wealthier districts. He did not know why.

He had already ignored the wish of *Aoishenis-Ahâre* —

Most Aged Father – and yet he could not leave well enough alone. He had not been told all and nearly spilled the blood of his people, even though it ran through the flesh of a half-blood mongrel. And the *majay-hì* would not keep company with a traitor. It was not possible.

As dusk settled, the half-blood renegade and his companions had entered the house across the way. Sgäile settled in to watch. For a while, nothing happened. Then a tall man ran from the house, carrying the gray-robed woman over his shoulder, and disappeared into a sewer grate. A short while later the renegade, the human female, and the small boy appeared. The boy ran off down the street, and now the armored woman went straight to the same sewer grate and disappeared below the city.

Sgäile waited longer, but the renegade half-blood did not emerge. Neither did the *majay-hì*. He slipped from his hiding place and approached the house, the front door half-open.

Snapping a stiletto into his right hand, he stepped inside and walked silently along the hall past the base of the stairs, watching in all directions. As he passed an archway to his right, he spotted a headless body upon the floor. The room was a shattered mess all around.

Sgäile froze in place, listening in the dark, but he heard no sounds in the house. When he turned back to the front door, he looked at the wall at the bottom of the stairs.

The wall had a crack in it.

More than a crack; it was a portal in the stone that had not been fully closed.

Sgäile pulled the door open and slipped inside and downward.

19

Chane splashed along the dark sewer tunnel, carrying Wynn and following the ankle-deep flow toward the bay. At the city's low side, he could emerge into the poor district inside the third ring and disappear into the side streets. With luck, Toret would take his second death at the hands of the dhampir and the half-blood, and he would be finally free.

Wynn choked from either the stench or the pounding of his shoulder into her stomach as he slogged through the seawater used to flush the city's bowels.

'Chane, please,' she uttered. 'Put me down.'

He glanced behind but saw nothing except mortared stone walls, and so he carefully set her on her feet. She still clutched the glowing crystal in her hand.

'We must hurry,' he urged her. 'If Toret escapes and pursues us, he will kill you. Or order me to do so, and it is beyond my power to disobey his commands.'

He gripped her wrist lightly, the long sword still in his other hand, and pulled her along. The quarrel wound in his chest still burned, as did the gashes on his leg from the hound's teeth. Wynn tried to pull away, and he tightened his grip, not allowing her to stop.

'What are you saying?' she asked, both frightened and confused. 'Let go of me. I will only slow your escape.'

He turned on her, as if by sheer will he could cow her into obedience, but then anger washed from him.

Her robe's hem was soaked, dragging at her with its weight, and in his grip, he could feel her shake. Chill water did not affect him, but she was alive and suffered from it. At the sight of her round, soft face, he knew the cold was only part of the cause.

Dried tear tracks marred her cheeks, and her small lips quivered with each short breath, expelling vapor into the dank air. Brown eyes stared back at him, but not as the visitor come to share intellectual curiosities, a hunger for knowledge, and a cup of mint tea in a quiet room, side by side.

She looked upon him with fear.

But Chane did not release his grip.

'The creature who attacked you on the stairs is my maker,' he said flatly, 'who made me his kin and slave, and I cannot refuse his commands. He can sense where his creation has gone – and track me. If he finds me, you will die, one way or another.'

'So you . . . are a vampire?' Wynn asked softly. 'You killed those people . . . did those things?'

'To survive,' he answered. 'Toret raised me to this state because he needed money and protection. I could offer both. I never asked for this, but I accept what I am, as does any other being.'

'So it is not your fault?' she said.

Could she understand?

'A matter of perspective,' he responded. 'Something for the philosophers among your guild.'

He looked back along the tunnel, feeling urgency take hold again, and resumed his flight. Wynn tried to keep up with him now.

'You could put me up the next grate,' she suggested between panting breaths. 'Please, Chane, let me go.'

'Toret, or even Sapphire, may still try to catch up,' he answered, 'It is too dangerous yet.'

'But you said if Toret finds you, you must obey him.'

When he did not answer her, she cried out, 'If you are a killer, then why are you protecting me?'

Chane pulled her faster through the filthy water.

'Because your life is not wasted in mindless drudgery,' he growled, as if the answer were all too obvious. 'Most mortals are little more than cattle, and their loss affects nothing.'

She jerked back, surprising him enough that he almost stopped.

'You saved me because I'm a sage?' she asked. 'Because my head is full of knowledge you find useful?'

'Of course,' he responded.

But this was a half-truth, and the rest was not appropriate for the time or place. When he looked back again, the tunnel was not empty. A light flickered in the distance.

'A torch,' Wynn said. 'Would Sapphire or Toret carry a torch?'

'No,' he replied.

'Then it is either Magiere or Leesil, or both. Release me and flee.'

Chane glanced at Wynn.

He could let her go, and that might slow the dhampir or the half-elf for a short while. But they would not turn back now, even if they found Wynn safe and unharmed. It had not occurred to him to use Wynn as a tool or a hostage, but such a ruse might soon be necessary.

Chane pulled Wynn after him until he reached an intersection where the tunnel connected with a wider passage. It looked to be one of the main flow routes down to the bay with elevated stone walkways along its sides. At one far corner was an iron ladder mounted into the stone that led up a vertical shaft. It likely led to a grate in one of the city's streets. Chane lifted Wynn onto the walkway to the left of where they had come out and stepped up beside her.

'Be silent,' he said. 'And put the crystal out of sight.'

'Chane, do not do this,' she urged.

He shot her a glare and held up the long sword between them. Wynn cowered back against the wall and tucked the crystal into her pocket. Chane settled in front of her near the corner, watching the far wall of the tunnel they'd come down for reflections of light that would tell him the pursuer drew near.

So far, this dhampir had proved less than effective in his scheme to destroy Toret. He was through with schemes.

Toret dropped out of the cellar's passage and down into the sewer tunnel. He looked both ways through the dark but couldn't detect any sign of Sapphire. She had a good start, and he now had a decision to make.

He could head toward the poor districts of the outer ring or closer to the exits to the bay. But which way had Sapphire taken? He'd told her to head for the sea, but she could be . . . unpredictable.

As her maker, he could sense her presence for a limited distance. His powers had never developed like Teesha's or Rashed's, but he could almost 'feel' where Sapphire was if he focused.

Toret closed his eyes, pictured Sapphire – and felt nothing.

Sapphire wouldn't head toward the poor side. She liked the rich districts after nightfall. He'd hoped she might try for somewhere with fewer people out and about. Perhaps the middle merchant district, where most shops would be closed for the night. He turned south along the tunnel.

Wading through mucky water slowed his progress, but with Sapphire's blue velvet gown soaked, it would slow her as well. He traveled more quickly than she would, and yet neither saw nor sensed her. Perhaps he'd chosen the wrong way? Was she foolish enough to head upslope to the inner ring?

When he turned about to reconsider, there was torch-light down the tunnel behind him.

Sapphire wasn't carrying a torch.

Had the hound led the half-blood to the cellar? That beast had tracked Rashed straight to the warehouse back in Miiska. It made sickening sense. He tensed, caught between fear and anger.

Leesil, with his cursed luck, was onto him.

Toret fled along the tunnel, searching for a place to lie in wait. If he was to escape this time, he had to make sure no one could track him again.

He would see that hound rot with the refuse beneath the city.

Chap jumped from Toret's cellar and landed with a splash in the center of the sewer.

'Which way?' Leesil asked.

The hound growled and headed southward against the flow of water. Leesil hopped down, the stench assaulting his nose. Beneath the smell of waste was the distinct odor of brine. He shifted the sack with Sapphire's head to the back of his belt, and quickly followed Chap.

Ratboy wouldn't leave this city – at least not in one piece.

The fine white hairs on Leesil's neck prickled with the strange sensation of being watched. He looked behind, holding the torch out. The light revealed only dank walls and slow-running water. He tried putting the torch behind himself, so his half-elven eyes could sift more easily through the shadows, but he saw nothing.

Chap waded onward, and Leesil followed again, each passing moment a sharp edge sliding across his nerves.

And still they moved on, approaching numerous intersecting tunnels. Each time, he called Chap back long enough to check them carefully. When the way was clear, he let Chap lead again, watching to see if the hound turned. But the dog continued straight south, even at the occasional wider flow ways leading down toward the bay.

After a while, Leesil wondered if Chap truly followed a trail. Magiere's topaz, hanging about his neck, glowed with only a dim aura. There was an undead down here, but they weren't gaining any ground. How could Chap track Ratboy through running water?

Ahead, the tunnel floor slanted sharply upward beyond a wide archway. As he came closer, he spotted a line of jagged points along the opening's top edge and a matching archway at the top of the slope. Raised stone walkways lined both sides of the rise, and Leesil could hear the continuous splash of running water from somewhere above. Chap passed through, working his way up, and a yellow shimmer reflected off the dank walls around Leesil. He looked down.

The topaz brightened right before his eyes.

'Chap, come back!' Leesil called.

A rattle of chains echoed down the rising passage, and the archway's spikes descended rapidly toward Leesil's head. He lurched back in reflex.

Leesil thought he glimpsed a flickering shape roll under the iron gate's edge just before it splashed into the water, and then a spray of salt water made him shield his face. Upslope, Chap broke into battle cry, and the eerie wail echoed through the sewers.

Holding his torch high, Leesil peered through the gate up the passage. Past the upper archway, the floor leveled off out of sight in a large, round chamber. He couldn't see if there were other entrances or passages leading into it. Chap's snarl sounded from above, but the hound was beyond view over the slope's top lip.

A familiar voice echoed down to him.

'Too bad the gate missed you.' Ratboy's high-pitched laugh rolled along the walls. 'But now you get to watch me slaughter your beast, and you'll never track us again.'

'Chap, come back to the gate!' Leesil shouted, but he already heard the splashing of feet in shallow water and knew Ratboy was closing.

Chap was a born tracker and fighter, like the bear hounds of the Warlands, bred by petty lords and tyrants for hunting mountain bears. Those hounds would go to any length to track their prey and threw themselves head-long into battle if not controlled. Many died on their first hunt. Chap was even more willful than those mere beasts.

The gate was here for a reason, though Leesil couldn't fathom why. Deeper inside the sewers, it had been over-looked by the city guard when they sealed the outer spill-ways. He looked about for a way to open it but only spotted brackets on the walls to either side. Jamming his torch into one, he gripped the gate with both hands and strained to lift it. The barrier wouldn't budge.

Chap's snarl grew loud again amidst a flurry of splashes.

'Leave him,' Leesil shouted. 'Back away to me.'

Even if Chap did as he commanded, Ratboy wouldn't abandon this chance to kill the hound.

A flicker of shadow across the upper archway made Leesil pause from straining at the gate. The chamber's darkness above was too severe even for his eyes. He snatched the torch and threw it through the gate onto the left walkway, as far up as he could. Framed in the upper archway was the capering figure of Ratboy maneu-vering around Chap, the hound's silvery coat tinged to gold in the torchlight.

Ratboy dodged and swung down with a thick short sword, barely missing Chap's neck.

'*Valhachkasej'â!*' Leesil cursed, wishing he'd grabbed Vàtz's crossbow before the boy had left.

Chap dashed inside Ratboy's guard. Spinning around behind, the hound snapped teeth along the back of Ratboy's knee. The undead cried out but turned with the dog and kicked out hard, catching Chap in the side. The hound tumbled back out of sight with a cascade of splashes.

Snarling, Ratboy faced into the chamber with sword raised.

Leesil drew his right blade and chopped down on the gate's crossbars. Steel clanged against iron, leaving only a minor gash.

Ratboy glanced toward him, sharp teeth bared in a sneer, and then turned back to Chap. Leesil struck the gate again and again, but Ratboy gave no more notice.

From beyond the upper archway's right side, a silvery flutter skimmed through the air.

Ratboy's head snapped sideways as he staggered. He righted himself and reached up with his free hand.

A stiletto of bright metal protruded from the base of his neck.

Leesil stopped his assault, lost in confusion. He'd have done that himself if he'd thought it would do any good.

'Stop,' a smooth, lilting voice ordered.

The echo from the upper chamber made it impossible for Leesil to tell where the voice came from. A gray specter slid forward into view.

Standing to the upper archway's right was a gray-clad figure, cowl up and cloak corners tied around its waist. Coiled between the fingers of its left fist was a silvery wire glinting in the torchlight. It was like the garrote in Leesil's own toolbox, and recognition filled him.

This was the *anmaglâhk* from the previous night.

The elf had followed him and must have been the shadow he'd glimpsed slipping under the gate before it closed. The stiletto had been nothing more than a ploy to gain Ratboy's attention.

'What's this?' Ratboy uttered, as he slid the stained blade from his neck. 'A new playmate?'

'You are not my concern,' the elf said calmly. 'Leave the hound.'

At those words, Ratboy appeared uncertain, but Leesil couldn't believe what he was hearing. He unsheathed his second blade.

'Kill him!' he yelled at the elf. 'Fire or decapitation is the only way.'

The elf gave him no notice. His cowled head turned toward the back of the chamber as he said, 'Please, stand with me.'

Chap came into view as he circled in to stand a pace or two back on the elf's side of the archway. The man looked to the hound, holding his hands open to his sides, and said something in Elvish that Leesil couldn't follow.

'He's an undead,' Leesil spit in frustration. 'Take his head, now.'

The torch's crackle was the only sound for the span of two breaths.

Ratboy screamed out, dropping his sword and stiletto as he lunged at the elf. He collided into the elf, and both collapsed down in a spray of water.

Leesil expected Chap to fly into the battle, but the hound held his place, snarling in frustration as he watched the two flail. Ratboy's hand rose up, fingers hooked, and he slashed down at the elf's neck, fingernails shredding the side of the cowl. The elf's gray-clad leg whipped up and around the front of Ratboy's throat.

Leesil's view was obscured again by the splash of Ratboy toppling, and he saw little more than a whirl of wet bodies and water thrown into the air. When it ended, the elf was behind Ratboy, who sat or knelt with the garrote whipped around his neck.

The elf's hands jerked apart, and the wire closed instantly, cutting into Ratboy's throat.

'Don't let go,' Leesil called out. 'Finish it.'

Even with just torchlight, Leesil saw the line around Ratboy's throat darken as black fluids began to seep out.

Ratboy reached back and grabbed the sides of the elf's cloak. He jerked the elf over the top of himself. As the elf passed in front, Ratboy kicked out, sending the taller man slamming against the side of the archway. But the elf lost only one grip on the garrote handles, and as the wire lashed free of Ratboy's neck, it bit deeper.

Ratboy scuttled back, holding his throat. His gaze never strayed from the tall gray figure as he fumbled in the water to recover his sword.

'Go,' the elf said again. 'Go hunt humans. Leave the *majay-hì*.'

Chap inched toward the wiry undead.

Still clutching his throat, Ratboy passed one last hateful glance toward Leesil, turned, and ran out of view.

'No!' Leesil screamed out and smashed his blades against the gate.

Hunger boiled up from Magiere's stomach.

Torch held high, she slowed at the intersection ahead and aimed her crossbow toward the arched opening. When the blade flashed out from her left, she quickly swiped it aside with the torch and sidestepped into the intersection.

Chane stood on a walkway with Wynn directly behind him. He pulled her around in front of himself with one hand clamped over her mouth. The sage was so small that her head barely reached his collarbone. Magiere felt her teeth begin to ache.

'Let her go,' she ordered.

She tossed the torch to the far side walkway and drew her falchion. To her surprise, his voice was calm and polite.

'Is Toret dead?'

She didn't care about his questions or anything but seeing his head come off, and she took two steps toward him through the water.

'Take your hand off her. Unless you want to fight with one arm.'

'I doubt you could accomplish that without severely wounding your friend.'

For an answer, Magiere squeezed the crossbow's firing lever. The quarrel pierced Chane's exposed calf, already marred from Chap's teeth, and he cried out as smoke rose around the embedded shaft. Chane's grip faltered as he folded in pain, reaching for the quarrel, and Wynn lunged away along the wall.

Magiere threw the empty crossbow onto the walkway at the sage's feet. It would have been a perfect moment to press Chane, but until Wynn was better protected, Magiere couldn't afford to rush the tall undead. As Chane jerked the quarrel from his leg and stepped into the tunnel's running water, Magiere cut the quiver's strap with her falchion and tossed the quarrels after the crossbow.

'Load it,' she ordered Wynn, stepping forward to put herself between the sage and the undead nobleman.

She could feel a shift in Chane's presence. Before, at the inn and in the house, she'd sensed hunger and evasion. She saw a hint of determination.

'Stop it! Both of you,' Wynn called. 'Chane, she is

unique – do not harm her. Magiere, none of this is his fault. Toret took him without permission.'

Pointless words, but as Magiere glared over to silence her, Wynn was fitting one of the last two quarrels into the crossbow.

'When I tell you,' Magiere said, 'shoot him.'

It was unlikely Wynn had any skill with the weapon, but the words would play upon Chane well enough. The undead circled, looking for an opening.

'She will not fire at me,' he said with quiet certainty. 'You are wasting your breath.'

'At least I have breath to waste,' she replied.

It had never occurred to her that Wynn was anything other than a hostage, but there was apparently something more between these two. But as Magiere matched Chane's maneuvers, she saw the sage point the crossbow at the undead.

He rolled his arm over and up and swung downward, trying Rashed's old trick of brute strength to crash through Magiere's guard. The force was immense, and Magiere dropped halfway to one knee as she blocked. He wasn't playing anymore.

But she never had been.

Magiere deflected and slashed low at his legs. When he retreated, she spun backward through the water for distance. He charged immediately, swinging the sword down as she rose to her feet. This time she dodged and slashed again for his leg. He tried to step away, but the falchion's tip cut across his left knee. He grunted, and as he buckled from the burn of her blade, he slashed upward.

The long sword's point cut partway through Magiere's hauberk below the collar and sliced her left shoulder. She staggered back, regaining her feet as the pain flared.

Chane favored his wounded leg; and Magiere felt blood

seeping into her shirt at the shoulder. She needed him off guard for a moment.

'Wynn, shoot him!' she called.

Chane tried to circle but was now limping. At the sight of her blood, his irises dilated, turning crystalline. She felt hunger grow in him, and something else as well.

Desire.

Chane took pleasure in killing, in feeding, in the last moments of his victim's lives.

Why hadn't Wynn fired?

He rushed forward and, at the last second, swung low with his sword.

When Magiere dipped her falchion to block, his free hand snapped out around her wrist. On momentum, he thrust her back against the wall.

Magiere let the hunger rush through her flesh. She thrust her fist into his jaw.

His head snapped back so hard that his body arched away from her, and he lost his grip on her sword arm. His eyes widened as he reeled, and his teeth were stained with his own black fluids.

Magiere swung her freed blade down at his head.

Chane blocked, and the steel clang echoed sharply. He pressed on her throat, forcing Magiere into the wall again.

Blades locked between them, Magiere slapped her free hand around his throat, and her fingers squeezed into cold flesh. Her back came away from the wall.

Chane slowly lost ground, and then set himself, pushing harder, trying to lever the long sword around her falchion toward her face.

In a quick spasm, his eyes and seeping mouth widened as he cried out and pulled away.

The sudden release threw Magiere off balance, and she stumbled. When she regained her footing, Chane was trying desperately to reach a smoking quarrel protruding from his lower back. He looked overwhelmed with shock more than pain as the smoke rose up from his body.

'Wynn . . . ?' he whispered in confusion.

Magiere saw the young sage already reloading the last quarrel. In that moment of distraction, Chane slashed out wildly with his sword and sliced Magiere across the right thigh.

Her weight gave, and she splashed down to one knee. But Chane staggered as well, smoke still rising from the quarrel in his back. He moaned, clutching at the shaft.

Magiere braced with the falchion to get back up, but she couldn't keep weight on her wounded leg for too long. Chane was in no better shape. If she could get close enough for one swing . . .

'Aim for his head!' she yelled to Wynn.

But Wynn stood frozen in place. Tears ran down her cheeks.

The world slowed to a stop and all three stared at each other in silence.

If Wynn would simply fire, there would too much pain for Chane to defend or flee. If Wynn did not, Magiere's wounded leg might stop her from catching him.

Chane searched Wynn's face as if looking for something in it.

'If you take a step toward Magiere – or try to cast your magic,' Wynn whispered, 'I will shoot.'

Chane took one stumbling step back, disbelief on his face.

'He's a killer – a monster,' Magiere shouted to the sage. 'Shoot him!'

Their positions were all wrong. If Magiere tried to close, she would simply be in Wynn's line of fire.

'Wynn?' she snarled. 'Pull the lever, damn you.'

But Wynn didn't move or take her eyes off of the undead.

Chane looked at her. The crystal of his irises faded to deep brown as a strange loss passed across his face. The tall undead turned and fled down the tunnel.

The dank air caught in Magiere's chest as she tried to stumble after her prey and nearly fell in the sewer water. She turned to Wynn.

'What have you done?'

'He may be a killer,' Wynn whispered with effort as the crossbow sagged in her arms. 'But I am not. Not like that. He spared me – and you.'

'He didn't have a choice!' Magiere snapped back.

Wynn dropped the crossbow with a flinch, as if discarding something repugnant to the touch. She stepped down into the water and lifted Magiere's free arm over her shoulders.

'You made me believe we hunted savage beasts,' the sage said accusingly.

'You stupid . . . girl,' Magiere answered. What lunacy this woman had developed amid dusty books and isolation from the real world. 'That's all they are.'

'Then why did he let me live?'

'You were his tool.'

'No,' Wynn said firmly. 'Now we must leave and see to your wounds.'

Magiere drew a long breath, prepared to tell this idiot what she thought of her grand ethics, and the sound of footsteps resonated into the intersection.

'So much for your mercy,' she said. 'He's coming back to finish this.'

She was about to shove Wynn away when she realized the footfalls were against stone and not splashing through the water. Slow and even, they came from up the wide flow way toward the city's center rather than down the tunnel into which Chane had fled.

Magiere's night vision was almost gone. Hunger had faded with the fury to call back her sight, leaving only frustration and fatigue. She barely made out the dark figure moving along the left-side stone walkway, and heard his voice echo to her.

'A moment, if you please.'

Hollow and cultured – and familiar in a way that made Magiere tense.

A figure of medium height stepped into the far reach of the torchlight, wearing a black cloak over dark clothes that obscured him from view. With black-gloved hands, he pulled his cowl back, and even in the low torchlight, Magiere caught the streaks of white at his temples. Her leg gave again, and she leaned on Wynn.

'Welstiel?'

'Not quite what I expected,' he said, ignoring her puzzlement as he glanced down the side tunnel Chane had taken. 'But your skills are increasing. And I suppose this was still a worthwhile lesson. Never depend on anyone beside yourself, except perhaps for the half-blood or the *majay-hì*.'

His voice. It was strangely familiar, urgently so, aside from when she'd last seen him in Miiska.

'What are you doing here?' she asked.

Again he ignored her and looked at Wynn. 'Leave.'

Magiere felt Wynn's grip around her waist tighten. Welstiel lifted one black-gloved hand to point down the side tunnel.

His earlier words came back to Magiere – *a moment, if you please*.

She shoved Wynn in the direction Welstiel pointed and stumbled over to snatch the loaded crossbow, cradling it across her sword arm.

'Run now,' Magiere ordered. 'Find Leesil.'

Wynn looked between Magiere and Welstiel in confused panic, then turned and slogged away into the tunnel.

Magiere leveled the crossbow directly at Welstiel.

Leesil watched in frustration and rage as Ratboy vanished.

Chap trotted down the slope to him, pushing his nose through the iron bars. At least he was all right. As much as Leesil should thank the elf for this, he was too angry.

'Open the damn gate!' he shouted.

The elf gazed at him from the top of the passage and turned aside out of view. Leesil heard rattling gears and chains, and the gate slowly lifted. When it was but halfway up, he ducked under and hurried up the walkway, picking up his torch along the way and gripping it along with the blade in his left hand. Chap followed close behind him.

The chamber was a large half circle, its flat side holding the archway entrance. Along this same wall, to either side, were narrow passageways. Ratboy had likely fled down the one to the left, and Leesil saw the elf standing on the right side, cranking a metal wheel. The man flipped a lever, locking the mechanism used to open the gate.

The walls reached up to four times the height of a man. High in the curved wall, a wide chute spilled a steady but light fall of water to the chamber floor. The smell of brine thickened here, and Leesil guessed this place was beneath the salt mill, where excess seawater was pumped in to flush the sewers.

'We're going after him,' he said to the elf. 'Are you coming?'

Chap began softly growling at the mouth of the left passageway, and the elf watched him with a puzzled expression that made Leesil briefly follow his gaze.

'You are alike,' the elf said. 'You care for only one thing – to kill the dead. Why?'

Leesil had no time for this. Ratboy was escaping yet again.

'Because they prey upon the living,' he answered quickly. 'No one else will . . . can hunt them, so we do.'

'Humans,' Sgäile said, as if spitting out something foul to the taste. 'They feed on humans, are spawned from them. That creature serves his purpose in thinning the blight upon this world. These humans have even failed to remember their own folly that brought the world to the edge of death in their long-forgotten past.'

'Then why didn't you kill me, a half-human?' Leesil asked in spite. 'Why did you come after me at all?'

'An error of judgment was made – we do not kill our own,' the elf said with difficulty, though his study of Chap made Leesil believe there was more to it.

'Slaughter, you mean,' Leesil retorted. 'That's what you do, just like these monsters.' And he pointed down the passage Ratboy had taken.

'Is this why you abandoned your parents – to hunt the humans' dead?'

Leesil tensed. What did this elf know of his past?

'I left because my life was a horror, and I could no longer do as Darmouth forced me. I know they both were executed because of me.'

'I care not what happened to your human sire,' elf replied. 'But Cuirin'nên'a is a traitor to her people and their future. She will never again teach another our ways. And it matters little if you choose to waste yourself in such meaningless pursuit.'

Chap snarled and lunged at the elf, and the man backed away two steps. But Leesil was only barely aware of this. For a moment he couldn't breathe.

Father had called mother Nein'a, and that was close to the name the elf had spoken.

Chap lunged again with a snap of teeth, backing the elf against the wall. The *anmaglâhk* looked at Leesil as if he were something unpleasant that couldn't be discarded.

'I came to you for one reason,' he said with reluctance, not letting Chap slip from his field of view. 'To tell you that you must never step in our way, or our shared blood will not save you from the fate of a traitor.'

Leesil waved Chap back, and the hound retreated several steps. The elf moved away from the wall, side-stepping toward the sloped passage.

'What is your name?' Leesil asked.

'Sgäilsheilleache á Oshâgäirea gan'Coilehkrotall,' he replied, as if challenging Leesil to even try to repeat it. 'Sgäile, if that is easier for you to speak, though it gains you nothing. I am not known to anyone you will ever meet.'

He stepped partway down the slant before looking back.

'You were my task, but you are no threat to us. You are *anmaglâhk*, but not yet a traitor. Go your way and do not interfere with ours.'

Sgäile turned and disappeared into the sewers.

Chap's growl pulled Leesil's awareness back. The hound stood at the narrow passage down which Ratboy had fled. Leesil was about to follow but stopped and faced down the slope.

Sgäile's words rushed together in his mind and spread an anguish that nearly made him cry out. He ran down the slope, footfalls splashing in the open tunnel, but the elf was gone.

We do not kill our own. . . . She will never again teach another our ways.

If the elves wouldn't kill their own but still punished a traitor . . .

Where was this Cuirin'nên'a – what had truly happened to his mother?

Toret ran, arms swinging wildly, barely clutching his short sword.

Elves – cursed elves everywhere.

He turned with the flow of water, heading toward the bay.

The quarrel wound in his head still seared, and the elf's wire had cut deeply into his throat. His damaged eye was not fully healed, and he needed to feed.

All of his lessons with Chane seemed useless. Master of his own family and house, he'd wanted to take Rashed's place. Such a role begged for skill at arms. But even with superior strength and speed, he couldn't match in two moons what took a swordsman years of practice. What a fool he'd been.

Chane, on the other hand, could fend for himself, yet the coward had left him with the dhampir and the halfblood. Toret simply wanted to find Sapphire and leave this place behind.

He ran hard. Sapphire must have escaped into the city near the bay, but he still couldn't sense her presence no matter where he turned. What if she'd managed somehow to find her way completely out of the city? That would explain his lack of connection.

Ahead, the tunnel roof curved downward, creating the illusion of meeting with the sewer floor. As he approached, he noted the passage dipped steeply downward. Water at his feet rushed faster. When he crested the slope, he looked toward the tunnel's end and saw the opening to the bay.

An iron gate was closed over the exit. He heard voices – many voices.

Toret crept a little farther along the tunnel wall and

crouched to listen. City guards stood outside the sealed spill-way to the bay. By voices, he counted at least seven or more men. Toret crept back up the slope to the level tunnel and began backtracking.

The other bay opening would be similarly guarded, so likely Sapphire had escaped into the city itself. If she'd followed the same path he had, there were any number of shafts she could have climbed up to the street. Most likely, she'd have traveled as far as possible through the tunnels and then used the last ladder shaft to slip out to hide in the city. She must be frightened out there all alone.

At the next intersection, he found the iron bars of a ladder leading up. Any way out would have to do. He reached for an iron rung, and a flicker of yellow light danced across the wall.

Toret flattened against the stone wall and glanced back down the tunnel.

The light came from a glowing stone on the half-blood's neck as he and the hound splashed into the inter-section.

Leesil tossed his torch onto the closest tunnel walkway and stood before Toret with both blades out. The hound snarled, his fur wet and matted.

Toret no longer cared if the half-blood died or not. He was tired of all this and wanted nothing more than to find Sapphire and flee this city. In the kingdoms of the Suman Empire, he and his love could feed at will, safe in each other's company. All he need do was scramble up the rungs, and he would be into the streets before that half-blood could blink. If Toret was nothing else, he was quick.

Leesil's face was expressionless. 'Wait.'

The half-blood shifted both blades to one hand and

pulled a dark blue velvet drawstring bag from behind his back. Puzzlement passed through Toret as Leesil clumsily pulled an object from the bag and held it up.

Sapphire's head hung from the half-blood's grip, with black fluids smeared from her gaping mouth across her pale cheeks.

Leesil steeled himself for Ratboy's screaming assault.

The small undead merely lowered his sword arm until the blade point dipped into the flowing water. He stared blankly with his one good eye and his head slowly turned from side to side in denial.

'You couldn't,' he said weakly. 'She was in the sewer ahead of me. It's a trick.'

Leesil flung the head and shifted his second blade back to his free hand.

Sapphire's head struck Ratboy in the stomach, and he closed his arms around it, still clinging to his sword.

'Take a closer look,' Leesil said.

Ratboy looked upon Sapphire's blond curls matted with her own black fluids. For a moment, he didn't react, still denying what he held in his hands. His pale face suddenly twisted in a soundless, tearless sob.

'That's for Beth-rae,' Leesil spit out. 'You cut her throat with your nails back in Miiska. Remember? And Eliza. You left her dead in her own backyard for her brother, Brenden, to find.'

Rage welled in Leesil again for all the lives Ratboy had destroyed.

'How does it feel,' he whispered, 'to lose?'

This time, Ratboy did cry out. The head slipped from his hands as he rushed forward, swinging wildly with his sword.

Leesil controlled his hatred as he sidestepped. All he

needed was a clear shot at the monster's neck. Chap howled and closed in.

'Stay back!' Leesil ordered.

The hound snarled in frustration but retreated, circling behind Leesil.

Ratboy swung again – and again. Leesil blocked, the short sword glancing and sliding away along the curves of his blades.

This butchering whelp wasn't skilled, but he was strong and enraged, and Leesil feared becoming locked in a stalemate until he was too exhausted to continue. Undeads seemed to possess endless stamina. But as he circled, forcing Ratboy to keep changing positions, he saw the undead falter once.

Leesil heard Chap growling from behind, but the hound stayed clear. Ratboy struck hard. As Leesil blocked, he dropped to one knee in the water. He kicked out with his free leg to the inside of Ratboy's knee.

The joint gave a muffled crackle on impact, but Ratboy only stumbled and struck again. Leesil rose up inside the downward stroke, his blocking blade's edge up. When the blow connected, there was no clang of steel.

Ratboy's wrist struck the blade's edge, and Leesil slashed outward.

Hand and sword flew away in the water. The undead jerked up his arm to strike again and then gaped in disbelief at the stump of his wrist.

Leesil kicked out to Ratboy's other knee, letting his whole weight drop down and drive the blow home. A resounding crack followed as his boot collided with bone. His outstretched foot dropped through the water to the tunnel floor, and he shifted his weight to it. He slashed his second blade across, waist level, and Ratboy retreated two steps.

Ratboy's movements were halting and unstable, but he showed no sign of outright pain, only angry disbelief. The lower half of his tunic hung loose from the cut, and his sunken stomach was slick with his own black blood.

Leesil lifted his left blade at guard, the right low and ready. Ratboy lunged, and his one remaining hand lashed out.

It was so fast that Leesil couldn't block or duck in time. Thin, cold fingers closed on his throat as fingernails bit into his skin.

The grip faltered briefly, squeezed painfully tight, and then faltered again.

Gasping for air, Leesil realized what was happening. The small-boned bastard was bleeding out, weakening. Undeads were not inexhaustible after all.

Ratboy opened his mouth, head thrusting forward. Sharp teeth and fangs rushed at Leesil's face, and he jammed his right blade upward. Its point pierced the underside of Ratboy's jaw, snapping his mouth closed. Ratboy's head barely flinched, but it was enough, and Leesil sliced up with his left blade.

It cut halfway through the forearm of the hand about his throat, and the grip released.

The undead swung wildly with the stump of his right arm, and Leesil ducked aside, slipping to Ratboy's flank. He dropped his right blade and braced his free hand against his left forearm as he swung the remaining blade back.

Ratboy turned his head, open mouth dribbling dark fluids.

Leesil swung down with his full weight. Bone ground on steel as his weapon severed straight through Ratboy's neck.

The headless body splashed down.

Leesil fell to his knees with a second splash, panting. Anger and dark delight washed from him in the bite of cold water. The tunnel became instantly quiet but for the soft sound of lapping liquid running against the walk-ways.

Finished – but Leesil felt his past failures only partially rectified.

Exhaustion took him, and he remained there for a long while with his head down, trying to regain his breath. What finally stirred him was Chap's warm and wet tongue upon his cheek.

Leesil crawled slowly to his feet and sheathed one blade, then felt through the water for the other until he found it. Both blades in place, he turned about, searching for the heads, and spotted Chap standing on the walkway next to the torch. Both heads rested before his front paws, as did the sack. Leesil gathered the trophies with a sense of release instead of triumph.

The moment he finished tying the sack to the back of his belt, Chap took off down the tunnel toward where they had first entered. Leesil followed without questioning the hound's decision.

They had to find Magiere.

20

Magiere studied Welstiel. He looked much the same as he had in Miiska, composed and controlled. She looked at his black leather gloves and cloak, and his voice echoed in her thoughts.

A moment, if you please.

Lord Au'shiyn's dead face surfaced in her mind. His murderer had used those very words to draw the Suman's attention.

'You,' she whispered aloud, still uncertain what her senses now demanded she believe. 'Your voice . . . your hands.'

He was calm and detached, still the cryptic mentor he'd played for her back in Miiska. Magiere tried to find the hunger inside that always warned of an undead's presence, but it wouldn't stir.

'Did you follow Ratboy here, or did he follow you?' she asked.

He frowned as if such a question were childish.

'I am not one of them,' he said. 'I have been preparing you for what lies ahead. You would have never battled these creatures without inspiration, and now look what you've become. So much more than you were, even since your awakening in Miiska.'

What did he mean by inspiration? Nausea threatened to creep in upon the tail of Magiere's bewilderment.

'You arranged this?' she asked, a sickening awareness growing. 'And what happened in Miiska as well?'

'A simple matter,' he answered, 'of making sure you were the one to purchase the vacant tavern.'

Confusion began to feed slowly into outrage.

The council of Bela, Chap's hidden manipulations, the elves seeking Leesil's life, and now Welstiel. How many had played Leesil and herself like puppets, tugging their strings from both near and far?

Welstiel waved his hand, apparently growing frustrated with her. 'All but a means to an end, and you have nearly reached that end. The rest you will learn on our journey, and so I've come for you. The conjuror is unpredictable, and I wanted to be present in case he became a true danger.'

He was mad, but Magiere was uncertain what to do. Her gaze kept returning to the black gloves.

'I'm not going anywhere with you,' she said.

'You haven't heard where we are going,' he responded.

'I don't care.'

The torchlight flickered off his smooth face.

'I watched you at your game on the open road. Not often, but enough to follow your progress – and ambition. You are not like other mortals – you do not think like a mortal. When forced, you do what is necessary. What you earned from those peasants was a pittance. What the council offered you is nothing compared to what I seek, and that which I trained you to achieve.'

Magiere flinched as he pointed a black-gloved hand at her.

Her shoulder still bled, but the wound was not threatening. Her thigh was more of a concern, as she couldn't put full weight on her leg. Looking at Welstiel, she remembered how undeads seemed to heal themselves through sheer will once they had fed. She focused her thoughts on the slash across her thigh.

The bleeding stopped, though she could still feel the open wound, and she tentatively settled more weight into the leg.

'I am not speaking of money,' he went on. 'But power. In the ice-capped mountains of this continent is an object long forgotten, guarded by "old ones" – possibly the oldest vampires in existence. You were bred to be a hunter, but you will learn nothing more battling these city-dwelling Noble Dead. I must teach you how to truly use the raw skills you have acquired.'

His voice, words, and manner recalled her visions and the sensations of Chesna's and Au'shiyn's final moments.

'I know you,' he said. 'You take risks if the reward is enough, but you have no idea what I offer to make you a part of.'

After all she and Leesil had been through to track down the murderer, the pieces of the puzzle suddenly pointed elsewhere. It should have been Chane. The gloves, the dark cloak, and the noble bearing all fit. Even the voice she'd heard in her vision could have been his. Perhaps even the formal words were but a coincidence.

A moment, if you please.

Magiere looked into Welstiel's composed and stern face and remembered the impressions she'd felt in Chane's presence. The mage undead reveled in the kill, enjoyed the death of his victims.

But the killer had not.

Magiere looked to the crossbow's quarrel. Like all those prepared by Leesil before their hunt, it smelled faintly of garlic. There was one way to settle this mystery.

Leesil ran behind Chap, and the tunnel again seemed endless. He had to trust that Chap could pick up Magiere's trail once they reached the house of the undeads. How the dog could follow anything in this stinking sewer was baffling.

Chap pulled up short, and Leesil stepped past him

before stopping. The hound stood poised, staring down the tunnel, and before Leesil could speak, he took off again at a run. From a distance ahead, Leesil heard splashing footfalls. When he saw Wynn coming, relief filled him.

Glowing crystal in hand, she stumbled to a stop and let out a shallow whimper before rushing toward them. Robe soaked to her thighs, she gripped Leesil's arms with her small hands.

'Hurry,' she gasped out. 'I think Magiere is in trouble.'

'Chane?' he asked.

'No – he escaped.'

A rush of panic struck Leesil.

'What happened to Magiere?' he asked more harshly.

'She is all right,' Wynn replied. 'But there is someone else.' Her hands squeezed tighter on his arms. 'It is Welstiel, and I think Magiere is troubled. She told me to run and find you.'

'Welstiel?' Leesil answered with puzzlement. What was that deluded man doing in Bela, and why had he followed Magiere into the sewers?

'Come quickly,' Wynn urged. 'She is down this tunnel.'

Chap bolted ahead. Leesil followed, pulling Wynn along behind him as he called out, 'Chap, stay in sight.'

The dog paused, yipped once, and continued at a slower pace. Wynn's fatigue and soaked robe slowed them too much, but Leesil wouldn't leave her behind. The three of them moved as quickly as possible.

'Not far now,' Wynn panted once.

Ahead was an opening in the tunnel that flickered faintly with torchlight.

Chap stopped there, staring off to the right. But it was from the left side of the wide crossing of tunnels that Leesil saw Magiere inching forward through the shallow water, crossbow pointed in the direction the hound gazed.

She was soaked, and her hauberk had been severed near the left shoulder. The wound bled, and there was another gash across her right thigh.

Leesil handed off his torch to Wynn and pulled both his blades as he came up behind Chap. To the right on the farside walkway stood Welstiel. His striking face, dark hair, and white temples were unmistakable even in the dim light.

Magiere's eyes flicked briefly in Leesil's direction and then back to Welstiel.

'It's him,' she breathed. 'He killed Chesna to get us here.'

Leesil didn't understand any of this. An undead had butchered Lanjov's daughter, not this obsessive man who babbled about the Noble Dead. Leesil glanced at the topaz upon his chest, but there wasn't the faintest glow coming from the stone. Chap didn't react as if a vampire were present and merely stood with his head swiveling between Magiere and the black-clad gentleman.

Welstiel looked at Leesil with a slight frown.

'She is distraught. I was simply here to make certain she was able to handle the conjuror. I have assisted you in the past. Now, I am here to make you both an offer.'

Wynn listened as well, but she hung back as Leesil stepped into the intersection toward Magiere, watching her closely.

Her eyes were intense and unblinking as she watched Welstiel. She gripped the crossbow so tightly her fingernails were whiter than her skin.

'Magiere,' Leesil said, stepping closer. 'He's not the one. It was Chane.'

She sidestepped away from him and took another

advancing step toward Welstiel, who began to back away.

'Magiere . . .' Leesil said gently, and pointed to the topaz with the tip of one blade. 'No light, see? And Chap, he would know.'

Her eyes flicked only briefly toward him and the hound.

'One way to be certain,' she said, and her grip closed on the lever.

'No!' Leesil shouted.

He slashed at the crossbow, but the quarrel was already away. It struck Welstiel in the chest. In panic, Leesil turned to rush toward the man.

Smoke curled up from Welstiel's chest as he stumbled back against the tunnel wall.

'No,' Leesil whispered.

'Take his head!' Magiere shouted, her voice echoing through the sewers. 'He murdered Chesna.'

Chap snarled, crystal-blue eyes turning to Leesil.

How was this possible? Leesil had seen no glow in the amulet. Chap hadn't sensed this. Even Magiere wasn't afflicted with the rage she succumbed to in the presence of an undead. But only an undead burned at the touch of garlic.

Leesil rushed at Welstiel as he shouted to Chap.

'Take him, now!'

Chap lunged out, splashing past him. Welstiel's hand clamped over the quarrel, and he jerked it out. Leesil saw Welstiel's lips move, and strange words buzzed in his head. Welstiel's free hand snapped out, scattering a fine white powder into the air. The smoke around the man grew in a billowing cloud that welled out to fill the tunnel.

It thickened around Leesil until he could no longer see beyond an arm's length. He tried striking at Welstiel's last position, but his blade only clanged against stone.

Then he saw what looked like the quarrel floating in the smoke, and it suddenly shot past him.

A cry of angered pain came from behind.

'Magiere!' Leesil shouted, and he spun about, thrashing his way into the clearer air of the intersection.

Magiere had dropped the crossbow and now gripped her upper arm below the wounded shoulder. She was still on her feet, but slumped as he reached her, head dropping upon his shoulder. Leesil quickly lifted her hand. The quarrel had grazed her, leaving a bleeding gash in her arm.

Gray smoke boiled from the tunnel, and he heard Chap choking inside of it.

'Get out, Chap,' he shouted. 'Back the way we came.'

'No,' Wynn said. 'To the ladder and up to the street.'

'He'll get away,' Magiere said, choking. 'You can't lose him.'

But Leesil stared into the billowing gray cloud rolling toward them and couldn't tell if Welstiel was even in the tunnel anymore.

Wynn waded across to the ladder, urging them to follow, and Chap came lunging out of the smoke. Leesil sheathed his blades and guided Magiere to the ladder. She seemed able to climb well enough with one hand. Leesil reached down and lifted Chap and proceeded to climb as well.

The shaft was tall, and its narrow width helped steady him as he climbed the rungs with one hand, holding on to Chap with the other. Three times the sack of heads at his back caught on the wall, and he stopped to twist himself free of the snag. When he reached the top, Wynn and Magiere grabbed hold of the hound and pulled him through the open grate, and Leesil crawled out to lie panting on the street's cobblestones. He gulped in mouthfuls of fresh air.

Magiere stared down at the ground, expressionless. The sound of running feet and voices traveled up the street, and Leesil rolled to his knees, hands dropping to this blades. But it was only three of the guard rushing toward them.

'Chetnik's men,' he said in relief. 'I'll have them fetch a wagon so we can get you back to the guild.'

Magiere neither looked up nor answered.

Chane limped through the shadows of the residential district near their home when he experienced an unexpected hollow sensation inside his mind. It was almost painful in its intensity, as if something had been ripped out of his head. Just as suddenly, it vanished.

His thoughts felt clear and crisp, more than he remembered in recent times. He paused for a moment, and even stepped out openly into the street to look about.

There was no one present. Even in his own thoughts, he was alone. He smiled and closed his eyes.

He had not had any conception of what freedom would feel like when it came. He had not known if he would feel anything at all, but the realization now settled upon him.

Toret was dead.

Chane's smile vanished.

He was injured and homeless and certainly unwelcome at the sages' guild. The dhampir and her people, as well as the sages, now knew his identity, and it would not be long before others would hear of it as well.

'Wynn,' he whispered.

Chane wandered the dark streets. All that remained were belongings he could carry, if he reached the house. He could no longer stay in Bela.

Between the deep slash on his knee, the hole in his

chest, and the burning wound in his back where Wynn had shot him, he could not face another conflict. His rat would still be in its cage on his desk. As he stood out back, near the servants' entrance, he reached into the animal's limited mind and listened. The house was quiet and still. Drawing his sword, he entered the open back door, and listened on his own.

Nothing. The house seemed to be empty.

He walked through the dining chamber, past Tihko's body on the table and around the wolf's corpse. When he came upon the parlor, there was Sapphire's headless, velvetclad body lying in a pool of congealing black fluids. He turned back to the stairs and downward into the cellar.

He reeked of the sewers and so changed his clothing first, then quickly packed what belongings he could into a small chest and sack. He had hidden some money in a purse behind a drawer in his desk. On his desk sat a small cold lamp that Wynn had given to him. Taking the crystal out, he fingered it for a moment and slipped it into his cloak. He packed only his most necessary texts and materials, and remembered the day his mother had given him his first book on metaphysics. He wondered if it might still be in his room at home in their manor to the north.

Tonight he said good-bye to the only existence he had known since the night Toret had raised him from death. He had never thought of returning to the family keep, but realized that as well was now left behind forever. Finally, he took the rat from its cage and slipped it into the cloak's pocket. With one hand, he grabbed both the sack and small chest, a strap about its girth, and left his room.

Out in the cellar again, he stared up the stairs as he heard booted feet walking slowly on the floor above.

Chane set his baggage down and drew his sword as he climbed the steps. Reaching the exit to the main floor, he slipped the rat out the door and directed it along the wall to the dining chamber.

Through the rodent's eyes, he expected to see city guards come to check on the hunter's story, or perhaps her half-blood returning for some reason. Instead, he saw that Toret's visitor with black hair and white temples stood examining the dead raven upon the table.

Chane tried to sense him through his familiar but felt nothing. It was as if the man were an illusion, not truly there. He watched the stranger idly poke the wolf's corpse with the toe of his boot and then walk down to the parlor. Chane followed, sending the rat along the hallway wall. The visitor stared only a moment at Sapphire's body.

The stranger inspected the whole house, stopping only briefly to note Tibor's body and severed head on the second floor. When it was apparent he was heading for the cellar, Chane slipped quietly into the hidden door at the bottom of the stairs and waited.

It took more time for the rat to catch up, but when it did, the man was in Chane's room. He glanced at the empty cage, paged through several texts, and then picked up Chane's sewer-soaked clothes from the floor. He frowned and dropped them.

When the stranger's inspection was finished, he went back up to the parlor and studied Sapphire's body. Chane had no idea what this man wanted, but there was purpose to his inspection. When the stranger headed for the front door, Chane set a simple task into the rat's thoughts with an image of the man.

Follow – watch.

Chane pulled out of the familiar's mind and waited until he was certain the stranger was well away from the house. Then he climbed to the main floor and slipped through the rear kitchen door.

Magiere sat numbly upon the sage's kitchen table, her armor removed and her ruined shirtsleeve cut away. Domin Tilswith carefully spread oily salve across her shoulder, arm, and leg. Neither the old man's comforting presence nor the salve did anything for the turmoil of her thoughts.

If this night's suffocating revelations settled in her mind all at once, she wouldn't be able to keep from screaming – or weeping.

Leesil hovered near, asking if he could do anything. Wynn kept pushing him out of the way as she assisted the older sage. Chap sat at the floor before her, looking up intently. Every now and then, his tail twitched.

Apparently, Vàtz was still at the guard barracks. Once he arrived with Magiere's message, Captain Chetnik had forced him to stay inside for his own safety. It seemed the captain had been more successful than she in getting the little whelp to obey.

Magiere gazed around the kitchen at the herbs and pots hanging everywhere, the fire crackling in the hearth, and the cold lamps hung about for good light. She looked at Leesil's pleasant, tan face, and knew she should be glad, at least in part. They'd taken two undeads and managed to survive. Leesil had the heads for proof.

But proof of what? Chesna's murderer had escaped, as had Chane, making Magiere little more than the charlatan who once bedazzled peasants out of their last coins.

While Wynn dressed her wounded leg, the young sage talked feverishly with the domin in their own language. All wounds finally tended, Tilswith smiled at Magiere.

'Done,' he said with confidence. 'You heal soon.'

Magiere looked tiredly into his eyes and lined face.

She wondered if he was speaking of more than just her body. The old sage turned to Leesil.

'Teeth?' he asked, pointing to the base of Leesil's neck. 'And bruise.'

For a moment, Leesil appeared puzzled, lifting a hand up to feel. Then he winced. The domin motioned for him to sit beside Magiere, and Leesil became the object of ministrations. As Wynn helped Leesil remove his armor, Tilswith suddenly turned his curiosity back to Magiere.

'This man – Noble Dead – who kill Chesna. You know him?'

'Yes,' Magiere said bitterly. 'We know him.'

Leesil looked at her in concern. 'There's no way we could have guessed. None of this is our fault.'

'Isn't it?' she asked. 'Dunction, our tavern's previous owner, also mysteriously "disappeared" one night. Somehow Welstiel made certain I would buy the Sea Lion, and we would end up in Miiska, stumbling upon disappearing townsfolk and uncovering Ratboy, Rashed, and Teesha.'

Realization spilled across Leesil's long features.

'He knew what I was before I did,' Magiere added. 'Watched us on the game. And I think he knows a great deal more about my past, about what I am, than he's told us. He's been playing us . . . like everyone else.'

Tilswith was listening carefully as he dressed Leesil's wound. 'Why? Why he know these and want you learn?'

Magiere remembered Welstiel's urgency in the sewers.

'Something he's after,' she said thoughtfully. 'Something old, a long-forgotten object that will give him power, and he thinks it's guarded by ancient Noble Dead. He's been preparing me for that task.'

Tilswith stopped and looked her full in the face. 'This he say? Exact he say?'

'Yes,' she answered with a frown. 'What does it matter?'

Wynn had frozen in place as well. She and Domin Tilswith began speaking rapidly again in their own tongue, agitated and perhaps arguing. Finally Tilswith ended with a shake of his head, and Wynn turned slowly to Magiere.

'He told you an object of great power was guarded by ancient undeads, and he has been preparing you to assist him in attaining this?'

'What is this about?' Leesil asked.

Tilswith shrugged. 'Not certain. But if he undead, can hide self from hound, and seek object, you must find first. This thing not be in his hand.'

For a moment, his words, like part of an overheard conversation, didn't fully settle upon Magiere as having anything to do with her.

Leesil sighed deeply. 'Oh, spiteful deities.'

'Are you suggesting Leesil and I go after him?' Magiere asked. 'We wouldn't even know where to look. Chap can't even track him.'

Tilswith pondered this for a moment with an appraisal of Chap. All eyes in the room followed his gaze.

Chap glanced about at all of them and began to fidget, slowly sliding his butt backward across the floor, not able to meet anyone's gaze. The old sage grunted.

'Track . . . no,' Tilswith said. 'But Welstiel first to know *majay-hì*, yes? And elf hunt Leesil stop because hound here. Chap has part in all.'

At his mention, Chap lowered his head.

'He your guide,' Tilswith added, bright green eyes warm as he delivered a disapproving frown to Chap. 'From his mistake to Wynn, you three meant to be. Dhampir, *majay-hì*, and one half-elf in all land? Now find why – and what – to Welstiel.'

The room was silent for a moment. Wynn took up where her domin left off.

'Some of our guild see a time of convergence approaching, though we do not all agree on what it means or what it will be . . . or even if it will be. We have seen strange occurrences over the decades but without a clear connection.'

She hesitated.

'From what little you have told us,' she said, 'both you and Leesil hide pasts filled with regrets. It is the time to choose your own path and stop letting others choose it for you. Centuries ago, the fabled war cost the world so much in the Forgotten. Knowledge, great works, even civilization faded so utterly that we know little of what happened before, during, or following that conflict. If this Welstiel discovered a power of that time, he will continue to seek it – with or without you. Find it before he does. If he murdered Chesna just to bring you here, think what he would do to get it and to use it.'

Everything the sages said made sense, but it was too much to ask. Magiere simply wanted to go home. Each time she stepped outside the life she wanted, unwillingly doing whatever was asked, some far greater burden fell upon her.

'We didn't even finish our task here,' she said, and took a deep breath that was hard to let out. 'Not only did we chase the wrong undead, but we let Welstiel escape and Chane as well.'

Tilswith blinked in surprise, and Leesil threw up his arms in disgust, then winced at the pain such action sent through his wounds.

'Take money for Miiska,' Tilswith insisted. 'No other could take Noble Dead. You make city safe. You refuse Welstiel so he not stay here – find other way to that he seek.'

Leesil clearly agreed. 'That pack of stuffed pheasants

on the council used what happened in our town to drag you into this. I've got two heads in a satchel, and there's a third in that house we can add to it.'

She let his words sink in but wondered if they were motivated by guilt over burning down the warehouse to save her life.

'What about Chane?' she asked.

Wynn averted her eyes at the name.

'Chane is scholar,' Tilswith answered, 'but we know he is too Noble Dead. Small chance he come to us and small chance we help him. He not stay in Bela, not take risk.' He held up his hands with a shrug, as if the answer were obvious. 'So task done. All Noble Dead gone.'

'I will take the bankdraft to Miiska for you,' Wynn added, 'and seek out the baker you mentioned named Karlin.'

The sages truly believed the situation was resolved, but this was all happening too fast for Magiere. Now they expected her and Leesil and Chap to somehow stop Welstiel from finding whatever he sought, though no one knew what or where this thing was. When she closed her eyes, she could still feel the last moments of Chesna and Au'shiyn, and how their killer felt nothing – no pity, no regret, not even satisfaction.

Welstiel hadn't even fed on them. He'd murdered them as bait to draw her in. For a moment, Magiere felt anger's heat return. As much as Welstiel knew of her nature, how much did he know of the means by which she was brought into this world? Dhampir, the child of a vampire with hidden knowledge and a mortal mother Magiere had known only from a wooden marker in a village graveyard.

And how far back in her life did Welstiel's meddling reach? There were possibilities in that she did not want to think upon.

Leesil leaned close to her. 'There's actually something more I haven't told you.'

Magiere's dampened anger flared at the thought that he'd once more left something until after the fact.

'Back on the ship that brought us here,' he continued, 'I spoke with the thug locked in the cargo hold. Master Poyesk hired those men to stop you from returning with the bankdraft. Karlin has to be warned how far Poyesk will go to prevent the new warehouse from being built.'

Magiere's wounds started to ache as if the numbing salve had worn off, and the pain merely added to her ire.

'Damn you, Leesil.'

'You had too much to deal with already,' he snapped back at her. 'And some of it you wouldn't even face.'

He dropped his eyes, head down, and Magiere's anger waned. He looked tired and sad. There was more to his reaction than the tangle of deceptions they'd unraveled since leaving Miiska. Part of his exasperation had more to do with her.

'Not to worry,' Wynn said matter-of-factly. 'You can tell me exactly what to say or you can write a letter. I promise that Karlin will be made aware of all.'

Magiere longed only for home, but the sages' words plagued her. She – and Leesil and Chap – weren't finished. She wanted answers for her past, her future, and why she was here.

With Leesil close but ignoring her, she felt suddenly tired of talk. All she wanted now was to be out of this crowded room and to be alone with him.

'We don't have that bankdraft yet,' she said. 'We can't decide anything until that's settled.'

The two sages said their good-nights and quietly left. Leesil lifted Magiere's good arm over his shoulders, winced once as it settled around his neck, and led her toward their barracks room. Chap ambled along behind them, sore and stiff, but otherwise well enough.

As Leesil settled Magiere upon the lower bunk, he still appeared lost inside himself.

'I'm sorry,' Magiere said. 'I've been weighed down by all that's happened since before we even left home.'

'Yes . . .' he whispered. 'But leave that for the moment. There's something else you need to know. Something that happened tonight in the sewers.'

Magiere held her breath, unsure if she could take anything more.

'My mother . . .' he whispered, somehow afraid to speak it aloud, 'may be alive.'

Magiere grabbed his arm and pulled him down to crouch in front her. Before she could ask the first urgent question, he told her of his encounter with the elf – the *anmaglâhk* – who called himself Sgäile. Nagging suspicion grew when she heard how the elf cowered back as Chap intimidated him into partially answering Leesil's questions.

'Maybe they imprisoned her for what she taught me,' Leesil finished. 'Though from watching Sgäile, she didn't have time to teach me everything of their ways, or she chose not to. I think she may have gotten away from Darmouth, and if I'm right, the elves don't kill their own – even a traitor, so-called.'

Chap watched them both with keen attention. Magiere thought she saw the hound wrinkle his jowls at the mention of the elven assassin.

'She was the one who gave me Chap,' Leesil reminded her.

A new sorrow settled upon Magiere. Leesil's guilt over his parents, so long hidden, had been tossed back in his face with the uncertainty of his mother's fate.

'If she's alive, we'll find her,' she promised. 'We'll find out why all of this has happened to us.'

As quickly as this journey had started, the day the council letter arrived in Miiska, the days to come settled in her mind. Home would have to wait.

'Us,' Leesil answered, with a soft laugh that made Magiere uncomfortable. 'That is another puzzle entirely. And I know the crux of it, now.'

He looked at her with sorrow, as if she'd betrayed him with some secret he'd uncovered. Magiere tensed, frightened.

Leesil held out his left wrist, the scars of her teeth plain to see. She shoved his arm away and shrank back.

'All the distance you placed between us,' he said accusingly. 'This is why.'

'Leesil, not now,' she warned him.

'I told you before,' he said. 'I'm not that easy to kill.'

Magiere's stomach lurched as memory rushed at her upon his words. She felt his flesh between her teeth the night he burned the warehouse. She tasted his blood in her mouth as she swallowed it down, the only thing she desired in that moment. Not anyone's – only his.

'Yes, you are,' she shouted. 'You can't make this so simple!'

Leesil hung back, confused. 'What do you mean . . . ?'

'Neither of us really knows what I am,' Magiere answered. 'You're here with me now, and I wouldn't wish it any other way. But each time you try to make it more than that, it becomes dangerous, unnatural, and you—'

'What?' Leesil snapped at her. 'I'm not the one holding secrets now. You tell me what's so—'

'Because I can kill you,' Magiere said through her teeth, and her anger added vicious bite to her words. 'And worst of all, you'd let me!'

She wanted to slap him, shake him from this foolish blindness that had almost cost him his life. It was better to finally have done with it, once and for all, and she spit out every word.

'The night you saved me from the warehouse, you just slit yourself open and fed me without a thought. If Brenden hadn't been there to pull you away, you would have stayed there and died in my teeth. I'd have awoken with you dead in my arms. Not once did you think of it – don't even try to deny it, because you didn't. That's how easy it is to kill you, Leesil. And you'd let me be the one to do it.'

Magiere could no longer look at him. Between the memory of his blood in her mouth and the heated rage in her flesh came the pain of final loss.

Leesil dropped to one knee, leaning toward her.

'Neither of us knew what was happening that night,' he said. 'You no less than me. How could we, how could I? But we're beyond that, and we're not those same people anymore.'

He put one hand to her cheek, and as much as Magiere felt the urge to pull aside, she couldn't bring herself to harm him any more than she just had.

'I've lived three lives,' he said. 'As a child in the Warlands, knowing only deceit and death. Then roaming the countryside alone but for Chap. Finally, the game with you, from the night we met . . . with Chap's meddling. I'm looking at a fourth life now. Any life begins by simply living it. And I say again – I won't die on you.'

Before she could stop him, Leesil placed both hands upon her cheeks, and pressed his mouth against hers.

Magiere stiffened in revulsion as the touch mixed with the lingering memory of the night he fed her. But the blood faded from her taste.

His mouth was warm and soft for that brief moment, and beneath the swirl of fear and sorrow, she felt another loss when he pulled away.

'I will never leave you,' he whispered. 'But I can't stay adrift between lives. You will have to decide — for both of us, it seems — since you already think you know what I can and can't do.'

Without another word; Leesil crawled tiredly up into the top bunk and out of sight.

It was a long while before Magiere lay back upon her bed, numbed with a maelstrom of emotions in the room's silence. Chap lay quietly on the floor, now and again lifting his head to look at her.

Sometime during the night, Magiere drifted off, but only after she could hear the comforting sound of Leesil's slumbering breaths from above.

21

Leesil rose in the morning with his stomach churning. Only severe fatigue had brought sleep in the night, as his thoughts tumbled into dreams – or nightmares. Not of death or the repulsive lessons of his childhood, but of his mother, locked away for years somewhere unknown, and of Magiere's sadly confused eyes as he left her sitting upon her bed. So it came as only a minor shock when Magiere announced there was more to be done before they were finished with the undead of Bela.

From his perspective, they need only retrieve the head of the undead they'd found mysteriously struck down on the house's second floor. With Wynn and Chap along again, they returned by coach to the three-story stone house. As Magiere entered, she immediately began shattering furniture with her falchion.

'There are too many things we've found to be false in hunting these creatures, like the stake through Sapphire's heart,' she explained. 'We need to be certain this is all done with.'

Though she winced in pain from her wounded shoulder, as before it seemed to be healing more quickly than it should. When she dumped a divan's remains in the street, oiled them, and lit the pile ablaze, Leesil understood, though he wasn't certain this was the best place. Wynn was aghast, but Magiere silenced any objection with a dour shake of her head. They'd continually stumbled upon false superstitions in their hunts, and Leesil understood leaving nothing to chance.

'I'll get more wood,' she said quietly. 'Start bringing out the bodies.'

Leesil nodded, and signaled Chap to follow him. Before he stepped back into the house, he looked at Magiere standing near the fire, hair bound in a tail, and the flames feeding blood-glimmers into her black hair in the early-morning light. She was tired and worn in her damaged armor, falchion on her hip, but she gazed pensively into the pyre. Leesil felt suddenly afraid he'd pushed her too far the night before. He turned into the house.

Stopping short of the parlor and Sapphire's body, he glanced to the cellar stairs. If there were any uncertainty for the demise of an undead, there was one he wanted to be certain of first. He headed down to the passage into the sewers.

Leesil didn't relish a return to the city's underbelly, but the distance seemed shorter somehow, as Chap led the way. They found Ratboy's body lodged against the walkway a little way down from the intersection where Leesil had taken his head. The severed hand seemed to have been washed away.

'He looks dead to me,' Leesil said.

Chap yipped once in agreement, but they weren't about to argue with Magiere. Leesil dragged the waterlogged corpse all the way back and dropped it next to Sapphire's in the parlor. He was about to climb to the second floor, and instead returned to crouch next to Sapphire's corpse.

A thin, raised line in the congealed black fluids on the carpet had caught his attention. Leesil slipped out a stiletto and poked at it. It shifted slightly, and he hooked it with the blade's tip to pull it out.

It was a necklace covered by dark ichor. He wiped it with the skirt of the blue gown, and before him hung a gold pendant with a sapphire the size of his small fingernail.

Leesil stared at it in thought, knowing just how Magiere would react if she caught him pilfering the dead – or the undead, for that matter. There might be long months ahead, and what the council would pay them needed to go to Miiska.

Spoils of war, he thought, and finished roughly wiping it off before tucking it into his hauberk. He would deal with Magiere later, when objections were pointless. If later still remained a possibility in her mind. Then another thought occurred to him.

A gown with a matching stone. And if there were other gowns . . . ?

He was about to head upstairs when Wynn scurried through the front door.

'You have to stop this,' she urged. The outright dread upon her face was plain to see. 'You cannot let Magiere burn bodies in the middle of a public street!'

Leesil was about to answer when Magiere stepped through the door behind the young sage.

'You find Ratboy?' she asked him.

Leesil nodded. 'He's in the parlor. I'll bring the third one down, the one we found already dead last night.'

'Time to finish this,' Magiere added. 'People are already out and about, and that's not such a terrible thing – though they may not agree when they see what we're doing.'

She headed back outside and down to the pyre.

Leesil sensed there was more to this than burning undeads to be certain of their destruction. Wynn looked at him uncomfortably. While the little scholar respected Magiere, she would never understand all of it.

'She hates to admit it,' Leesil said. 'But deep inside,

Magiere likes the drama of a good show. She's angry that these creatures lived comfortably amidst the wealthy, and none of these fools appeared to know or care enough to realize what was happening. We'll shake them out of their complacency.'

'Oh . . .' Wynn answered. 'Is she still angry with me over Chane?'

For a moment, Leesil tried to find some way to spare her feelings, to understand what she had done. But he couldn't.

'You were wrong, Wynn. You should've done anything in your power to help Magiere take his head.'

Wynn stepped back, and it was perhaps the first time he'd seen her grow cold and harsh.

'I had a place among you in this,' she said. 'You, Magiere, and Chap possess strength and courage beyond anyone I have known, but you lack conscience. I was that conscience last night. Not all beings of a kind are the same, Leesil. And I believe it is possible not all Noble Dead are the same.'

Her answer surprised him. He appreciated how she stood by her convictions, even if she was completely naive.

'If you still want to help,' he said, 'go out there and keep people away from Magiere as best you can. One wrong word and . . . well, you know her enough to guess the worst.'

Wynn sighed deeply, still not at all pleased, but she nodded and headed out to the street.

Leesil didn't stop at the body on the second floor. Instead, he opened the doors there to briefly inspect the rooms, but neither held what he looked for. It was in the last room of the top floor that he reached his goal. He entered and pulled aside the thick curtains and shutters to let in the daylight.

The room was decorated in peach and white, and Leesil grimaced at the décor. He inspected the closet and confirmed his suspicions – gowns of varied hues, all of costly fabrics and frills. He wasted no time and rummaged through the wardrobe and vanity and found what he sought. The walnut box was only slightly ornate, and inside were trinkets, earrings, and necklaces, all seasoned with stones and gems, some of which he couldn't identify.

He closed the box.

No one would miss it, not from a place such as this, but he thought of Magiere and the horrifying scene they were creating in the street. He thought of people who'd never know where their friends and family disappeared to in the night. He thought of the council, who'd still be hiding all this from their citizens, if not for the pyre about to be fed.

Leesil slipped the box back into the drawer with a better purpose for it in mind.

Back at the body on the second floor, he opened the sack with the two heads and was about to add the third when he noticed a wad of cloth caught beneath Toret's head. He pulled it out of the sack to discover it was a satchel or purse.

Inside was a small collection of pennies, groats, shills, and even one sovereign, the assortment roughly equal in both silver and gold. One more thing for Magiere to get angry about, and he shoved the purse into his hauberk with the necklace.

He added the third head to his sack, and hauled the corpse down the stairs. He left it in the foyer and dragged Toret's out first.

People watched from their windows, a few gathered upon the street at a safe distance, but no one approached. As Leesil approached the blaze, Magiere grabbed Toret's legs, and they tossed the headless corpse upon the pyre.

Sparks rose in the air, and Wynn recoiled. Chap merely sat near the street's edge, watching intently. Leesil returned to the house.

When the last body was fed to the flames, people crowded together at either end of the street. Smoke thickened in the morning air, carrying with it the stench of burning flesh.

Chap suddenly barked and stood up.

Leesil saw Captain Chetnik in a wagon coming straight toward them through the crowd. Vàtz was seated next to the captain, and several guards sat behind. The crackling roar of the pyre and mill of the crowds had masked the wagon's approach.

As the wagon halted, Chetnik appeared stunned by the sight on the street. He jumped out, imposing with his wide girth and white surcoat and mass of dark curling hair hidden beneath the three-crested helmet. He strode purposefully toward Magiere.

'Have you lost all reason?' he demanded.

Magiere stood with arms crossed, facing the fire.

Leesil reached into the sack and pulled out Ratboy's head. 'Look in its mouth.'

Chetnik leaned away. He'd rarely spoken to Leesil, and he stopped, uncertain. Cautiously, the captain reached out and pushed back the head's stiffened, pale lips to reveal long, canine eyeteeth.

'We have bodies to burn,' Leesil said. 'It's the only way to be certain.'

Chetnik's eyes flew up to Leesil's face and then to Magiere.

'You might have chosen a more discreet location. I would have helped.'

'Yes,' Magiere said coldly. 'We should have quietly

slipped away with all proof, so no one had to acknowl-
edge anything happened at all.'

Chetnik ran a hand over his face, trying to resume his
professional posture. 'Well enough. I understand.'

Leesil realized then, that of all the people they'd dealt
with in this city, aside from the sages, Chetnik was one
of the few who cared what happened to its citizens, even
the commoners. In time, word of this grisly scene would
spread, and people would know what had happened. No
more secrets and lies from the council. After that, well,
Leesil didn't envy the captain when family and friends
of the missing came looking for him.

'Is there anything more that needs to be done?' the
captain asked grudgingly.

'We need to see the council immediately,' Leesil
answered. 'Can you get us in?'

Chetnik sighed. 'Get in the wagon. There's a meeting
this morning.'

Magiere turned from the pyre without a word, and
Wynn followed her at a safe distance with Vàtz. As the
captain was about to join them, Leesil stopped him to
speak privately.

'On the third floor of the house is the female's room.
When the rest of this is finished, go there yourself and see
what you find. Sell it all, and use the money for those who
suffered loss. It won't bring back their dead, but it might
help them get on with their lives. I doubt the council will
do much, even now that all of this is out in the open.'

Chetnik appeared suspicious for a moment. Then, with
a firm clench of his square jaw, he nodded.

As they drove away, the bodies blackened in the flames.
Chetnik left two guards to watch the fire, with instruc-
tions to keep it burning until nothing but ash remained.

★   ★   ★

Magiere followed the captain down the long hall toward the ornate doors of the council chamber. Leesil was beside her, and Chap, Wynn, and even Vàtz hurried along behind them.

'I take it this'll be as ugly as that scene you made in the street,' Chetnik growled over his shoulder.

Magiere made no reply.

Chetnik grunted his approval. 'Good enough.'

The effeminate secretary, Doviak, scurried after them, nearly shouting, 'Sir, you cannot bring them in without an appointment!'

The captain ignored him and, fortunately, the little man didn't try to step in the way.

Magiere's respect for Chetnik increased. Bela's city officials were a loathsome lot, but the guards' captain had a brain and a backbone behind his sense of duty to the people. Such a rarity left Magiere sad and stirred more guilt for all the years she and Leesil had preyed upon the poor.

The captain grabbed both latches and jerked the council room doors open. Magiere stepped straight up to the near end of the long oval table as Leesil joined her.

The men of Bela's council gasped at their arrival. The councilmen, in their fine black tunics and cloaks, with their perfectly clipped and combed hair, stared in astonishment at the ragged band invading their sacred space. Surprise quickly faded from several faces to be replaced with anger, followed by exclamations of outrage and indignation at the intrusion. At the table's far end, Lanjov stood up.

Magiere hadn't seen him since the morning Au'shiyn's body was found. He looked haggard beneath his proper attire, and his hair appeared lead gray rather than the polished steel she remembered from her first day in Bela.

'Mistress Magiere,' Lanjov said politely. 'An appointment for an audience is customary, and Captain Chetnik knows this.'

'It's done,' she responded, ignoring the admonishment. 'We want our bankdraft, and I want your guarantee that this boy's uncle' – she gestured back to Vàtz – 'has his inn rebuilt and paid for by the city. In the course of our task, the inn was burned down by an undead.'

Sputters broke out around the table, but Lanjov looked at her in a mix of anxiety and hope.

'You found Chesna's killer? You destroyed the creature plaguing Bela?'

'Creatures,' Magiere corrected.

'Really?' replied an older gentleman in anger, and he stood up. 'And I assume you have proof of these *vampires* you claim to have destroyed?'

Magiere glanced toward Leesil, and her partner smiled. For a moment, that expression brought her a chill. There was still a dark nature inside of him, much as there was in her.

Leesil gripped the sack's bottom and snapped it forward across the table.

Three heads rolled down the polished surface, tumbling to a stop along the way at various places. Covered in grime, with black fluids congealed in mouths, hair, and neck stumps, their dead eyes stared out at the fine gentlemen all around. Ratboy's half-opened mouth exposed sharp fangs.

Several men rose or lurched away, covering their mouths with hands or handkerchiefs. Lanjov dropped in his chair and then froze. Captain Chetnik crossed his arms with a disapproving moan.

Magiere spoke calmly. 'Would anyone like to further question Lanjov's offer?'

*   *   *

In the aftermath, and much to Leesil's satisfaction, the council quickly fulfilled all their requests – and politely suppressed their relief when Magiere announced she was leaving immediately. As they stepped outside and off the royal grounds, Wynn had the bankdraft in her hand, as well as a short note Leesil had penned to Karlin. Of course, nothing could be done to punish Poyesk without further proof, but at least Karlin would be warned.

'Take the wagon and horses,' Chetnik suddenly offered with a wry smile. 'I'm sure I can pass on the expense somehow. You'll need them if you intend to leave by land. This has certainly been an entertaining morning.'

Leesil looked up at the captain in mild surprise and then simply held out his hand. The captain shook it. He was about to approach Magiere but seemed to think better of it.

'Well, I'd best tend to that other matter you mentioned,' he said. With a nod to Leesil, he strode off down the street, motioning his guards to follow.

Magiere stood silent, facing the inland side of Bela, looking at the open land beyond the outer wall.

'So when do I get my cut?' Vàtz suddenly piped in.

'You'll get it,' Leesil growled.

'We'll need to resupply,' Magiere said, but the exhaustion in her voice suggested such an effort was almost beyond her. 'And we'll leave this afternoon, get out of Bela and find an inn. Vàtz, what's left of the coins I gave you?'

The boy handed her the purse she'd given him the night before, and he rolled his shoulders. It was empty. Magiere grew wearier right before Leesil's eyes. With reluctance, and then resignation, he reached inside his hauberk, pulled out the stained purse, and handed it to her.

Magiere opened it to look inside with first relief, followed by suspicion, and then, as expected, anger.

'Don't ask. I'll explain later,' he said before she could cut into him.

He wanted to absolve her of any mundane duties and could see that she desperately needed time alone.

'I'll take the wagon,' he added, 'and gather our things. You head out and follow the main route through the central land side gate. If I don't catch you beforehand, wait for me at the first inn that's on the main road outside the city's reach.'

Magiere relaxed a little. Nodding once, she turned and headed up the street without even a good-bye to the sage or the boy. She paused once to look back at Leesil and then was gone.

'Get in the wagon, and I'll take you back to the barracks,' Leesil told Wynn and Vàtz. 'I have one more favor to ask.'

He called to Chap, who was exchanging sniffs with the horses, and the hound ducked around back of the wagon to hop up beside the boy and the sage.

It was a short ride, and, with Wynn's help, they transferred Leesil and Magiere's chest and other scant belongings into the wagon, along with a few food supplies and blankets. Domin Tilswith was off on a regular visit to badger the council for better facilities, and so Leesil stood outside the barracks with only Wynn and Vàtz. He reached inside his hauberk, lifted out Sapphire's necklace, and handed it to the sage.

'Sell this,' he said. 'And Vàtz, you help her get a fair price. Take payment in gold only, as I'm guessing its value in silver would be too bulky to carry.'

'You coming back?' the boy asked.

'Only if you can't find me where I told Magiere to

wait,' he explained. 'At the first inn outside the city's reach. Tomorrow you can bring the coins to me there.'

He paused, considering how much they owed these two for their help.

'You hold back two gold sovereigns from whatever you get. One for your guild, Wynn, to help out here until the council gives in to your needs. The other is for you, Vàtz.'

For the first time Leesil could remember since their meeting on the docks, Vàtz stood in silence, mouth gaping open. It was more than the boy could earn in years at his present endeavors. Leesil patted him on the shoulder and turned to Wynn.

'I appreciate you helping uncover Chap's little secret.'

Wynn smiled shyly, and her oval olive face blushed. She lunged forward to wrap her arms about him. Leesil held her for a moment before gently disentangling himself.

'I hope Magiere will forgive me,' Wynn said quietly. 'Though she was wrong concerning Chane.'

'She already has,' Leesil said with a smile. 'She just doesn't know it yet. At times she's rather slow that way.'

As he climbed into the wagon and snapped the reins, Chap clambered forward onto the seat next to him, and he called out one last time: 'Give our best to Karlin, and with luck, we'll see you again . . . someday.'

He left them both waving as the wagon rolled down the road and out through the gatehouse of the middle ring wall.

Leesil traveled the rest of the way out of the city with thoughts dull and thick in his head. Nothing had changed – nothing that mattered, anyway. There was the money for Miiska, of course, but Magiere still remained far away from him. He'd promised to stay by her, no matter that she now chose for everything to remain as it was between them.

The road grew quieter as they passed through the city's landward gate and the cottages, shops, and buildings that spread beyond Bela's outer wall. All the way into the nearest farmland, even Chap remained quiet. Past the open fields, barren in autumn, the wagon rolled into the first outlying village with an inn on the main road. How Magiere had gotten this far ahead Leesil could only guess. Perhaps she'd actually spent money for a coach.

As they pulled up, Chap jumped out to scurry into the brush around the nearby field. Leesil unloaded the chest, and the hound came back briefly, looking to him and then back at the field.

'Go on,' he said. 'Just don't be long.'

Chap licked Leesil's hand once, and he was off into the wild grass. Leesil hauled the chest into the inn.

The innkeeper was a solid old woman who informed him that the black-haired swordswoman he sought had already taken a room. He asked the innkeeper to tend the wagon and horses, and she showed him the way to the back of the inn through a narrow hallway. As he approached, a door opened.

In it stood Magiere, armor and sword removed, and hair untied, hanging loose about her shoulders. She stepped aside, holding the door for him.

Leesil set the chest at the foot of a narrow bed. The small room was dark and lit by one oil lamp. Rough burlap curtains were pulled closed over a shuttered window with no glass. It appeared Magiere now wished to hide from the world as well as from him.

'I paid for only one room,' she said quietly. Shutting the door, she leaned against it, head slightly down.

'It's all right,' he answered. 'There'll be more coin in the morning.'

'What?' she asked. 'How? From where?'

He shook his head, not wanting to deal with her any further at the moment.

'I'll explain tomorrow while we prepare for travel,' he answered. 'I can sleep on the floor. We have spare blankets in the wagon.'

Magiere gave him a bewildered frown. Her pale brow remained wrinkled as she stepped closer, searching his face. Leesil suppressed a shudder that threatened to shatter his self-control. Perhaps now she'd at least tell him and be done with it.

She took his face in both hands, scowling at him. Before he could ask what he'd done now, she leaned in and pressed her mouth hard against his.

Leesil stiffened as he grabbed her by the shoulders and held her away just far enough to look her in the eyes.

Magiere looked startled at his reaction. Then her large brown eyes softened as she pulled the scarf from his head and combed her fingers through his hair.

'It we're to live that fourth life of yours, it seems we must now hunt our own pasts . . . and Chap's,' she whispered. There was some fear in her face, and perhaps a bit of sadness, but also warmth. 'This still feels strange, but you've put all your trust in me, and I've not done the same for you. It's time I changed that.'

Leesil's mind went blank. All he felt was relief as he pressed close to kiss Magiere again. Then suddenly, he stopped.

'I think I need a bath.'

'Later,' she said. 'For now, we rest.'

Magiere carefully pulled aside his hauberk's collar, checking the bandage, and helped him slip out of his armor. She turned down the lamp until the flame extinguished, and Leesil felt her hand again upon the side of his face.

'I don't think this is going to get us any rest,' he remarked in the dark.

'Leesil . . .' she answered with a sigh. 'Just be quiet for a little while.'

He wanted to laugh aloud and let go of everything but her. And as always, at the best moments in his life, joy stirred his natural humor.

'Magiere . . .'

'Leesil, shut up.'

'Just one little thing.'

'What?' she said crossly.

'Um . . . no biting.'

Two hands slammed his shoulders, and he tumbled onto the small bed. He felt Magiere drop on top of him, pressing close.

'Not funny.'

Her answer came with all the irritation he'd so long become accustomed to.

As always, an angry Magiere was most often the true Magiere.

Epilogue

Chap stood outside the back of the inn, staring across the field to the bordering line of trees as dusk settled in. Northern Belaski was cool in midautumn, but the tall fir and cedar trees remained full and green. He'd returned several times to listen beneath the window of one room inside, and now, finally, the voices of his companions within faded.

The hound's crystalline eyes stared steadily across the field. He tensed but didn't growl, nor did his long blue-gray fur stand up beyond the rustle caused by the evening breeze.

He felt a hollowness beyond the edge of the woods. Something waited, though he could neither see nor smell it. But it was there. An emptiness in the dark.

Chap turned for a moment to look at the window of the room Leesil and Magiere now occupied. Then he settled himself on the ground against the wall of the inn, watching across the field.

Welstiel stood deep within the trees, idly fingering the brass ring on his finger beneath his glove. Across the fallow field, he watched smoke rise from the chimney of an outlying inn.

Careful planning had not worked out quite as expected, but it appeared Magiere and Leesil might soon be following the course he had so meticulously set. The dhampir and her half-blood would not be returning home. Perhaps there was still a use for Magiere, whether she was willing or not.

His premature, failed offer might work to his benefit. Would she seek out the location of the old ones for him? He could simply follow her, and she would play her part, even if her reasons differed from those he had counted on.

Welstiel stepped back into the forest, feeling the black, scaled coils of his slumber, as if even now they circled about him in the darkness. He did not relish his next meeting with the patron in his dreams.

Something moved in the grass near his feet, and he looked down. A small animal darted away into the brush, and he caught only a glimpse of its naked tail. Likely a rat, though they seldom ranged to the woods with autumn closing in. A louder *snap* sounded behind him, and he turned, on guard.

A tall figure with red-brown hair stepped from behind a gnarled cedar. He wore a well-tailored cloak and a long sword. Welstiel glanced down at the path of the rat.

'I see we both have an interest in the dhampir's whereabouts,' Chane remarked politely. 'I've always found common interest a suitable beginning for conversation.'

Welstiel despised his own kind, but perhaps there was a use for this creature in the coming days. Without response, he stepped through the trees and headed for the outward road.

Chane followed quietly behind.